Mac

MEAN SPIRITS & YOUNG BLOOD

Meg Cabot is the author of the phenomenally successful The Princess Diaries series. With vast numbers of copies sold around the world, the books have topped the US and UK bestseller lists for weeks and won several awards. Two movies based on the series have been massively popular throughout the world.

Meg is also the author of the bestselling Airhead trilogy, *All American Girl*, *All American Girl: Ready or Not*, *How to Be Popular*, *Jinx*, *Teen Idol*, *Avalon High*, *Tommy Sullivan Is a Freak*, The Mediator series and the Allie Finkle series as well as many other books for teenagers and adults. She and her husband divide their time between New York and Florida.

Visit Meg Cabot's website at
www.megcabot.co.uk

2 GHOSTLY **Mediator** BOOKS IN 1

MEAN SPIRITS & YOUNG BLOOD

Meg Cabot

MACMILLAN

Mean Spirits first published in the USA 2001 as *Reunion* under author
name Jenny Carroll, by Simon Pulse, an imprint of Simon & Schuster.
First published in the UK 2005 as *Mean Spirits* by Macmillan Children's Books

Young Blood first published in the USA 2001 as *Darkest Hour* under author
name Jenny Carroll, by Simon Pulse, an imprint of Simon & Schuster.
First published in the UK 2005 as *Young Blood* by Macmillan Children's Books

This edition published 2010 by Macmillan Children's Books
a division of Macmillan Publishers Limited
20 New Wharf Road, London N1 9RR
Basingstoke and Oxford
Associated companies throughout the world
www.panmacmillan.com

ISBN 978-0-330-51951-9

3 5 7 9 8 6 4

A CIP catalogue record for this book is available from
the British Library.

Typeset by Intype Libra Ltd
Printed and bound in the UK by CPI Mackays, Chatham ME5 8TD

Mediator

Mean Spirits

In memory of J. V. C.

One

'Now this,' Gina said, 'is the life.'

I was forced to agree with her. The two of us were stretched out in our bikinis, taking in the rays and balmy seventy-five-degree weather on Carmel Beach. It was March, but you wouldn't have known it by the way the sun was pouring down on us.

Well, this *was* California, after all.

'I mean it,' Gina said. 'I don't know how you do it every day.'

I had my eyes closed. Visions of tall, icy Diet Cokes were dancing in my head. If only they had waiter service on the beach. It was the one thing missing, really. We'd already finished all of the sodas in our cooler, and it was a really long walk up the stairs from the beach to Jimmy's Quick Mart.

'Do what?' I murmured.

'Go to school,' Gina said, 'when you've got this fabulous beach just a mile or so away.'

'It *is* hard,' I admitted, my eyes still closed. 'But graduating from high school continues to be considered one of life's important achievements. I mean, I've heard that without a high school diploma, one doesn't have a hope of acquiring one of those high-powered service positions at Starbucks that I know I'll be angling for upon graduation.'

'Seriously, Suze,' Gina said. I felt her stir next to me, and opened my eyes. Gina had leaned up on her elbows, and was scanning the beach through her Ray Bans. 'How can you *stand* it?'

How, indeed? It *was* gorgeous. The Pacific stretched out as far as the eye could see, turquoise blue darkening to navy the closer it got to the horizon. The waves were huge, crashing up against the yellow sand, tossing surfers and boogie boarders into the air as if they were pieces of driftwood. To our far right rose the green cliffs of Pebble Beach. To our left, the huge, seal-strewn boulders that were the stepping stones for what eventually turned into Big Sur, a particularly rugged section of the Pacific coastline.

And everywhere, the sun beat down, burning away the fog that earlier that day had threatened to ruin our plans. It was perfection. It was paradise.

If only I could have gotten someone to bring me a drink.

'Oh, my God.' Gina tilted her Ray Bans and peered over the rims. 'Check *this* out.'

I followed her gaze through the tortoiseshell lenses of my Donna Karans. The lifeguard, who'd been sitting in his white tower a few yards away from our towels, suddenly leaped from his chair, his orange flotation device clutched in one hand. He landed with catlike grace in the sand, then suddenly took off toward the waves, his muscles rippling beneath his darkly tanned skin, his long blond hair flowing behind him.

Tourists fumbled for their cameras while sunbathers sat up for a better look. Gulls took off in startled flight, and beachcombers hurried to move out of the lifeguard's way. Then, with his lean, muscular body making a perfect arc in the air, he dove into the waves, only to come up yards away, swimming hard and fast for a kid who was caught in an undertow.

2

To my amusement, I saw that the kid was none other than Dopey, one of my stepbrothers, who'd accompanied us to the beach that afternoon. I recognized his voice instantly – once the lifeguard had pulled him back to the surface – as he vehemently cursed at his rescuer for attempting to save his life, and embarrassing him in front of his peers.

The lifeguard, to my delight, cursed right back at him.

Gina, who'd watched the drama unfold with rapt attention, said, lazily, 'What a spaz.'

Clearly, she had not recognized the victim. Gina had, much to my astonishment, informed me that I was incredibly lucky, because all my stepbrothers were so 'cool'. Even, apparently, Dopey.

Gina had never been particularly discriminating where boys were concerned.

Now she sighed, and leaned back against her towel.

'That,' she said, shoving her sunglasses back into place, 'was extremely disturbing. Except for the part when the hot lifeguard ran past us. That I enjoyed.'

A few minutes later, the lifeguard came trudging back in our direction, looking no less handsome in wet hair than he had in dry. He swung himself up to his tower, spoke briefly into his radio – probably putting out a B.O.L.O on Dopey: Be On the Look Out for an extremely stupid wrestler in a wetsuit, showing off for his stepsister's best friend from out of town – then returned to scanning the waves for other potential drowning victims.

'That's it,' Gina declared suddenly. 'I am in love. That lifeguard is the man I am going to marry.'

See what I mean? Total lack of discrimination.

'You,' I said disgustedly, 'would marry any guy in a swimsuit.'

'That's not true,' Gina said. She pointed at a particularly hairy-backed tourist sitting in a Speedo a few yards away with his sunburned wife. 'I do not, for instance, wish to marry him.'

'Of course not. He's taken.'

Gina rolled her eyes. 'You're so weird. Come on, let's go get something to drink.'

We climbed to our feet and found our shorts and sandals, then wriggled into them. Leaving our towels where they were, we picked our way across the hot sand toward the steep steps that led up to the parking lot where Sleepy had left the car.

'I want,' Gina declared, when we'd reached the pavement, 'a chocolate shake. Not one of those fancy gourmet ones they sell around here, either. I want a completely fake, chemically enhanced one, like they have at Mickey D's.'

'Yeah, well,' I said, trying to catch my breath. It was no joke, climbing up all those steps. And I'm in pretty good shape. I do a kick-boxing tape practically every night. 'You're going to have to go into the next town for it because there aren't any fast food places around here.'

Gina rolled her eyes. 'What kind of hick town is this?' she complained in mock outrage. 'No fast food, no traffic lights, no crime, no public transportation.'

But she didn't mean it. Since her arrival from New York City the day before, Gina had been agog at my new life: envious of my bedroom's glorious ocean view, enraptured by my new stepfather's culinary abilities, and not in the least contemptuous of my stepbrothers' attempts to impress her. She hadn't once, as I'd expected her to, told either Sleepy or Dopey, both of whom seemed to be vying for her attentions, to get lost.

'Jesus, Simon,' she'd said when I'd questioned her about it, 'they're hotties. What do you expect me to do?'

Excuse me? My stepbrothers, hotties?

I think *not*.

Now, if it was hotties you wanted, you didn't have to look any further than the guy who manned the counter at Jimmy's, the little convenience store right across from the stairs to the beach. Dumb as an inflatable pool toy, Kurt – that was his name, I swear to God – was nevertheless stunning, and after I'd placed the sweating bottle of Diet Coke I'd secured from the refrigerated case on the counter in front of him, I gave him the old hairy eyeball. He was deeply absorbed in a copy of *Surf Digest*, so he didn't notice my leering gaze. I guess I was sun-drunk, or something, because I just kept standing there staring at Kurt, but what I was really doing was thinking about someone else.

Someone whom I really shouldn't have been thinking about at all.

I guess that's why when Kelly Prescott said hi to me, I didn't even notice. It was like she wasn't even there.

Until she waved a hand in my face and went, 'Hello, earth to Suze. Come in, Suze.'

I tore my eyes off Kurt and found myself looking at Kelly, sophomore class president, radiant blonde and fashion plate. She was in one of her dad's dress shirts, unbuttoned to reveal what she wore beneath it, which was an olive-green bikini made out of yarn. There were skin-coloured inserts so you couldn't see her bare skin through the holes in the crochet.

Standing next to Kelly was Debbie Mancuso, my stepbrother Dopey's sometime girlfriend.

'Oh, my God,' Kelly said. 'I had no idea you were at the beach today, Suze. Where'd you put your towel?'

'By the lifeguard tower,' I said.

5

'Oh, God,' Kelly said. 'Good spot. We're way over by the stairs.'

Debbie went, way too casually, 'I noticed the Rambler in the parking lot. Is Brad out on his board?'

Brad is what everyone but me calls my stepbrother Dopey.

'Yeah,' Kelly said. 'And Jake?'

Jake is the stepbrother I call Sleepy. For reasons unfathomable to me, Sleepy, who is in his senior year at the Mission Academy, and Dopey, a sophomore like me, are considered to be these great catches. Obviously, these girls have never seen my stepbrothers eat. It is truly a revolting sight.

'Yeah,' I said. And since I knew what they were after, I added, 'Why don't you two join us?'

'Cool,' Kelly said. 'That'd be gr—'

Gina appeared, and Kelly broke off mid-sentence.

Well, Gina is the kind of girl people break off mid-sentence to admire. She's nearly six feet tall, and the fact that she'd recently had her hair done into a mop of prickly-looking copper-coloured tendrils, forming a four- or five-inch aura all the way around her head, only made her look taller. She also happened to have on a black vinyl bikini, over which she'd tugged on shorts that appeared to be made from the pull-tabs off of a lot of soda cans.

Oh, and the fact that she'd been out in the sun all day had darkened her normally café au lait skin to the colour of espresso, always startling when combined with a nose ring and orange hair.

'Score,' Gina said excitedly, as she thumped a six-pack down on to the counter next to my Diet Coke. 'Yoo Hoo, dude. The perfect chemical compound.'

'Um, Gina,' I said, hoping she wasn't going to expect me

to join her in consuming any of those bottles. 'These are some friends of mine from school, Kelly Prescott and Debbie Mancuso. Kelly, Debbie, this is Gina Augustin, a friend of mine from New York.'

Gina's eyes widened behind her Ray Bans. I think she was astonished by the fact that I had, since moving out here, actually made some friends, something I had certainly not had many of, besides her, back in New York. Still, she managed to control her surprise and said, very politely, 'How do you do?'

Debbie murmured, 'Hi,' but Kelly got straight to the point: 'Where did you get those awesome shorts?'

It was while Gina was telling her that I first noticed the four kids in evening wear hanging out near the suntan lotion rack.

You might be wondering how I'd missed them before. Well, the truth of the matter is that, up until that particular moment, they hadn't been there.

And, then, suddenly, there they were.

Being from Brooklyn, I've seen far stranger things than four teenagers dressed in formal wear in a convenience mart on a Sunday afternoon at the beach. But since this wasn't New York, but California, the sight was a startling one. Even more startling was that these four were in the act of heisting a twelve-pack of beer.

I'm not kidding. A twelve-pack, right in broad daylight with them dressed to the nines, the girls with wrist corsages, even. Kurt's no rocket scientist, it's true, but surely they couldn't think he would simply let them walk out of there with this beer – particularly in prom wear.

Then I lifted up my Donna Karans in order to get a better look at them.

And that's when I realized it.

Kurt wasn't going to be carding these kids. No way.
Kurt couldn't see them.
Because they were dead.

Two

Yeah, all right. So I can see and talk to the dead. That's my 'special' talent. You know, that 'gift' we're all supposedly born with, the one that makes us unique from everyone else on the planet, but which so few of us actually ever discover.

I discovered mine at around the age of two, which was approximately when I met my first ghost.

See, my special gift is that I'm a mediator. I help guide the tortured souls of the newly dead to their afterlife destinations – wherever that happens to be – generally by cleaning up whatever messes they left behind when they croaked.

Some people might think this is really cool – you know, having the ability to talk to the dead. Allow me to assure you that it so isn't. First of all, with a few exceptions, the dead generally don't have anything all that interesting to say. And secondly, it's not like I can go around bragging about this unusual talent to my friends. Who'd believe me?

So, anyway, there we were at Jimmy's Quick Mart: me, Kurt, Gina, Kelly, Debbie and the ghosts.

Whoopee.

You might be wondering why Kurt, Gina, Debbie and Kelly didn't run screaming out of the store at this point. You know, seeing as how, on second glance, these kids were obviously ghouls. They were giving off that special *Look at me! I'm dead!* glow that only spooks have.

But of course Kurt, Gina, Debbie and Kelly couldn't see these ghosts. Only I could.

Because I'm the mediator.

It's a crummy job, but somebody has to do it.

Only I have to tell you, at that particular moment, I wasn't too keen to.

This was because the ghosts were behaving in a particularly reprehensible manner. They were trying, as near as I could tell, to steal beer. Not a noble pursuit at any time, and, if you think about it, an especially stupid one if you happen to be dead. Don't get me wrong – ghosts do drink. In Jamaica, people traditionally leave glasses of coconut rum for Chango Macho, the *espiritu de la buena suerte*. And in Japan, fishermen leave sake out for the ghosts of their drowned brethren. And you can take my word for it, it isn't just evaporation that makes the level of liquid in those containers go down. Most ghosts enjoy a good drink, when they can get one.

No, what was stupid about what these ghosts were doing was the fact that they were obviously quite new at the whole being dead thing, and so they weren't real coordinated yet. It isn't easy for ghosts to lift things, even relatively light things. It takes a lot of practice. I've known ghosts who got really good at rattling chains and chucking books and even heavier stuff – usually at my head, but that's another story.

But for the most part, a twelve-pack of beer is way beyond your average new ghost's abilities, and these clowns were not about to pull it off. I would have told them so, but since I was the only one who could see them – and the twelve-pack, which was hovering behind the lotion rack, just

10

out of range of everybody else's vision but mine – it might have looked a little strange.

But they got the message without my saying anything. One of the girls – a blonde in an ice-blue sheath dress – hissed, 'That one in the black is looking at us!'

One of the boys – they were both in tuxedos, both blond, both muscular; your basic interchangeable jock-type – went, 'She is not. She's looking at the Bain de Soleil.'

I pushed my DKs all the way to the top of my head so they could see that I really was glaring at them.

'Shit,' the boys said at the same time. They dropped the pack of beer as if it had suddenly caught on fire. The sudden explosion of glass and beer caused everyone in the store – well, except for me, of course – to jump.

Kurt, behind the counter, looked up from his copy of *Surf Digest* and asked, 'What the hell?'

Then Kurt did a very surprising thing. He reached under the counter and pulled out a baseball bat.

Gina observed this with great interest.

'You go, homey,' she said to Kurt.

Kurt didn't seem to hear these words of encouragement. He ignored us, and strode over to where the pack of beer lay behind the lotion rack. He looked down at the foaming mess of broken glass and cardboard and asked, again, plaintively, 'What the hell?'

Only this time, he didn't say *hell*, if you get my meaning.

Gina wandered over to look at the wreckage.

'Now, that's just a shame,' she said, toeing one of the bigger shards with her platform sandal. 'What do you think caused it? Earthquake?'

When my stepfather, driving Gina back to our house from the airport, had asked her what she most hoped to experience while in California, Gina had replied without

11

hesitation, 'The big one.' Earthquakes were the one thing we didn't get a lot of back in New York.

'There wasn't no quake,' Kurt said. 'And these beers are from the fridge against that wall back there. How'd they get all the way up here?' he wanted to know.

Kelly and Debbie joined Gina and Kurt in surveying the damage and wondering at its cause. Only I hung back. I could, I suppose, have offered an explanation, but I didn't think anyone was going to believe me – not if I told the truth, anyway. Well, Gina probably would have. She knew a little bit – more than anybody else I knew, with the exception, maybe, of my youngest stepbrother, Doc, and Father Dom – about the mediator thing.

Still, what she knew wasn't much. I've always sort of kept my business to myself. It simplifies things, you know.

I figured it would be wisest if I just stayed out of the whole thing. I opened my soda and took a deep swallow. Ah. Potassium benzoate. It always hits the spot.

It was only then, my attention wandering, that I noticed the headline on the front of the local paper. *Four Dead*, it proclaimed, *in Midnight Plunge*.

'Maybe,' Kelly was saying, 'somebody took it out and was gonna buy it, and at the last minute, changed their mind, and left it on the shelf right there—'

'Yeah,' Gina interrupted enthusiastically. 'And then an earthquake shook it off!'

'There wasn't no earthquake,' Kurt said. Only he didn't sound as sure as before. 'Was there?'

'I kind of felt something,' Debbie said.

Kelly said, 'Yeah, I think I did, too.'

'Just for a minute there,' Debbie said.

'Yeah,' Kelly said.

'Damn!' Gina put her hands on her hips. 'Are you telling me there was an actual earthquake just now, and *I missed it.*'

I took a copy of the paper off of the pile and unfolded it.

Four seniors from Robert Louis Stevenson High School were tragically killed in a car accident last night as they were returning home from a spring formal. Felicia Bruce, 17; Mark Pulsford, 18; Josh Saunders, 18; and Carrie Whitman, 18, were declared dead at the scene after a head-on collision along a treacherous stretch of California Highway 1 caused their vehicle to careen past a protective guardrail and into the sea below.

'What'd it feel like?' Gina demanded. 'So I'll know if there's another one.'

'Well,' Kelly said. 'This wasn't a very big one. It was just . . . well, if you've been through enough of them, you can just sort of tell, you know? It's like a feeling you get, on the back of your neck. The hair there kind of raises up.'

'Yeah,' Debbie said. 'That's just how I felt. Not so much that the ground was moving *underneath* me, but like a cold breeze moved *through* me real fast.'

'Exactly,' Kelly said.

A thick fog, which rolled in from the sea after midnight last night, causing poor visibility and dangerous driving conditions along the area of the coastline known as Big Sur, is said to have contributed to the accident.

'That doesn't sound like any earthquake I've ever heard of,' Gina declared, the scepticism in her voice plainly evident. 'That sounds more like a ghost story.'

'But it's true,' Kelly said. 'Sometimes we get tremors that

13

are so little, you can't really feel them. They're very local-
ized. For instance, two months ago there was a quake that
brought down a sizeable portion of a breezeway at our
school. And that was it. No other damage was reported anywhere else.'

Gina looked unimpressed. She didn't know what I did,
which was that that chunk of the school's roof had caved in
not because of any earthquake, but because of a supernatural
occurrence brought about during an altercation between me
and a recalcitrant ghost.

'My dog always knows when there's going to be a quake,'
Debbie said. 'She won't come out from under the pool
table.'

'Was she under the pool table this morning?' Gina wanted to know.

'Well,' Debbie said. 'No . . .'

The driver of the other vehicle, a minor whose name
has not been made available by the police, was injured
in the accident, but was treated and released from
Carmel Hospital. It is unknown at this time whether
alcohol played a part in the accident, but police say
they will be investigating the matter.

'Look,' Gina said. She bent down and picked something up
from the wreckage at her feet. 'A sole survivor.'

She held up a lone bottle of Bud.

'Well,' Kurt said, taking the bottle from her. 'That's something, I guess.'

The bell above the door to Jimmy's tinkled, and suddenly my two stepbrothers, followed by two of their surfer
friends, streamed in. They'd changed out of their wetsuits
and abandoned their boards somewhere. Apparently, they

were taking a beef jerky break, since it was toward the canisters of these, sitting on the counter, that they headed upon entering.

'Hi, Brad,' Debbie said in this very flirty voice.

Dopey broke away from the beef jerky long enough to say hi back in an extremely awkward manner – awkward because even though it was Debbie that Dopey was semi-seeing, it was Kelly he really liked.

What was worse, though, was that since Gina's arrival, he'd been flirting with her outrageously, too.

'Hi, Brad,' Gina said. Her voice wasn't flirty at all. Gina never flirted. She was very straightforward with boys. It was for this reason that she had not been without a date on a Saturday night since the seventh grade. 'Hi, Jake.'

Sleepy, his mouth full of beef jerky, turned around and blinked at her. I used to think Sleepy had a drug problem, but then I found out that that's how he always looks.

'Hey,' Sleepy said. He swallowed, and then did an extraordinary thing – well, for Sleepy, anyway.

He smiled.

This was really too much. I'd lived with these guys for almost two months, now – ever since my mom married their dad, and moved me all the way across the country so that we could all live together and be One Big Happy Family – and during that time, I'd seen Sleepy smile may-be twice. And now here he was drooling all over my best friend.

It was sick, I tell you. Sick!

'So,' Sleepy said. 'You girls goin' back down? To the water, I mean?'

'Well,' Kelly said, slowly. 'I guess that depends—'

Gina cut to the chase.

'What are you guys doing?' she asked.

15

'Goin' back down for about another hour,' Sleepy replied. 'Then we're gonna stop and get some 'za. You in?'

'I could deal,' Gina said. She looked at me questioningly. 'Simon?'

I followed the direction of her gaze, and saw she'd noticed the newspaper in my hands. I hastily put it back.

'Sure,' I said. 'Whatever.'

I figured I'd better eat while I still could. I had a feeling I was going to be pretty busy soon.

Three

'Ah,' Father Dominic said. 'The RLS Angels.'

I didn't even glance at him. I was slumped in one of the chairs he keeps in front of his desk, playing with a Gameboy one of the teachers had confiscated from a student, and which had eventually found its way into the bottom drawer of the principal's desk. I was going to keep Father Dom's bottom desk drawer in mind when Christmas rolled around. I had a good idea where Sleepy and Dopey's presents were going to come from.

'Angels?' I grunted, and not just because I was losing badly at Tetris. 'There wasn't anything too angelic about them, if you ask me.'

'They were very attractive young people, from what I understand.' Father Dom started shifting around the piles of paper he had all over his desk. 'Class leaders. Very bright young things. I believe it was their principal who dubbed them the RLS Angels in his statement to the press concerning the tragedy.'

'Huh.' I tried to angle an oddly shaped object into the small space allotted for it. 'Angels who were trying to lift a twelve-pack of Bud.'

'Here.' Father Dom found a copy of the paper I'd looked at the day before, only he, unlike me, had taken the trouble to open it. He turned to the obituaries where there were photos of the deceased. 'Take a look and see if they are the young people you saw.'

I passed him the Gameboy. 'Finish this game for me,' I said, taking the paper from him.

Father Dominic looked down at the Gameboy in dismay. 'Oh, my,' he said. 'I'm afraid I don't—'

'Just rotate the shapes to make them fit in the spaces at the bottom. The more rows you complete, the better.'

'Oh,' Father Dominic said. The Gameboy binged and bonged as he frantically pushed buttons. 'Oh, dear. Anything more complicated than computer solitaire, and I'm afraid—'

His voice trailed off as he became absorbed in the game. Even though I was supposed to be reading the paper, I looked at him instead.

He's a sweet old guy, Father Dominic. He's usually mad at me, of course, but that doesn't mean I don't like him. I was, in fact, growing surprisingly attached to him. I'd found that I couldn't wait, for instance, to come rushing in and tell him all about those kids I'd seen at the Quick Mart. I guess that's because, after sixteen years of not being able to tell anybody about my 'special' ability, I finally had someone to unload on, Father Dom having that same 'special' ability – something I'd discovered my first day at the Junipero Serra Mission Academy.

Father Dominic, however, is a way better mediator than I am. Well, maybe not better. But different, certainly. See, he really feels that ghosts are best handled with gentle guidance and earnest advice – same as the living. I'm more in favour of a sort of get-to-the-point approach that tends to involve my fists.

Well, sometimes these dead folks just won't *listen*.

Not all of them, of course. Some of them are extremely good listeners. Like the one who lives in my bedroom, for instance.

But lately, I've been doing my best not to think about him any more than I have to.

I turned my attention to the paper Father Dom had passed me. Yep, there they were, the RLS Angels. The same kids I'd seen the day before in Jimmy's, only in their school photos they weren't dressed in their formal wear.

Father Dom was right. They were attractive. And bright. And leaders. Felicia, the youngest, had been head of the varsity cheerleading team. Mark Pulsford had been captain of the football team. Josh Saunders had been senior class president. Carrie Whitman had been last season's home-coming queen – not exactly a leadership position, but one that was elected democratically enough. Four bright, attractive kids, all dead as doornails.

And up, I happened to know, to no good.

The obituaries were sad and all, but I hadn't known these people. They attended Robert Louis Stevenson High School, our school's bitterest rival. The Junipero Serra Mission Academy, which my stepbrothers and I attend, and of which Father Dom is principal, is always getting its academic and athletic butt kicked by RLS. And while I don't possess much school spirit, I've always had a thing for underdogs – which the Mission Academy, in comparison with RLS, clearly is.

So I wasn't about to get all choked up about the loss of a few RLS students. Especially not knowing what I knew.

Not that I knew so much. In fact, I didn't really know anything at all. But the night before, after coming home from "za' with Sleepy and Dopey, Gina had succumbed to jet lag – we're three hours behind New York, so around nine

19

o'clock, she more or less passed out on the daybed my mother had purchased for her to sleep on in my room during her stay.

I didn't exactly mind. The sun had pretty much wiped me out, so I was perfectly content to sit on my own bed, across the room from hers, and do the geometry homework I'd assured my mother I'd finished well before Gina's arrival.

It was around this time that Jesse suddenly materialized next to my bed.

'Shhh,' I said to him when he started to speak, and pointed toward Gina. I'd explained to him, well in advance of her arrival, that Gina was coming all the way from New York to stay for a week, and that I'd appreciate it if he laid low during her visit.

It's not exactly a joke, having to share your room with its previous tenant – the *ghost* of its previous tenant, I should say, since Jesse has been dead for a century and a half or so.

On the one hand, I can totally see Jesse's side of it. It isn't his fault someone murdered him – at least, that's how I suspect he died. He – understandably, I guess – isn't too anxious to talk about it.

And I guess it also isn't his fault that, after death, instead of going off to heaven, or hell, or on to another life, or wherever it is people go after they die, he ended up sticking around in the room in which he was killed. Because in spite of what you might think, most people do not end up as ghosts. God forbid. If that were true, my social life would be so over . . . not that it's so great to begin with. The only people who end up being ghosts are the ones who've left behind some kind of unfinished business.

I have no idea what business it is that Jesse left unfinished – and the truth is, I'm not so sure he knows, either. But it doesn't seem fair that if I'm destined to share my bedroom with the ghost of a dead guy, the dead guy has to be so cute.

I mean it. Jesse is way too good-looking for my peace of mind. I may be a mediator, but I'm still human, for crying out loud.

But anyway, there he was, after I'd told him very politely not to come around for a while, looking all manly and hot and everything in the nineteenth-century outlaw outfit he always wears. You know the kind: with those tight black pants and the white shirt open down to *there* . . .

'When is she leaving?' Jesse wanted to know, bringing my attention away from the place where his shirt opened, revealing an extremely muscular set of abs, up to his face – which, I probably don't have to point out, is totally perfect, except for this small white scar in one of his dark eyebrows.

He didn't bother whispering. Gina couldn't hear him.

'I told you,' I said. I, on the other hand, had to whisper since there was every likelihood I might be overheard. 'Next Sunday.'

'That long?'

Jesse looked irritated. I would like to say that he looked irritated because he considered every moment I spent with Gina a moment stolen from him, and deeply resented her because of that.

But to be honest, I highly doubt that was the case. I'm pretty sure Jesse likes me, and everything . . .

But only as a friend. Not in any special kind of way. Why should he? He's one hundred and fifty years old – a hundred and seventy if you count the fact that he'd been twenty or so when he died. What could a guy who'd lived through a hundred and seventy years of stuff possibly see in a sixteen-year-old high school sophomore who's never had a boyfriend and can't even pass her driving exam?

21

Not a whole heck of a lot.

Let's face it, I knew perfectly well why Jesse wanted Gina gone.

Because of Spike.

Spike is our cat. I say 'our' cat, because even though ordinarily animals can't stand ghosts, Spike has developed this strange affinity for Jesse. His affection for Jesse balances out, in a way, his total lack of regard for me, even though I'm the one who feeds him, and cleans out his litter box, and, oh, yes, rescued him from a life of squalor on the mean streets of Carmel.

Does the stupid thing show me one iota of gratitude? No way. But Jesse, he adores. In fact, Spike spends most of his time outdoors, and only bothers coming around whenever he senses Jesse might have materialized.

Like now, for instance. I heard a familiar thump on the porch roof – Spike landing there from the pine tree he always climbs to reach it – and then the big orange nightmare was scrambling through the window I'd left open for him, mewing piteously, like he hadn't been fed in ages.

When Jesse saw Spike, he went over to him and started scratching him under the ears, causing the cat to purr so loudly I thought he might wake Gina up.

'Look,' I said. 'It's just for a week. Spike will survive.'

Jesse looked up at me with an expression that seemed to suggest that he thought I'd slipped down a few notches on the IQ scale.

'It's not Spike I'm worried about,' he said.

This only served to confuse me. I knew it couldn't be *me* Jesse was worrying about. I mean, I guess I'd gotten into a few scrapes since I'd met him – scrapes that, more often than not, Jesse'd had to bail me out of. But nothing was going on just then. Well, aside from the four dead kids I'd seen that afternoon in Jimmy's.

'Yeah?' I watched as Spike threw his head back in obvious ecstasy as Jesse scratched him underneath the chin. 'What is it, then? Gina's very cool, you know. Even if she found out about you, I doubt she'd run screaming from the room, or anything. She'd probably just want to borrow your shirt sometime, or something.'

Jesse glanced over at my house guest. All you could really see of Gina was a couple of lumps beneath the comforter, and a lot of bright copper curls spread out across the pillows beneath her head.

'I'm certain that she's very . . . cool,' Jesse said, a little hesitantly. Sometimes my twenty-first-century vernacular throws him. But that's OK. His frequent employment of Spanish, of which I don't speak a word, throws me. 'It's just that something's happened—'

This perked me right up. He looked pretty serious about it, too. Like maybe what had happened was that he'd finally realized that I was the perfect woman for him, and that all this time he'd been fighting an overwhelming attraction for me, and that he'd finally had to give up the fight in the light of my incredible irresistibility.

But then he had to go and say, 'I've been hearing some things.'

I sank back against my pillows, disappointed.

'Oh,' I said. 'So you've sensed a disturbance in the Force, have you, Luke?'

Jesse knit his eyebrows in bewilderment. He had no idea, of course, what I was talking about. My rare flashes of wit are, for the most part, sadly wasted on him. It's really no wonder he isn't even the tiniest bit in love with me.

I sighed and said, 'So you heard something on the ghost grapevine. What?'

Jesse often picked up on things that were happening on what I like to call the spectral plane, things that often don't have anything to do with him, but which usually end up involving me, most often in a highly life-threatening – or at least horribly messy – way. The last time he'd 'heard some things', I'd ended up nearly being killed by a psychotic real estate developer.

So I guess you can see why my heart doesn't exactly go pitter-pat whenever Jesse mentions he's heard something.

'There are some newcomers,' he said, as he continued to pet Spike. 'Young ones.'

I raised my eyebrows, remembering the kids in the prom wear at Jimmy's. 'Yes?'

'They're looking for something,' Jesse said.

'Yeah,' I said. 'I know. Beer.'

Jesse shook his head. He had a sort of distant expression on his face, and he wasn't looking at me, but sort of past me, as if there were something very far away just beyond my right shoulder.

'No,' he said. 'Not beer. They're looking for someone. And they're angry.' His dark eyes came sharply into focus and bored into my face. 'They're very angry, Susannah.'

His gaze was so intense, I had to drop my own. Jesse's eyes are such a deep brown, a lot of the time I can't tell where his pupils end and irises begin. It's a little unnerving. Almost as unnerving as the way he always calls me by my full name, Susannah. No one except Father Dominic ever calls me that.

'Angry?' I looked down at my geometry book. The kids I saw hadn't looked a bit angry. Scared, maybe, after they'd realized I could see them. But not angry. He must, I thought, have been talking about someone else.

'Well,' I said. 'OK. I'll keep my eyes open. Thanks.'

Jesse looked like he'd wanted to say more, but all of a sudden, Gina rolled over, lifted up her head, and squinted in my direction.

'Suze?' she said sleepily. 'Who you talking to?'

I said, 'Nobody.' I hoped she couldn't read the guilt in my expression. I hate lying to her. She is, after all, my best friend. 'Why?'

Gina hoisted herself up on to her elbows and gaped at Spike. 'So that's the famous Spike I've been hearing so much about from your brothers? Damn, he *is* ugly.'

Jesse, who'd stayed where he was, looked defensive. Spike was his baby, and you just don't go around calling Jesse's baby ugly.

'He's not so bad,' I said, hoping Gina would get the message and shut up.

'Are you on crack?' Gina wanted to know. 'Simon, the thing's only got one ear.'

Suddenly, the large, gilt-framed mirror above the dressing table started to shake. It had a tendency to do this whenever Jesse got annoyed – really annoyed.

Gina, not knowing this, stared at the mirror with growing excitement. 'Hey!' she cried. 'All right! Another one!'

She meant an earthquake, of course, but this, like the one before, was no earthquake. It was just Jesse letting off steam.

Then the next thing I knew, a bottle of fingernail polish Gina had left on the dressing table went flying, and, defying all gravitational law, landed upside down in the suitcase she had placed on the floor at the end of the daybed, around seven or eight feet away.

I probably don't need to add that the bottle of polish – it

was emerald green – was uncapped. And that it ended up on top of the clothes Gina hadn't unpacked yet.

Gina let out a terrific shriek, threw back the comforter, and dove to the floor, trying to salvage what she could. I, meanwhile, threw Jesse a very dirty look.

But all he said was, 'Don't look at me like that, Susannah. You heard what she said about him.' He sounded wounded. 'She called him ugly.'

I growled, '*I* say he's ugly all the time, and you don't ever do that to *me*.'

He lifted the eyebrow with the scar in it, and then said, 'Well, it's different when you say it.'

And then, as if he couldn't stand it a minute longer, Jesse abruptly disappeared, leaving a very disgruntled-looking Spike – and a confused Gina – behind.

'I don't understand this,' Gina said as she held up a one-piece leopard-print bathing suit that was now hopelessly stained. 'I don't understand how that happened. First the beer, in that store today, and now this. I tell you, California is *weird*.'

Reflecting on all this in Father Dominic's office the next morning, I supposed I could see how Gina must have felt. I mean, it probably seemed to her like things had gone flying around an awful lot lately. The common denominator, which Gina still hadn't noticed, was that they only went flying around when *I* was present.

I had a feeling that, if she stuck it out for the whole week, she'd catch on. And fast.

Father Dominic was engrossed in the Gameboy I'd given him. I put down the obituary page and said, 'Father Dom.'

His fingers flew frantically over the buttons that manipulated the game pieces. 'One minute, please, Susannah,' he said.

'Uh, Father Dom?' I waved the paper in his general direction. 'This is them. The kids I saw yesterday.'

'Um-hmmm,' Father Dominic said. The Gameboy beeped.

'So, I guess we should keep an eye out for them. Jesse told me—' Father Dominic knew about Jesse, although their relationship was not, shall we say, the closest: Father D had a real big problem with the fact that there was, basically, a boy living in my bedroom. He'd had a private chat with Jesse, but although he had come away from it somewhat reassured – doubtless about the fact that Jesse obviously hadn't the slightest interest in me, amorously speaking – he still grew noticeably uncomfortable whenever Jesse's name came up, so I tried to mention it only when I absolutely had to. Now, I figured, was one of those times.

'Jesse told me he felt a great, um, stirring out there.' I put down the paper and pointed up, for want of a better direction. 'An angry one. Apparently, we have some unhappy campers somewhere. He said they're looking for someone. At first I figured he couldn't mean these guys' – I tapped the paper – 'because all they seemed to be looking for was beer. But it's possible they have another agenda.' A more murderous one, I thought, but didn't say out loud.

But Father Dom, as he often did, seemed to read my thoughts.

'Good heavens, Susannah,' he said, looking up from the Gameboy screen. 'You can't be thinking that these young people you saw and the stirring Jesse felt have anything to do with one another, can you? Because I must say, I find that highly unlikely. From what I understand, the Angels were just that . . . true beacons in their community.'

Jeez. Beacons. I wondered if there was anybody who'd

ever refer to *me* as a beacon after I was dead. I highly doubted it. Not even my mother would go that far.

I kept my feelings to myself, however. I knew from experience that Father D wasn't going to like what I was thinking, let alone believe it. Instead, I said, 'Well, just keep your eyes open, will you? Let me know if you see them around. The, er, Angels, I mean.'

'Of course.' Father Dom shook his head. 'What a tragedy. Poor souls. So innocent. So young. Oh. Oh, my.' He sheepishly held up the Gameboy. 'High score.'

That's when I decided I'd spent quite enough time in the principal's office for one day. Gina, who attended my old school back in Brooklyn, had a different spring break from the Mission Academy's, so while she was getting to spend her vacation in California, she had to endure a few days following me around from class to class – at least until I could figure out a way for us to ditch without getting caught. Gina was back in world civ with Mr Walden, and I hadn't any doubt that she was getting into all sorts of trouble while I was gone.

'All righty then,' I said, getting up. 'Let me know if you hear anything more about those kids.'

'Yes, yes,' Father Dominic said, his attention riveted to the Gameboy once again. 'Bye for now.'

As I left his office, I could have sworn I heard him say a bad word after the Gameboy let out a warning beep. But that would have been so unlike him, I must have heard wrong.

Yeah. Right.

Four

When I got back to world civ, Kelly Prescott, my friend Adam, Rob Kelleher – one of the class jocks, and a good buddy of Dopey's – and this quiet kid whose name I could never remember were just finishing up their presentation on the Nuclear Arms Race: Who Will Come in First?

It was a bogus assignment, if you asked me. I mean, with the fall of communism in Russia, who even cared?

I guess that was the point. We *should* care. Because as the charts Kelly's group was holding up revealed, there were some countries who had way more bombs and stuff than we did.

'OK,' Kelly was saying, as I came in and laid my hall pass on Mr Walden's desk before going to my seat. 'Like, as you can see, the US is pretty well stocked for missiles, and stuff, but as far as tanks, the Chinese have been way better at building up their military—' Kelly pointed to a bunch of little red bombs on her chart. 'And they could totally annihilate us if they wanted to.'

'Except,' Adam pointed out, 'that there are more privately owned handguns in America than there are in the whole of the Chinese army, so—'

'So what?' Kelly demanded. I could sense that there was some division amongst the ranks of this particular group.

'What good are handguns against tanks? I am so sure we are all going to stand around and shoot off our handguns at the tanks the Chinese are running us over with.'

Adam rolled his eyes. He hadn't exactly been thrilled to be assigned to a group with Kelly.

'Yeah,' Rob said.

The grade for the group projects was split, with thirty percent counting toward participation. I guess that 'Yeah' had been Rob's contribution.

The kid whose name I didn't know didn't say anything. He was a tall, skinny kid with glasses. He had the kind of pasty white skin that made it obvious he didn't get to the beach much. The Palm Pilot in his shirt pocket revealed why.

Gina, who was sitting behind me, leaned forward and presented me with a note, written on a page of the spiral notebook in which she'd been doodling.

Where the hell have you been? she wanted to know

I picked up a pen and wrote back, *I told you. Principal wanted to see me.*

About what? Gina asked. *Have you been up to your old tricks again???*

I didn't blame her for asking. Let's just say that at our old school, back in Brooklyn, I'd been forced to skip class a lot. Well, what do you expect? I'd been the only mediator for all five boroughs of New York. That's a lot of ghosts! Here at least I had Father D to help out once in a while.

I wrote back, *Nothing like that. Father Dom is our student council advisor. I had to check with him about some of our recent expenditures.*

I thought this would be such a boring topic that Gina would drop it, but she totally didn't.

So? What were they? Gina demanded. *Your expenditures, I mean.*

30

Suddenly, the notebook was snatched from my hands. I looked up, and saw CeeCee, who sat in front of me in homeroom and this class, and who had become my best friend since I'd moved to California, scribbling in it furiously. A few seconds later, she passed it back.

Did you hear? CeeCee had written in her sprawling cursive. *About Michael Meducci, I mean?*

I wrote back, *I guess not. Who's Michael Meducci?*

CeeCee, when she'd read what I'd written, made a face, and pointed at the kid standing in the front of the room, the pasty-looking one with the Palm Pilot.

Oh, I mouthed. Hey, I'd only started attending the Mission Academy two months earlier, in January. So sue me already if I didn't know everybody by name yet.

CeeCee bent over the notebook, writing what seemed to be a novel. Gina and I exchanged glances. Gina looked amused. She seemed to find my entire West Coast existence highly entertaining.

Finally CeeCee surrendered the notebook. In it she had scrawled, *Mike was the one driving the other car in that accident on the Pacific Coast Highway Saturday night. You know, the one where those four RLS students died.*

Whoa, I thought. It totally pays to be friends with the editor of the school paper. Somehow, CeeCee always manages to ferret out everything about everyone.

I heard he was coming back from a friend's house, she wrote. *There was this fog, and I guess they didn't see each other until the last minute, when everybody swerved. His car went up an embankment, but theirs crashed through the guard rail and plunged two hundred feet into the sea. Everyone in the other car died, but Michael escaped with just a couple of sprained ribs from when the air bag deployed.*

I looked up and stared at Mike Meducci. He didn't look like a kid who had, only just that weekend, been involved in

31

an accident that had killed four people. He looked like a kid who'd maybe stayed up too late playing video games or participating in a *Star Wars* chat room on the Internet. I was sitting too far away to tell if his fingers, holding on to the chart, were shaking, but there was something about the strained expression on his face that suggested to me that they were.

It's especially tragic, CeeCee scribbled, *when you consider the fact that only last month, his little sister – you don't know her; she's in eighth grade – almost drowned at some pool party and has been in a coma ever since. Talk about a family curse . . .*

'So, in conclusion,' Kelly said, not even attempting to make it look like she wasn't reading off an index card, and rushing her words all together so you could hardly tell what she was saying, 'America-needs-to-spend-way-more-money-building-up-its-military-because-we-have-fallen-way-behind-the-Chinese-and-they-could-attack-us-any-time-they-wanted-to-thank-you.'

Mr Walden had been sitting with his feet propped up on his desk, staring over the tops of our heads at the sea, which you can see quite plainly through the windows of most of the classrooms at the Mission Academy. Now, hearing the sudden hush that fell over the classroom, he started, and dropped his feet to the floor.

'Very nice, Kelly,' he said, even though it was obvious he hadn't listened to a word she'd been saying. 'Anybody have questions for Kelly? OK, great, next group—'

Then Mr Walden blinked at me. 'Um,' he said, in a strange voice. 'Yes?'

Since I hadn't raised my hand, or in any way indicated that I had anything to say, I was somewhat taken aback by this. Then a voice behind me said, 'Um, I'm sorry, but that conclusion – that we, as a country, need to start building up our military arsenal in order to compete with the Chinese – sounds grossly ill conceived to me.'

I turned around slowly in my chair to stare at Gina. She had a perfectly straight expression on her face. Still, I knew her:

She was bored. This was the kind of thing Gina did when she was bored.

Mr Walden sat up eagerly in his chair and said, 'It seems that Miss Simon's guest disagrees with the conclusion you all have come up with, Group Seven. How would you like to respond?'

'Ill conceived in what way?' Kelly demanded, not consulting with any of the other members of her group.

'Well, I just think the money you're talking about would be better spent on other things,' Gina said, 'besides making sure we have as many tanks as the Chinese. I mean, who cares if they have more tanks than we do? It's not like they're going to be able to drive them over to the White House and say, "OK, surrender now, capitalist pigs." I mean, there's a pretty big ocean between us, right?'

Mr Walden was practically clapping his hands with glee. 'So how do you suggest the money be better spent, Miss Augustin?'

Gina shrugged. 'Well, on education, of course.'

'What good,' Kelly wanted to know, 'is an education, when you've got a tank bearing down on you?'

Adam, standing beside Kelly, rolled his eyes expressively. 'Maybe,' he ventured, 'if we educate future generations better, they'd be able to avoid war altogether, through creative diplomacy and intelligent dialogue with their fellow man.'

'Yeah,' Gina said. 'What he said.'

'Excuse me, but are you all on crack?' Kelly wanted to know.

Mr Walden threw a piece of chalk in Group Seven's direction. It hit their chart with a loud noise, and bounced off. This was not unusual behaviour on Mr Walden's part. He frequently threw chalk when he felt we were not paying proper attention, particularly after lunch when we were all somewhat dazed from having ingested too many corn dogs.

What was not usual, however, was Mike Meducci's reaction when the chalk hit the poster board he was holding. He let go of the chart with a yell, and ducked – actually ducked, with his hands up over his face – as if a Chinese tank was rolling toward him.

Mr Walden did not notice this. He was still too enraged.

'Your assignment,' he bellowed at Kelly,' 'was to make a persuasive argument. Demanding to know whether detractors of your position are on crack is not arguing persuasively.'

'But seriously, Mr Walden,' Kelly said, 'if they would just look at the chart, they'd see that the Chinese have way more tanks than we do, and all the education in the world isn't going to change that—'

It was at this point that Mr Walden noticed Mike coming out of his defensive hunch.

'Meducci,' he said flatly. 'What's with you?'

Mr Walden, I realized, did not know how Mike had spent his weekend. Maybe he didn't know about the comatose sister, either. How CeeCee had managed to find out these things that even our teachers did not know was always a mystery to me.

'N-nothing,' Mike stammered, looking pastier than ever. There was something weird about his expression, too. I couldn't put my finger on what, exactly, was wrong with it, but something more than just typical geek embarrassment. 'S-sorry, Mr W-Walden.'

Scott Turner, one of Dopey's friends, seated a few desks away from me, muttered, 'S-sorry, Mr W-Walden,' in a whispered falsetto, but still audibly enough for him to be heard by everyone in the room – especially by Michael, whose pale face actually got a little bit of colour into it as the snickers reached him.

As vice president of the sophomore class, it is my duty to instil discipline in my fellow classmates during student council meetings. But I take my executive responsibilities quite seriously, and tend to correct the behaviour of my more rambunctious peers whenever I feel it necessary to do so, not just during assemblies of the student council.

So I leaned over and hissed, 'Hey, Scott.'

Scott, still laughing at his own joke, looked over at me. And stopped laughing abruptly.

I'm not exactly sure what I was going to say – it was going to have something to do with Scott's last date with Kelly Prescott and a pair of tweezers – but Mr Walden unfortunately beat me to it.

'Turner,' he bellowed. 'I want a thousand-word essay on the battle at Gettysburg on my desk in the morning. Group Eight, be prepared to give your report tomorrow. Class dismissed.'

There is no bell system at the Mission Academy. We change classes on the hour, and are supposed to do so quietly. All of the classroom doors at the Mission Academy open into arched breezeways that look out into a beautiful courtyard containing all these really tall palm trees and this fountain and a statue of the Mission's founder, Junipero Serra. The Mission, being something like three hundred years old, attracts a lot of tourists, and the courtyard is the highlight of their tour, after the basilica.

The courtyard is actually one of my favourite places to sit and meditate about stuff like . . . oh, I don't know: how I've had the misfortune to be born a mediator, and not a normal girl, and why I can't seem to get Jesse to like me, you know, in that special way. The sound of the bubbling fountain, the chirping of the sparrows in the rafters of the breezeway, the buzz of hummingbird wings around the plate-sized hibiscus blossoms, the hushed chatter of the tourists – who feel the grandeur of the place, and lower their voices accordingly – all make the Mission courtyard a restful place to sit and ponder one's destiny.

It was also, however, a favourite place for novices to stand and wait for innocent students to slip up by talking too loud-ly between classes.

No novice has ever been created that could keep Gina quiet, however.

'Dude, that was so bogus,' she complained loudly as we walked toward my locker. 'What kind of conclusion was *that*? I am so sure the Chinese are going to come rolling over here in tanks and attack us. How are they going to get here, anyway? By way of Canada?'

I tried not to laugh, but it was hard. Gina was outraged.

'I know that girl is your class president,' she went on, 'but talk about dumb blondes . . .'

CeeCee, who'd been walking beside us, growled, 'Watch it.' Not, as I'd thought, because, being an albino, CeeCee is the blondest of blondes, but because a novice was staring daggers at us from the courtyard.

'Oh, good, it's you,' Gina said when she noticed CeeCee, completely missing her warning glance at the novice, and not lowering her voice a bit. 'Simon, CeeCee here says she's going to the mall after school.'

'My mom's birthday,' CeeCee explained apologetically. She knows how I feel about malls. Gina, who'd always had something of a selective memory, had apparently forgotten. 'Gotta get her some perfume or a book or something.'

'What do you say?' Gina asked me. 'You want to go with her? I've never been to a real California mall. I want to check it out.'

'You know,' I said as I worked the combination to my locker door, 'the Gap sells the same old stuff all over the country.'

'Hello,' Gina said. 'Who cares about the Gap? I'm talking about hotties.'

'Oh.' I got rid of my world civ book, and fished out my bio, which I had next. 'Sorry. I forgot.'

'That's the problem with you, Simon,' Gina said, leaning against the locker next to mine. 'You don't think enough about guys.'

I slammed my locker door closed. 'I think a lot about guys.'

'No, you don't.' Gina looked at CeeCee. 'Has she even been out with one since she got here?'

'Sure, she has,' CeeCee said. 'Bryce Martinson.'

'No,' I said.

CeeCee looked up at me. She was a little shorter than me. 'What do you mean, no?'

'Bryce and I never actually went out,' I explained, a little uncomfortably. 'You remember, he broke his collar bone—'

'Oh, yeah,' CeeCee said. 'In that freak accident with the crucifix. And then he transferred to another school.'

Yeah, because that freak accident hadn't been an accident at all: the ghost of his dead girlfriend had dropped that crucifix on him, in a totally unfair effort to keep me from going out with him.

Which unfortunately had worked.

Then CeeCee said, brightly, 'But you definitely went out with Tad Beaumont. I saw you two together at the Coffee Clutch.'

Gina, excited, asked, 'Really? Simon went out with a guy? Describe.'

CeeCee frowned. 'Gee,' she said. 'It didn't end up lasting very long, did it, Suze? There was some accident with his uncle, or something, and Tad had to go live with relatives in San Francisco.'

Translation: After I'd stopped Tad's uncle, a psychotic serial killer, from murdering us both, Tad moved away with his father.

That's gratitude for you, huh?

'Gosh,' CeeCee said, thoughtfully. 'Bad things seem to happen to the guys you go out with, huh, Suze?'

Suddenly feeling a little depressed, I said, 'Not all of them,' thinking of Jesse. Then I remembered that Jesse:

(a) was dead, so only I could see him – hardly good boyfriend material – and

(b) had never actually asked me out, so you couldn't exactly say we were dating.

It was right about then that something whizzed by us so fast, it was only a khaki blur, followed by the faintest trace of slightly familiar-smelling men's cologne. I looked around and saw that the blur had been Dopey. He was holding Michael Meducci in a headlock while Scott Turner shoved a finger in his face and snarled, '*You*'re writing that essay for me, Meducci. Got that? A thousand words on Gettysburg by tomorrow morning. And don't forget to double-space it.'

I don't know what came over me. Sometimes I am simply

seized by impulses over which I have not the slightest control.

But suddenly I'd shoved my books at Gina and stalked over to where my stepbrother stood. A second later I held a pinchful of the short hairs at the back of his neck.

'Let him go,' I said, twisting the tiny hairs hard. This method of torture, I'd discovered recently, was much more effective than my former technique of punching Dopey in the gut. He had, over the past few weeks, greatly built up the muscles in his abdominal wall, undoubtedly as a defence against just this sort of occasion.

The only way he could keep me from grabbing him by the short hairs, however, was to shave his head, and this had apparently not occurred to him.

Dopey, opening his mouth to let out a wail, released Michael right away. Michael staggered away, scurrying to pick up the books he'd dropped.

'Suze,' Dopey cried, 'let go of me!'

'Yeah,' Scott said. 'This doesn't concern you, Simon.'

'Oh, yes, it does,' I said. 'Everything that happens at this school concerns me. Want to know why?'

Dopey already knew the answer. I had drilled it into him on several previous occasions.

'Because you're the vice president,' he said. 'Now let me freakin' go, or I swear I'll tell Dad—'

I let him go, but only because Sister Ernestine showed up. The novice had apparently run for her. It's become official Mission Academy policy to send for back-up whenever fights break out between Dopey and me.

'Is there a problem, Miss Simon?'

Sister Ernestine, the vice principal, is a very large woman, who wears an enormous cross between her equally sizeable breasts. She has an uncanny ability to evoke terror wherever she goes, merely by frowning. It is a talent I admire and hope to emulate someday.

'No, Sister,' I said.

Sister Ernestine turned her attention toward Dopey. 'Mr Ackerman? Problem?'

Sullenly, Dopey massaged the back of his neck. 'No, Sister,' he said.

'Good,' Sister Ernestine said. 'I'm glad the two of you are finally getting along so nicely. Such sibling affection is an inspiration to us all. Now hurry along to class, please.'

I turned and joined CeeCee and Gina, who'd stood watching the whole thing.

'Jesus, Simon,' Gina said with disgust as we headed into the bio lab. 'No wonder the guys around here don't like you.'

Five

'Girl,' Gina said. 'That is so you.'

CeeCee looked down at the outfit Gina had talked her into purchasing, then had goaded CeeCee into putting on for our inspection.

'I don't know,' she said, dubiously.

'It's you,' Gina said, again. 'I'm telling you. It's so you. Tell her, Suze.'

'It's pretty flicking,' I said truthfully. Gina had the touch. She had turned CeeCee from fashion challenged to fashion plate.

'But you won't be able to wear it to school,' I couldn't help pointing out. 'It's too short.' I'd learned the hard way that the Mission Academy's dress code, while fairly lenient, did not condone miniskirts under any circumstances. And I highly doubted Sister Ernestine would approve of CeeCee's new, navel-revealing faux-fur-trimmed sweater, either.

'Where am I going to wear it, then?' CeeCee wanted to know.

'Church,' I answered with a shrug.

CeeCee gave me a very sarcastic look. I said, 'Oh, all right. Well, you can definitely wear it to the Coffee Clutch. And to parties.'

CeeCee's gaze, behind the violet lenses of her glasses, was

tolerant. 'I don't get invited to parties, Suze,' she reminded me.

'You can always wear it to my house,' Adam offered helpfully. The startled look CeeCee threw him pretty much assured me that however much she'd spent on the outfit – and it had to have cost several months' allowance, at least – it had been worth it: CeeCee had had a secret crush on Adam McTavish for as long as I'd known her, and probably much longer than that.

'All right, Simon,' Gina said, lowering herself into one of the hard plastic chairs that littered the food court. 'What were you up to while I was coordinating Ms Webb's spring wardrobe?'

I held up my bag from Music Town. 'I bought a CD,' I said lamely.

Gina, appalled, echoed, 'A *what*?'

'A CD.' I hadn't even wanted to buy one, but sent out into the wilds of the mall with instructions to return with a new purchase, I had panicked, and headed into the first store I saw.

'You know malls give me sensory overload,' I said, by way of explanation.

Gina shook her head at me, her copper curls swaying. 'You can't really get mad at her,' she said to Adam. 'She's just so cute.'

Adam shifted his attention from CeeCee's sassy new outfit to me. 'Yeah,' he said. 'She is.' Then his gaze slipped past me, and his eyes widened. 'But here come some people I'm not sure will agree.'

I turned my head and saw Sleepy and Dopey sauntering toward us. The mall was like Dopey's second home, but what Sleepy was doing here, I could not imagine. All of his free time, between school and delivering pizzas – he was saving up for a Camaro – was usually spent surfing. Or sleeping.

Then he slumped down into a chair near Gina's, and said, in a voice I'd never heard him use before, 'Hey, I heard you were here.'

Suddenly all became clear.

'Hey,' I said to CeeCee, who was still gazing rapturously in Adam's direction. She was trying to figure out, I could tell, just what precisely he'd meant when he'd said she could wear her new outfit to his house. Had he been sexually harassing her – as she clearly hoped – or merely making conversation?

'Yeah?' CeeCee asked. She didn't even bother to turn her head in my direction.

I grimaced. I could see I was all alone on this one.

'You got your mom's present yet?' I demanded.

CeeCee said, faintly, 'No.'

'Good.' I dropped my CD into her lap. 'Hang on to this. I'll go get her Oprah's latest pick of the month. How about that?'

'That sounds great,' CeeCee said, still without so much as a glance at me, although she did wave a twenty in the air.

Rolling my eyes, I snatched the bill, then stomped off before I burst a blood vessel from screaming as hard as I could. You'd have screamed, too, if you'd seen what I had as I left the food court, which was Dopey trying desperately to squeeze a chair in between Sleepy and Gina.

I don't get it. I really don't. I mean, I know I probably come off as insensitive and maybe even a little weird, what with the mediator thing, but deep down, I am really a caring person. I am very fair-minded and intelligent, and sometimes I'm even funny. And I know I'm not a dog. I mean, I fully blow-dry my hair every morning, and I have been told on more than one occasion (OK, by my mom, but it still counts) that my eyes are like emeralds. So what gives? How come Gina has *two* guys vying for her attention, while I can't even get one? I mean, even dead guys don't seem to like me so much, and I don't think they have a whole lot of options.

I was still mulling over this in the bookstore as I stood in line for the cashier, the book for CeeCee's mother in my hands. That was when something brushed my shoulder. I turned around and found myself staring at Michael Meducci.

'Um,' he said. He was holding a book on computer programming. He looked, in the fluorescent lights of the bookstore, pastier than ever. 'Hi.' He touched his glasses nervously, as if to assure himself they were still there. 'I thought that was you.'

I said, 'Hi, Michael,' and moved up a space in the line.

Michael moved up with me. 'Oh,' he said. 'You know my name.' He sounded pleased.

I didn't point out that up until that day, I hadn't. I just said, 'Yeah,' and smiled.

Maybe the smile was a mistake. Because Michael stepped a little closer, and gushed, 'I just wanted to say thanks. You know. For what you did to your, um, stepbrother today. You know. To make him let me go.'

'Yeah,' I said again. 'Well, don't worry about it.'

'No, I mean it. Nobody has ever done anything like that for me – I mean, before you came to school at the Mission, no one ever stood up to Brad Ackerman. He got away with everything. With murder, practically.'

'Well,' I said. 'Not any more.'

'No,' Michael said with a nervous laugh. 'No, not any more.'

The person ahead of me stepped up to the cashier, and I moved into her place. Michael moved, too, only he went a little too far, and ended up colliding with me. He said, 'Oh, I'm sorry,' and backed up.

'That's okay,' I said. I began to wish, even if it had meant risking a brain hemorrhage, that I'd stayed with Gina.

'Your hair,' Michael said in a soft voice, 'smells really good.'

Oh, my God. I thought I was going to have an aneurism right there in line. *Your hair smells really good? Your hair smells really good?* Who did he think he was? James Bond? You don't tell someone their hair smells good. Not in a *mall*.

Fortunately, the cashier yelled, 'Next,' and I hurried up to pay for my purchase, thinking that by the time I turned around again, Michael would be gone.

Wrong. So wrong.

Not only was he still there, but it turned out he already owned the book on computer programming – he was just *carrying it around* – so he didn't even have to make a stop at the cashier's counter . . . which was where I'd planned on ditching him.

No. Oh, no. Instead, he followed me right out of the store.

Okay, I told myself. The guy's sister is in a coma. She went to a pool party, and ended up on life support. That's gotta screw a person up. And what about the car accident? The guy was just in a horrifying car accident. It's entirely possible that he may have killed four people. Four people! Not on purpose, of course. But four people, dead, while you yourself escaped perfectly unscathed. That and the comatose sister . . . well, that's gotta give a guy issues, right?

So cut him a little slack. Be a little nice to him.

The trouble was that I had already been a little nice to

him, and look what had happened: he was practically stalking me.

Michael followed me right into Victoria's Secret, where I'd instinctively headed, thinking no boy would follow a girl into a place where bras were on such prominent display. Boy, was I ever wrong.

'So, what'd you think,' Michael wanted to know as I stood there fingering a cheetah print number in rayon, 'about our group report? Do you agree with your, uh, friend that Kelly's argument was fatuous?'

Fatuous? What sort of word was *that?*

A saleslady came up to us before I had a chance to reply. 'Hello,' she said, brightly. 'Have you noticed our sales table? Buy three pairs of panties, get a fourth pair free.'

I couldn't believe she'd said the word *panties* in front of Michael. And I couldn't believe that Michael just kept standing there *smiling!* I couldn't even say the word *panties* in front of my *mother!* I whirled around and headed out of the store.

'I don't normally come to the mall,' Michael was saying. He was sticking to me like a leech. 'But when I heard you were going to be here, well, I thought I'd come over and see what it's all about. Do you come here a lot?'

I was trying to head in the general direction of the food court, in the vague hope that I might be able to ditch Michael in the throng in front of Chick Fill-A. It was tough going, though. For one thing, it looked as if just about every kid in the peninsula had decided to go to the mall after school. And for another, the mall had had one of those events, you know, that malls are always having. This one had been some kind of screwed-up Mardi Gras, with floats and gold masks and necklaces and all. I guess it had been a success, since they'd left a lot of the stuff up, like these big

46

shiny purple and gold puppets. Bigger than life-size, the puppets were suspended from the mall's glass atrium ceiling. Some of them were fifteen or twenty feet long. Their appendages dangled down in what I suppose was intended to be a whimsical manner, but in some cases made it hard to manoeuvre through the crowds.

'No,' I said in reply to Michael's question. 'I try never to come here. I hate it.'

Michael brightened. 'Really?' he gushed, as a wave of middle schoolers poured around him. 'Me, too! Wow, that's really a coincidence. You know, there aren't a whole lot of people our age who dislike places like this. Man is a social animal, you know, and as such is usually drawn toward areas of congregation. It's really an indication of some biological dysfunction that you and I aren't enjoying ourselves.'

It occurred to me that my youngest stepbrother, Doc, and Michael Meducci had a lot in common.

It also occurred to me that pointing out to a girl that she might be suffering from a biological dysfunction was not exactly the way to win her heart.

'Maybe,' Michael said, as we dodged a large puppet hand dangling down from an insanely grinning puppet head some fifteen feet above us, 'you and I could go somewhere a bit quieter. I have my mom's car. We could go get coffee or something, in town, if you want—'

That's when I heard it. A familiar giggle.

Don't ask me how I could have heard it over the chatter of the people all around us, and the piped-in mall Muzak, and the screaming of some kid whose mother wouldn't let him have any ice cream. I just heard it, is all.

Laughter. The same laughter I'd heard the day before at Jimmy's, right before I'd spotted the ghosts of those four dead kids.

And then the next thing I knew, there was a loud snap – the kind of sound a rubber band that's been stretched too tightly makes when it breaks. I yelled, 'Look out!' and tackled Michael Meducci, knocking him to the ground.

Good thing I did, too. Because a second later, exactly where we'd been standing, crashed a giant grinning puppet head.

When the dust settled, I lifted my face from Michael Meducci's shirt front and stared at the thing. It wasn't made of papier mâché, like I'd thought. It was made of plaster. Bits of plaster were everywhere; clouds of it were still floating around, making me cough. Chunks of it had been wrenched from the puppet's face, so that, while it was still leering at me, it was doing so with only one eye and a toothless smile.

For half a beat, there was no sound whatsoever, except for my coughing and Michael's unsteady breathing.

Then a woman screamed.

All hell broke loose after that. People fell over themselves in an effort to get out from under the puppets overhead, as if all of them were going to come crashing down at once.

I guess I couldn't exactly blame them. The thing had to have weighed a couple hundred pounds, at least. If it had landed on Michael, it would have killed, or at least badly hurt, him. There was no doubt in my mind about that.

Just as there was no doubt, even before I spotted him, who owned the jeering voice that drawled a second later, 'Well, look what we have here. Isn't this *cozy*?'

I looked up and saw that Dopey – along with a breathless Gina, CeeCee, Adam and Sleepy – had all hurried over.

I didn't even realize I was still lying on top of Michael until Sleepy reached down and pulled me off.

'Why is it,' my stepbrother asked in a bored voice, 'that

you can't be left alone for five minutes without something collapsing on top of you?'

I glared at him as I stumbled to my feet. I have to say, I really can't wait until Sleepy goes away to college.

'Hey,' Sleepy said, reaching down to give Michael's cheeks a couple of slaps, I suppose in some misguided attempt to bring him around, though I doubt this is a method espoused by the Emergency Medical Services. Michael's eyes were closed, and even though I could see he was breathing, he didn't look good.

The slaps worked, though. Michael's eyelids fluttered open.

'You OK?' I asked him worriedly.

He didn't see the hand I stretched out toward him. He'd lost his glasses. He fumbled around for them in the plaster dust.

'M-my glasses,' he said.

CeeCee found them and picked them up, brushing them off as best she could before handing them back to him.

'Thanks.' Michael put the glasses on, and his eyes, behind the lenses, got very large as he took in the carnage around us. The puppet had missed him, but it had managed to take out a bench and a steel trash can without any problem whatsoever.

'Oh, my God,' Michael said.

'I'll say,' Adam said. 'If it hadn't been for Suze, you'd have been crushed to death by a giant plaster puppet head. Kind of a sucky way to die, huh?'

Michael continued to stare at the debris. 'Oh, my God,' he said again.

'Are you all right, Suze?' Gina asked, laying a hand on my arm.

I nodded. 'Yeah, I think so. No broken bones, anyway. Michael? How about you? You still in one piece?'

'How would he be able to tell?' Dopey asked with a sneer, but I glared at him, and I guess he remembered how hard I can pull hair, since for once he shut up.

'I'm fine,' Michael said. He shoved away the hands Sleepy had stretched out to help him to his feet. 'Leave me alone. I said I was fine.'

Sleepy backed up. 'Whoa,' he said. 'Excuse me. Just trying to help. Come on, G. Our shakes are melting.'

Wait a minute. I threw a startled glance in the direction of my best friend and eldest stepbrother. *G?* Who's *G?*

CeeCee fished a bag out from underneath the waves of shiny purple and gold material. 'Hey,' she said delightedly. 'Is this the book you got for my mom?'

Sleepy, I saw, was walking back toward the food court, his arm around Gina. *Gina. My best friend!* My best friend appeared to be allowing my stepbrother to buy her shakes and put his arm around her! And call her G!

Michael had climbed to his feet. Some mall cops arrived just about then and went, 'Hey, there, guy, take it easy. An ambulance is on its way.'

But Michael, with a violent motion, shrugged free of them, and, with a last, inscrutable look at the puppet head, stumbled away, the mall cops trailing after him, obviously concerned about the likelihood of a concussion . . . or a lawsuit.

'Wow,' CeeCee said, shaking her head. 'That's gratitude for you. You save the guy's life, and he takes off without even a thank you.'

Adam said, 'Yeah. How is it, Suze, that whenever something is about to come crashing down on some guy's head, you always know it and tackle him? And how can I get

50

something to crash down on my head so that you have to tackle me?'

CeeCee whacked him in the gut. Adam pretended it had hurt, and staggered around comically for a while before nearly tripping over the puppet, and then stopping to stare down at it.

'I wonder what caused it,' Adam said. Some mall employees were there now, wondering the same thing, with many nervous glances in my direction. If they'd known my mom was a television news journalist, they probably would have been falling all over themselves in an attempt to give me free gift certificates to Casual Corner and stuff.

'I mean, it's kind of weird if you think about it,' Adam went on. 'The thing was up there for weeks, and then all of a sudden Michael Meducci stands underneath it, and—'

'Bam,' CeeCee said. 'Kind of like . . . I don't know. Someone up there has got it out for him, or something.'

Which reminded me. I looked around, thinking I might catch a glimpse of the owner of that giggle I'd heard, just before the puppet had come down on us.

I didn't see anyone, but that didn't matter. I knew who'd been behind it.

And it sure hadn't been any angel.

Six

'Well,' Jesse said when I told him about it later that night. 'You know what you have to do, don't you?'

'Yeah,' I said sullenly, my chin on my knees. 'I have to tell her about that time I found that nudie magazine under the front seat of the Rambler. That oughtta make her change her mind about him real quick.'

The scarred eyebrow went up. 'Susannah,' he said. 'What are you talking about?'

'Gina,' I said, surprised he didn't know. 'And Sleepy.'

'No,' Jesse said. 'I meant about the boy, Susannah.'

'What boy?' Then I remembered. 'Oh. You mean Michael?'

'Yes,' Jesse said. 'If what you're telling me is true, he is in a lot of danger, Susannah.'

'I know.' I leaned back on my elbows. The two of us were sitting out on the roof of the front porch, which happened to stick out beneath my bedroom windows. It was kind of nice out there, actually, under the stars. We were high enough up so that no one could see us – not that anyone but me and Father Dom could see Jesse, anyway – and it smelled good because of the giant pine tree to one side of the porch. It was the only place, these days, that we could sit and talk without fear of being interrupted by people. Well, just one person, actually: my house guest, Gina.

'So, what are you going to do about it?' In the moonlight, Jesse's white shirt looked blue. So did the highlights in his black hair.

'I have no idea,' I said.

'Don't you?'

Jesse looked at me. I hate it when he does that. It makes me feel . . . I don't know. Like he's mentally comparing me with someone else. And the only someone else I could think of was Maria de Silva, the girl Jesse was on his way to marry when he died. I had seen a portrait of her once. She was one hot babe, for the 1850s. It's no fun, let me tell you, being compared to a chick who died before you were even born.

And always had a hoop skirt to hide the size of her butt under.

'You're going to have to find them,' Jesse said. 'The Angels. Because if I'm right, that boy will not be safe until they are persuaded to move on.'

I sighed. Jesse was right. Jesse was always right. It was just that tracking down a bunch of partying ghosts was so not what I wanted to be doing while Gina was in town.

On the other hand, hanging around with me was not exactly proving to be what Gina wanted to do.

I stood up and walked carefully across the roof tiles, then stooped to peer through the bay windows into my bedroom. The daybed was empty. I picked my way back down to where Jesse was sitting, and slumped down beside him again.

'Jeez,' I said. 'She's still in there.'

Jesse looked down at me, the moonlight playing around the little smile on his face. 'You cannot blame her,' he said, 'for being interested in your brother.'

'Stepbrother,' I reminded him. 'And yes, I can. He's vermin. And he's got her in his lair.'

Jesse's smile grew broader. Even his teeth, in the moonlight, looked blue. 'They are only playing computer games, Susannah.'

'How do you know?' Then I remembered. He was a ghost. He could go anywhere. 'Well, sure. The last time you looked, maybe. Who knows what they're doing now?'

Jesse sighed. 'Do you want me to look again?'

'*No.*' I was horrified. 'I don't care what she does. If she wants to hang around with a big loser like Sleepy, I can't stop her.'

'Brad was there, too,' Jesse pointed out. 'Last time I looked.'

'Oh, great. So she's hanging out with two losers.'

'I don't understand why you are so unhappy about it,' Jesse said. He had stretched out across the tiles, contented as I'd ever seen him. 'I like it much better this way.'

'What way?' I groused. I couldn't get quite as comfortable. I kept finding prickly pine needles beneath my butt.

'Just the two of us,' he said with a shrug. 'Like it's always been.'

Before I had a chance to reply to what – to me, anyway – seemed an extraordinarily heartfelt and perhaps even romantic admission, headlights flashed in the driveway, and Jesse looked past me.

'Who's that?'

I didn't look. I didn't care. I said, 'One of Sleepy's friends, I'm sure. What was that you were saying? About how you like it being just the two of us?'

But Jesse was squinting through the darkness. 'This is not a friend of Jake's,' he said. 'Not bringing with him so much . . . fear. Could this be the boy, Michael, perhaps?'

'*What?*'

I swung around and, clinging to the edge of the roof, watched as a minivan pulled up the driveway and parked behind my mother's car.

A second later, Michael Meducci got out from behind the wheel, and with a nervous glance at my front door, began heading toward it, his expression determined.

'Oh, my God,' I cried, reeling back from the roof's edge. 'You're right! It's him! What do I do?'

Jesse only shook his head at me. 'What do you mean, what do you do? You know what to do. You've done this hundreds of times before.' When I only continued to stare at him, he leaned forward, until his face was just a couple of inches from mine.

But instead of kissing me like I'd hoped, for one wild heart-pounding moment, he would, he said, enunciating distinctly, 'You're a mediator, Susannah. Go mediate.'

I opened my mouth to inform him that I highly doubted Michael was at my house because he wanted help with his poltergeist problem, considering he couldn't know I was in the ghostbusting business. It was much more likely that he was here to ask me out. On a date. Something that I was sure had never occurred to Jesse, since they probably didn't have dates back when he'd been alive, but which happened to girls in the twenty-first century with alarming regularity. Well, not to me, necessarily, but to most girls, anyway.

I was about to point out that this was going to ruin our wonderful opportunity to be alone together when the door-bell rang, and deep inside the house, I heard Doc yell, 'I'll get it!'

'Oh, God,' I said, and dropped my head down into my hands.

'Susannah,' Jesse said. There was concern in his voice. 'Are you all right?'

I shook myself. What was I thinking? Michael Meducci was not at my house to ask me out. If he'd wanted to ask me out, he would have called like a normal person. No, he was here for some other reason. I had nothing to worry about. Nothing at all.

'I'm fine,' I said, and got slowly to my feet.

'You don't sound fine,' Jesse said.

'I'm fine,' I said. I started crawling back into my room, through the open window Spike used.

I had wiggled most of the way in when the inevitable thump on my door occurred. 'Enter,' I said from where I lay, collapsed against the window seat, and Doc opened the door and stuck his head into my room.

'Hey, Suze,' he whispered. 'There's a *guy* here to see you. I think it's that guy you all were talking about at dinner. You know, the guy from the mall.'

'I know,' I said to the ceiling.

'Well,' Doc said, fidgeting a little. 'What should I do? I mean, your mom sent me up here to tell you. Should I say you're in the shower, or something?' Doc's voice became a little dry. 'That's what girls always have their brothers say when my friends and I try calling them.'

I turned my head and looked at Doc. If I'd had to choose one Ackerman brother to be stuck with on a desert island, Doc would definitely have been my pick. Red haired and freckle faced, he hadn't quite grown into his enormous ears yet, but at only twelve he was by far the smartest of my stepbrothers.

The thought of any girl making up an excuse to avoid talking to him made my blood boil.

His statement tweaked my conscience. Of course I wasn't

56

going to make up an excuse. Michael Meducci may be a geek. And he may not have acted with any real class earlier that day at the mall. But he was still a human being.

I guess.

I said, 'Tell him I'll be right down.'

Doc look visibly relieved. He grinned, revealing a mouthful of sparkling braces. 'Okay,' he said, and disappeared.

I climbed slowly to my feet, and sauntered over to the mirror above my dressing table. California had greatly improved both my complexion and my hair. My skin – only slightly tanned thanks to SPF 15 sunblock – looked fine without any make-up, and I'd given up trying to straighten my long brown hair, and simply let it curl. A single hit of lip gloss, and I was on my way. I didn't bother changing out of my cargo pants and T-shirt. I didn't want to overwhelm the guy, after all.

Michael was waiting for me in the living room, his hands shoved in his pants pockets, looking at the many school portraits of me and my stepbrothers that hung upon the wall. My stepfather was sitting in a chair he never sat in, talking to Michael. When I walked in he dried up, then climbed to his feet.

'Well,' Andy said after a few seconds of silence. 'I'll just leave the two of you alone, then.' Then he left the room, even though I could tell he didn't want to. Which was kind of strange, since Andy usually takes only the most perfunctory interest in my affairs, except when they happen to involve the police.

'Suze,' Michael said when Andy was gone. I smiled at him encouragingly since he looked like he was about to expire from nervousness.

'Hey, Mike,' I said easily. 'You okay? No permanent injury?'

He said with a smile that I suppose he meant to match mine, but which was actually pretty wan, 'No permanent injury. Except to my pride.'

In an effort to diffuse some of the nervous energy in the room, I flopped down on to one of my mom's armchairs – the one with the Pottery Barn slip cover she was always yelling at the dog for sleeping on – and said, 'Hey, it wasn't your fault the mall authority did a shoddy job of hanging up their Mardi Gras decorations.'

I watched him carefully to see how he replied. Did he know? I wondered.

Michael sank into the armchair across from mine. 'That's not what I meant,' he said. 'I meant that I'm ashamed of the way I acted today. Instead of thanking you, I – well, I behaved ungraciously, and I just came by to apologize. I hope you'll forgive me.'

He didn't know. He didn't know why that puppet had come down on him, or he was the best damned actor I'd ever seen.

'Um,' I said. 'Sure. I forgive you. No problem.'

Oh, but it was a problem. To Michael, it was apparently a great big problem.

'It's just that—' Michael got up out of the chair and started pacing around the living room. Our house is the oldest one in the neighbourhood – there's even a bullet hole in one of the walls, left over from when Jesse had been alive, when our house was a haven for gamblers and gold rushers and fiancés on their way to meet their brides. Andy had rebuilt it almost from scratch – except for the bullet hole, which he'd framed – but the floorboards still creaked a little under Michael's feet as he paced.

'It's just that something happened to me this weekend,'

Michael said to the fireplace, 'and ever since then . . . well, strange things have been happening.'

So he did know. He knew *something*, anyway. This was a relief. It meant I didn't have to tell him.

'Things like that puppet falling down on you?' I asked, even though I already knew the answer.

'Yeah,' Michael said. 'And other things, too.' He shook his head. 'But I don't want to burden you with my problems. I feel badly enough about what happened.'

'Hey,' I said with a shrug. 'You were shaken up. It's understandable. No hard feelings. Listen, about what happened to you this weekend, do you want to—'

'No.' Michael, usually the quietest of people, spoke with a forcefulness I'd never heard him use before. 'It's not understandable,' he said vehemently. 'It's not understandable, and it's not excusable, either. Suze, you already – I mean, that thing with Brad earlier today—'

I stared at him blankly. I had no idea what he was getting at. Although, looking back on it, I should have. I really should have.

'And then when you saved my life at the mall . . . It's just that I was trying so hard, you know, to show you that that's not who I am – the kind of guy who needs a girl to fight his battles for him. And then you did it *again* . . .'

My mouth dropped open. This was not going at all the way it was supposed to go.

'Michael,' I began, but he held up a hand.

'No,' he said. 'Let me finish. It's not that I'm not grateful, Suze. It's not that I don't appreciate what you're trying to do for me. It's just that . . . I really like you, and if you would agree to go out with me this Friday night, I'll show you that I am not the snivelling coward I've acted like so far in our relationship.'

59

I stared at him. It was as if the gears in my mind had slowed suddenly to a halt. I couldn't think. I couldn't think what to do. All I could think was, *Relationship?* What *relationship?*

'I've already asked your father,' Michael said from where he stood in the centre of our living room. 'And he said it was all right as long as you were home by eleven.'

My father? He'd asked my *father?* I had a sudden picture of Michael talking to my dad, who'd died over a decade earlier, but who frequently shows up in ghost form to torture me about my bad driving skills, and other things like that. He'd have gotten an enormous kick, I knew, out of Michael – one I'd never likely hear the end of.

'Your stepfather, I mean,' Michael corrected himself, as if he'd read my thoughts.

But how could he have read my thoughts when they were in such confusion? Because this was wrong. It was all wrong. It wasn't supposed to go like this. Michael was supposed to tell me about the car accident, and then I would say, in a kind voice, that I already knew. Then I'd warn him about the ghosts, and he either wouldn't believe me, or he'd be eternally grateful, and that would be the end of it – except, of course, I'd still have to find the RLS Angels and quell their murderous wrath before they managed to get their mitts on him again.

That's how it was *supposed* to go. He wasn't supposed to *ask me out.* Asking me out was not part of the programme. At least, it had never gone like that before.

I opened my mouth – not in astonishment this time, but to say, *Gee, no, Michael, I'm sorry, but I'm busy this Friday . . . and every Friday for the rest of my life, incidentally –* when a familiar voice beside me said, quickly, 'Think before you say no, Susannah.'

I turned my head, and saw Jesse sitting in the armchair Michael had vacated.

'He needs your help, Susannah,' Jesse went on, swiftly, in his deep, low voice. 'He is in very grave danger from the spirits of those he killed – however accidentally. And you are not going to be able to protect him from a distance. If you alienate him now, he'll never let you close enough to help him later when he's really going to need you.'

I narrowed my eyes at Jesse. I couldn't say anything to him, of course, because Michael would hear me and think I was talking to myself, or worse. But what I really wanted to say was, Look, this is taking everything a little too far, don't you think?

But I couldn't say that. Because, I realized, Jesse was right. The only way I was going to be able to keep an eye on the Angels was by keeping an eye on Michael.

I heaved a sigh, and said, 'Yeah, okay. Friday's fine.'

I won't describe what Michael said after that. The whole thing was just too excruciatingly embarrassing for words. I tried to remind myself that this was probably what Bill Gates was like in high school, and look at him now. I bet all the girls who knew him back then are really kicking themselves now for having turned down his invitations to prom, or whatever.

But to tell you the truth, it didn't do much good. Even if he had a trillion dollars like Bill Gates, I still wouldn't let Michael Meducci put his tongue in my mouth.

Michael left eventually, and I made my way grumpily back up the stairs – well, after enduring an interrogation from my mother, who came out as soon as she heard the front door close and demanded to know who Michael's parents were, where he lived, where we'd be going on our date and why wasn't I more excited? A boy had asked me out!

61

Returning at last to my room, I noticed that Gina was back. She was lying on the daybed, pretending to read a magazine, and acting like she had no idea where I'd been. I walked over, snatched it away from her and hit her over the head with it a few times.

'OK, OK,' she said, throwing her arms up over her head and giggling. 'So I know already. Did you say yes?'

'What was I supposed to say?' I demanded, flopping down on to my own bed. 'He was practically crying.'

Even as I said it, I felt disloyal. Michael's eyes, behind the lenses of his glasses, had been very bright, it was true. But he had not actually been crying. I was pretty sure.

'Oh, my God,' Gina said to the ceiling. 'I can't believe you're going out with a geek.'

'Yeah,' I said, 'well, you haven't exactly been exercising much discrimination lately yourself, G.'

Gina rolled over on to her stomach and looked at me seriously. 'Jake's not as bad as you think, Suze,' she said. 'He's actually very sweet.'

I summed up the situation in one word: '*Ew.*'

Gina, with a laugh, rolled on to her back again. 'Well, so what?' she asked. 'I'm on vacation. It's not like it could possibly go anywhere anyway.'

'Just promise me,' I said, 'that you aren't going to . . . I don't know. Get full frontal with one of them, or anything.'

Gina just grinned some more. 'What about you and the geek? You two going to be doing any lip-locking?'

I picked up one of the pillows from my bed and threw it at her. She sat up and caught it with a laugh. 'What's the matter?' she wanted to know. 'Isn't he The One?'

I leaned back against the rest of my pillows. Outside, I heard the familiar thump of Spike's four paws hitting the porch roof. 'What one?' I asked.

'You know,' Gina said. 'The One. The one the psychic talked about.'

I blinked at her. 'What psychic? What are you talking about?'

Gina said, 'Oh, come on. Madame Zara. Remember? We went to her at that school fair in like the sixth grade. And she told you about being a mediator.'

'Oh.' I lay perfectly still. I was worried if I moved or said anything much, I would reveal more than I wanted to. Gina knew . . . but only a little. Not enough to really understand.

At least, that's what I thought then.

'You don't remember what else she said?' Gina demanded. 'About you, I mean? About how you were only going to have one love in your life, but that it was going to last until the end of time?'

I stared at the lace trim of the canopy that hung over my bed. I said, my throat gone mysteriously dry, 'I don't remember that.'

'Well, I don't think you heard much of what she said after that bit about you being a mediator. You were in shock. Oh, look. Here comes that . . . cat.'

Gina avoided, I noticed, supplying any descriptives for Spike, who climbed in through the open window, then stalked over to his food bowl and cried to be fed. Apparently, the memory of what had happened the last time she'd called the cat a name – the thing with the fingernail polish – was still fresh in Gina's mind. As fresh, apparently, as what that psychic had said all those years ago.

One love that would last until the end of time.

I realized, as I picked up Spike's bag of food, that my palms had broken out into a cold sweat.

'Wouldn't you die,' Gina asked, 'if it turned out your one true love was Michael Meducci?'

'Totally,' I replied, automatically.

But it wasn't. If it was true – and I had no reason to doubt it, since Madame Zara had been right about the mediator thing, the only person in the world, with the exception of Father Dominic, who had ever guessed – then I knew perfectly well who it was.

And it wasn't Michael Meducci.

Seven

Not that Michael didn't try.

The next morning he was waiting for me in the parking lot as Gina, Sleepy, Dopey, Doc and I stumbled out of the Rambler and started making our way toward our various lines for assembly. Michael asked if he could carry my books. Telling myself that the RLS Angels could show up at any time and attempt to murder him again, I let him. Better to keep an eye on him, I thought, than to let him wander into God only knew what.

Still, it wasn't all that fun. Behind us, Dopey kept doing a very convincing imitation of someone throwing up.

And later, at lunch, which I traditionally spend with Adam and CeeCee – though this particular day, since Gina was in our midst, we had been joined by her groupies, Sleepy, Dopey and about a half dozen boys I didn't know, each of whom was vying desperately for Gina's attention – Michael asked if he could join us. Again, I had no choice but to say yes.

And then when, strolling toward the Rambler after school, it was suggested that we use the next four or five hours of daylight to its best advantage by doing our home-work at the beach, Michael must have been nearby. How else could he have known to show up at the Carmel Beach, beach chair in tow, an hour later?

'Oh, God,' Gina said from her beach towel. 'Don't look now, but your one true love approacheth.'

I looked. And stifled a groan. And rolled over to make room for him.

'Are you mental?' CeeCee demanded, which was an interesting question coming from her, considering the fact that she was seated in the shade of a beach umbrella – no big deal, and perfectly understandable, considering the number of times she'd been taken to the hospital with sun poisoning.

But she was also wearing a rain hat – the brim of which she'd pulled well down – long pants and a long-sleeved T. Gina, stretched out in the sun beside her like a Nubian princess, had lifted a casual brow and inquired, 'Who are you supposed to be? Gilligan?'

'I mean it, Suze,' CeeCee said as Michael came nearer. 'You better nip this one in the bud, and fast.'

'I can't,' I grumbled, shifting my textbooks over in the sand to make room for Michael and his beach chair.

'What do you mean, you *can't*?' CeeCee inquired. 'You had no trouble telling Adam to get lost these past two months. Not,' she added, her gaze straying toward the waves where all the guys, including Adam, were surfing, 'that I don't appreciate it.'

'It's a long story,' I said.

'I hope you aren't doing it because you feel sorry for him about that whole thing with his sister,' CeeCee said grumpily. 'Not to mention those dead kids.'

'Shut up, will you,' I said. 'He's coming.'

And then he was there, dropping his stuff all over the place, spilling cold soda on Gina's back and taking an inordinately long time to figure out how his beach chair worked. I bore it as well as I could, telling myself, You are all that is keeping him from becoming a geek pancake.

But I gotta tell you, it was sort of hard to believe, out there in the sun, that anything bad – like vengeance-minded ghosts – even existed. Everything was just so . . . right.

At least until Adam, claiming he needed a break – but really, I noticed, taking the opportunity to plunge down into the sand next to us and show off his four or five chest hairs – threw down his board. Then Michael looked up from his calculus book – he was taking senior math and science classes – and said, 'Mind if I borrow that?'

Adam, the easiest going of men, shrugged and said, 'Be my guest. Wave face is kinda flat, but you might be able to pick off some clean ones. Water's cold, though. Better take my suit.'

Then, as Gina, CeeCee and I watched with mild interest, Adam unzipped his wetsuit, stepped out of it, and, dressed only in swim trunks, handed the black rubber thing to Michael, who promptly removed his glasses and stripped off his shirt.

One of Gina's hands whipped out and seized my wrist. Her fingernails bit into my skin.

'Oh, my God,' she breathed.

Even CeeCee, I noticed with a quick glance, was staring, completely transfixed, at Michael Meducci as he stepped into Adam's wetsuit and zipped it up.

'Would you,' he asked, dropping to one knee in the sand beside me, 'hang on to these?'

He slipped his glasses into my hands. I had a chance to look into his eyes, and noticed for the first time that they were a very deep, very bright blue.

'Sure thing,' I heard myself murmur.

He smiled. Then he got back to his feet, picked up Adam's board, and, with a polite nod to us girls, trudged out into the waves.

'Oh, my God,' Gina said again.

Adam, who'd collapsed into the sand beside CeeCee, leaned up on an elbow and demanded, 'What?'

When Michael had joined Sleepy, Dopey and their other friends in the surf, Gina turned her face slowly toward mine. 'Did you see that?' she asked.

I nodded dumbly.

'But that – that—' CeeCee stammered. 'That defies all logic.'

Adam sat up. 'What are you guys talking about?' he wanted to know.

But we could only shake our heads. Speech was impossible.

Because it turned out that Michael Meducci, underneath his pen protector, was totally and completely buff.

'He must,' CeeCee ventured, 'work out like three hours a day.'

'More like five,' Gina murmured.

'He could bench press *me*,' I said, and both CeeCee and Gina nodded in agreement.

'Are you guys,' Adam demanded, 'talking about *Michael Meducci*?'

We ignored him. How could we not? For we had just seen a god – pasty skinned, it was true, but perfect in every other way.

'All he needs,' Gina breathed, 'is to come out from behind that computer once in a while and get a little colour.'

'No,' I said. I couldn't bear the thought of that perfectly sculpted body marred by skin cancer. 'He's fine the way he is.'

'Just a little colour,' Gina said again. 'I mean, SPF 15 and he'll still get a little brown. That's all he needs.'

'No,' I said again.

'Suze is right,' CeeCee said. 'He's perfect the way he is.'

'Oh, my God,' Adam said, flopping back disgustedly into the sand. '*Michael Meducci.* I can't believe you guys are talking that way about *Michael Meducci.*'

But how could we help it? He was perfection. OK, so he wasn't the best surfer. That, we realized, while we watched him get tossed off Adam's board by a fairly small wave that Sleepy and Dopey rode with ease, would have been asking for too much.

But in every other way, he was one hundred percent genuine hottie.

At least until he was knocked over by a middling to large-size wave and did not resurface.

At first we were not alarmed. Surfing was not something I particularly wanted to try – while I love the beach, I have no affection at all for the ocean. In fact, quite the opposite: the water scares me because there's no telling what else is swimming around in all that murky darkness. But I had watched Sleepy and Dopey ride enough waves to know that surfers often disappear for long moments, only to come popping up yards away, usually flashing a big grin and an OK sign with their thumb and index finger.

But the wait for Michael to come popping up seemed longer than usual. We saw Adam's board shoot out of a particularly large wave, and head, riderless, toward the shore. Still no sign of Michael.

This was when the lifeguard – the same big blond one who'd attempted to rescue Dopey; we had stationed ourselves close to his chair, as had become our custom – sat up straight, and suddenly lifted his binoculars to his face.

I, however, did not need binoculars to see what I saw next. And that was Michael finally breaking the surface after having been down nearly a minute. Only no sooner had he come up than he was pulled down again, and not by any undertow or rip tide.

No, this I saw quite clearly: Michael was pulled down by a rope of seaweed that had somehow twined itself around his neck . . .

And then I saw there was no 'somehow' about it. The seaweed was being held there by a pair of hands.

A pair of hands belonging to someone in the water beneath him.

Someone who had no need to surface for air. Because that someone was already dead.

Now, I'm not going to tell you that I did what I did next with any sort of conscious thought. If I'd been thinking at all, I'd have stayed exactly where I was and hoped for the best. All I can say in defence of my actions is that, after years and years of dealing with the undead, I acted purely on instinct, without thinking anything through.

Which was why, as the lifeguard was charging through the surf toward Michael, his little orange flotation device in hand, I leaped up and followed.

Now, maybe I've seen the movie *Jaws* one too many times, but I have always made it a point never to wade further than waist-deep into the ocean – any ocean. So when I found myself surging toward the spot where I'd last seen Michael, and felt the sand shelf I'd been running on give out beneath me, I tried to tell myself that the lurch my heart gave was one of adrenalin, not fear.

I tried to tell myself that, of course. But I didn't believe me. When I realized I was going to have to start swimming, I completely freaked. I swam, all right – I know how to do that, at least. But the whole time I was thinking, Oh, my God, please don't let anything gross, like an eel, touch me on any part of my body. Please don't let a jellyfish sting me. Please don't let a shark swim up from underneath me and bite me in half.

But as it turned out, I had way worse things to worry about than eels, jellyfish or sharks.

Behind me, I could hear voices shouting dimly. Gina and CeeCee and Adam, I figured, in the part of my brain that wasn't paralysed with fear. Yelling at me to get out of the water. What did I think I was doing, anyway? The lifeguard had the situation well in hand.

But the lifeguard couldn't see – or fight – the hands that were pulling Michael down.

I saw the lifeguard – who had no idea, I'm sure, that some crazy girl had dove in after him – let the enormous wave approaching us gently lift his body and propel him that much closer to where Michael had disappeared. I tried his technique, only to end up sputtering, with a mouthful of saltwater. My eyes were stinging, and my teeth starting to chatter. It was really, really cold in the water without a wetsuit.

And then, a few yards away from me, Michael suddenly resurfaced, gasping for breath and clawing at the rope of seaweed around his neck. The lifeguard, in two easy strokes, was beside him, shoving the orange flotation device at him, and telling him to relax, that everything was going to be all right.

But everything was not going to be all right. Even as the lifeguard was speaking, I saw a head bob up beside Michael. Though his wet hair was plastered to his face, I still recognized Josh, the ringleader of the RLS Angels – a ghostly little group so hell-bent on mischief making . . . and evidently worse.

71

I couldn't speak, of course – my lips, I was sure, were turning blue. But I could still punch. I pulled my arm back and let go of a good one, packed with all the panic I felt at finding myself with nothing but water beneath my feet.

Josh either didn't remember me from Jimmy's or the mall, or didn't recognize me with my hair all wet. In any case, he'd been paying no attention to me at all.

Until my fist connected solidly with his nasal cartilage, that is.

Bone crunched quite satisfyingly under my knuckles, and Josh let out a pain-filled shriek that only I could hear.

Or so I thought. I'd forgotten about the other angels.

At least until I was abruptly pulled under the waves by two sets of hands that had wrapped around my ankles.

Let me just mention something here. While to the rest of humanity, ghosts have no actual matter – most of you walk right through them all the time and don't even know it; maybe you feel a cold spot, or you get a strange chill, like Kelly and Debbie did at the convenience mart – to a mediator, they are most definitely made of flesh and bone. As illustrated by my slamming my fist into Josh's face.

But because they have no matter where humans are concerned, ghosts must resort to more creative methods of harming their intended victims than, say, wrapping their hands around their necks. It was for that reason that Josh was using seaweed instead. He could pick up the seaweed – with an effort, like the beer in the Quick Mart. And he could wrap *that* around Michael's neck. Mission accomplished.

I, on the other hand, being a mediator, was not subject to the laws governing human-ghost contact, and, accordingly, they quickly made use of their unexpected advantage.

OK, I realized then that I had made a bad mistake. It is one thing to fight bad guys on land, where, I must admit, I am quite resourceful and – I feel I can say without bragging – quite agile.

But it is quite another thing altogether to try to fight something underwater. Particularly something that does not need to breathe as often as I do. Ghosts do breathe – some habits are hard to break – but they don't need to, and sometimes, if they've been dead long enough, they realize it. The RLS Angels hadn't been dead very long, but they'd died underwater, so you might say they had a head start on their spectral peers.

Given those circumstances, I saw my situation progressing in one of either of two ways: either I was going to give up, let my lungs fill with water and drown, or I was going to completely freak out, strike at anything that came near me and make those ghosts sorry they'd ever chosen not to go into the light.

I don't suppose it will come as any big surprise to anyone – with the exception of myself, maybe – that I chose the second option.

The hands that were wrapped around my ankles, I realized – though it took me a while; I was pretty disoriented – were connected to bodies, attached to which, presumably, were heads. There is nothing so unpleasant, I know from experience, as a foot to the face. And so I very promptly, and with all my strength, kicked in the direction that I supposed those faces might be, and was gratified to feel soft facial bones give way beneath my heels.

Then with my arms, which were still free, I gave a mighty stroke, and broke back through the water's surface, gulping in a huge lungful of air – and checking to make sure Michael had gotten well and truly away, which he had; the lifeguard was towing him back to shore – before I dove down again, in search of my attackers.

73

I found them easily enough. They were still in their prom wear, and the girls' dresses were floating all around them like seaweed. I grabbed a handful of one, tugged it toward me, and saw, in the murky water, the very startled face of Felicia Bruce. Before she had a chance to react, I plunged a thumb into her eye. She screamed, but since we were underwater, I didn't hear a thing. I just saw a trail of bubbles racing for the water's surface.

Then someone grabbed me from behind. I reacted by thrusting my head back, as hard as I could, and was delighted to feel my skull make very hard contact with my attacker's forehead. The hands that had been holding me instantly let go, and I spun around, and saw Mark Pulsford swimming hastily away. Some football player he'd been, if he couldn't take a simple head butt.

I felt the urgent need to breathe, so I followed the last of the bubbles from Felicia's scream, and resurfaced just as the ghosts did, too.

We all bobbed there on the surface: me, Josh, Felicia, Mark and a very white-faced Carrie.

'Omigod,' Carrie said. Her teeth, unlike mine, weren't chattering. 'It's that girl. That girl from Jimmy's. I told you she can see us.'

Josh, whose broken nose had sprung, cartoon-like, back into place, was nevertheless wary of me. Even if you happen to be dead, getting your nose broken hurts a lot.

'Hey,' he said to me as I treaded water. 'This isn't your fight, okay? Stay out of it.'

I tried to say, 'Oh, yeah? Well, listen up. I'm the mediator, and you guys have a choice. You can go on to your next life with your teeth in or your teeth out. Which is it going to be?'

Only my own teeth were chattering so hard, all that came

out was a bunch of weird noises that sounded like, Oah? Esup. Imameator an—

You get the picture.

Since Father Dominic's technique – reasoning – didn't appear to be working in this particular instance, I abandoned it. Instead, I reached out and grabbed the rope of seaweed they'd tried to strangle Michael with and flung it around the necks of the two girls, who were treading water close to each other, and to me. They looked extremely surprised to find themselves lassoed like a couple of sea cows.

And I can't really tell you what I was thinking, but it's probably safe to say my plan – though somewhat haphazardly formed – involved towing them both back to shore where I intended to beat the crap out of them.

While the girls clawed at their necks and attempted to escape, the boys came at me. I didn't care. I was furious all of a sudden. They had ruined my nice time at the beach and tried to drown my date. Granted I wasn't particularly fond of Michael, but I certainly didn't want to see him drowned before my eyes – particularly not now that I knew what a hottie he was under his sweater vest.

Holding on to the girls with one hand, I thrust out the other and managed to grab Josh by – what else? – the short hairs on the back of his neck.

Though this proved highly effective – in that he promptly began thrashing in pain – I'd neglected two things. One was Mark, who continued to swim free. And the other was the ocean, which was still churning waves at me. Any sensible person would have been looking out for these things, but I, in my anger, was not.

Which was why a second later, I was promptly sucked under.

Let me tell you, there are probably pleasanter ways to die

75

than choking on a lungful of saltwater. It burns, you know? I mean, it is, after all, *salt*.

And I coughed down a lot of it, thanks first to the wave, which bowled me under. And then I swallowed a lot more when Mark grabbed hold of my ankle, and kept me under.

One thing I have to admit about the ocean: it's very quiet down there. I mean, really. No more shrieking gulls, crashing of the waves, shouts from the surfers. No, under the sea, it's just you and the water and the ghosts who are trying to kill you.

Because, of course, I'd held on to the ends of the seaweed I was using to tow the girls. And I hadn't let go of Josh's hair, either.

I kind of liked it, I discovered, under there. It wasn't so bad, really. Except for the cold, and the salt, and the horrible realization that at any moment, a twenty-foot killer shark could swoop under me and bite my leg off, it was, well, almost pleasant.

I suppose I lost consciousness for a few seconds. I mean, I'd have had to, to have held on to those stupid ghosts so tightly, and think being held under tons and tons of saltwater was pleasant.

The next thing I knew, something was tugging at me, and it wasn't one of the ghosts. I was being tugged *toward* the surface, where I could see the last rays of the sun winking across the waves. I looked up, and was surprised to see a flash of orange and a lot of blond hair. Why, I thought, wonderingly, it's that nice lifeguard. What's he doing here?

And then I became greatly concerned for him, because, of course, there were a lot of bloodthirsty ghosts around, and it was entirely possible one of them might try to hurt him.

But when I looked around, I found, to my astonishment,

that all of them had disappeared. I was still holding the rope of seaweed, and my other hand was still clenched as if on someone's hair. But there was nothing there. Just sea water.

The chickens, I thought to myself. The lousy chickens. Came up against the mediator and found out you couldn't take it, huh? Well, let that be a lesson to you! You don't mess with the mediator.

And then I did something that will probably live on in mediator infamy for the rest of time:

I blacked out.

Eight

OK, I don't know if any of you have ever lost consciousness before, so let me just say here real quickly:

Don't do it. Really. If you can avoid situations in which you might lose consciousness, please do so. Whatever else you do, do not pass out. Trust me. It is not fun. It is not fun at all.

Unless, of course, you're guaranteed to wake up having mouth-to-mouth performed on you by a totally hot California lifeguard. Then I say go for it.

That was my experience when I opened my eyes that afternoon on the Carmel Beach. One second I was sucking in lungfuls of saltwater, and the next I was lip-locked with Brad Pitt. Or at least someone who looked very much like him.

Could this, I asked myself, my heart turning over in my chest, be my one true love?

Then the lips left mine, and I saw that it wasn't my true love at all, but the lifeguard, his long blond hair falling wetly around his tanned face. The skin around his blue eyes crinkled with concern – the ravages of sun; he should have used Coppertone – as he asked, 'Miss? Miss, can you hear me?'

'Suze,' I heard a familiar voice – Gina? but what was Gina doing in California? – say. 'Her name is Suze.'

'Suze,' the lifeguard said, giving my cheeks a couple of rather rough little taps. 'Blink if you can understand me.'

This, I thought, could not possibly be my one true love. He seems to think I'm a moron. Also, why does he keep hitting me?

'Oh, my God.' CeeCee's voice was more high-pitched than usual. 'Is she paralysed?'

To prove to them I wasn't paralysed, I started to sit up.

Then promptly realized this had been a bad decision.

I think I only threw up once. To say that I spewed like Mount St Helens is a gross exaggeration on Dopey's part. It is true that a great deal of sea water came up out of me after I tried to sit up. But fortunately, I avoided throwing it up on both myself and the lifeguard, sending most of it neatly into the sand beside me.

After I was done throwing up, I felt a great deal better.

'Suze!' Gina – who I suddenly remembered was in California visiting me – was on her knees beside me. 'Are you all right? I was so worried! You just laid there so still . . .'

Sleepy was a lot less sympathetic.

'What the hell were you thinking?' he demanded. 'Did Pamela Anderson die and leave an opening on the *Baywatch* rescue squad, or something?'

I looked up at all the anxious faces around me. Really, I'd had no idea so many people cared. But there were Gina and CeeCee and Adam and Dopey and Sleepy and some of their surfer friends and a few tourists, snapping pictures of the real live drowned girl, and Michael and . . .

Michael. My gaze snapped back toward him. Michael, who was in so much danger, and hardly seemed aware of it. Michael, who, as he stood dripping over me, seemed unconscious of the fact that around his throat was a great red welt where the seaweed had bit into his skin. It looked painfully inflamed.

'I'm all right,' I said, and started to stand up.

'No,' the lifeguard said. 'There's an ambulance on its way. Stay where you are until the dudes from EMS have checked you out.'

'Um,' I said. 'No, thank you.'

Then I stood up and moved toward my towel, which still rested where I'd left it beside Gina's, a little further up the beach.

'Miss,' the lifeguard said, hurrying after me. 'You were unconscious. You nearly drowned. You've got to be checked out by EMS. It's procedure.'

'You really,' CeeCee said as she jogged along beside me, 'should let them check you out, Suze. Rick says he thinks both you and Michael might have been victims of a Portuguese man-of-war.'

I blinked at her. 'Rick? Who's Rick?'

'The lifeguard,' CeeCee said with exasperation. Apparently, while I'd been unconscious, everyone had gotten to know one another. 'That's why he had them hang out the yellow flag.'

I squinted and peered up at the flag that now fluttered from the top of the lifeguard's chair. Usually green, except when rip tides or extreme undertows were reported, it flew bright yellow, urging beachgoers to use caution in the water.

'I mean, look at Michael's neck,' CeeCee continued. I looked obligingly at Michael's neck.

'Rick says when he got there, there was something around my neck,' Michael said. He couldn't, I noticed, seem to meet my gaze. 'He thought it was a giant squid, at first. But that couldn't be, of course. There's never been one spotted this far north before. So he thought it must have been a man-of-war.'

I didn't say anything. I was quite certain that Rick really did believe that Michael had been the victim of a Portuguese man-of-war. The human mind will do whatever it must to trick itself into believing anything but the truth – that there might be something else out there, something unexplainable . . . something not quite normal.

Something *para*normal.

So the rope of seaweed that had been wrapped around Michael's throat became the arm of a giant squid, and then, later, the stinging tentacle of a jellyfish. It certainly couldn't have been what it had appeared to be: a piece of seaweed being used with deadly intent by a pair of invisible hands.

'And look at your ankles,' CeeCee said.

I looked down. Around both my ankles were bright red marks, like rope burns. Only they weren't rope burns. They were the places Felicia and Carrie had grabbed me, trying to drag me down to the ocean floor, and to certain death.

Those stupid girls needed manicures, and badly.

'You're lucky,' Adam said. 'I've been stung by a man-of-war before, and it hurts like a—'

His voice trailed off as he noticed Gina listening intently. Gina, who had four brothers, had certainly heard every swear word in the book, but Adam was much too gentle-manly to utter any in front of her.

'A lot,' he finished up. 'But you guys don't seem to have been hurt too badly. Well, except for that whole drowning thing.'

I reached for my towel, and did my best to wipe off the sand that seemed to be coating me all over. What had that lifeguard done, anyway? Dragged me through the stuff?

'Well,' I said. 'I'm OK now. No harm done.'

Sleepy, who'd followed me over along with everybody else, went, exasperatedly, 'It is not OK, Suze. Do what the lifeguard tells you. Don't make me have to call Mom and Dad.'

I looked at him in surprise. Not because I was mad about his threatening to rat me out, but because he'd called my mother *Mom*. He'd never done it before. My stepbrothers' own mother had died years and years ago.

Well, I thought to myself. She *is* the best mother in the world.

'Go ahead and call them,' I said. 'I don't care.'

I saw Sleepy and the lifeguard exchange meaningful looks. I hurried to find my clothes, and started to wiggle into them, pulling them on right over my damp bikini. I wasn't trying to be difficult. Really, I wasn't. It's just that I totally could not afford a trip to the hospital just then, and the three-hour wait it would entail. In those three hours, I was fairly certain the RLS Angels were going launch another attack against Michael . . . and I could not in good conscience leave him to their devices.

'I am not,' Sleepy said, folding his arms across his chest, a motion that caused the rubber of the wetsuit he was still wearing to squeak audibly, 'taking you home unless you let the EMS guys check you out first.'

I turned toward Michael, who looked extremely surprised when I asked him, politely, 'Michael, would *you* mind taking me home?'

Now he seemed to have no problem meeting my gaze. His eyes very wide behind his glasses – he'd evidently found them where I'd abandoned them on my towel – he stammered, 'Of c-course!'

This caused the lifeguard to shake his head in disgust and stomp away. Everyone else just stood around looking at me as if I were demented. Gina was the only one who came up to me as I was gathering up my books and preparing to follow Michael to where his car was parked.

'You and I,' she whispered, 'are going to be doing some talking when you get home.'

I regarded her with what I hoped was an innocent look. The last slanting rays of the sun had set her aura of copper-coloured curls glowing like a flaming halo.

'What do you mean?' I asked.

'You *know* what I mean,' she said meaningfully.

And then she turned around and sauntered back over to where Sleepy stood, regarding me worriedly.

The truth was, I *did* know what she meant. She meant Michael. What was I doing, messing around with a boy like Michael, who was so obviously not my one true love?

But the thing was, I couldn't tell her. I couldn't tell her that Michael was being stalked by four ghosts with murderous intent, and that it was my sacred duty as a mediator to protect him.

Although considering what happened later on that night, I probably should have.

'So,' I said, as soon as Michael got the car – his mother's minivan again; his car, he explained, was still in the shop – going. 'We need to talk.'

Michael, now that he was back in his glasses and clothes, wasn't nearly the intimidatingly buff male specimen he'd been without them. Like Superman when he was in his Clark Kent attire, Michael had turned back into a stammering geek.

Only I couldn't help noticing, as he stammered, how nicely he filled out that sweater vest.

'Talk?' He gripped the wheel quite tightly as we sat in

83

what, for Carmel, represented rush-hour traffic: a single tour bus and a Volkswagen filled with surfboards. 'W-what about?'

'About what happened to you this weekend.'

Michael turned his head sharply to look at me, then just as quickly turned back to face the road. 'W-what do you m-mean?' he asked.

'Come off it, Michael,' I said. I figured there was no point in being gentle with him. It was like a Band-Aid that needed to come off: either you did it with agonizing slowness, or you got it over with, hard and quick. 'I know about the accident.'

The tour bus finally started moving. Michael put his foot on the gas.

'Well,' he said after a minute, a wry smile on his face, though he kept his eyes on the road, 'you must not blame me too much, or you wouldn't have asked for a ride.'

'Blame you for what?' I asked him.

'Four people died in that accident.' Michael picked up a half-empty can of Coke from the cup holder between our seats. 'And I'm still alive.' He took a quick swallow and put the can back. 'You be the judge.'

I didn't like his tone. It wasn't that it was self-pitying. It was that it wasn't. He sounded hostile. And he wasn't stammering any more, I noticed.

'Well,' I said carefully. Like I mentioned, Father Dominic is the one who's good at reasoning. I'm more like the muscle of our little mediator family. I knew I was venturing out into deep and troubled waters – if you'll excuse the pun.

'I read in the paper today that your breath test came back negative for alcohol,' I said cautiously.

'So?' Michael exploded, startling me a little. 'What does that prove?'

I blinked at him. 'Well, that you, at least, weren't drinking and driving.'

He seemed to relax a little. He said, 'Oh.' Then he asked, tentatively, 'Do you want . . .'

I looked at him. We were driving along the coastline, and the sun, sinking into the water, had cast everything into either brilliant orange or deep shadow. The light reflecting off the lenses of Michael's glasses made it impossible to read his expression.

'Do you want to see where it happened?' he asked all in a rush, as if he wanted to get the words out before he changed his mind.

'Um, sure,' I said. 'If you feel like you want to show me.'

'I do.' He turned his head to look at me, but once again, I couldn't read his eyes behind his glasses. 'If you don't mind. It's weird, but . . . I really feel like you might understand.'

Ha! I thought smugly to myself. Take that, Father Dom! All your nagging about how I always hit first and talk later. Well, look at me now!

'Why did you do it?' Michael asked abruptly, interrupting my self-congratulations.

I threw a startled glance in his direction. 'Do what?' I genuinely hadn't the slightest idea what he was talking about.

'Go in,' he said in that same quiet voice, 'after me.'

'Oh.' I cleared my throat. 'That. Well, you see, Michael . . .'

'Never mind.'

'When I glanced over at him, I saw he was smiling.

'Don't worry about it,' he said. 'You don't have to tell me. I know.' His voice dropped about an octave. I looked over at him in alarm. 'I know.'

And then he reached across the Coke can, nestled in the

cup holder between our seats, and dropped his right hand over my left.

Oh, my God! I felt my stomach lurch all over again, just like it had back down at the beach.

Because suddenly it was all very clear to me. Michael Meducci didn't just have a crush on me. Oh, no. It was much, much worse than that:

Michael Meducci thinks *I* have a crush on *him*.

Michael Meducci thinks I *more* than just have a crush on him. Michael Meducci thinks I'm in love with him.

I had just one thing to say, and since I couldn't say it out loud, I said it in my head:

EEEEW!

I mean, he might have looked good in a bathing suit and all, but Michael Meducci still wasn't exactly . . .

Well, Jesse.

And that, I thought with a sigh, is pretty much how my love life is going to go from now on, isn't it?

Nine

Carefully, I tried to pull my hand out from under Michael's.

'Oh,' he said, lifting his hand off mine so he could grip the wheel. 'It's coming up. Where the accident happened, I mean.'

Hideously relieved, I glanced to my right. We were moving along Highway 1 at quite a little clip. The sands of Carmel Beach had turned into the majestic cliffs of Big Sur. A few more miles down the coast, and we'd hit redwood groves and Point Sur Lighthouse. Big Sur was a haven for hikers and campers, and just about anybody who liked magnificent views and breathtaking natural beauty. Me, I'll take the views, but nature leaves me cold . . . especially after a little poison oak incident that had occurred a week or two after I'd arrived in California.

And don't even get me started on ticks.

Big Sur – or at least the pretty much one-lane road that winds along it – also hosts quite a few hairpin curves. Michael eased around a completely blind one just as a Winnebago, coming from the other direction, came thundering around the other side of this massive cliff. There wasn't exactly room for both vehicles, and considering that all that was separating us from the sheer drop-off to the sea was a metal guard rail, it was a bit disconcerting. Michael, however, backed up – we hadn't been going that fast – and then pulled over, allowing the Winnebago to ease by with only a foot or so of room to spare.

'Jeez,' I said, glancing back at the huge RV. 'That's kind of dangerous, huh?'

Michael shrugged. 'You're supposed to honk,' he said, 'as you round that corner. To let anyone behind that rock thing know you're there. That guy didn't know, obviously, because he's a tourist.' Michael cleared his throat. 'That's what happened, um, on Saturday night.'

I sat up straighter in my seat.

'This—' I swallowed. '—is where it happened?'

'Yeah,' Michael said. There was no change in the inflection of his voice at all. 'This is it.'

And indeed it was. Now that I knew to look for them, I could plainly see the black skid marks the wheels of Josh's car had left as he'd tried to keep from going over. A large section of the guard rail had already been replaced, the metal shiny and new just where the skid marks ended.

I asked, in a quiet voice, 'Can we stop?'

'Sure,' Michael said.

There was a scenic overlook around the corner, not a hundred yards away from where the cars had narrowly missed each other. Michael pulled into it and turned off the engine.

'Observation point,' he said, pointing to the wooden sign in front of us that said, *Observation point. No Littering.* 'A lot of kids come here on Saturday night.' Michael cleared his throat and looked at me meaningfully. 'And park.'

I have to say, up until that moment I really had no idea I was capable of moving as fast as I did getting out of that car. But I was unbuckled and out of that seat quicker than you could say *ectoplasm*.

The sun had almost completely set now, and it was already growing chilly. I hugged myself as I stood on tip-toe to look over the edge of the cliff, my hair whipping my face in the wind off the sea, which was much wilder and cooler up here than it had been back down on the beach. The rhythmic pulse of the sea below us was loud, much louder than the engines of the cars going by on Highway 1.

There were, I noticed, no gulls. No birds of any kind.

That should, of course, have been my first clue. But as usual, I missed it.

Instead, all I could concentrate on was how sheer the drop was. Hundreds of feet, straight down, into waves churning against giant boulders knocked down from the cliffsides during various earthquakes. Not exactly the kind of cliff you'd catch anyone – not even Elvis back in his Acapulco prime – diving off.

Strangely, at the bottom of the place where Josh's car had gone off of the road was a small, sandy beach. Not the kind you'd go to sunbathe, but a nice picnic area, if you were willing to risk your neck climbing down to get there.

Michael must have noticed my gaze, since he said, 'Yeah, that's where they landed. Not in the water. Well, at least, not right away. Then high tide came in, and—'

I shuddered and looked away.

'Is there some way,' I wondered aloud, 'to get down there?'

'Sure,' he said, and pointed at an open section of the guard rail. 'Over there. It's a trail. Hikers are the only ones who use it, mostly. But sometimes tourists try it. The beach down there is amazing. You never saw such huge waves. Only it's too dangerous to surf. Too many rip tides.'

I looked at him curiously in the purpling twilight. 'You've

been down there?' I asked. The surprise in my voice must have been evident.

'Suze,' he said with a smile. 'I've lived here all my life. There aren't a whole lot of beaches I haven't been to.'

I nodded, and pulled at a strand of hair that had found its way into my mouth thanks to the wind. 'So, what,' I asked him, 'happened, exactly, that night?'

He squinted at the road. It was dark enough now that the cars travelling on it had switched on their lights. Occasionally, the glow of one swept his face as he spoke. Again, it was difficult to see his eyes behind the reflection of the light against the lenses of his glasses.

'I was coming home,' he said, 'from a workshop at Esalen—'

'Esalen?'

'Yeah. The Esalen Institute. You've never heard of it?' He shook his head. 'My God, I thought it was known world-wide.' My expression must have been pretty blank, since he said, 'Well, anyway, I was at a lecture there. "Colonization of Other Worlds, and What It Means for Exterrestrials Here on Earth."'

I tried not to burst out laughing. I was, after all, a girl who could see and speak to ghosts. Who was I to say there wasn't life on other planets?

'Anyway, I was driving home – it was pretty late, I guess – and they came barrelling around that corner, didn't honk, nothing.'

I nodded. 'So what did you do?'

'Well, I swerved to avoid them, of course, and ended up going into that cliff there. You can't see it because it's dark out now, but my front bumper took out a big chunk of the side of the hill. And they . . . well, they swerved the other way, and it was foggy, and the road might have been a little slick, and they were going really fast, and . . .'

He finished, tonelessly, with another shrug. 'And they went over.'

I shuddered again. I couldn't help it. I had met these kids, remember. They hadn't exactly been at their best – in fact, they'd been trying to kill me – but still, I couldn't help feeling sorry for them. It was a long, long way down.

'So what did you do?' I asked.

'Me?' He seemed strangely surprised by the question. 'Well, I hit my head, you know, so I blacked out. I didn't come around until someone pulled over and checked on me. That's when I asked what happened to the other car. And they said, "What other car?" And I thought they'd, you know, driven away, and I have to admit, I was pretty hacked. I mean, that they hadn't bothered to call an ambulance for me, or anything. But then we saw the guard rail . . .'

I was getting really cold now. The sun was completely gone, although the western sky was still streaked violet and red. I shivered and said, 'Let's get in the car.'

And so we did.

We sat there staring at the horizon as it turned a deeper and deeper shade of blue. The headlights from the cars that went by occasionally lit up the interior of the minivan. Inside the car it was much quieter, without the wind and the sound of the waves below us. Another wave of extreme tiredness passed over me. I could see by the glow of the clock in the dashboard that soon it would be dinnertime. My stepfather Andy had a very strict rule about dinner. You showed up. Period.

'Look,' I said, breaking the stillness. 'It sounds horrible, what happened. But it wasn't your fault.'

He looked at me. In the green glow from the instruments

91

in the dash, I could see that his smile was rueful. 'Wasn't it?' he asked.

'No,' I said sternly. 'It was an accident, plain and simple. The problem is . . . well, not everyone sees it that way.'

The smile disappeared. 'Who doesn't see it that way?' he demanded. 'The cops? I gave them my statement. They seemed satisfied. They took a blood sample. I tested completely negative for alcohol, for all drugs. They can't possibly—'

'Not,' I said quickly, 'the cops.' How, I wondered, was I going to put this? I mean, the guy was obviously one of those UFO geeks, so you'd think he wouldn't have a problem with ghosts, but you never knew.

'The thing is,' I began, carefully, 'I've kind of noticed that since the accident this weekend, you've been a bit . . . danger prone.'

'Yeah,' Michael said. All of a sudden, his hand was on mine again. 'If it wasn't for you, I might even be dead. That's twice now you've saved my life.'

'Ha ha,' I said nervously, pulling my hand away, and pretending I had another hair in my mouth so I needed to use that particular hand, you know, to brush it away. 'Um, but seriously, haven't you kind of, I mean, wondered what was going on? Like why all of a sudden so many . . . *things* were happening to you?'

He smiled at me again. His teeth, in the glow of the speedometer, looked green. 'It must be fate,' he said.

'OK,' I said. *Why me?* 'Not those kind of things. I mean *bad* kind of things. Like at the mall. And at the beach just now . . .'

'Oh,' he said. Then he shrugged those incredibly strong shoulders. 'No.'

'OK,' I said yet again. 'But if you were to think about it,

don't you think one sort of logical explanation might be . . . angry spirits?'

His smile faded a little. 'What do you mean?'

I heaved a sigh. 'Look, that wasn't a jellyfish back there, and you know it. You were being pulled under, Michael. By something.'

He nodded. 'I know. I haven't quite . . . I'm used to undertows, of course, but that was—'

'It wasn't an undertow. And it wasn't jellyfish. And I just . . . well, I think you should be careful.'

'What are you saying?' Michael asked. He peered at me curiously. 'It almost sounds like you're suggesting that I've been the victim of some kind of . . . demonic force.' He laughed. In the quiet of the car, his laugh was loud. 'Brought on by the deaths of those kids who almost ran me off of the road? Is that it?'

I looked out my window. I couldn't see anything except the huge purple shadows of the steep cliffs around us, but I kept looking anyway. 'Yes,' I said. 'That's exactly it.'

'Suze.' Michael reached for my hand again, and this time, he squeezed it. 'Are you trying to tell me that you believe in ghosts?'

I looked at him. I looked him straight in the eye. And I said, 'Yes, Michael. Yes, I am.'

He laughed again. 'Oh, come on,' he said. 'Do you honestly think that *Josh Saunders* and his friends are capable of communicating from beyond the grave?'

Something in the way he said Josh's name caused me to . . . I don't know. But I didn't like it. I didn't like it at all.

'I mean—' Michael let go of my hand, then leaned forward and switched on the ignition. 'Face facts. The guy was a dumb jock. The most impressive thing he ever did was plunge off of a cliff with another dumb jock, and their equally low-wattage girlfriends. It's not necessarily such a bad thing they're gone, you know? They were just taking up space.'

My jaw sagged. I felt it. And yet there didn't seem to be anything I could do about it.

'And as for any of them being able to summon up any sort of powers of darkness,' Michael said, putting vocal quotes around the words *powers of darkness*, 'to avenge their pitifully stupid deaths, well, thanks for the warning, but I think that whole *I Know What You Did Last Summer* thing has pretty much been played out, don't you?'

I stared at him. Really stared at him. I couldn't believe it. So much for Mr Sensitive. I guess he only stammered and blushed when his own life was being threatened. He didn't seem to care very much about anybody else's.

Unless maybe he was going out with them on Friday night, as was illustrated by his comment as we were about to pull out on to the highway again:

'Hey,' he said with a wink. 'Buckle up.'

Ten

I flung myself into my seat just as everybody else was picking up their forks.

Ha! Not late! Not technically, since no one had actually started eating yet.

'And where have you been, Suze?' my mother asked, lifting a basket of rolls and passing it directly to Gina. Good thing, too. Otherwise, given the way my brothers ate, that thing would be empty before it ever reached her.

'I went,' I said as Max, my stepbrothers' extremely large, extremely slobbery dog, dropped his head down upon my lap, his traditional station at mealtimes, and rolled his soft brown eyes up at me, 'on a drive.'

'With whom?' my mother asked in that same mild tone, the one that indicated that if I didn't answer carefully, I could potentially be in serious trouble.

Before I could say anything, Dopey went, 'Michael Meducci,' and made some gagging noises.

Andy raised his eyebrows. 'That boy who was here last night?'

'That'd be the one,' I said, shooting Dopey a dirty look that he ignored. Gina and Sleepy, I noticed, had taken care to sit beside each other and were strangely quiet. I wondered, if I dropped my napkin and leaned down to pick it up, what I'd see going on underneath the table. Probably, I thought to myself, something I did not particularly care to see. I kept my napkin tightly in my lap.

'Meducci,' my mother murmured. 'Why is that name familiar to me?'

'Doubtlessly,' Doc said, 'you are thinking of the Medicis, an Italian noble family that produced three popes and two queens of France. Cosimo the Elder was the first to rule Florence, while Lorenzo the Magnificent was a patron of the arts, with clients that included Michelangelo and Botticelli.'

My mother looked at him curiously. 'Actually,' she said, 'that's not what I was thinking.'

I knew what was coming. My mom has a memory like a steel trap. She needs it, of course, in her line of work. But I knew it was only a matter of time before she figured out where she'd heard Michael's name before.

'He was the one who was in that accident this weekend,' I said, to hasten the inevitable. 'The one where those four RLS students were killed.'

Dopey dropped his fork. It made quite a clatter as it landed on his plate.

'Michael *Meducci?*' He shook his head. 'No way. That was *Michael Meducci?* You are shitting me.'

Andy said, sharply, 'Brad. Language, please.'

Dopey said, 'Sorry,' but his eyes, I noticed, were very bright. 'Michael Meducci,' he said again. 'Michael Meducci killed Mark Pulsford?'

'He didn't kill anybody,' I snapped. I could see I should have kept my mouth shut. Now it was going to be all over school. 'It was an accident.'

'Really, Brad,' Andy said. 'I'm sure the poor boy didn't mean to kill anyone.'

'Well, I'm sorry,' Dopey said. 'But Mark Pulsford was like one of the best quarterbacks in the state. Seriously. He had a scholarship to UCLA, the whole thing. That guy was really cool.'

'Oh, yeah? Then what was he doing hanging around you?' Sleepy, in a rare moment of wit, grinned at his brother.

'Shut up,' Dopey said. 'We happen to have partied together.'

'Right,' Sleepy said with a sneer.

'We did,' Dopey insisted. 'Last month, in the Valley. Mark was the bomb.' He grabbed a roll, stuffed most of it into his mouth, then said around the doughy mass, 'Until Michael Meducci came along and murdered him, that is.'

I noticed that Gina was observing me with one eyebrow – one only – raised. I ignored her.

'The accident wasn't Michael's fault,' I said. 'At least, he hasn't been charged with anything.'

My mother laid down her own fork. 'The investigation into the accident,' she said, 'is still ongoing.'

'As many accidents as they've had,' my stepfather said as he rolled a few spears of asparagus on to my mother's plate, then passed the platter of them to Gina, 'on that section of highway, you would think somebody would do something to improve the road conditions.'

'The narrow stretch of highway,' Doc said conversationally, 'along the one-hundred-mile stretch of seacoast known as Big Sur has traditionally been considered treacherous – even highly dangerous. Frequently enshrouded with coastal fog, this winding and narrow mountainous road is, thanks to historical preservationists, unlikely to be expanded. The very isolation of the area is what has held such appeal for the many poets and artists who have made their homes there, including Robinson Jeffers, who found the splendour of the bleak wilderness highly appealing.'

I blinked at my youngest stepbrother. His photographic memory could, at times, be annoying, but for the most part it was highly useful, particularly when term paper time came rolling around.

'Thanks,' I said, 'for that.'

Doc smiled, revealing a mouthful of food-encrusted braces. 'Don't mention it.'

'The worst part of it,' Andy said, continuing his rant on the safety conditions on Highway 1, 'is that young drivers seem irresistibly drawn to that particular stretch of road.'

Dopey, shoveling wild rice into his mouth as if it were the first food he'd seen in weeks, snickered and said, 'Well, duh, Dad.'

Andy looked at his middle-born son. 'You know, Brad,' he said mildly. 'In America – and, I'm told, much of Europe – it is considered socially acceptable to occasionally lay down our fork between bites, and spend some time actually chewing.'

'That's where the action is,' Dopey said, laying down his fork as his father had suggested, but compensating by speaking with his mouth full.

'What action?' my stepfather asked curiously.

Sleepy, who generally didn't speak unless absolutely forced to, had grown almost garrulous since Gina's arrival. 'He means the Point,' Sleepy said.

My mother looked confused. 'The point?'

'The Point,' Sleepy corrected her. 'The observation point. It's where everybody goes to make out on Saturday night. At least' – Sleepy chuckled to himself – 'Brad and his friends.'

Dopey, far from taking offence at this slanderous remark,

98

waved an asparagus spear as if it were a cigar while he explained, 'The Point is the bomb.'

'Is that,' Doc asked interestedly, 'where you take Debbie Mancuso?' and then he winced in pain as one of his shins was brutally assaulted beneath the table. 'Ow!'

'Debbie Mancuso and I are not going out!' Dopey bellowed.

'Brad,' Andy said. 'Do not kick your brother. David, do not invoke Miss Mancuso's name at the dinner table. We've talked about this. And Suze?'

I looked up with raised eyebrows.

'I don't like the idea of you getting into a car with a boy who was involved in a fatal accident, whether it was his fault or not.' Andy looked at my mother. 'Do you agree?'

'I'm afraid I'm going to have to,' my mother said. 'I feel bad about it. The Meduccis have certainly been through some trying times lately—' When my stepfather looked at her questioningly, my mother said, 'Their little girl was the one who almost drowned a few weeks ago. You remember.'

'Oh.' Andy nodded. 'At that pool party. There was no parental supervision—'

'And plenty of alcohol,' my mother said. 'Poor thing apparently drank too much and fell in. Nobody noticed – or if they did, nobody did anything about it. Not until it was too late. She's been in a coma ever since. If she lives, it will be with severe brain damage. Suze.' My mother laid down her fork. 'I don't think it's a good idea for you to be seeing this boy.'

Ordinarily, this would have cheered me up considerably. I mean, I wasn't exactly looking forward to going out with the guy.

But I sort of had to. I mean, if I was to have any hope at all of keeping him from slipping into a nerd coffin.

'Why?' I carefully swallowed a mouthful of salmon. 'It's not Michael's fault his sister's an alcoholic who can't swim. And what were her parents thinking, anyway, letting an eighth grader go to a party like that?'

'That,' my mother said, her mouth tightening, 'is not the issue here, and you know it. You're just going to have to call that young man and tell him that your mother absolutely forbids you to get into a vehicle with him. If he wants to come here and spend the evening with you watching videos or whatever, that's fine. But you are not getting into a car with him.'

My eyes widened. *Here?* Spend the evening *here?* Under Jesse's watchful eye? Oh, God, just what I needed. The image these words conveyed filled me with such horror, the forkful of salmon I'd had poised before my lips fell into my lap, where it was instantly vacuumed up by a long canine tongue.

My mother touched my hand. 'Suze,' she said softly. 'I really mean it. I don't want you getting into a car with that boy.'

I looked at my mother curiously. It's true that in times past I have been forced to disobey her, largely due to circumstances beyond my control. But she didn't know that. That I had disobeyed her, I mean. For the most part, I'd managed to keep my transgressions to myself – except for the occasions I'd been brought home by the police, incidents so few they are hardly worth mentioning.

But since that had not been the case in this situation, I didn't quite understand why she felt it necessary to repeat her edict concerning Michael Meducci.

'Okay, Mom,' I said. 'I got it the first time.'

'It's just something I feel very strongly about,' she said.

I looked at her. It wasn't that she appeared . . . well, guilty.

But she definitely knew something. Something she wasn't letting on.

This was not particularly surprising. A television journalist, my mother was often privy to information not necessarily meant for release to the public. She wasn't one of those reporters you hear about, either, who'd do anything to get the 'big' story. If a cop told my mother something – and they often do; my mother, even though she's forty-something, is still pretty hot, and just about anybody would tell her anything she wanted to know if she licked her lips enough – he could depend on her not mentioning it on air if he asked her not to. That's just how she is.

I wondered what, exactly, she knew about Michael Meducci and the accident that had killed the four Angels.

Enough, apparently, to keep her from wanting me to hang around with him.

I didn't exactly think she was being particularly unfair to him, either. I couldn't help remembering what Michael had said in the car, right before pulling back out on to the highway: *They were just taking up space.*

Suddenly, I didn't blame those kids so much for trying to drown him.

'Okay, Mom,' I said. 'I get it.'

Apparently satisfied, my mother turned back to her salmon, which Andy had grilled to perfection and served with a delicate dill sauce.

'So how are you going to break it to him?' Gina asked a half hour later as she helped me load the dishwasher after dinner – having brushed aside my mother's insistence that, as a guest, she did not have to do this.

'I don't know,' I said hesitantly. 'You know, the whole Clark Kent thing aside—'

'Geeky on the outside, dreamy in the middle?'

'Yeah. In spite of that – which is hard to resist, believe me – he's still kind of got this quality that strikes me as . . .'

'Stalkery?' Gina said, rinsing the salad bowl before handing it to me to put in the dishwasher rack.

'Maybe that's it. I don't know.'

'It was very stalkery how he showed up here last night,' she said. 'Without even calling first. Any guy ever tried to do that to me' – she waved her fingers in the air and then snapped them – 'and he is so gone.'

I shrugged. It was different back east, of course. In the city, you simply do not stop by someone's place without calling first. In California, I'd noticed, 'drive-bys' were more socially acceptable.

'But don't even act,' Gina went on, 'like you care, Simon. You don't like that guy. I don't know what, exactly, you've got going on with him, but it definitely isn't anything gonadal.'

I thought, fleetingly, of how pleasantly surprised we'd all been when Michael had taken his shirt off. 'It might have been,' I said with a sigh.

'Please.' Gina handed me a fistful of silverware. 'You and Supergeek? No. Now, tell me. What is going on with you and this guy?'

I looked down at the silverware I'd been shoving into the dishwasher. 'I don't know,' I said. I couldn't tell her the truth, of course. 'There's just . . . I've got this feeling that there's more to this accident thing than he's letting on. My mom seems to know something about it. Did you notice?'

'I noticed,' Gina said, not really grimly, but not happily, either.

'Well, so . . . I just can't help wondering what really happened. The night of the wreck. Because . . . well, that wasn't a jellyfish this afternoon, you know.'

Gina just nodded. 'I didn't think so. I suppose this all has something to do with that mediator thing, huh?'

'Sort of,' I said uncomfortably.

'Right. Which might also explain that little mishap with the fingernail polish the other night?'

I couldn't say anything. I just kept thrusting the silverware into the plastic compartments in the dishwasher door. Forks, spoons, knives.

'All right.' Gina turned off the water in the sink and dried her hands on a dish towel. 'What do you want me to do?'

I blinked at her. 'Do? You? Nothing.'

'Come on. I know you, Simon. You didn't miss home-room seventy-nine times last year because you were enjoying a leisurely breakfast over at the Mickey D's. I know perfectly well you were out there fighting the undead, making this world a safer place for children, and all that. So what do you want me to do? Cover for you?'

I bit my lip. 'Well,' I said hesitantly.

'Look, don't worry about me. Jake said he'd take me on his delivery run – which holds a certain appeal, if you can stand getting down and dirty in a car full of pepperoni and pineapple pizzas. But if you want, I can stay here and hang with Brad. He's invited me to a video screening of his favourite movie of all time.'

I sucked in my breath. 'Not *Hellraiser III* . . . ?'

'Indeed.'

Gratitude washed over me like one of those waves that had knocked me senseless. 'You would do that for me?'

'For you, Simon, anything. So what's it going to be?'

'OK.' I threw down the dish towel I'd been holding. 'If you would just stay here and pretend like I'm upstairs in my room with cramps, I will worship you forever. They don't ask questions about cramps. Say that I'm in the bathtub, and then maybe a little while later, say I went to bed early. If anyone calls, will you take it for me?'

'As you wish, Queen Midol.'

'Oh, Gina.' I grabbed her by the shoulders and gave her a little shake. 'You are the best. You understand? The *best*. Don't throw yourself away on my stepbrothers: you could do so much better.'

'You just don't see it,' Gina said, shaking her head wonderingly. 'Your stepbrothers are *hot*. Well, except for that little red-headed one. And hey—' This she added as I was headed to the phone to make a call to Father Dominic. '— I expect compensation, you know.'

I blinked at her. 'You know I only get twenty bucks a week allowance, but you can have it—'

Gina made a face. 'I don't want your money. But a thorough explanation would be nice. You never would give me one. You always just dodged the question. But this time, you owe me.' She narrowed her eyes. 'I mean, I am going to sit through a screening of *Hellraiser III* for you. You owe me *big* time. And yes,' she added, before I could open my mouth, 'I won't tell anybody. I promise not to call the *Enquirer* or *Ripley's Believe It or Not*.'

I said, with what dignity I could muster, 'I wouldn't have thought otherwise.'

Then I picked up the phone and dialled.

Eleven

'So what is it, exactly,' I said as I swung the flashlight back and forth across the sandy trail, 'that I'm supposed to be looking for?'

'I'm not sure,' Father Dominic, a few steps ahead of me, said. 'You'll know, I expect, when you find it.'

'Great,' I muttered.

It was no joke trying to climb down a mountainside in the dark. If I had known this was what Father Dom was going to suggest when I called, I probably would have put off phoning him. I probably would have just stayed home and watched *Hellraiser III* instead. Or at least attempted to finish my geometry homework. I mean, really. I had already nearly died once that day. The Pythagorean theorem hardly seemed threatening in comparison.

'Don't worry,' I heard a guy's voice behind me, laced with tolerant amusement, say. 'There's no poison oak.'

I turned my head and gave Jesse a very sarcastic look, even though I doubted he could see it. The moon – if there was one – was hidden behind a thick wall of clouds. Tendrils of fog crept along the cliffside we were climbing down, gathering thickly in the dips the trail made, swirling whenever I set my foot down in it, as if it were recoiling at the prospect of touching me. I tried not to think about movies I'd seen in which horrible things happened to people out in such heavy fog. You know the movies I'm talking about.

At the same time, I tried not to think about all the poison oak that might be brushing up against me. Jesse had been joking, of course, but in his usual way, he had read my mind: I have a real thing about disfiguring skin rashes.

And don't even get me started about snakes, which I had every reason to believe might be curled up all along this sorry excuse for a path, just waiting to take a chunk out of the soft fleshy part of my calf just above my Timberlands.

'Yes,' I heard Father Dom say. The fog had rushed in and swallowed him up, and I could see only the faint pinprick of yellow his flashlight made in front of me. 'Yes, I can see that the police have already been here. This must be where a section of the guard rail fell. You can see its imprint in the broken weeds.'

I staggered blindly along, using the beam from my flash-light primarily to hunt for snakes, but also to make sure I didn't step off the trail and plunge the several hundred feet or so into the churning surf below. Jesse had already reached out twice to steer me gently away from the edge of the path when I'd strayed from it while eyeing a suspicious branch.

Now I nearly staggered off it after colliding hard with Father Dom, who'd stopped in the middle of the trail and crouched down. I hadn't seen him at all, and both he and Jesse had to reach out and grab various articles of my clothing in order to right me again. This was not a little embarrassing.

'Sorry,' I muttered, mortified at my own clumsiness. 'Um, what are you doing, Father D?'

Father Dominic smiled in that infuriatingly patient way of

his, and said, 'Examining some of the evidence from the accident. You mentioned that your mother seemed to know something about it, and I have a feeling that I know what.'

I zipped my windbreaker up more fully, so that my neck was no longer exposed to the chilly night air. It may have been springtime in California, but it couldn't have been more than forty degrees out there on that cliff. Fortunately, I had brought along gloves – mainly as protection, it must be admitted, from potential contact with poison oak – but they were doing double duty now, keeping my fingers from freezing.

'What do you mean?' I hadn't thought to bring along a hat, and so my ears felt like icicles, and my hair kept whipping around in the cold wind off the sea and smacking me in the eyes.

'Look at this.' Father Dominic shined his flashlight along a section of the earth, about six feet long, where the dirt was churned up, and the grass broken. 'This, I think, is where the guard rail ended up. But do you notice anything odd about it?'

I pulled some hair out of my mouth and kept my eyes peeled for snakes. 'No.'

'That particular section of rail seems to have come down in one piece. A vehicle would have to be moving at considerable speed to break through such strong metal fencing, but the fact that the entire section seems to have given way suggests that the metal rivets holding it in place must have snapped.'

'Or they were loosened,' Jesse suggested quietly.

I blinked up at him. Being dead, Jesse wasn't suffering half as much discomfort as I was. The cold didn't affect him, although the wind was catching on his shirt quite a bit, pulling it out and affording me glimpses of his chest, which,

I probably don't need to add, was every bit as buff as Michael's, only not quite as pale.

'Loosened?' For the second time that day, my teeth had started to chatter. 'What would cause something like that? Rust?'

'I was thinking something a little more man-made, actually,' Jesse said quietly.

I looked from the priest to the ghost, then back again. Father Dominic looked as perplexed as I felt. Jesse had not exactly been invited along on this little expedition, but he had shown up as I'd made my way down the driveway to the spot where Father D had said he'd pick me up. Father Dominic's reaction to the news I'd imparted – about the attempt on Michael's life at the beach, and his odd comments in the car later – had been swift and immediate. We needed, he declared, to find the RLS Angels, and fast.

And the easiest way to do that, of course, was to visit the place where their lives had been lost, a locale, Jesse pointed out, best not visited alone at night by a sixty-year-old priest and a sixteen-year-old girl.

I have no idea what Jesse thought he was protecting us from by coming along: bears? But there he was, and apparently, he had a way better idea than I did about what was going on.

'What do you mean, man-made?' I demanded. 'What are you talking about?'

'I just think it's strange,' Jesse said, 'that a whole section of this railing would give way like that, while the rest – as we saw when we inspected it a little while ago – didn't even bend upon the impact.'

Father Dominic blinked. 'You're suggesting that someone might have loosened the rivets in anticipation of a vehicle striking it. Is that it, Jesse?'

Jesse nodded. I got what he was driving at, but only after a minute or so.

'Wait a minute,' I said. 'Are you saying you think *Michael* purposely loosened that section of guard rail so that he could run Josh and the others over the cliff?'

'Someone certainly did,' Jesse said. 'It might well have been your Michael.'

I took umbrage at that. Not at the suggestion that Michael might have done something so heinous, but at Jesse calling him *my* Michael.

'Wait just a minute—' I began. But Father Dominic rather uncharacteristically interrupted me.

'I have to agree with Susannah, Jesse,' Father Dominic said. 'Certainly it appears that the rail did not perform the function it was intended to. In fact, a rather serious flaw in its design seems to have occurred. But to suggest that someone might have purposefully tampered with it . . . '

'Susannah,' Jesse said. 'Didn't you say that Michael seems to dislike the people who died in the accident?'

'Well,' I said, 'he did tell me he thought that they were a waste of space. But honestly, Jesse, in order for what you're suggesting to work, Michael would have had to know Josh and those guys were coming. How could he have known that? And he'd have had to wait for them, and then when they started to round the corner, he'd have had to purposefully put down the gas . . . '

'Well,' Jesse said with a shrug. 'Yes.'

'Impossible.' Father Dominic straightened up, brushing dirt from the knees of his trousers. 'I refuse even to consider such a possibility. That boy, a cold-blooded murderer? You don't know what you're saying, Jesse. Why, he's got the highest grade point average in school. He's a member of the Chess Club.'

I patted Father Dominic on the shoulder. 'Hate to break it to you, Father D,' I said, 'but chess players can kill people, just like anyone else.' Then I looked down at the gouge mark, in the earth where the guard rail had lain. 'The real question is why?' I asked. 'I mean, *why* would he do something like that?'

'I think,' Jesse said, 'if we hurry, we might be able to find out.'

He pointed. We looked. The clouds overhead had parted enough to allow us to see the tiny slice of beach at the bottom of the cliff. The moonlight picked out four ghostly forms huddled in a circle around a pitiful little campfire.

'Oh, God,' I said as the clouds closed in again, quickly obscuring the sight. 'All the way down there? I know I'm going to get bitten.'

Father Dominic had already started hurrying down the rest of the trail. Jesse, behind me, asked curiously, 'Bitten by what, Susannah?'

'A snake, of course,' I said, avoiding a root that had looked a bit snakelike in the beam from my flashlight.

'Snakes,' Jesse said – and I could tell by his voice that he was restraining an urge to laugh, 'don't come out at night.'

This was news to me. 'They don't?'

'Not usually. And particularly not on cold, wet nights like this. They like the sun.'

Well, that was a relief. Still, I couldn't help wondering about ticks. Did ticks come out at night?

It seemed to take forever – and I was sure that I'd wake up with shin splints – but we eventually reached the bottom of the path, though the last fifty feet or so were so steep, I practically sprinted down them, and not on purpose, either.

There on the beach, the sound of the waves was much, much louder – loud enough to completely drown out the sound of our approach. The smell of salt was heavy in the air. I realized, as our feet sank into the wet sand – well, except for Jesse's – why it was I hadn't seen any gulls earlier in the evening: animals, including birds, don't like ghosts.

And there were a lot of ghosts on this particular beach.

They were singing. I am not kidding you. They were singing around their sulky little fire. You won't believe what they were singing, either. 'Ninety-nine Bottles of Beer on the Wall.' Seriously. They were on fifty-seven.

I tell you, if that's how I end up spending eternity when I die, I hope some mediator comes along and puts me out of my misery. I really do.

'OK,' I said, slipping off my gloves and jamming them in my pockets. 'Jesse, you take the guys. I'll take the girls. Father D, you just make sure none of them makes a run for the waves, all right? I've already been swimming once today, and believe me, that water's cold. I am not going in after them.'

Father Dominic caught my arm as I started striding toward the firelit group.

'Susannah!' he cried, looking genuinely shocked. 'Surely you can't . . . you aren't seriously suggesting that we—'

'Father D.' I gawked up at him. 'Earlier this afternoon, those jerks over there tried to drown me. Pardon me if I feel that sauntering up to them and asking them if they'd like to join us for root beer floats isn't such a good idea. Let's go kick some supernatural butt.'

Father Dominic only clutched my arm tighter. 'Susannah, how many times do I have to tell you? We are mediators. Our job is to intercede on behalf of troubled souls, not cause them more pain and grief by committing acts of violence upon them—'

'I'll tell you what,' I said. 'Jesse and I will hold them down while you do the interceding. Because, believe me, that's the only way they're going to listen. They aren't real communicative.'

'Susannah,' Father Dom said again.

But this time, he didn't get to finish whatever it was he was going to say. That's because all of a sudden, Jesse went, 'Stay here, both of you, until I say it's all right to move.'

And then he started striding across the beach toward the ghosts.

Huh. I guess he'd gotten sick of listening to the two of us arguing. Well, you couldn't really blame him.

Father Dominic looked worriedly after Jesse. 'Oh, dear,' he said. 'You don't think he's going to do anything . . . rash, do you, Susannah?'

I sighed. Jesse never did anything rash.

'No,' I said. 'He's probably just going to try to talk to them. It's better this way, I guess. I mean, he's a ghost, they're ghosts . . . they've got a lot of stuff in common.'

'Ah,' Father Dominic said, nodding. 'Yes, I see. Very wise. Very wise indeed.'

The Angels were at seventeen bottles of beer on the wall by the time they noticed Jesse.

One of the boys swore quite colourfully, but before any of them had time to dematerialize, Jesse was speaking – and in such a low voice that Father D and I couldn't hear him above the sound of the waves. We could only watch as Jesse – glowing a little, the way ghosts tend to – spoke to them, and then, slowly, after a little while, lowered himself into the sand, still talking.

Father Dominic, watching the proceedings intently, murmured, 'Excellent idea, sending Jesse in first.'

I shrugged. 'I guess.'

I guess my disappointment that I'd missed out on what probably would have been a first-class brawl must have shown, since Father D tore his gaze from the group around the campfire, and grinned down at me.

'With a little help from Jesse, we just might make a mediator of you yet,' he said.

As if he had a clue as to how many ghosts I'd mediated out of existence before I'd ever even met either of them, I thought. But I didn't say it out loud.

'And how,' Father Dominic asked quietly, 'is your little friend Gina occupying herself while you're out tonight?'

'Oh,' I said. 'She's covering for me.'

Father Dominic raised his eyebrows – and his voice – in surprised disapproval. 'Covering for you? Your parents don't know you're here?'

'Oh, yeah, Father D,' I said sarcastically. 'I told my mom I was coming out to Big Sur to deal with the ghosts of some dead teenagers. Please.'

He looked troubled. Being a priest, Father D frowns on dishonesty, particularly when it involves parents, whom his ilk are always encouraging us to honour and obey. But I figure if God really wanted me heeding that particular rule, He wouldn't have made me a mediator. The two things just don't mix, you know?

'But evidently,' Father Dominic said, 'you had no trouble telling Gina.'

'I didn't, actually. Tell her, I mean. She kind of just . . . knows. I mean, once she and I went to this psychic, and . . .' My voice trailed off. Talking about Madame Zara reminded me of what Gina had told me, about the whole one single love of a lifetime thing. Was it true? I wondered. Could it possibly be true? I shivered, but this time, it had nothing to do with the cold.

'I see,' Father Dominic said. 'Interesting. You feel comfortable telling your friends about your extraordinary ability, but not your own mother.'

We had had this argument before – recently, in fact – so I just rolled my eyes at him. 'Friend,' I corrected him. 'Not *friends*. Gina knows. Nobody else. And she doesn't know *all* of it. She doesn't, for instance, know about Jesse.'

Father Dominic glanced in the direction of the bonfire once again. Jesse appeared to be deeply engrossed in his conversation with Josh and the others. Their faces, orange in the firelight, were all turned in his direction, their gazes locked on him. It was strange they had built that fire. They couldn't feel it, any more than they could get drunk from the beer they'd tried to steal, or drown in the water they'd been under. I wondered why they had gone to the trouble. It had probably taken a lot of kinetic power to light it.

All four of them glowed with the same subtle light Jesse gave off – not enough to see by on a dark night like this, but enough to tell they weren't quite . . . well, *human* was the wrong word, because of course they were human. Or had been, anyway.

I guess the word I'm looking for is *alive*.

'Father D,' I said, abruptly. 'Do you believe in psychics? I mean, are they real? Like mediators?'

Father Dominic said, 'I'm sure some of them are.'

'Well,' I went on in a rush before I could change my mind. 'This psychic Gina and I went to once, she knew I was a mediator. I didn't tell her, or anything. She just knew. And she said this weird thing. At least, Gina says she did. I don't remember it. But according to Gina, she said I would only have one true love.'

Father Dominic looked down at me. Was it my imagination, or did he look amused? 'Were you planning on having a great many?'

'Well, not exactly,' I said, a little embarrassed. You would have been, too. I mean, come on. The guy was a priest. 'But it's kind of weird. This psychic – Madame Zara – she said a bunch of stuff about how I'd just have this one love, but that it would last for, like, my whole life.' I swallowed. 'Or maybe it was all eternity. I forget.'

'Oh,' Father Dominic said, not looking amused any more. 'Dear.'

'That's what I said. I mean . . . well, she probably didn't know what she was talking about. Because that sounds kind of bogus, right?' I asked hopefully.

But much to my disappointment, Father D said, 'No, Susannah. It does not sound bogus. Not to me.'

He said it in such a way . . . I don't know. Something about the way he said it made me ask, curiously, 'Were you ever in love, Father D?'

He started fumbling around in his coat pockets. 'Um,' he said.

I knew what he was looking for so intently: a pack of cigarettes. I also knew he wasn't going to find any – he had quit smoking years ago, and kept only one pack for emergencies. And that, I happened to know, was back in his office at the school.

I also knew, from the fact that he'd started looking for them at all, that Father D was stressed. He only felt an urge to smoke when things weren't quite going how he'd planned.

He had been in love. I could totally tell by the way he was avoiding meeting my gaze.

I wasn't really surprised. Father Dominic was old, and a priest, and everything, but he was still a hottie, in a senior citizen, Sean Connery kind of way.

'There was, I believe,' he said finally, when his search came up negative, 'a young woman. At one time.'

Aha. I pictured Audrey Hepburn, for some reason. You know, in that movie that's always on, the one where she played a nun. Maybe Father Dom and his one true love had met in priest and nun school! Maybe their love had been forbidden like in the movie!

'Did you know her before you took your, um, orders, or whatever they're called?' I asked, trying to sound casual. 'Or after?'

'Before, of course!' He sounded shocked. 'For heaven's sake, Susannah.'

'I was just wondering.' I kept my gaze on Jesse over by the campfire, so Father D wouldn't be too embarrassed thinking I was staring at him, or anything. 'I mean, we don't have to talk about it, if you don't want to.' Only I couldn't help it. 'Was she—'

'I was your age,' Father Dominic said, as if he wanted to hurry up and get it over with. 'In high school, like you. She was a little younger.'

I had trouble picturing Father Dominic in high school. I didn't even know what colour his hair had been before it turned the snowy white it was now.

'It was . . .' Father D went on, a faraway look in his bright blue eyes. 'It . . . well, it would never have worked.'

'I know,' I said. Because suddenly I did know. I don't know how I knew, but something in the way he said it never would have worked just told me, I guess. 'She was a ghost, right?'

Father Dominic inhaled so sharply that for a second I thought he was having a heart attack, or something.

But before I had a chance to jump in and start CPR, Jesse got up from the fire, and started coming toward us.

'Oh, look,' Father Dominic said with obvious relief. 'Here comes Jesse.'

116

I had gotten over the annoyance I used to feel at Jesse when he'd appear suddenly, usually when I least expected – or wanted – him to. Now I was almost always glad to see him.

Except at that particular moment. At that particular moment, I wished Jesse was far, far away. Because I had a feeling I was never going to get Father D to open up about this particular subject again.

'All right,' Jesse said, when he'd come close enough to speak to us. 'I think they'll listen to you now, Father, without trying to bolt. They're quite frightened.'

'They sure didn't act very frightened when they were trying to kill me this afternoon,' I muttered.

Jesse looked down at me, a trace of amusement in his dark eyes – though what's so funny about me practically drowning, I don't know.

'I think,' he said, 'if you listen to what they have to say, you'll understand why they behaved the way they did.'

'We'll see about that,' I said with a sniff.

Twelve

I guess I was in kind of a bad mood because of Jesse interrupting my little heart-to-heart with Father Dominic. But that was no reason for him to come up behind me as I was walking toward the group around the fire and whisper, 'Behave,' in my ear.

I flashed him a look of annoyance. 'I always do,' I said.

You know what he did then? He laughed! And not in a very nice way, either. I couldn't believe it.

When I got close enough to the group to be able to make out the expressions on their faces, I didn't see anything to convince me they weren't still the same ghosts who'd tried to kill me – twice – in two days.

'Wait a minute,' Josh said when he recognized me. He climbed quickly to his feet, and pointed accusingly at me. 'That's the bitch who—'

Jesse stepped quickly into the firelit circle. 'Now,' he said, 'I told you who these people were—'

'You said they were going to help us,' Felicia wailed from where she sat, the skirt of her evening dress poofing up all around her. 'But that girl there kicked me in the face this afternoon!'

'Oh,' I said, 'like you weren't trying to drown me at the time?'

Father Dominic stepped quickly between me and the ghosts and said, 'My children, my children, do not be alarmed. We are here to help you, if we can.'

Josh Saunders, stunned, said, 'You can see us?'

'I can,' Father Dominic said solemnly. 'Susannah and I are, as I'm sure Jesse explained, mediators. We can see you, and we want to help you. Indeed, it is our responsibility to help you. Only, you must understand, it is also our responsibility to ensure that you don't harm anyone. That is why Susannah tried to stop you earlier today, and, if I understand correctly, the day before.'

This caused Mark Pulsford to say a bad word. Felicia Bruce elbowed him and said, 'Cut it out. That guy's a priest.'

Mark said, belligerently, 'He is not.'

'He is so,' Felicia said. 'Can't you see the little white thingie around his neck?'

'I *am* a priest.' Father Dominic hastened to cut the argument short. 'And I am telling you the truth. You can call me Father Dominic. And this is Susannah Simon. Now, we understand that the four of you feel a bit of resentment toward Mr Meducci—'

'Resentment?' Josh, still standing, glared at Father Dominic. '*Resentment?* It's because of that jerk that we're all dead!'

Only he didn't say *jerk*.

Father Dominic raised his white eyebrows, but Jesse said, calmly, 'Why don't you tell the father what it was you told me, Josh, so that he and Susannah can begin to understand.'

Josh, his bowtie hanging loosely around his neck, and the first few buttons of his dress shirt undone, lifted a hand and ran his fingers frustratedly through his short blond hair. He had obviously been, in life, an extremely good-looking boy.

119

Blessed with looks, intelligence and wealth (his parents had to have money if they could afford to send him to Robert Louis Stevenson School, which was as expensive as it was exclusive), Josh Saunders was having trouble adjusting to the only misfortune that had ever befallen him in his short, happy life:

His untimely death.

'Look,' he said. The sounds of the waves, and now the crackle of the little fire they'd made, were easily drowned out by his deep voice. Had he lived, Josh might have been anything, I thought to myself, from professional athlete to president. He exuded that kind of confidence.

'On Saturday night we went to a dance,' he said. 'A *dance*, OK? And afterward, we thought we might go for a drive, and park—'

Carrie chimed in: 'We always park at the Point on Saturday night.'

'The observation point,' Felicia explained.

'It's so pretty,' Carrie said.

'Really pretty,' Felicia said with a quick glance at Father Dominic.

I stared at them. Who were they kidding? We all knew what they were doing parked at the observation point.

And it wasn't looking at the view.

'Yeah,' Mark said. 'Plus no cops ever come by, and make us move. You know?'

Ah. Such honesty was refreshing.

'All right,' Josh said. He had shoved his hands in his trouser pockets. Now he took them out, and held them, palms toward us. 'So we went for this drive. Everything's going fine, right? Same as any other Saturday night. Only it wasn't the same. Because this last time, when we went around the corner – you know, that hairpin curve up there – something rammed us—'

'Yeah,' Carrie said. 'No lights, no warning, nothing. Just bam.'

'We went right into the guard rail,' Josh said. 'No big deal. We weren't going very fast. I thought, Shit, I crushed the fender. And I started to back up. But then he hit us again—'

'Oh, but surely—' Father Dominic began.

Josh, however, went on as if the priest hadn't spoken.

'And the second time he hit us,' Josh said, 'we just kept on going.'

'As if the guard rail wasn't even there,' Felicia put in.

'We went straight over.' Josh slipped his hands back into his pockets. 'And woke up down here. Dead.'

There was silence after that. At least no one spoke. There was still the sound of the waves, of course, and the crackling of the fire. Spray from the sea, blown by the wind, was coating my hair and forming little ice crystals in it. I moved closer to the fire, thankful for its warmth . . .

And realized, all in a rush, why the RLS Angels had gone to the trouble of building it. Because that's what they'd have done if they'd still been alive. They'd have built a fire for warmth. So what if they could no longer feel its heat? It didn't matter. That's what live people would have done.

And all they wanted was to be alive again.

'Troubling,' Father Dominic said. 'Very troubling. But surely, my children, you can see that it was just an accident—'

'An accident?' Josh glared at Father D. 'There was nothing *accidental* about it, Father. That guy – that Michael guy – came at us *on purpose*.'

'But that's ridiculous,' Father Dominic said. 'Perfectly ridiculous. Why on earth would he do such a thing?'

'Simple,' Josh said with a shrug. 'He's jealous.'

'Jealous?' Father Dominic looked appalled. 'Perhaps you aren't aware of this, young man, but Michael Meducci, whom I have known since he was in the first grade, is a very gifted student. He is well liked by his fellow classmates. Why in heaven's name would he – No. No, I'm sorry. You're mistaken, my boy.'

I wasn't sure which universe Father Dom was living in – the one where Michael Meducci was well liked by his fellow classmates – but it sure wasn't this one. As far as I knew, no one at the Mission Academy liked Michael Meducci – or even knew him, outside of the chess club. But then, I had only been there a few months, so maybe I was wrong.

'He may be gifted,' Josh said, 'but he's still a geek.'

Father Dominic blinked at him. 'Geek?' he ventured.

'You heard me.' Josh shook his head. 'Look, Father, face facts. Your boy Meducci is nothing. *Nothing. We*' – he pointed at himself, then gestured toward his friends – 'on the other hand, were *it*. The most popular people in our school. Nothing happened at RLS unless it had our seal of approval. A party wasn't a party until *we* got there. A dance wasn't a dance unless Josh, Carrie, Mark and Felicia – the RLS "Angels" – were there. OK? Are you getting the picture now?'

Father Dominic looked confused. 'Um,' he said. 'Not quite.'

Josh rolled his eyes. 'Is this guy for real?' he asked me and Jesse.

Jesse said, without smiling, 'Very much so.'

'OK,' Josh said. 'Then let me put it to you this way. This Meducci guy? He may have the sparkling GPA. But so what? That's nothing. I've got a 4.0. I hold the school record in the high jump. I belong to the National Honour Society. I play forward on the basketball team. I've been president of the student council for three years in a row, and for a lark, this spring I tried out for – and got – the lead in the school drama society's production of *Romeo and Juliet*. Oh, and guess what? I was accepted to Harvard. Early decision.'

Josh paused to take a breath. Father Dominic opened his mouth to say something, but Josh barrelled right along.

'How many Saturday nights,' Josh asked, 'do you think Michael Meducci has sat alone in his room playing video games? Huh? Well, let me put it to you another way: do you know how many *I*'ve spent caressing a joystick? None. Want to know why? Because there's never been a Saturday night when I didn't have something to do – a party to go to or a girl to take out. And not just any girl, either, but the hottest, most popular girls in school. Carrie here' – he gestured at Carrie Whitman, sitting in the sand in her ice-blue evening gown – 'models part-time up in San Francisco. She's done commercials. She was homecoming queen.'

'Two years in a row,' Carrie pointed out in her squeaky voice.

Josh nodded. 'Two years in a row. Are you starting to get it now, Father? Is Michael Meducci dating a model? I don't think so. Is Michael Meducci's best friend like mine, Mark over there, captain of the football team? Does Michael Meducci have a full athletic scholarship to UCLA?'

Mark, obviously not the group genius, went, with feeling, 'Go Bruins.'

'What about me?' Felicia demanded.

Josh said, 'Yes, what about Mark's girlfriend, Felicia? Head cheerleader, captain of the dance team, and, oh yeah, winner of a National Merit Scholarship because of her superior grades. So, keeping all that in mind, let's ask that question again, shall we? Why would a guy like Michael Meducci want people like us dead? Simple: he's jealous.'

123

The silence that swept in after this statement was almost as penetrating as the smell of brine permeating the air. No one said a word. The Angels looked too self-righteous to speak, and Father Dom seemed stunned by their revelations. Jesse's feelings on the subject were unclear; he looked a little bored. I guess to a guy born over a hundred and fifty years ago, the words *National Merit Scholarship* don't mean much.

I pried my tongue from where it had been stuck to the roof of my mouth. I was very thirsty from my long hike down, and I certainly wasn't looking forward to the climb back up to Father Dom's car. But I felt compelled, despite my discomfort, to speak.

'Or,' I said, 'it could be because of his sister.'

Thirteen

Everyone – from Father Dom to Carrie Whitman – blinked at me in the firelight.

'Excuse me?' Josh said. Only his tone was more impatient than polite.

'Michael's sister,' I said. 'The one who's in the coma.'

Don't ask me what made me think of it. Maybe it was Josh's reference to parties – how no party began until he and the other Angels got there. That started me thinking of the last party I'd heard about – the one where Michael's sister had fallen into the pool and nearly drowned. Some party that must have been. Had the police broken it up after the ambulance arrived?

Father Dominic's shaggy white eyebrows went up. 'You mean Lila Meducci? Yes, of course. How could I have forgotten about her? It's tragic – very tragic – what happened to her.'

Jesse piped up for the first time in some minutes. 'What happened to her?' he asked, lifting his chin from the knee he'd been resting it on, his foot propped up against the boulder he was sitting on.

'An accident,' Father Dom said, shaking his head. 'A terrible accident. She tripped and fell into a swimming pool and very nearly drowned. Her parents are losing hope that she'll ever regain consciousness.'

I grunted. 'That's one version of the story, anyway,' I said. Michael's parents had obviously cleaned it up for the principal of their daughter's school.

'You left out the part,' I went on, 'about how she was at a party in the Valley when it happened. And that she was completely blotto when she went under.' I narrowed my eyes at the four ghosts seated on the opposite side of the fire. 'So was everybody else at this particular party, apparently, since nobody noticed what happened to her until she'd been under long enough to curdle her brain.' I looked at Jesse. 'Did I mention the fact that she's only fourteen years old?'

Jesse, still sitting on the boulder, his hands around the propped up knee, looked at the Angels. 'I don't suppose any of you,' he said, 'would know something about this.'

Mark looked disgusted. 'How would any of us know about some geek's sister getting wasted at a party?' he demanded.

'Perhaps because one – or all – of you happened to be at the party at the time?' I suggested sweetly.

Father Dominic looked startled. 'Is this true?' He blinked down at the Angels. 'Do any of you know anything about this?'

'Of course not,' Josh said – too quickly, I thought. Felicia's 'As if' was not very convincing, either.

It was Carrie who gave it away, though.

'Even if we did,' she demanded with unfeigned indignation, 'what would it matter? Just because some stupid wannabe drank herself into a coma at one of our parties, how does that make *us* responsible?'

I stared at her. Felicia, I remembered, was the National

Merit Scholar. Carrie Whitman had only been homecoming queen. Twice.

'How about, just for starters,' I said, 'making alcohol available to an eighth grader?'

'How were we supposed to know how old she was?' Felicia asked, not very nicely. 'I mean, she had enough make-up slathered on, I could have sworn she was forty.'

'Yeah,' Carrie said. 'And that particular party was by invitation only. I certainly never issued an invitation to any *eighth grader.*'

'If you want to hold someone responsible,' Felicia said, 'how about the idiot who brought her in the first place?'

'Yeah,' Carrie said angrily.

'I don't think Susannah is the one holding you responsible for what happened to Michael's sister.' Jesse's voice, after the shrillness of the girls, sounded like distant thunder. It shut the others up quite effectively. 'Michael, I believe, is the one who killed you for it.'

Father Dominic made a soft noise as if Jesse's words had sunk, like a fist, into his stomach.

'Oh, no,' he said. 'No, surely you can't think—'

'It makes more sense,' Jesse said, 'than this one's argument' – he nodded briefly at Josh – 'that Michael did it out of jealousy because he has no . . . what is it? Oh, yes. Dates on Saturday night.'

Josh looked uncomfortable. 'Well,' he said, tugging on his evening jacket's lapels. 'I didn't know the skank they fished out of Carrie's pool was Meducci's sister.'

'This,' Father Dominic said, 'is too much. Simply too much. I am . . . I am *appalled* by all of this.'

I glanced at him, surprised by what I heard in his voice. It was – if I wasn't mistaken – pain. Father Dominic was actually hurt by what he'd just heard.

'A young girl is in a coma,' he said, his blue-eyed gaze very bright as it bored into Josh, 'and you call her names?'

Josh had the grace to look ashamed of himself. 'Well,' he said, 'it's just a figure of speech.'

'And you two.' Father Dominic pointed at Felicia and Carrie. 'You break the law by serving alcohol to minors, and dare to suggest that it is the girl's own fault she was harmed by it?'

Carrie and Felicia exchanged glances.

'But,' Felicia said, 'nobody else got hurt, and they were all drinking, too.'

'Yeah,' Carrie said. 'Everybody was doing it.'

'That doesn't matter.' Father Dominic's voice was shaking with emotion now. 'If everyone else jumped off the Golden Gate Bridge, would that make it right?'

Whoa, I thought. Father D obviously needed a little refresher course in student discipline if he thought that old line still had any punch.

And then my eyes widened as I noticed that Father Dominic was now pointing at me. *Me?* What had *I* done?

I soon found out.

'And you,' Father Dominic said. 'You still insist that what happened to these young people was not an accident, but deliberate murder!'

My jaw sagged. 'Father D,' I managed to say when I'd levered it back into place. 'Excuse me, but it's pretty obvious—'

'It isn't.' Father Dominic dropped his arm. 'It isn't obvious to me. So the boy had motive? That doesn't make him a killer.'

I glanced at Jesse for help, but it was apparent from his startled expression that he was as baffled by Father Dominic's outburst as I was.

128

'But the guard rail,' I tried. 'The loosened bolts—'

'Yes, yes,' Father Dominic said, quite testily for him. 'But you're missing the most important point, Susannah. Supposing Michael did lie in wait for them. Perhaps he did intend, when they turned that corner, to ram them. How was he able to tell, in the dark, that he had the right car? Tell me that, Susannah. Anyone could have come around that corner. How could Michael have known he had the right car? *How?*'

He had me there. And he knew it. I stood there, the wind from the sea whipping hair into my face, and looked at Jesse. He looked back at me, and gave a little shrug. He was at as much of a loss as I was. Father Dom was right. It didn't make any sense.

At least until Josh said, 'The Macarena.'

We all looked at him.

'I beg your pardon?' Father Dominic said. Even in anger, he was unerringly polite.

'Of course!' Felicia scrambled to her feet, tripping over her evening gown's long skirt. 'Of course!'

Jesse and I exchanged yet another confused look. 'The what?' I asked Josh.

'The Macarena,' Josh said. He was smiling. Smiling, he didn't look anything like the guy who'd tried to drown me earlier that day. Smiling, he looked like what he was – a smart, athletic eighteen-year-old in the prime of his life.

Except that his life was over.

'I was driving my brother's car,' he explained, still grinning. 'He's away at college. He said I could use it while he was gone. It's bigger than my car. The only thing is, he had this stupid thing put in so that when you honk the horn it plays the Macarena.'

'It's *so* embarrassing,' Carrie informed us.

'And the night we were killed,' Josh went on, 'I laid on the horn as we were turning that corner – the one Michael was waiting behind.'

'You're supposed to honk when you go around those hairpin curves,' Felicia said, excitedly.

'And it played the Macarena.' Josh's smile vanished as if wiped away by the wind. 'And that's when he hit us.'

'No other car horn on the peninsula,' Felicia said, her expression no longer excited, 'plays the Macarena. Not any more. The Macarena was only hot for about the first two weeks after it came out. Then it became totally lame. Now they only play it at weddings and stuff.'

'That's how he knew.' Josh's voice was no longer filled with indignation. Now he merely sounded sad. His gaze was locked on the sea – a sea that was too dark to be distinguishable from the cloudy night sky. 'That's how he knew it was us.'

Frantically, I thought back to what Michael had told me, a few hours earlier, in his mother's minivan. *They came barrelling around that corner.* That's what he'd said. *Didn't honk. Nothing.*

Only now Josh was saying they *had* honked. That not only had they honked, but that they had honked in a particular way, a way that distinguished Josh's car horn from all others . . .

'Oh,' Father Dominic said, sounding as if he wasn't feeling well. 'Dear.'

I totally agreed with him. Except . . .

'It still doesn't prove anything,' I said.

'Are you kidding?' Josh looked at me as if *I* was the crazy one – like he wasn't wearing a tuxedo on the beach. 'Of course it does.'

'No, she's right.' Jesse pushed himself off the boulder and

came to stand beside Josh. 'He has been very clever, Michael has. There is no way to prove – in a court of law, anyway – that he has committed a crime here.'

Josh's jaw dropped. 'What do you mean? He killed us! I'm standing here telling you so! We honked the horn, and he purposefully rammed us and pushed us over the cliff.'

'Yes,' Jesse said. 'But your testimony will not hold up in a court of law, my friend.'

Josh looked close to tears. 'Why not?'

'Because it is the testimony,' Jesse said evenly, 'of a dead man.'

Stung, Josh stabbed a finger in my direction. '*She*'s not dead. *She* can tell them.'

'She can't,' Jesse said. 'What is she supposed to say? That she knows the truth about what happened that night because the ghosts of the victims told her? Do you think a jury will believe that?'

Josh glared at him. Then, his gaze falling to his feet, he muttered, 'Well, fine then. We're right back to where we started. We'll just take the matter into our own hands, right, guys?'

'Oh, no, you don't,' I said. 'No way. Two wrongs do not make a right – and three most definitely don't.'

Carrie glanced from me to Josh and back again. 'What's she talking about?' she wanted to know.

'You are not,' I said, 'going to avenge your deaths by killing Michael Meducci. I am sorry. But that is just not going to happen.'

Mark, for the first time all evening, rose to his feet. He looked at me, then at Jesse, and then at Father Dom. Then he went, 'This is *bogus*, man,' and started stalking off down the beach.

'So the geek's just going to get away with it?' Josh, his jaw

131

set, glared menacingly at me. 'He kills four people, and he gets off scot-free?'

'Nobody said that.' Jesse, in the firelight, looked more grim-faced than I'd ever seen him. 'But what happens to the boy isn't up to you.'

'Oh, yeah?' Josh was back to sneering. 'Who's it up to, then?'

Jesse nodded at Father Dominic and me. 'Them,' he said quietly.

'*Them?*' Felicia's voice rose on a disgusted note. '*Why them?*'

'Because they are the mediators,' Jesse said. In the orange glow from the fire, his eyes looked black. 'It's what they do.'

Fourteen

The only problem was that the mediators couldn't figure out just how, exactly, to handle the situation.

'Look,' I whispered as Father Dominic dropped a white candle into the box I was holding, and dug out a purple one. 'Let me just call the police with an anonymous tip. I'll tell them I was driving along Big Sur that night, and that I saw the whole thing, and that it was no accident.'

Father Dominic screwed the purple candle into the place where the white one had been.

'And do you think the police follow up on every anonymous tip they receive?' He didn't bother whispering because there was no one to overhear us. The only reason I'd lowered my voice was because the basilica, with all its gold leaf and majestic stained glass, made me really nervous.

'Well, at least maybe they'll get suspicious.' I followed Father Dominic as he climbed down from the stepladder, folded it up, and moved to the next Station of the Cross. 'I mean, maybe they'll start looking into it a little more, bring Michael in for questioning, or something. I swear he'd crack if they'd just ask the right questions.'

Father Dominic lifted the skirt of his black robe as he climbed back on to the ladder.

'And what,' he asked, swapping another white candle for

one of the purple ones in the box I was holding, 'would the right questions be?'

'I don't know.' My arms were getting tired. The box I was carrying was really heavy. Normally the novices would have been the ones changing the candles. Father Dominic, however, had been unable to keep still since our little field trip the night before, and had volunteered his services to the monsignor. *Our* services, I should say, since he'd dragged me out of religion class to help. Not that I minded. Being a devout agnostic, I wasn't getting all that much out of religion class, anyway – something Sister Ernestine hoped to rectify before I graduated.

'I think that the police,' Father Dom said as he gave the candle a determined twist since it didn't seem to be fitting too easily into the holder, 'can get along fine without our help. If what your mother said was true, the police seem suspicious enough of Michael already that it shouldn't be much longer before they bring him in for questioning.'

'But what if my mom's just overreacting?' I noticed a tourist nearby, in madras and an Izod, admiring the stained glass windows, and lowered my voice even more. 'I mean, she's a mom. She does that. Supposing the police don't really suspect anything at all?'

'Susannah.' The candle successfully in place, Father Dominic climbed back down the ladder, and looked at me with an expression that appeared to be a mingling of exasperation and affection. There were, I noticed, purple shadows under Father Dom's eyes. We had both been pretty wiped after our long hike down to the beach and then back up again – not to mention the emotional wear and tear we'd experienced while we'd been down there.

Still, Father Dominic seemed to have sprung back with more vigour than you might expect for a guy in his sixties. *I* could barely walk, my shins ached so badly and I couldn't stop yawning since our little tête-à-tête with the Angels had lasted until well past midnight. Father Dom, except for the shadows beneath his eyes, seemed almost sprightly, bubbling over with energy.

'Susannah,' he said again, less exasperatedly, and more affectionately this time. 'Promise me you will do nothing of the kind. You will not call the police with any anonymous tips.'

I shifted the box of candles in my arms. It had certainly seemed like a good idea when I'd come up with it around four that morning. I'd lain awake almost all night wondering what on earth we were going to do about the RLS Angels and Michael Meducci.

'But—'

'And you will not, under any circumstances' – Father Dominic, apparently noticing my problem with the box, lifted it easily from my arms and set it down on the step-ladder's top rung – 'attempt to speak with Michael yourself about any of this.'

That, of course, had been Plan B. If the whole anonymous tip thing to the cops didn't pan out, I'd planned on cornering Michael and sweet-talking – or beating, whichever proved most effective – a confession out of him.

'You will let me handle this,' Father Dominic said loudly enough so that the tourist in the madras, who'd been about to take a picture of the altar, hastily lowered his camera and moved away. 'I intend to speak to the young man, and I can assure you that if he is indeed guilty of this heinous crime—' I sucked in my breath, but Father Dominic held up a warning finger.

'You heard me,' he said, a bit more quietly, but only because he'd noticed that one of the novices had slipped

135

into the church carrying more black material to drape over the basilica's many statues of the Virgin Mary. They would remain cloaked in that manner, I had gathered, until Easter. Religion. That is some wacky stuff, let me tell you.

'If Michael is guilty of what those young people say he is, then I will convince him to confess.' Father Dominic looked like he meant it, too. In fact, I hadn't even done anything, but somehow, looking at his stern expression, I wanted to confess. Once I had taken five dollars from my mother's wallet to buy a jumbo bag of Skittles. Maybe I could confess that.

'Now,' Father Dominic said, pulling back the sleeve of his black robe and looking at his Timex. They don't pay priests enough for them to be able to get cool watches. 'I am expecting Mr Meducci to join me here momentarily, so you need to move along. It would be best for him not to see us together, I think.'

'Why not? He has no idea we spent most of last night in conversation with his victims.'

Father Dominic put a hand in the centre of my back and pushed. 'Run along now, Susannah,' he said in a fatherly sort of voice.

I went, but not very far. As soon as Father D's back was turned, I ducked down into a pew and crouched there, waiting. Waiting for what, I couldn't say. Well, all right, I could say: I was waiting for Michael. I wanted to see if Father D really would be able to get him to confess.

I didn't have to wait long. About five minutes later, I heard Michael's voice say, not too far from where I was hiding, 'Father Dominic? Sister Ernestine said you wanted to speak to me.'

'Ah, Michael.' Father Dominic's voice conveyed none of the horror that I knew he felt over the prospect of one of his

136

students being a possible murderer. He sounded relaxed and even jovial.

I heard the box of candles rattle.

'Here,' Father Dominic said. 'Hold those, will you?'

He had, I realized, just handed Michael the box I'd been holding.

'Uh,' Michael said. 'Sure, Father Dominic.'

I heard the scrape of the stepladder being folded again. Father Dom was picking it up and moving to the next Station of the Cross. I could still hear him, however . . . barely.

'I've been worried about you, Michael,' Father Dominic said. 'I understand that your sister isn't showing much sign of improvement.'

'No, Father,' Michael said. His voice was so soft, I could hardly hear it.

'I'm very sorry to hear that. Lila is a very sweet girl. I know you must love her very much.'

'Yes, Father,' Michael said.

'You know, Michael,' Father Dominic said. 'When bad things happen to the people we love, we often . . . well, sometimes we turn our backs on God.'

Aw, geez, I thought, from my pew. That wasn't the way. Not with *Michael*.

'Sometimes we become so resentful that this terrible thing has happened to someone who doesn't deserve it that we not only turn our backs on God, but we might even begin contemplating . . . well, things we wouldn't ordinarily con-template if the tragedy hadn't occurred. Like, for instance, revenge.'

All right, I thought. Getting better, Father D.

'Miss Simon.'

Startled, I looked around. The novice who had come in

to finish draping the statues was staring at me from the end of my pew.

'Oh,' I said. I slithered up off of my knees and into the seat. Father Dominic and Michael, I saw, had moved so that their backs were to me. They were too far away to overhear us.

'Hi,' I said to the novice. 'I was just, um, looking for an earring.'

The novice didn't appear to believe me.

'Don't you have religion with Sister Ernestine right now?' she asked.

'Yes, Sister,' I said. 'I do.'

'Well, hadn't you better get to class, then?'

Slowly, I rose to my feet. It wouldn't have mattered, even if I hadn't gotten caught. Father Dominic and Michael had moved too far away for me to have heard anything anyway.

I walked, with what dignity I could, toward the end of the pew, pausing when I reached the novice before moving on.

'Sorry, Sister,' I said. Then, striving to break the awkward silence that ensued, during which the novice stared at me in mute disapproval, I added, 'I like your, um . . .'

But since I couldn't remember what they call that dress they all wear, the compliment fell a little flat, even though I thought I'd sort of saved it at the end by gesturing toward her and going, 'You know, your thing. It's very figure flattering.'

But I guess that's the wrong thing to say to somebody who is in training to be a nun, since the novice got very red in the face and said, 'Don't make me have to report you again, Miss Simon.'

Which I thought was sort of harsh, considering I'd been trying, anyway, to be nice. But whatever. I left the church and headed back to class, taking the long way, through the brightly sunlit courtyard, so I could soothe my frazzled nerves by listening to the sound of the burbling fountain.

My nerves soon shot back up to frazzled, however, when I spotted another one of the novices standing by the statue of Father Serra, delivering a little lecture to a group of tourists about the missionary's good works. In order to avoid being spotted out of class without a hall pass (why hadn't I thought to ask Father D for one? I'd been thrown by the whole candle thing), I ducked into the girls' room, where I was met by a cloud of grey smoke.

Which meant only one thing, of course.

'Gina,' I said, stooping over so I could figure out which stall she was in by looking under the doors. 'Are you insane?'

Gina's voice came floating out from one of the stalls on the end, near the window, which she'd strategically opened.

'I do not,' she said, throwing open the stall door, and then hanging on to it while she puffed, 'believe so.'

'I thought you quit smoking.'

'I did.' Gina joined me on the window sill, on to which I'd hauled myself. The Mission, having been built in like the year 1600 or something, was made of this really thick adobe, so all the windows were set back two feet into the stone. This supplied built-in window seats that, if they were a little high, were at least very cool and comfortable.

'I only smoke now in emergencies,' Gina explained. 'Like during religion class. You know I am philosophically opposed to organized religion. How about you?'

I raised my eyebrows. 'I don't know,' I said. 'Buddhism has always struck me as kind of cool. That whole rein-carnation thing is very appealing.'

'That's Hinduism, you dink,' Gina said. 'And I was talk-ing about smoking.'

'Oh. OK. No, I never got the hang of it. Why?' I grinned

at her. 'Didn't Sleepy tell you about the time he caught me trying to smoke?'

She frowned prettily. 'He did not. And I wish you wouldn't call him that.'

I made a face. 'Jake, then. He was pretty peeved about it. You better not let him catch you at it, or he'll dump you like a hot potato.'

'I highly doubt that,' Gina said with a mysterious smile.

She was probably right. I wondered what it would be like to be Gina, and have every boy you met fall madly in love with you. The only boys who fell madly in love with me were boys like Michael Meducci. And he wasn't even technically in love with me. He was in love with the idea that I was in love with him. Something I still couldn't think about, by the way, without shuddering.

I heaved a dejected sigh and looked out the window. About a mile of sloping, cypress-tree-dotted landscape stretched to the sea, teal blue and sparkling in the bright afternoon sunlight.

'I don't see how you can stand it.' Gina exhaled a plume of grey smoke. She was back to talking about religion class, I could tell from her tone. 'I mean, it must all *really* seem bogus to you, considering the whole mediator thing.'

I shrugged. I had gotten home too late the night before for Gina and I to have our 'talk'. She'd been sound asleep when I snuck back into the house. Which was just as well, since I'd been exhausted.

Not exhausted enough, however, to fall asleep.

'I don't know,' I said. 'I mean, I haven't got the slightest idea where the ghosts go after I send them packing. They just . . . go. Maybe to heaven. Maybe on to their next life. I doubt I'll ever know until I die myself.'

Gina aimed her next plume of smoke out the window.

'You make it,' she said, 'sound like a trip. Like when we die, we're just moving to a new address.'

'Well,' I said. 'Personally, I think that's how it works. Just don't ask me to tell you what that address is. Because that I don't know.'

'So.' Her cigarette finished, Gina stamped it out on the adobe beneath us, then flung the butt expertly over the closest stall door and into the toilet. I heard the plop, and then the sizzle. 'What was that all about last night, anyway?'

I told her. About the RLS Angels, and how they thought Michael had killed them. I told her about Michael's sister, and the accident out on the Pacific Coast Highway. I told her about how Josh and his friends were looking to avenge their deaths, and about how Father Dominic and I had argued with them, long into the night, until we'd finally convinced them to let us try to bring Michael to justice the old-fashioned way – you know, utilizing the appropriate law enforcement agencies, and not a paranormal contract killing.

There was only one thing I didn't tell her, and that was about Jesse. For some reason, I just couldn't bring myself to mention him. Maybe because of what the psychic had said. Maybe because I was afraid Madame Zara was right, that I really was this giant loser who was only going to fall in love with one person my entire life, and that person was a guy who:

(a) did not love me back, and

(b) wasn't exactly someone I could introduce to my mother, since he wasn't even alive.

Or maybe it was simply because . . . well, maybe because Jesse was a secret I wanted to hug to myself, like some stupid girl with a crush on Carson Daly, or somebody. Maybe someday I'd take to standing underneath my bedroom window with a big sign that says *Jesse, will you go to prom with me?* like all those girls who stand around outside the MTV studios, though I sincerely hope someone would shoot me or something before it comes to that.

When I was through, Gina sighed, and said, 'Well, it just goes to show. The cute ones always do end up being psychotic murderers.'

She meant Michael.

'Yeah,' I said. 'But he's not even that cute. Except with his clothes off.'

'You know what I mean.' Gina shook her head. 'What are you going to do if he doesn't confess to Father Dominic?'

'I don't know.' This was something that had contributed to my insomnia of the night before. 'I guess we'll just have to get some proof.'

'Oh, yeah? Where you gonna find that? The evidence store?' Gina yawned, looked at her watch, and then hopped off the window sill. 'Two minutes until lunch,' she said. 'What do you think it will be today? Corn dogs again?'

'It always is,' I said. The Mission Academy was not exactly known for the culinary excellence of its cafeteria. That was because it didn't have one. We ate lunch outside, out of these vendor wagons. It was bizarre, even to a couple of chicks from Brooklyn who had seen it all . . . as was illustrated by Gina's total lack of surprise about everything that I'd just told her.

'What I want to know,' she said as we made our way out of the girls' room and into the soon-to-be-flooded-with-humanity breezeway, 'is why you never said anything about any of this stuff before. You know, the mediator stuff. It wasn't as if I didn't know.'

You *don't* know, I thought. Not the worst part, anyway.

'I was afraid you'd tell your mother,' was what I said out

142

loud. 'And that she'd tell my mother. And that my mother would stick me in the loony bin. For my own good, of course.'

'Of course,' Gina said. She blinked down at me. 'You are an idiot. You know that, don't you? I never would have told my mother. I never tell my mother anything, if I can avoid it. And I certainly wouldn't ever have told her – or anybody else, for that matter – about the mediator thing.'

I shrugged uncomfortably. 'I know,' I said. 'I guess . . . well, back then I was pretty uptight about everything. I guess I've loosened up some since then.'

'They say California does that to people,' Gina observed.

And then the Mission clock struck twelve. All of the classroom doors around us were flung open, and a flood of people started streaming toward us.

It only took about thirty seconds for Michael to find and then glom on to me.

'Hey,' he said, not looking at all like somebody who had just confessed to a quadruple murder. 'I've been looking for you. What are you doing after school today?'

'Nothing,' I said quickly, before Gina could open her mouth.

'Well, the insurance company finally came through with a rental for me,' Michael said, 'and I was thinking, you know, if you wanted to go back to the beach, or something . . . '

Back to the beach? Did this guy have amnesia, or what? You'd think after what had happened to him the last time he'd gone to the beach, it'd be the one place he *wouldn't* want to go.

Still, though he didn't know it, he'd be perfectly safe there. This was on account of Jesse. He was keeping an eye on the Angels while Father Dom and I tried our hand at bringing their alleged killer to justice.

It was as I was mulling over a reply to this offer that I caught a glimpse of Father Dominic as he came toward us down the breezeway. Right before he was pulled into the teachers' lounge by an enthusiastically gesticulating Mr Walden, he shook his head. Michael was standing with his back to him, so he didn't see. But Father Dom's message to me was clear:

Michael hadn't confessed.

Which meant only one thing: it was time to bring in the professionals.

Me.

'Sure,' I said, looking from Father Dom back to Michael. 'Maybe you can help me with my geometry homework. I don't think I'm ever going to get the hang of this stupid Pythagorean theorem. I swear I'm going to flunk out after that last quiz.'

'The Pythagorean theorem isn't hard,' Michael said, looking amused by my frustration. 'The sum of the squares of the lengths of the sides of a right triangle is equal to the square of the length of the hypotenuse.'

I went, 'Huh?' in this helpless way.

'Look,' Michael said. 'I aced geometry. Why don't you let me tutor you?'

I looked up at him in what I hoped he would mistake for worshipfulness. 'Oh, would you?'

'Sure,' he said.

'Can we start today?' I asked. 'After school?' I should get an Oscar. I really should. I had the whole helpless female thing totally down. 'At your house?'

Michael only looked a little taken aback. 'Um,' he said. 'Sure.' Then, when he'd recovered from his surprise, he added, slyly, 'My parents won't be home, though. My dad'll be at work, and my mom spends most of her time at the

144

hospital. With my sister. You know. I hope that won't be a problem.'

I did everything but flutter my eyelashes at him. 'Oh, no,' I said. 'That'll be fine.'

He looked pleased – and yet at the same time a little uncomfortable.

'Um,' he said, as the hordes of people pushed past us. 'Look, about lunch. I can't sit with you today. I've got some stuff to do. But I'll meet you here right after last period. OK?'

I went, 'OK,' in this total imitation of Kelly Prescott at her most school-spirited. It must have worked, since Michael went away looking dazed, but pleased.

That was when Gina grabbed my arm, pulled me into a doorway, and hissed, 'What are you, high? You're going to the guy's *house? Alone?*'

I tried to shake her off. 'Calm down, G,' I said. Sleepy's nickname for her was kind of catchy, loath as I was to admit anything my stepbrother had come up with might have any sort of merit. 'This is what I do.'

'Hang out with possible murderers?' Gina looked sceptical. 'I don't think so, Suze. Did you clear this with Father Dominic?'

'G,' I said. 'I'm a big girl. I can take care of myself.'

She narrowed her eyes. 'You didn't, did you? What are you, freelancing? And don't call me G.'

'Look,' I said, in what I hoped was a soothing tone. 'Chances are, Michael won't say a word about it to me. But he's a geek, right? A computer geek. And what do computer geeks do when they're planning something?'

Gina still looked angry. 'I don't know,' she said. 'And I don't care. I'm telling—'

'They write stuff down,' I said calmly. 'On their computer.

Right? They keep a journal, or they brag to people in chat rooms, or they pull up schematics of the building they want to blow up, or whatever. So even if I can't get him to admit anything, if I can get some time alone with Michael's computer, I bet I can—'

'G!' Sleepy strolled up to us. 'There you are. You doing lunch now?'

Gina's lips were pressed together in annoyance with me, but Sleepy did not appear to notice this. Neither did Dopey, who showed up a second later.

'Hey,' he said breathlessly. 'What are you guys just standing here for? Let's go eat.'

Then he noticed me and sneered. 'Suze, where's your shadow?'

I said with a sniff, 'Michael will be unable to join us for lunch today, having been unavoidably detained.'

'Yeah,' Dopey said, and then he made a rude remark pertaining to Michael's having been detained by an inability to get certain parts of his body back into his pants. This was apparently an allusion to Michael's lack of coordination and not an intimation that he was more endowed than the average sixteen-year-old male.

I chose to ignore this remark, as did Gina, though I think this was because she hadn't even heard it.

'I sure hope you know what you're doing,' was all she said, and it was clear she was not speaking to either of my stepbrothers, which puzzled them enormously. Why would any girl bother speaking to *me* when she could be speaking to *them*?

'G,' I said with some surprise. 'What do you take me for? An amateur?'

'No,' Gina said. 'A fool.'

I laughed. I really did think she was just being funny. It

wasn't until much later that I realized there wasn't anything amusing about it at all.

Because it turned out Gina was one hundred percent right.

Fifteen

Here's the thing about killers. If you know one, I'm sure you'll agree with me:

They can't help bragging about what they've done.

Seriously. They are totally vain. And that, generally, is their undoing.

Look at it from their point of view: I mean, here they are, and they've gotten away with this terrific crime. You know, something totally ingenious that no one would ever think to pin on them.

And they can't tell anybody. They can't tell a soul.

That's what gets them almost every time. Not telling anyone – not letting anyone in on their brilliant secret – well, that just about kills them.

Don't get me wrong. They don't want to get caught. They just want somebody to appreciate the brilliance of this thing they've done. Yes, it was a heinous – sometimes even unthinkable – crime. But look. *Look.* They did it *without getting caught.* They fooled the police. They fooled everybody. They *have* to tell somebody. They have to. Otherwise, what's the point?

This is just a personal observation, of course. I have met quite a few killers in my line of work, and this is the one thing they all seem to have in common. Only the ones who

148

kept their mouths shut were the ones who managed to keep from getting caught. Everybody else? Slammer city.

So it seemed to me that Michael – who already believed that I was in love with him – just might decide to brag to me about what he'd done. He'd already started to, a little, when he'd told me how Josh and people like him were just a 'waste of space'. It seemed likely that, with a little prompting, I could get him to elaborate . . . maybe to the tune of a confession that I could then turn around and give to the police.

What's that you're saying? Guilty? Won't I feel guilty for snitching on this guy who had, after all, only been trying to get back at the kids who'd let his sister hurt herself so badly?

Yeah. Right. Listen, I don't do guilt. In my book, there are two kinds of people. Good ones and bad ones. As far as I was concerned, in this particular case, there wasn't a single good person to be found. Everybody had done something reprehensible, from Lila Meducci crashing that party and getting herself trashed in the process, to the RLS Angels for throwing the drunken free-for-all in the first place. Maybe some of them had committed crimes a little more heinous than the others – Michael's killing four people comes to mind – but frankly, in my mind . . . they all sucked.

So, in answer to your question, no, I didn't feel guilty about what I was about to do. The way I saw it, the sooner Michael got what was coming to him, the sooner I could get back to what was really important in life: lying on the beach with my best friend, soaking up some rays.

It was as I was in the girls' room just after last period let out, applying eyeliner in the mirror above the sinks – I have found that wringing confessions from potential murderers is easier when I am looking my best – that I got my first indication that the afternoon was not going to go exactly as I'd planned.

The door opened and Kelly Prescott walked in, followed by her shadow, Debbie Mancuso. They were not, apparently, there either to relieve or coif themselves, since all they did was stand there and stare at me in a hostile manner.

I looked at their reflections in the mirror and went, 'If this is about funding for a class trip to the wine country, you can forget it. I already spoke to Mr Walden about it, and he said it was the most ludicrous thing he'd ever heard of. Six Flags Great Adventure, maybe, but not the Napa Valley. Wineries *do* card, you know.'

Kelly's upper lip curled. 'This isn't about *that*,' she said in a disgusted tone of voice.

'Yeah,' Debbie said. 'This is about your *friend*.'

'My friend?' I had extracted a hairbrush from my backpack, and now I ran it through my hair, feigning unconcern. And I wasn't concerned. Not really. I could handle anything Kelly Prescott and Debbie Mancuso dished out. Only I didn't exactly feel like dealing with this, on top of everything else that had happened lately. 'You mean Michael Meducci?'

Kelly rolled her eyes. 'As if. Why you would ever want to be seen with *that*, I cannot imagine. But we happen to be talking about this Gina person.'

'Yeah,' Debbie said, her eyes narrowed to angry little slits.

Gina? Oh, *Gina*. Gina, who had stolen both Kelly's and Debbie's inamoratos. Suddenly all became clear.

'When is she going back to New York?' Kelly demanded.

'Yeah,' Debbie said. 'And where is she sleeping? Your room, right?'

Kelly elbowed her, and Debbie went, 'Well, don't act like you don't want to know, Kel.'

Kelly shot her friend an annoyed look, and then asked me, 'There hasn't been any . . . well, bed-hopping, has there?'

Bed-hopping?

'Not to my knowledge,' I said. I thought about messing with them, but the thing was, I really did feel for them. I know if some superhot femme fatale ghost had come along and stolen Jesse from me, I'd have been plenty peeved. Not that Jesse had ever even been mine to begin with.

'No bed-hopping,' I said. 'Footsie under the dinner table, maybe, but no bed-hopping that I know of.'

Debbie and Kelly exchanged glances. I could see they were relieved.

'And she's leaving when?' Kelly asked.

When I said 'Sunday,' both girls let out a little sigh. Debbie went, 'Good.'

Now that she knew she wouldn't have to put up with her much longer, Kelly was willing to be gracious about Gina. 'It isn't that we don't like her,' she said.

'Yeah,' Debbie said. 'It's just that she's . . . you know.'

'I know,' I said in what I hoped was a comforting manner.

'It's just because she's new,' Kelly said. Now she was getting defensive. 'That's the only reason they like her. Because she's different.'

'Sure,' I said, putting my hairbrush back.

'I mean, so she's from New York?' Kelly was really warming to her subject. 'Big deal. I mean, I've been to New York. It wasn't so great. It was really dirty, and there were these disgusting pigeons and bums everywhere.'

'Yeah,' Debbie said. 'And you know what I heard? In New York, they don't even have fish tacos.'

I almost felt sorry for Debbie then.

'Well,' I said, shouldering my backpack. 'It's been a pleasure. But now I gotta go, ladies.'

I left them there, dipping their pinkies into little pots of lip gloss and then leaning into the mirror to apply it.

Michael was waiting for me exactly where he'd said he would be. You could tell the eyeliner was doing its job, since he got very flustered and went, 'Hi, uh, do you, uh, want me to take your backpack?'

I cooed, 'Oh, that would be lovely,' and let him take it. With two backpacks slung over his shoulders, mine and his own, Michael looked a bit odd, but then, he always did – at least with his clothes on – so this was no big surprise. We started down the cool, shady breezeway – empty now that most everybody had left for the day – and then stepped out into the warm yellow sunlight of the parking lot. The sea, just beyond it, winked at us. The sky overhead was cloudless.

'My car's over there,' Michael said, pointing at an emerald green sedan. 'Well, not my car, really. But the one the rental agency loaned me. It's not a bad little number, actually. Has some punch to it.'

I smiled at him, and he tripped over a loose piece of concrete. He would have fallen flat on his face if he hadn't saved himself at the last minute. My lipstick, I could see, was performing as well as the eyeliner.

'Let me just, uh, find the keys,' Michael said as he fumbled around in his pockets.

I told him to take his time. Then I pulled out my DKs and turned my face toward the sun, leaning against the hood of his rental car. How, I wondered, to best bring it up? Maybe I should suggest we stop by the hospital to see his little sister? No, I wanted to get to his house as soon as possible so I could start reading his email. Would I even know how to access his email? Probably not. But I could call CeeCee. She'd know. Could you talk on the phone and access someone's email at the same time? Oh, God, why wouldn't my mom let me get a cellphone? I was practically the only sophomore without one – Dopey excepted, of course.

It was while I was wondering about this that a shadow fell over my face, and suddenly I could no longer feel the warmth of the sun. I opened my eyes, and found myself staring up at Sleepy.

'What,' he demanded in the same somnambulistic manner in which he did everything, 'do you think you're doing?'

I could feel my cheeks getting red. And it wasn't because of the sun, either.

'Getting a ride home with Michael,' I said meekly. I could see out of the corner of my eye that Michael, over on the driver's side of the car, had finally found the keys, and had frozen with them in his hand, the driver side door open.

'No, you're not,' Sleepy said.

I couldn't believe it. I couldn't believe he was doing this to me. I was so embarrassed, I thought I was going to die.

'Slee—' I started to say, then stopped myself just in time. '*Jake*,' I said, under my breath. 'Cut it *out*.'

'No,' Jake said. '*You* cut it out. You remember what Mom said.'

Mom. He'd called my mother *Mom*. What was going on here?

I lowered my sunglasses and looked past Jake. Gina, along with Dopey and Doc, stood on the far side of the parking lot, leaning against the side of the Rambler and staring in my direction.

Gina. She'd told on me. She'd told on me to *Sleepy*. I couldn't believe it.

'Slee – I mean, Jake,' I said. 'I appreciate your concern. I really do. But I can take care of myself—'

'No.' And to my surprise, he wrapped a hand around my arm, and started to pull. He was surprisingly strong, for

153

someone who gave the impression of being so tired all the time. 'You're coming home with us. Sorry, man.' This last he said to Michael. 'She's supposed to ride home with me today.'

Michael, however, did not appear to find this apology a satisfactory one. He put down both our backpacks, and, slipping his car keys back into his trouser pocket, took a step toward Sleepy.

'I don't think,' Michael said in a hard voice I'd never heard him use before, 'the lady wants to go with you.'

The lady? What lady? Then I realized with a start that Michael meant me. *I* was the lady!

'I don't care what she wants,' Sleepy said. His voice wasn't hard at all. It was simply very matter-of-fact. 'She's not getting into a car with you, and that's the end of it.'

'I don't think so.' Michael took another step toward Sleepy, and that's when I saw that both of his hands were curled into fists.

Fists! Michael was going to fight Sleepy! Over me!

This was very exciting. I'd never had two boys get into a fight over me before. The fact that one of the boys was my stepbrother, however, and held about as much romantic appeal for me as Max, the family dog, somewhat dampened my enthusiasm.

And Michael wasn't much of a catch, either, when you actually thought about it, being a potential murderer and all.

Oh, why did I have to have such a couple of losers fighting over me? Why couldn't Matt Damon and Ben Affleck fight over me? Now *that* would be truly excellent.

'Look, buddy,' Sleepy said, noticing Michael's fists. 'You don't want to mess with me, OK? I'm just going to take my sister here' – he dragged me off the hood of the car – 'and go. Got that?'

Sister? *Stepsister! Stepsister!* God, why can't anyone keep it straight?

'Suze,' Michael said. He hadn't taken his eyes off Sleepy. 'Just get in the car, OK?'

Well, this, I decided, had gone on long enough. Not only was I completely embarrassed, but I was getting hot, too. That afternoon sun was no joke. Suddenly, I just didn't have any ghost-busting energy left in me.

Plus I guess I didn't want to see anybody get hurt over something so completely lame.

'Look,' I said to Michael. 'I better go with him. Some other time, OK?'

Michael finally looked away from Sleepy. His gaze, when it landed on me, was odd. It was like he wasn't even really seeing me.

'Fine,' he said.

Then he got into his car without another word, and started the engine.

God, I thought. Be a baby about it, why don't you?

'I'll call you when I get home,' I shouted to Michael, though I doubt he heard me through the rolled-up windows. It would be difficult, I realized, to wring a confession out of him over the phone, but not, I thought, impossible.

Michael's tires squealed on the hot asphalt as he drove away.

'What a freakin' jerk,' Sleepy muttered as he dragged me across the parking lot. Only he didn't say *freakin'*. Or *jerk*. 'And you want to go out with this guy?'

I said sullenly, 'We're just friends.'

'Yeah,' Sleepy said. 'Right.'

'You,' Dopey said to me as Sleepy and I approached the Rambler, 'are so busted.'

This was one of his favourite things to say to me. He said it, as a matter of fact, whenever he had the slightest chance.

'Not technically, Brad,' Doc said thoughtfully. 'You see, she didn't actually get into the car with him. And that was what she was forbidden to do. Get into a car with Michael Meducci.'

'Shut up, all of you,' Sleepy said, heading for the driver's seat. 'And get in.'

Gina, I noticed, slipped automatically into the front passenger seat. Apparently, she didn't believe that when Sleepy had told us all to shut up, he meant her, too, since she went, 'How about we stop somewhere for ice cream on the way home?'

She was trying, I knew, to get me not to be mad at her. As if a chocolate-dipped twist would help. Actually, it sort of would, now that I thought about it.

'Sounds good to me,' Sleepy said.

Dopey, on my right – as usual, I'd ended up sitting on the hump in the middle of the backseat – muttered, 'I don't know what you see in that head case Meducci anyway.'

Doc said, 'Oh, that's easy. Females of any species tend to select the male partner who is best able to provide for her and any offspring which might result from their coupling. Michael Meducci, being a good deal more intelligent than most of his classmates, amply fulfils that role, in addition to which he has what is considered, by Western standards of beauty, an outstanding physique – if what I've overheard Gina and Suze saying counts for anything. Since he is likely to pass on these favourable genetic components to his children, he is irresistible to breeding females everywhere – at least, discerning ones like Suze.'

There was silence in the car . . . the kind of silence that usually followed one of Doc's speeches.

Then Gina said reverently, 'They really should move you up a grade, David.'

'Oh, they've offered,' Doc replied, cheerfully, 'but while my intellect might be evolved for a boy my age, my growth is somewhat retarded. I felt it was inadvisable to thrust myself into a population of males much larger than I, who might be threatened by my superior intelligence.'

'In other words,' Sleepy translated for Gina's benefit, 'we didn't want him getting his butt kicked by the bigger kids.'

Then he started the car, and we roared out of the parking lot at the usual high rate of speed that Sleepy, in spite of my private nickname for him, chooses to employ.

I was trying to figure out how I could make it clear that it wasn't so much that I wanted to breed with Michael Meducci, as get him to confess to having killed the RLS Angels, when Gina went, 'God, Jake, drive much?'

Which was sort of amusing since Gina, whose parents very wisely won't let her near their car, has never driven before in her life. But then I looked up and saw what she meant. We were approaching the front gates to the school, which were set at the base of a sloping hill that opened out into a busy intersection, at a higher rate of speed than was usual, even for Sleepy.

'Yeah, Jake,' Dopey said from beside me on the backseat. 'Slow down, you maniac.'

I knew Dopey was only trying to make himself look good in front of Gina, but he did have a point: Sleepy was going way too fast.

'It's not a race,' I said, and Doc started to say something about how Jake's endorphins had probably kicked in, due to his fight with me and his near-fight with Michael, and that that would account for his sudden case of lead foot . . .

At least until Jake said, in tones that weren't in the least drowsy, 'I can't slow down. The brakes . . . the brakes aren't working.'

This sounded interesting. I leaned forward. I guess I thought Jake was trying to scare us.

Then I saw the speed with which we were approaching the intersection in front of the school. This was no joke. We were about to plunge into four lanes of heavy traffic.

'Get out!' Jake yelled at us.

At first I didn't know what he meant. Then I saw Gina struggling to undo her seatbelt, and I knew.

But it was too late. We had already started down the dip that led past the gates, and on to the highway. If we jumped now, we'd be as dead as we were going to be the minute we plunged into those four lanes of oncoming traffic. At least if we stayed in the car, we'd have the questionable protection of the Rambler's steel walls around us—

Jake leaned on the horn, swearing loudly. Gina covered her eyes. Doc flung his arms around me, burying his face in my lap, and Dopey, to my great surprise, began to scream like a girl, very close to my ear . . .

Then we were sailing down the hill, speeding past a very surprised woman in a Volvo station wagon and then a stunned-looking Japanese couple in a Mercedes, both of whom managed to slam on their brakes just in time to keep from barrelling into us.

We weren't so lucky with the traffic in the far two lanes, however. As we went flying across the highway, a tractor trailer with the words *Tom Cat* emblazoned on the front grid came bearing down on us, its horn blaring. The words *Tom Cat* loomed closer and closer, until suddenly I couldn't see them any more because they were above the roof of the car . . .

It was at that point that I closed my eyes, so I wasn't sure

158

if the impact I felt was in my head because I'd been expecting it so strongly, or if we'd really been struck. But the jolt was enough to send my neck snapping back the way it did on roller coasters when the train-car suddenly took a violent ninety-degree turn.

When I opened my eyes again, however, I started to suspect the jolt hadn't been in my head since everything was spinning around, the way it does when you go on one of those teacup rides. Only we weren't on a ride. We were still in the Rambler, which was spinning across the highway like a top.

Until suddenly, with another sickening crunch, a loud crash of glass and another very big jolt, it stopped.

And when the smoke and dust settled, we saw that we were sitting halfway in and halfway out of the Carmel-by-the-Sea Tourist Information Bureau, with a sign that said *Welcome to Carmel!* pressed up against the windshield.

Sixteen

'They killed my car.'

That was all Sleepy seemed capable of saying. He had been saying it ever since we'd crawled from the wreckage of what had once been the Rambler.

'My car. They killed my car.'

Never mind that it hadn't actually been Sleepy's car. It had been the family car, or at any rate, the kids' car.

And never mind that Sleepy did not seem capable of telling us who this mysterious 'they' was, the 'they' he suspected of murdering his automobile.

He just kept saying it over and over again. And the thing was, the more he said it, the more the horror of it all sank in.

Because, of course, it wasn't the *car* someone had tried to kill. Oh, no. It was the people *in* the car that had been the intended victims.

Or, to be more accurate, one person. Me.

I really don't think I'm being at all vain. I honestly do think that it was because of me that the Rambler's brake line was clipped. Yes, it had been clipped, so all the brake fluid had eventually leaked out. The car, being older, even, than my mother – though not quite as old as Father D – did have only the single brake line, making it vulnerable to just that sort of attack.

Let me see now, who do I know who might like to see me perish in a fiery blaze . . . Oh, hang on, I know. How about Josh Saunders, Carrie Whitman, Mark Pulsford and Felicia Bruce?

Give that girl a prize.

I couldn't, of course, tell anyone what I suspected. Not the police who showed up and took the accident report. Not the EMS guys who couldn't believe that, beyond a few bruises, none of us were seriously hurt. Not the guys from Triple A who came to tow what was left of the Rambler away. Not Michael who, having left the parking lot just moments before us, had heard the commotion and turned back, and had been one of the first to try to help us out of the car.

And certainly not my mother and stepfather, who showed up at the hospital looking tight-lipped and pale-faced, and kept saying things like, 'It's a wonder none of you were hurt,' and, 'From now on, you're only driving the Land Rover.'

Which caused Dopey, anyway, to brighten up. The Land Rover was way roomier than the Rambler had ever been. I suppose he figured he wouldn't have as much trouble getting horizontal with Debbie Mancuso in the Land Rover.

'I just can't understand it,' my mother said, much later, after the X-rays and eye tests and poking and prodding were over, and the hospital personnel had finally let us go home. We sat in the dining room of Peninsula Pizza, the place Sleepy worked, which also happened to be one of the only places in Carmel you could get a table for six – seven, if you counted Gina – without a reservation. We must have looked, to an outsider, like one big, happy family (well, except for Gina, who sort of stuck out, though not as much as you might think) celebrating something, like a soccer game victory.

161

Only we knew that what we were celebrating was the fact that we were all still alive.

'I mean, it must be a miracle,' my mother went on. 'The doctors certainly think so. That none of you were more seriously hurt, I mean.'

Doc showed her his elbow, which he'd scraped on a piece of glass while slithering out of the car after it had come to a standstill. 'This could prove to be a very dangerous wound,' he said, in a wounded little boy voice, 'if it happens to become infected.'

'Oh, sweetie.' My mother reached out and stroked his hair. 'I know. You were so brave when they put in those stitches.'

The rest of us rolled our eyes. Doc had been playing up the injury thing all night. But it was making both him and my mother happy. She'd tried that hair-stroking thing with me, and I'd nearly broken my arm trying to get away.

'It wasn't a miracle,' Andy said, shaking his head, 'but simple dumb luck that you weren't all killed.'

'Dumb luck nothing,' Sleepy said. 'My superlative driving skills are what saved us.'

I hated to admit it, but Sleepy was right. (And where did he learn a word like *superlative*? Had he been studying for his SATs behind my back?) Except for the part where we'd crashed through the plate glass window, he'd driven that tank of a car – brakeless – like an Indy 500 pro. I guess I could sort of see why Gina wouldn't let go of his arm, and kept looking up at him in this worshipful way.

Out of my newfound respect for Sleepy, I didn't even look to see what he and Gina were doing in the back of the Land Rover on the way home.

But Dopey sure did. And whatever he saw back there put him in as foul a mood as I'd ever seen him.

His stomping around and turning up of Marilyn Manson in his room only served to annoy his father, however, who went from grateful humbleness over how close he'd come to losing his 'boys – and you, Suze. Oh, and Gina, too', to apoplectic rage upon hearing what he termed 'that noxious mind-poison'.

Alone in my room – Gina had disappeared to parts of the house unknown; well, OK, I knew where she was, I just didn't want to think about it – I did not mind the noise level in the hallway outside my door. It would keep, I realized, anybody from overhearing the very unpleasant conversation I was about to have.

'Jesse!' I called, switching on my bedroom lights and looking around for him. But both he and Spike were MIA. 'Jesse, where are you? I need you.'

Ghosts aren't dogs. They won't come when you call them. At least, they never used to. Not for me, anyway. Only lately – and this was something I hadn't exactly talked over with Father Dom. It was a little too weird to think about, if you asked me – the ghosts I knew had been popping up at the merest suggestion of them in my mind. Seriously. It seemed all I had to do was think about my dad, for instance, and poof, there he was.

Needless to say, this was quite embarrassing when I happened to be thinking about him while I was in the shower washing my hair, or whatever.

I kind of wondered if this had something to do with my mediator powers getting stronger with age. But if that were true, then it would stand to reason that Father Dom would be a way better mediator than me.

Only he wasn't. Different, but not better. Certainly not stronger. He couldn't summon a spirit with a single thought.

At least, I didn't think so.

Anyway, so even though ghosts don't come when you call them, Jesse always seemed to lately. He appeared before me with a shimmer, and then stood staring at me like I'd just stepped off the set of *Hellraiser III* in full costume. But may I say that I did not look half so dishevelled as I felt?

'*Nombre de Dios*, Susannah,' he said, paling visibly (well, for a guy who was already dead, anyway). 'What happened to you?'

I looked down at myself. All right, so my blouse was torn and dirty, and my thigh-highs had sort of lost their stick. At least my hair had that all-important windswept look.

'As if you didn't know,' I said sourly, sitting down on my bed and slipping out of my shoes. 'I thought you said you'd babysit them all day, until Father D and I had a chance to work on Michael.'

'Babysit?' Jesse knit his dark brows, revealing that he was unfamiliar with the word. 'I stayed with the Angels all day, if that's what you mean.'

'Oh, right,' I said. 'What are you saying? You went with them on their little field trip to the school parking lot to clip the Rambler's brake line?'

Jesse sat down next to me on the bed.

'Susannah.' His dark-eyed gaze was riveted to my face. 'Did something happen today?'

'You better believe it.' I told him what had gone down, though my explanation of exactly what had been done to the car was a little sketchy given my complete ignorance of all things mechanical, and Jesse's particular lack of knowledge about the workings of the automobile. Back when he'd been alive, of course, horse and buggy had been the only way to go.

When I was through, he shook his head.

'But, Susannah,' he said, 'it could not have been Josh and

the others. As I told you, I was with them all day. I only left them now because you called to me. They could not possibly have done what you are describing. I would have seen, and stopped them.'

I blinked at him. 'But if it wasn't Josh and those guys, then who could it have been? I mean, no one else wants me dead. At least, not at the moment.'

Jesse continued to stare down at me. 'Are you so sure you were the intended victim, Susannah?'

'Well, of course it was me.' I know it sounds weird, but I was almost offended at the idea that there might be someone else on the planet worthier of murdering than myself. I must say, I do pride myself on the number of enemies I've acquired. In the mediator business, I've always considered it a sign that things were going well if there were a bunch of people who wanted me dead.

'I mean, who else but me?' I gave a laugh. 'What, you think somebody's out to get *Doc*?'

Jesse, however, did not laugh.

'Think, Susannah,' he urged me. 'Isn't there anyone else who was in that car that someone might want to see badly hurt, or even dead?'

I narrowed my eyes at him. 'You know something,' I said flatly.

'No.' Jesse shook his head. 'But—'

'But what? God, I hate when you do the cryptic warning thing. Just tell me.'

'No.' He shook his head quickly. 'Think, Susannah.'

I sighed. There was no arguing with him when he got this way. You couldn't really blame him, I guess, for wanting to play Mr Miyagi to my Karate Kid. It wasn't like he had a whole lot of other stuff to do.

I exhaled gustily enough to send my bangs fluttering.

'OK,' I said. 'People who might not be too happy with someone – besides me – in that car. Let me see.' I brightened up. 'Debbie and Kelly aren't too happy about Gina. They had a nasty little interlude in the girls' room just before it happened. The car thing, I mean.'

Then I frowned. 'But I hardly think those two would clip a brake line to get her out of the way. In the first place, I doubt they even know what a brake line is, or where to find it. And in the second place, they might mess themselves up climbing under a car. You know, break a nail, or get oil in their hair, or whatever. Debbie probably wouldn't mind, but Kelly? Forget it. Plus they had to know they might end up killing Dopey and Sleepy, and they wouldn't want that.'

'Of course not,' Jesse said mildly.

It was the very tonelessness with which he uttered the words that cued me in.

'Dopey?' I shot him an incredulous look. 'Who'd want Dopey dead? Or Sleepy, for that matter? I mean, those guys are so . . . dumb.'

'Hasn't either of them,' Jesse asked in that same toneless manner, 'done anything that might make someone angry?'

'Well, sure,' I said. 'Not Sleepy so much, but Dopey? He's always doing asinine stuff like grabbing people in headlocks and throwing their books everywhere . . .' My voice trailed off.

Then I shook my head. 'No,' I said. 'That's impossible.'

Jesse only looked at me. 'Is it?' he said.

'No, you don't understand.' I stood up and started pacing my room. At some point during our conversation, Spike had slunk through the window. Now he sat on the floor at Jesse's feet, vigorously lashing himself with his sandpapery tongue.

'I mean, he was there,' I explained. 'Michael was there, right after it happened. He helped us out of the car. He . . .'

My last sight of Michael that evening had been just as the ambulance doors closed on me and Gina and Sleepy and Dopey and Doc. Michael's face had been pale – even more than usual – and concerned.

No. 'That just . . .' I got as far as Gina's daybed before I spun around to face Jesse again. 'That just can't be,' I said. 'Michael would never do something like that.'

Jesse laughed. There was no humour in the sound, however.

'Wouldn't he?' he wanted to know. 'I can think of four people who might have a very different opinion on the matter.'

'But why would he do it?' I shook my head again, emphatically enough to send the ends of my hair flying. 'I mean, Dopey's a butthead, it's true, but enough of one so that someone might feel compelled to *murder* him? Not to mention a bunch of innocent people along with him? Including *me*?' I raised my indignant gaze from the sight of Spike chewing on his own foot, trying to get the grime out from between his toes. 'Michael couldn't possibly want to see *me* dead. I'm the best chance he's got for a date to the prom!'

Jesse didn't say anything. And in the silence, I remembered something. And what I remembered took my breath away.

'Oh, God,' I said, and, clutching my chest, I sank down on to the daybed.

Jesse's neutral expression sharpened into one of concern.

'What is it, Susannah?' he asked worriedly. 'Are you ill?'

I nodded. 'Oh, yeah,' I said, staring unseeingly at the wall across from me. 'I think I'm going to be sick, Jesse . . . he asked me if I wanted to ride with him. Right before it happened. He was *insistent* I ride with him. In fact, when Sleepy

167

said I had to go with him or he'd tell Mom, I thought the two of them were going to get into a fist-fight.'

'Of course,' Jesse said in what was, for him, a very dry tone. 'His – what did you call it? Oh, yes – date for the prom was about to be exterminated.'

'Oh, God!' I stood up and started pacing again. 'Oh, God, why? Why *Dopey?* I mean, he's a jerk and all, but why would Michael want to kill him?'

Jesse said, quietly, 'Perhaps for the same reason he killed Josh and the others.'

I stopped dead in my tracks. Slowly, I turned my head to look at him. But I didn't see him. Not really. I was remembering something Dopey had said – weeks ago, it seemed like, but it had actually only been a night or two before. We'd been talking about the accident that had killed the RLS Angels, and Dopey had said something about Mark Pulsford. 'We happen to have partied together,' he'd said. 'Last month, in the Valley.'

At the same party in the Valley, I wondered, my blood suddenly running cold, where Lila Meducci had fallen into the pool?

A second later, without another word to Jesse, I'd ripped open the door to my room, taken the three strides across the hall to Dopey's room, and was banging on the door with all my might.

'Chill!' Dopey thundered from inside. 'I turned it down already!'

'It's not about the music,' I said. 'It's about something else. Can I come in?'

I heard the sound of barbells falling back into their stand. Then Dopey grunted, 'Yeah. I guess so.'

I laid my hand on the knob and turned it.

I'd like to point out something here. I have been in Doc's

room. Many times, in fact, as he is always the stepbrother I go to when I have a homework problem I cannot solve, in spite of the fact that he is three grades behind me. And I have even been in Sleepy's room since he usually needs actual physical shaking in order to wake him up in the morning in time to drive us all to school.

But I had never, ever been in Dopey's room before. Truth be told, I had always hoped I might never have a reason to cross that particular threshold.

Now, however, I had a reason. I took a deep breath and went in.

It was dark. This was because of Dopey's decision to paint three of his walls purple and one white, Mission Academy wrestling team colours. He had chosen a purple so dark it was almost black. The darkness of those three walls was only alleviated by the occasional poster of Michael Jordan urging the viewer to Just Do It.

The floor of Dopey's room was a deep carpet of dirty socks and underwear. The odour was pungent – a mixture of sweat and baby powder. Not unpleasant, necessarily, but not an odour I'd particularly want permeating my wardrobe. Dopey, however, did not seem to mind.

'Well?' He was stretched out on his back on a padded bench. Above his chest hung a set of barbells. I would not have liked to hazard a guess as to how much weight he was lifting, but allow me to assure you, with enough reps, I was quite sure he'd have no trouble heaving Debbie Mancuso out the window in the event of a fire. Which is all a girl really needs out of a boyfriend, if you ask me.

'Dope—' I took another deep breath. What was with the baby powder? Wait. Don't tell me. I don't want to know. 'Brad. Were you at that party in the Valley where Lila Meducci fell into the pool?'

Dopey had reached up and seized the barbell. Now he heaved it into the air, awarding me a glimpse of his excessively hairy armpits. I tried not to hurl at the sight of them.

'What are you talking about?' he grunted.

'Lila Meducci.'

Dopey had lowered the barbell until it was just above his chest. His biceps had bunched up into melon-sized balls. Allow me to point out that normally, the sight of a male bicep that size would have caused my knees to go weak. But then, these biceps were Dopey's, so all I could do was swallow hard and hope the slices of pepperoni pizza I'd downed for dinner would stay where they were.

'Michael's little sister,' I elaborated. 'She nearly drowned at a party out in the Valley last month. I was wondering if it was the same party you mentioned you'd been to, the one where you'd run into Mark Pulsford.'

Up went the barbells.

'Could have been,' Dopey said. 'I don't know. Why do you care?'

'Brad,' I said. 'It's important. I mean, if you were there, I think you would know. An ambulance must have shown up.'

'I guess,' he said between reps. 'I mean, I was pretty wasted.'

'You *guess* that a girl almost drowned in front of you?' I don't have much patience for Dopey under the best of circumstances. In this particular case, my tolerance for his stupidity had dipped to an all-time low.

Dopey let the barbell fall back into its stand with a clatter. Then he sat up and regarded me testily.

'Look,' he said. 'If I tell you I was there, what are you going to do? Go running to Mom and Dad, right? So why would I tell you? I mean, seriously, Suze. Why would I?'

Aside from my great surprise at hearing Dopey, too, mess

up and call my mother *Mom*, I was prepared for the question.

'I won't tell,' I said. 'I swear I won't tell, Brad. Only I have to know.'

He still looked suspicious. 'Why? So you can tell that creepy albino friend of yours, and she can put it in the school paper? "Brad Ackerman stood there like a schmo while a girl almost died." Is that it?'

'I swear it isn't,' I said.

He shrugged his heavy shoulders. 'Fine,' he said. 'You know what? I don't even care. It's not like my life doesn't already suck. I mean, I haven't got a hope of getting down to one-sixty-eight before sectionals, and it's pretty clear now that your friend Gina likes Jake better 'n me.' He eyed me. 'Doesn't she?'

I shifted my weight uncomfortably. 'I don't know,' I said. 'I think she likes both of you.'

'Yeah,' Dopey said sarcastically. 'That's why she's in here right now with me instead of locked in with Jake, doing whatever.'

'I'm sure they're just talking,' I said.

'Right.' Dopey shook his head. I was a bit stunned. I had never seen him looking so . . . human. Nor had I known he had goals. What was this 168 business? And did he really care that much about Gina that he would think his life sucked just because he didn't think she liked him back?

Weird. Really weird stuff.

'You want to know about that party in the Valley?' he asked. 'I was there. All right? Are you happy now? I was there. Like I said, I was wasted. I didn't see her fall in. I only noticed her as somebody was pulling her out.' Again, he shook his head. 'That was really uncool, you know? I mean, she shouldn't have been there in the first place. Nobody

171

invited her. If you can't hold your liquor, you got no business drinking, you know? But some of these girls, they'll do just about anything to get in with us.'

I knit my eyebrows. 'Us?'

He looked at me like I was stupid. 'You know,' he said. 'The jocks. The popular people. Meducci's sister – I didn't know it was her until your mom said it the other night at the dinner table – she was one of those girls. Always hanging around, trying to get one of us guys from the team to ask her out. So she could be popular, too, see?'

I saw. Suddenly, I saw only too well.

Which was why I left Dopey's room then without another word. What was there to say? I knew what I had to do. I guess I had known it all along. I just hadn't wanted to admit it.

But now I knew. Like Michael Meducci, I thought I had no other choice.

And like Michael Meducci, I needed to be stopped. Only I didn't think so. Not then.

Just like Michael.

Seventeen

Gina was in my room when I came back from my visit to Dopey. Both Jesse and Spike, however, were gone. Which was actually fine by me.

'Hey,' Gina said, looking up from the toenail she'd been painting. 'Where have you been?'

I strode past her and started wriggling out of my school clothes. 'Dopey's room,' I said. 'Look, cover for me, will you?' I stepped into a pair of jeans, then started lacing up my Timberland boots. 'I'm going to be out for a while. Just tell them I'm in the bathtub. It would help if you let the water run. Tell them it's cramps again.'

'They're going to start thinking you've got endometriosis, or something.' Gina watched as I tugged a black turtleneck sweater over my head. 'Where are you really going?'

'Out,' I said. I pulled on the windbreaker I'd worn the other night to the beach. This time I tucked a hat into my pocket, along with the gloves.

'Oh, sure. Out.' Gina shook her head, looking concerned. 'Suze, are you all right?'

'Of course I am. Why?'

'You've got kind of . . . well, a crazy look in your eye.'

'I'm fine,' I said. 'I figured it out, is all.'

'Figured what out?' Gina put the cap on her nail polish and stood up. 'Suze, what are you talking about?'

'What happened today.' I climbed up on to the window seat. 'With the brake line. Michael did it.'

'Michael *Meducci?*' Gina looked at me as if I were nuts. 'Suze, are you sure?'

'Sure as I'm standing here talking to you.'

'But why? Why would he do that? I thought he was in love with you.'

'With me, maybe,' I said with a shrug as I pushed the window open wider. 'But he's got a pretty big grudge against Brad.'

'Brad? What did Brad ever do to Michael Meducci?'

'Stand around,' I said, 'and let his little sister die. Well, almost, anyway. I'm out of here, OK, Gina? I'll explain everything when I get back.'

And then I slipped through the window, and climbed down to the porch roof. Outside, it was dark and cool and silent, except for the chirp of crickets and the far-off sound of the waves hitting the beach. Or was that the traffic down on the highway? I couldn't tell. After listening for a minute to make sure no one downstairs had heard me, I walked down the sloping roof to the gutter, where I squatted, ready to jump, knowing the pine needles below would cushion my landing.

'Suze!' A shadow blocked out the light streaming from the bay windows to my room.

I looked back over my shoulder. Gina was leaning out, looking anxiously after me.

'Shouldn't we—' She sounded, I noted in some distant part of my mind, frightened. 'I mean, shouldn't we call the police? If this stuff about Michael is true—'

I stared at her as if she'd suggested I . . . well, jump off the Golden Gate Bridge.

174

'The *police?*' I echoed. 'No way. This is between Michael and me.'

'Suze—' Gina shook her head so that her springy curls bounced. 'This is serious stuff. I mean, this guy is a murderer. I really think we need to call in the professionals here—'

'I am a professional,' I said, offended. 'I'm a mediator, remember?'

Gina did not look comforted by this piece of information. 'But . . . well, what are you going to do, Suze?'

I smiled at her reassuringly.

'Oh,' I said. 'That's easy. I'm going to show him what happens when somebody tries to kill someone I care about.'

And then I leaped off of the roof into the darkness.

I couldn't bring myself to take the Land Rover. Oh, sure, I was perfectly willing to commit what pretty much amount-ed to murder, but drive without a licence? No way! Instead, I hauled out one of the many ten speeds Andy had tucked away along the carport wall. A few seconds later, I was flying down the hill from our house, tears streaming from my eyes. Not because I was crying, or anything, but because the wind was so cold on my face as I sailed down into the Valley.

I called Michael from a pay phone outside the Safeway. An older woman – his mother, I suppose – answered. I asked if I could speak to Michael. She said, 'Yes, of course,' in that pleased way mothers use when their child gets his or her first call from a member of the opposite sex. And I would know. My mother uses that voice every time a boy calls me and she answers. You can't really blame her. It hap-pens so rarely.

Mrs Meducci must have tipped Michael off that it was a girl, since his voice sounded much deeper than usual when he said hello.

'Michael?' I said, just to be sure it was him and not his father.

'Suze?' he said in his normal voice. 'Oh, my God, Suze, I'm so glad it's you. Did you get my message? I must have called about ten times. I followed the ambulance to the hospital, but they wouldn't let me into the emergency room to see you. Only if you were admitted, they said. Which you weren't, right?'

'Nope,' I said. 'Fit as a fiddle.'

'Thank God. Oh, Suze, you don't have any idea how scared I was when I heard that crash and realized it was you—'

'Yeah,' I said shortly. 'It was scary. Listen, Michael, I'm in a jam of a different kind, and I was wondering if you could help me out.'

Michael said, 'You know I'd do anything for you, Suze.'

Yeah. Like try to kill my stepbrothers and my best friend.

'I'm stranded,' I said. 'At the Safeway. It's kind of a long story. I was wondering if there was any possible way—'

'I'll be there,' Michael said, 'in three minutes.' Then he hung up.

He was there in two. I'd barely had time to stash the bike between a couple of Dumpsters in the back of the store before I saw him pull up in his green rental sedan, peering into the brightly lit windows of the supermarket as if he expected to see me inside riding the stupid mechanical rocking horse, or whatever. I approached the car from the parking lot, then leaned over to tap on the passenger side window.

Michael whipped around, startled by the sound. When he saw it was me, his face – pastier than ever in the fluorescent lights – relaxed. He leaned over and opened the door.

'Hop in,' he said cheerfully. 'Boy, you don't know how glad I am to see you in one piece.'

'Yeah?' I slid into the front passenger seat, then slammed the door closed after I'd tucked my feet in. 'Well, me too. Happy to be in one piece, I mean. Ha ha.'

'Ha ha.' Michael's laugh, rather than being sarcastic, as mine had been, was nervous. Or at least I chose to think so.

'Well,' he said as we sat there in front of the supermarket, the motor running. 'You want me to take you, um, home?'

'No.' I turned my head to look at him.

You might be wondering what I was thinking at a moment like that. I mean, what goes through a person's head when they know they're about to do something that could result in another person's death?

Well, I'll tell you. Not a whole heck of a lot. I was thinking that Michael's rental car smelled funny. I was wondering if the last person who had used it had spilled cologne in it, or something.

Then I realized the smell of cologne was coming from Michael himself. He had apparently splashed on a little Carolina Herrera For Men before coming to get me. How flattering.

'I have an idea,' I said, as if I had only just then thought of it. 'Let's go to the Point.'

Michael's hands fell off the steering wheel. He hurried to right them, placing them at two and four o'clock, like the good driver he was.

'I beg your pardon?' he said.

'The Point.' I thought maybe I wasn't being alluring enough, or something. So I reached over and laid a hand on his arm. He was wearing a suede jacket. Beneath my fingertips, the suede felt very soft, and beneath the suede, Michael's bicep was as hard and as round as Dopey's had looked.

'You know,' I said. 'For the view. It's a beautiful night.'

Michael wasted no more time. He put the car in gear and began pulling out from the parking lot before I even had time to remove my hand.

'Great,' he said. His voice was maybe a little uneven, so he cleared his throat, and said, with a little more dignity, 'I mean, that sounds all right.'

A few seconds later, we were cruising along the Pacific Coast Highway. It was only ten o'clock or so, but there weren't many other cars on the road. It was, after all, a weeknight. I wondered if Michael's mother, before he'd left the house, had told him to be home at a certain time. I wondered if, when he didn't come home by curfew, she'd worry. How long, I wondered, would she wait before calling the police? The hospital emergency rooms?

'So nobody,' Michael said as he drove, 'was really hurt, right? In the accident?'

'No,' I replied. 'No one was hurt.'

'That's good,' Michael said.

'Is it?' I pretended to be looking out the passenger side window. But really I was watching Michael's reflection.

'What do you mean?' he asked quickly.

I shrugged. 'I don't know,' I said. 'It's just that . . . well, you know. Brad.'

'Oh.' He gave a little chuckle. There wasn't any real humour in it, though. 'Yeah. Brad.'

'I mean, I try to get along with him,' I said. 'But it's so hard. Because he can be such a jerk sometimes.'

'I can imagine,' Michael said. Pretty mildly, I thought.

I turned in my seat so that I was almost facing him.

'Like, you know what he said tonight?' I asked. Without waiting for a reply, I said, 'He told me he was at that party. The one where your sister fell. You know. Into the pool.'

178

I do not think it was my imagination that Michael's grip on the wheel tightened. 'Really?'

'Yeah. You should have heard what he said about it, too.'

Michael's face, in profile to mine, looked grim.

'What did he say?'

I toyed with the seatbelt I'd fastened around myself. 'No,' I said. 'I shouldn't tell you.'

'No, really,' Michael said. 'I'd like to know.'

'It's so mean, though,' I said.

'Tell me what he said.' Michael's voice was very calm.

'Well,' I said. 'All right. He basically said – and he wasn't quite as succinct as this, because, as you know, he's pretty much incapable of forming complete sentences – but basically he said your sister got what she deserved because she shouldn't have been at that party in the first place. He said she hadn't been invited. Only popular people were supposed to be there. Can you believe that?'

Michael carefully passed a pickup truck. 'Yes,' he said quietly. 'Actually, I can.'

'I mean, popular people. He actually said that. Popular people.' I shook my head. 'And what defines popular? That's what I'd like to know. I mean, your sister was unpopular why? Because she wasn't a jock? She wasn't a cheerleader? She didn't have the right clothes? What?'

'All of those things,' Michael said in the same quiet voice.

'As if any of that *matters*,' I said. 'As if being intelligent and compassionate and kind to others doesn't count for anything. No, all that matters is whether you're friends with the right people.'

'Unfortunately,' Michael said, 'that oftentimes appears to be the case.'

'Well,' I said. 'I think it's crap. I said so, too. To Brad. I was like, "So all of you just stood there while this girl

nearly died because no one invited her in the first place?"
He denied it, of course. But you know it's true.'

'Yes,' Michael said. We were driving along Big Sur now, the road narrowing while, at the same time, growing darker. 'I do, actually. If my sister had been . . . well, Kelly Prescott, for instance, someone would have pulled her out at once, rather than stand there laughing at her as she drowned.'

It was hard to see his expression since there was no moon. The only light there was to see by was the glow from the console in the dashboard. Michael looked sickly in it, and not just because the light had a greenish tinge to it.

'Is that what happened?' I asked him. 'Did people do that? Laugh at her while she was drowning?'

He nodded. 'That's what one of the EMS guys told the police. Everybody thought she was faking it.' He let out a humourless laugh. 'My sister – that was all she wanted, you know? To be popular. To be like them. And they stood there. They all just stood there laughing while she drowned.'

I said, 'Well. I heard everyone was pretty drunk.' Including your sister, I thought, but didn't say out loud.

'That's no excuse,' Michael said. 'But of course nobody did anything about it. The girl who had the party – her parents got a fine. That's all. My sister may never wake up, and all they got was a fine.'

We had reached, I saw, the turn-off to the observation point. Michael honked before he went around the corner. No one was on the other side. He swung neatly into a parking space, but he didn't switch off the ignition. Instead, he sat there, staring out into the inky blackness that was the sea and sky.

I was the one who reached over and turned the motor off. The dashboard light went off a second later, plunging us into absolute darkness.

180

'So,' I said. The silence in the car was pretty deafening. There were no cars on the road behind us. If I opened the window, I knew the sounds of the wind and waves would come rushing in. Instead, I just sat there.

Slowly, the darkness outside the car became less opaque. As my eyes adjusted to it, I could even make out the horizon where the black sky met the even blacker sea.

Michael turned his head. 'It was Carrie Whitman,' he said. 'The girl who had the party.'

I nodded, not taking my gaze off the horizon. 'I know.'

'Carrie Whitman,' he said again. 'Carrie Whitman was in that car. The one that went off the cliff last Saturday night.'

'You mean,' I said quietly, 'the car you pushed off the cliff last Saturday night.'

Michael's head didn't move. I looked at him, but I couldn't quite read his expression.

But I could hear the resignation in his voice.

'You know,' he said. It was a statement, not a question. 'I thought you might.'

'After today, you mean?' I reached down and undid my seatbelt. 'When you nearly killed me?'

'I'm so sorry.' He lowered his head, and finally, I could see his eyes. They were filled with tears. 'Suze, I don't know how I'll ever—'

'There was no seminar on extraterrestrial life at that institute, was there?' I glared at him. 'Last Saturday night, I mean. You came out here, and you loosened the bolts on that guard rail. Then you sat and waited for them. You knew they'd come here after the dance. You knew they'd come, and you waited. And when you heard that stupid horn, you rammed them. You pushed them over the side of that cliff. And you did it in cold blood.'

181

Michael did something surprising then. He reached out and touched my hair where it curled out from beneath the knit watch cap I was wearing.

'I knew you'd understand,' he said. 'From the moment I saw you, I knew you, out of all of them, were the only one who'd understand.'

I seriously wanted to throw up. I mean it. He didn't get it. He so didn't get it. I mean, hadn't he thought about his mother at all? His poor mother, who had been so excited because a girl had called him? His mother, who already had one kid in the hospital? Hadn't he thought how his mother was going to feel when it came out that her only son was a murderer? Hadn't he thought about that *at all*?

Maybe he had. Maybe he had, and he thought she'd be glad. Because he'd avenged what had happened to his sister. Well, almost, anyway. There were still a few loose ends in the form of Brad . . . and everyone else who'd been at that party, I suppose. I mean, why just stop at Brad? I wondered how he'd managed to secure the guest list, and if he intended to kill everyone on it or just a select few.

'How did you know, anyway?' he asked in what I suppose he meant to be this tender voice. But all it did was make me want to throw up even more. 'About the guard rail, I mean? And their car horn. That wasn't in the papers.'

'How did I know?' I jerked my head from his reach. 'They told me.'

He looked a little hurt at my pulling away from him. '*They* told you? Who do you mean?'

'Carrie,' I said. 'And Josh and Felicia and Mark. The kids you killed.'

His hurt look changed. It went from confused, to startled, and then to cynical, all in a matter of seconds.

'Oh,' he said with a little laugh. 'Right. The ghosts. You

tried to warn me about them before, didn't you? Right here, as a matter of fact.'

I just looked at him. 'Laugh all you want,' I said. 'But the fact is, Michael, they've been wanting to kill you for a while now. And after the stunt you pulled today with the Rambler, I am seriously thinking about letting them.'

He stopped laughing. 'Suze,' he said. 'Your strange fixation with the spirit world aside, I told you: today was an accident. You weren't supposed to be in that car. You were supposed to ride home with me. Brad was the one. Brad was the one I wanted dead, not you.'

'And what about David?' I demanded. 'My little brother? He's twelve years old, Michael. He was in that car. Did you want him dead, too? And Jake? He was probably delivering pizzas the night your sister was hurt. Should he die for what happened to her? Or my friend Gina? I guess she deserves to die, too, even though she's never even been to a party in the Valley.'

Michael's face was white against the bits of sky I could see through the window behind his head.

'I didn't mean for anyone to get hurt,' he said, in an oddly toneless voice. 'Anybody except for the guilty, I mean.'

'Well, you didn't do a very good job,' I said. 'In fact, you did a lousy job. You really messed up. And do you know why?'

I saw his eyelids, behind his glasses, narrow.

'I think I'm starting to,' he said.

'Because you tried to kill some people I happen to care about.' I swallowed. Something hard, that hurt, was growing in my throat. 'And that's why, Michael, it's going to stop. Right here. Right now.'

He continued to stare at me though those narrowed eyelids.

'Oh,' he said in the same expressionless voice. 'It's going to stop, all right. Believe me.'

I knew what he was driving at. I almost laughed. If it hadn't been for the painful lump in my throat, I would have.

'Michael,' I said. 'Don't even try. You so don't know who you're messing with.'

'No,' Michael said quietly. 'I guess I don't, do I? I thought you were different. I thought you, out of everyone at school, would be able to see things from my point of view. But I can see now that you're just like everybody else.'

'You don't have any idea,' I said, 'how much I wish I were.'

'I'm sorry, Suze,' Michael said, undoing his own seatbelt. 'I really thought you and I could be . . . well, friends, anyway. But I am getting the distinct impression that you don't approve of what I've been doing. Even though no one – *no one* – will miss those people. They really were wastes of space, Suze. They had nothing meaningful to contribute. I mean, look at Brad. Would it be such a tragedy if he simply ceased to exist?'

'It would,' I said, 'to his father.'

Michael shrugged. 'I suppose. Still, I think the world would be a better place without all the Josh Saunderses and Brad Ackermans.' He smiled at me. There was nothing, however, warm in that smile. 'You, however, disagree, I can see. It even sounds to me as if you're contemplating trying to stop me. And I really can't have that.'

'So what are you going to do?' I gave him a very sarcastic look. 'Kill me?'

'I don't want to,' he said. 'Believe me.'

Then he cracked his knuckles. Can I just tell you, I found this quite creepy. I mean, aside from the fact that cracking your knuckles in front of somebody is creepy, anyway, this was especially disturbing since it drew attention to the fact that Michael's hands were actually quite large, and were attached to these arms that I remembered from the beach were remarkably muscular, and filled with ropy sinews. I'm not exactly a delicate flower, but hands attached to a pair of arms like that could do a girl like me some serious damage.

'But I guess,' Michael said, 'you haven't left me with much choice, have you?'

Oh, sure. Blame the victim, why don't you?

I don't know if I said the words aloud, or simply thought them. I only know I went, 'Now would be a good time for Josh and his friends to show up,' and that a second later Josh Saunders, Carrie Whitman, Mark Pulsford and Felicia Bruce all appeared, standing in the gravel by the passenger side door of Michael's rental car.

They stood there blinking for a second, as if unsure what had happened. Then they looked beyond me, at the boy behind the steering wheel.

And that's when all hell broke loose.

Eighteen

Was it what I intended to happen all along?

I don't know. Certainly there'd been a moment in Dopey's room when I'd been seized by a kind of rage. It was rage, not bicycle pedals, that had propelled me down into the Valley, and rage that had prompted me to put that quarter into that pay phone and call Michael.

Some of that rage, however, dissipated when I spoke to Michael's mother. Yes, he was a murderer. Yes, he'd tried to kill me and a number of people I cared about.

But he had a mother. A mother who loved him enough to be excited because a girl was calling him, maybe for the first time in his life.

Still, I got into that car with him. I told him to drive to the Point, even though I knew what was there waiting for him. And I got him to admit it. All of it. Out loud.

And then I called them. There was no doubt about that. I called the RLS Angels. And when they showed up, all I did was calmly get out of the car.

That's right. I got out of the way. And I let them do what they'd been wanting to do for so long . . . since the night of their deaths, actually.

Look, I'm not proud of it. And I can't say that I stood there and watched it with any relish. When the seatbelt

Michael had removed suddenly wrapped around his throat, and his adjustable car seat started creeping inexorably toward the steering wheel, crushing his legs, I didn't feel good about it.

The Angels sure seemed to, however.

And they probably should have. Their telekinetic powers, I could see, had come a long way. They weren't messing around with any seaweed ropes or Mardi Gras decorations now. The force of their combined power was strong enough to have flicked on the rental car's lights and windshield wipers. Through the rolled-up windows, I could hear the radio blare to life. Britney Spears was bemoaning her latest heartache as Michael Meducci clawed at the seatbelt around his neck. The car had begun to rock and was lit eerily from inside, almost as if the dashboard lights were halogens that someone had set on bright.

And all the while, the RLS Angels stood there in total silence, their hands stretched out toward the car, and their gazes fixed on Michael. I mean, even for ghosts they looked spooky, glowing in that unearthly way, the girls in their long dresses and wrist corsages, and the boys in their tuxes. I shuddered, watching them, and it wasn't just from the cold breeze coming off the ocean, either.

I hate to say it, but it was Britney that broke the spell for me. I mean, she's likeable enough, but to have to die while listening to her? I don't know. It just seemed a bit harsh, somehow.

And then there was poor Mrs Meducci. She had already lost one child – well, more or less. Could I really just stand there and watch her lose another?

Minutes – maybe even seconds – before, the answer to that question might have been yes. But when it came down to it, I just couldn't. I couldn't, in spite of what Michael had

187

done. I simply had too many years of mediation behind me. Too many years, and too many deaths. I couldn't stand there and allow yet another one to occur right before my eyes.

Michael's face was contorted and purple, his glasses askew, when I finally shouted, '*Stop!*'

Instantly, the car stopped rocking. The windshield wipers stilled. Britney's voice was cut off mid-note, and Michael's car seat started sliding slowly back. The seatbelt loosened around his neck enough to allow him to gasp for air. He collapsed against the back of the seat, looking confused and frightened, his chest heaving.

Josh blinked at me like someone newly wakened from a trance. 'What?' he said, sounding annoyed.

I said, 'I'm sorry. But I can't let you do this.'

Josh and the others exchanged glances. Mark was the first to speak. He gave a little laugh and went, 'Oh, *right*.'

Then the radio blared to life again, and suddenly, the car was rocking on its shocks.

I reacted swiftly and decisively by hammering a fist into Mark Pulsford's gut. This threw off the Angels' concentration enough so that Michael was able to scrape open the driver's side door and throw himself out of the car before anything else could start strangling him. He lay in the gravel, moaning.

Mark, on the other hand, recovered all too quickly from my assault.

'You bitch,' he said, looking mightily offended. 'What gives?'

'Yeah.' Josh was clearly livid. His blue eyes were like shards of ice as they glinted at me. 'First you say we can't kill him. Then you say we can. Then you say we can't. Well, guess what? We're tired of this mediation crap. We're killing him, and that's the end of it.'

That was when the car started rocking with enough energy that it looked as if it was going to flip over, right on top of Michael.

'No!' I cried. 'Look, I was wrong, all right? I mean, he tried to kill me, too, and I'll admit, I went a little wacko. But believe me, this isn't the way—'

'Speak for yourself,' Josh said.

And a second later, I was flying backward through the air, blown off my feet by a blast of energy so strong, I was convinced Michael's car had blown up.

It wasn't until I landed hard in the dirt on the far side of the parking area that I realized it hadn't been the car exploding at all. It had merely been the combined force of the Angels' psychic power, thrown casually my way. I had been tossed aside as easily as an ant flicked off a picnic table.

I guess that's when I knew I was in some real trouble. I had, I realized, unleashed a monster. Or four of them, I should say.

I was struggling to get back up to my feet when Jesse materialized beside me, looking almost as angry as Josh.

'*Nombre de Dios*,' I heard him breathe as he took in the sight before him. Then he looked down at me. 'What is happening here?' he demanded, holding out a hand to help me up. 'I turn around for one second, and they are gone. Did you call them?'

Flinching – and not from pain – I took his hand, and let him pull me up.

'Yes,' I admitted, brushing myself off. 'But I didn't . . . well, I didn't mean for *this* to happen.'

Jesse looked at Michael, who was crawling across the parking lot, trying to get away from his gyrating car.

'*Nombre de Dios*, Susannah,' Jesse said again, incredulously. 'What did you expect to happen? You bring that boy *here*, of all places? And now you ask them not to kill him?' Shaking his head, Jesse started striding toward the Angels.

'You don't understand,' I protested, trotting after him. 'He tried to kill me. And Doc and Gina and Dopey and—'

'So you do *this*? Susannah, don't you know by now that you are not a killer?' Jesse's dark-eyed gaze bored into me. 'Kindly don't try to act like one. The only person who will end up getting hurt by it is you.'

I was so taken aback by the rebuke in his tone, tears filled my eyes. I mean it. Actual tears. Furious. That's what I told myself. I was crying because I was furious with him. Not because he'd hurt my feelings. Not at all.

But Jesse didn't notice my fury. He'd turned his back on me, and now he strode up to the Angels. A second later, the car stopped rocking, the windshield wipers and radio stilled, and the lights went dead. The Angels were strong, it was true. But Jesse had been dead a lot longer than they had.

'Get back to the beach,' Jesse said to them.

Josh actually laughed out loud.

'You're kidding me, right?' he said.

'I am not kidding you,' Jesse said.

'No way,' Mark Pulsford said.

'Yeah.' Carrie pointed at me. 'I mean, *she* called us. *She* said it was all right.'

Jesse did not turn his head in the direction Carrie was pointing. It was pretty clear he was disgusted with me.

'Now she says it is not,' Jesse informed them. 'You will do as she says.'

'Don't you get it?' Josh's eyes were flashing again, flashing

190

with the psychic energy he was so filled with. 'He killed us. He *killed* us.'

'And he will be punished for it,' Jesse said evenly. 'But not by you.'

'By who, then?' Josh demanded.

'By,' Jesse said, 'the law.'

'*Bullshit!*' Josh exploded. 'That is bullshit, man! We've been waiting all day for *the law!* The old man said that was what was going to happen, but I don't see this kid being taken away by any boys in blue. Do you? I don't think it's going to happen. So let us teach him a lesson *our* way.'

Jesse shook his head. It was a dangerous move with four angry, out-of-control young ghosts bearing down on him. But he did it anyway.

I took a step closer to Jesse as I saw the RLS Angels shimmer with rage. I stood on tiptoe so he could hear me when I whispered, 'I'll take the girls. You take the boys.'

'No.' Jesse's expression was grim. 'Leave, Susannah. While they are occupied with me, run for the road and flag down the next automobile you see. Then go with them to safety.'

Uh, yeah. Right.

'And leave you to deal with them alone?' I glared at him. 'What are you, nuts?'

'Susannah,' he hissed. 'You don't understand. They'll kill you—'

I laughed. I actually laughed, all my anger with him gone. Jesse was right. I didn't understand.

'Let them try,' I said.

That's when they rushed us.

I guess the Angels must have agreed upon an arrangement among themselves that was similar to the one I'd tried to make with Jesse, since the girls came at me and both boys went for Jesse. I wasn't too dismayed. I mean, two on one is kind of unfair, but, except for the whole telekinetic power thing, I felt we were pretty even. Carrie and Felicia hadn't been fighters when they'd been alive – that much was clear from the very first moment they tackled me – so they didn't have a real solid idea of where it was best to apply a fist in order to cause the most pain.

At least, that's what I thought before they started hitting me. The thing I hadn't counted on was the fact that these girls – and their boyfriends, too – were really, really mad.

And if you think about it, they had a right to be. OK, maybe they had been jerks when they'd been alive – they didn't exactly strike me as the kind of people I'd want to hang out with, with their obsession with partying and their elitist attitudes – but they'd been young. They would likely have grown into, if not thoughtful, then at least productive citizens.

Michael Meducci had put a stop to that, though. And they were spitting mad about it.

I guess you could argue that their own behaviour hadn't exactly been above reproach. I mean, they had thrown that party where Lila Meducci had been so seriously hurt, due not only to her own stupidity, but also their – and their parents' – negligence.

But that didn't seem to occur to them. No, as far as the RLS Angels were concerned, they'd been cheated. Cheated from their lives. And somebody was going to have to pay for that.

That someone was Michael Meducci. And anyone who tried to stand in the way of their achieving that goal.

Their wrath was exquisite. Really. I don't think I've ever been as completely, one hundred percent angry as those ghosts were. Oh, I've been mad, sure. But never that mad, and never for that long.

The RLS Angels were furious. And they took that fury out on Jesse and me.

I didn't even see the first blow. It spun me around the way that tractor trailer had spun the Rambler. I felt my lip split. Blood flew out in a fountain from my face. Some of it landed on the girls' evening gowns.

They didn't even notice. They just hit me again.

I don't want you to think I didn't hit back. I did. I was good. Really good.

Just not good enough. I had to reassess my whole theory on that two-on-one thing. It *wasn't* fair. Felicia Bruce and Carrie Whitman were killing me.

And there wasn't a blessed thing I could do about it.

I couldn't even look over to see if Jesse was bearing up any better than I was. Every time I turned my head, it seemed, another fist connected with it. Soon I couldn't see at all. My eyes had filled up with blood, which appeared to be streaming from a cut in my forehead. Either that or some blood vessels in my eyes had burst from the force of some of those blows. I hoped Jesse, at least, would be all right. It wasn't like he could die, or anything. Not like I could. The one thing that kept going through my head was, Well, if they kill me, then I'll finally know where everybody goes. Once a mediator has sent them packing, I mean.

At one point during Felicia and Carrie's assault, I tripped over something – something that was warm and somewhat soft. I wasn't sure what it was – I couldn't see it, of course – until it moaned my name.

'Suze,' it said.

At first I didn't recognize the voice. Then I realized Michael's throat must have been crushed by that seatbelt. All he could do was croak.

'Suze,' he wheezed. 'What's happening?'

The terror in his voice, I thought, showed that he was probably as frightened now as Josh, Carrie, Mark and Felicia had been when he'd rammed their car and sent them plummeting to their deaths. It served him right, I thought, in some distant part of my mind that wasn't concentrating on trying to escape the blows that were raining down on me.

'Suze,' Michael moaned, beneath me. 'Make it stop.'

As if I could. As if I had anything like control over what was happening to me. If I lived through this – which didn't seem likely – some big changes were going to be made. First and foremost, I was going to practice my kick-boxing a lot more faithfully.

And then something happened. I can't tell you what it was because, like I said, I couldn't see.

But I could hear. And what I heard was perhaps the sweetest sound I'd ever heard in my life.

It was a siren. Police or fire truck, ambulance or paramedic, I couldn't tell. But it was coming closer, and closer, and closer still, until suddenly, I could hear the vehicle's tires crunching on the gravel in front of me. The blows that had been raining down on me abruptly ceased, and I sagged against Michael, who was pushing at me feebly, saying, 'The cops. Get off me. It's the cops. I gotta go.'

A second later, hands were touching me. Warm hands. Not ghost hands. Human hands.

Then a man's voice was saying, 'Don't worry, miss. We've got you. We've got you. Can you stand up?'

I could, but standing caused waves of pain to go shooting through me. I recognized that pain. It was the kind of pain that was so intense, it seemed ridiculous . . . so ridiculous, I started to giggle. Really. Because it was just funny that anything could hurt that much. It meant, pain like that, that something, somewhere, was broken.

Then something soft was pressed beneath me, and I was told to lie down. More pain – burning, searing pain that left me chuckling weakly. More hands touched me.

Then I heard a familiar voice calling my name as if from somewhere very far away.

'Susannah. Susannah, it's me, Father Dominic. Can you hear me, Susannah?'

I opened my eyes. Someone had wiped the blood from them. I could see again.

I was lying on an ambulance gurney. Red and white lights were flashing all around me. Two emergency medical technicians were messing with the wound in my scalp.

But that wasn't what hurt. My chest. Ribs. I'd cracked a few. I could tell.

Father Dominic's face loomed over my gurney. I tried to smile – tried to speak – but I couldn't. My lip was too sore to move it.

'Gina called me,' Father Dominic said, I suppose in answer to the questioning look I'd given him. 'She told me you were going to meet Michael. I guessed – after she told me what you'd said about the accident today – that this was where you'd bring him. Oh, Susannah, how I wish you hadn't.'

'Yeah,' one of the EMTs said. 'Looks like he worked her over pretty good.'

'Hey.' His partner was grinning. 'Who you kidding? She gave as good as she got. Kid's a mess.'

Michael. They were talking about Michael. Who else could they be talking about? None of them – except Father Dominic – could see Jesse, or the RLS Angels. They could see only the two of us, Michael and me, both beaten, apparently, almost to death. Of course they assumed we'd done it to each other. Who else was there to blame?

Jesse. Reminded of him, my heart began to hammer in my broken chest. Where was Jesse? I lifted my head, looking around for him frantically in what had become a sea of uniformed police officers. Was Jesse all right?

Father Dominic misread my panic. He said, soothingly, 'Michael's going to be all right. A severely bruised larynx, and some cuts and bruises. That's all.'

'Hey.' The EMT straightened. They were getting ready to load me into the ambulance. 'Don't sell yourself short, kid.' He was talking to me. 'You got him real good. He won't be forgetting this little escapade for a long time to come, believe me.'

'Not with all the time he's going to be spending behind bars for this,' his partner said with a wink.

And sure enough, as they lifted me into the ambulance, I could see that Michael was sitting not, as I'd expected, in an ambulance of his own, but in the back of a squad car. His hands appeared to be cuffed behind his back. His throat may have been hurting him, but he was speaking. He was speaking rapidly and, if the expression on his face was any indication, urgently to a man in a suit I could only assume was a police detective of some kind. Occasionally, the man in the suit jotted something down on a clipboard in front of him.

'See?' The first EMT grinned down at me. 'Singing like a canary. You're not going to have to worry about running into him in school on Monday. Not for a real long time.'

Was Michael confessing? I wondered. And if so, what about? About the Angels? About what he'd done to the Rambler?

Or was he merely explaining to the detective what had happened to him? That he'd been attacked by some unseen, unmanageable force – the same force that had broken my ribs, split open my head and busted my lip?

196

The detective didn't look as if anything Michael was telling him was all that extraordinary. But I happen to know from experience that this is the way detectives always look.

Just as they were closing the ambulance doors, Father Dominic cried, 'Don't worry, Susannah. I'll tell your mother where to find you.'

Can I just tell you that if this was supposed to comfort me, it totally didn't.

But right after that the morphine kicked in. And I found that, happily, I didn't care any more.

Nineteen

'This,' Gina said, 'is so not how I pictured spending my spring break.'

'Hey.' I looked up from the copy of *Cosmo* she'd brought me. 'I said I was sorry. What more do you want?'

Gina seemed surprised by the vehemence in my tone.

'I'm not saying I haven't had *fun*,' she said. 'I'm just saying it's not how I pictured it.'

'Oh, right.' I tossed the magazine aside. 'Yeah, it's been real fun, visiting me in the hospital.'

I couldn't talk very fast with the stitches in my lip. Nor could I enunciate too well, either. I had no idea how I looked – my mother had instructed everyone, including the hospital staff, not to allow me access to mirrors, which of course led me to believe that I looked hideous; it had probably been a wise move, however, considering how I get when all I've got is a zit. Still, one thing for sure, I certainly *sounded* stupid.

'It's just for a few more hours,' Gina said. 'Until they get the results of your second MRI. If it comes out normal, you're free to go. And you and I can hit the beach again. And this time' – she glanced at the door to my private room to make sure it was all the way closed and no one could overhear her – 'there won't be any pesky ghosts to ruin everything.'

Well, that much was true, anyway. Michael's arrest, while anticlimactic, had nevertheless satisfied the Angels. They probably would have preferred to see him dead, but once Father Dominic convinced them of how miserable a sensitive boy like Michael was going to find the California penal system, they snapped right out of their murderous rage. They even asked Father Dominic to tell Jesse and me that they were sorry about the whole beating-us-into-a-bloody-pulp thing.

I, for one, was not exactly ready to forgive them, even after Father D had assured me that the Angels had moved on to their afterlife destinations – whatever those might be – and would be troubling me no more.

Jesse's opinion on the matter I did not know. He had not deigned to grace either Father Dom or me with his presence since the night the Angels had attacked us. He was, I feared, extremely upset with me. Seeing as how the whole thing had been my fault, I didn't exactly blame him. Still, I wished he'd stop by, if only to yell at me some more. I missed him. More, I knew, than was probably healthy.

Damn that Madame Zara, anyway, for being right.

'You should hear what everyone at school is saying about you,' Gina said. She was perched on the end of my hospital bed, already clad in her bikini, over which she'd thrown a leopard-print baby-doll dress. She wanted to waste as little time as possible when we finally got to the beach.

'Oh, yeah?' I tried to drag my thoughts from Jesse. It wasn't easy. 'What are they saying?'

'Well, your friend CeeCee's writing this story about you in the school paper . . . you know, the whole amateur sleuth angle of it all, how you caught on that it was Michael who'd committed all these heinous crimes and set out to trap him—'

199

'Something,' I said drily, 'that I'm sure she heard from you.'

Gina looked innocent. 'I don't know what you're talking about. Adam sent you those' – Gina pointed at an enormous bouquet of pink roses on the window sill – 'and Mr Walden, according to Jake, is taking up a collection to get you a complete set of Nancy Drew books. He apparently thinks you have a crime-solving fixation.'

Mr Walden was right about that. But my fixation wasn't about solving crimes.

'Oh, and your stepdad's thinking about buying a Mustang to replace the Rambler,' Gina informed me.

I made a face, then regretted it. It was hard to make expressions of any kind with my sore lip, not to mention the stitches in my scalp.

'A Mustang?' I shook my head. 'How are we all supposed to fit into a Mustang?'

'Not for you guys. For himself. He's giving you guys the Land Rover.'

Well, that, at least, made sense.

'What about . . .' I wanted to ask her about Jesse. After all, she was sharing a room with him – alone, thanks to my being held overnight in the hospital for observation. The thing is, she didn't know it. About Jesse, I mean. I still hadn't told her about him.

And now, well, there didn't seem to be any reason to. Not now that he wasn't speaking to me any more.

'What about Michael?' I asked instead. None of my other visitors – my mother and stepfather; Sleepy, Dopey, and Doc; CeeCee and Adam; even Father Dom – would tell me anything about him. The doctors had advised them that the topic might be 'too painful' for me to discuss.

As if. You want to know what's painful? I'll tell you what's

200

painful. Having two broken ribs, and knowing that for weeks, you're going to have wear a one-piece to the beach in order to hide the black and blue marks.

'Michael?' Gina shrugged. 'Well, you were right. What you said about him keeping stuff on his computer. The police got a warrant and confiscated his PC, and it was all there – journals, emails, the schematics of the Rambler's brake system. Plus they found the wrench he used. You know, on the bolts that held the guard rail in place? They matched the metal tracings. And the clippers he used to snip the Rambler's brake line. They got brake fluid off the blades. The boy didn't do such a good job cleaning up after himself, it appears.'

I'll say.

He was arrested on four counts of first-degree murder – the RLS Angels – and six counts of attempted murder: five for those of us who'd been in the Rambler the afternoon the brakes had given out, and one for what the police were convinced Michael had done to me out at the Point.

I didn't correct them. I mean, it wasn't like I was about to sit there and go, 'Uh, yeah, about my injuries? Yeah, Michael didn't inflict them. No, the ghosts of his victims did that because I wouldn't let them kill him.'

I figured it was just as well to let them go on thinking it was Michael who was responsible for my broken ribs and the fourteen stitches in my scalp . . . not to mention the two in my lip. I mean, after all, he'd been *going* to kill me. The Angels had just interrupted him. If you thought about it, they'd actually saved my life.

Yeah. So they could kill me themselves.

'So listen,' Gina was saying. 'Your grounding – you know, for sneaking out and getting into a car with Michael when your mother had told you expressly not to – isn't supposed

201

to start until after I leave. I say we spend the next four days at the beach. I mean, there's no way you're going to school. Not with broken ribs. You wouldn't be able to sit down. But you can certainly *lie* down, you know, on a towel. I should be able to talk your mom into letting you do *that*, at least.'

'Sounds good to me,' I said.

'Ex,' Gina said. She apparently meant excellent, only she'd shortened it – much in the way Sleepy often shortened words because he was too lazy to say all the syllables. Thus pizza became ''Za', Gina became 'G'. She had, I realized, more in common with Sleepy than I'd ever guessed.

'I'm going to get a Diet Coke,' she said, climbing down from my bed – careful not to jostle the mattress since the nurse had already come in twice and warned her not to. Like I hadn't consumed enough Tylenol with codeine to block out the pain. Somebody could have dropped a safe on my head and I probably wouldn't have felt it.

'You want?' Gina asked, pausing by the door.

'Sure,' I said. 'Just make sure—'

'Yeah, yeah,' she said over her shoulder as the door swung slowly shut behind her. 'I'll find a straw somewhere.'

Alone in my room, I adjusted the pillows behind me carefully, and then sat there, staring at nothing. People who are on as many painkillers as I was tend to do that a lot.

But I wasn't thinking about nothing. I was thinking, actually, about what Father Dominic had told me when he'd visited a few hours ago. In what could only be the cruelest of ironies, the morning after Michael's arrest, his sister, Lila Meducci, had wakened from her coma.

Oh, it wasn't like she'd sat up and asked for a bowl of Cheerios, or anything. She was still severely messed up. According to Father D, it was going to take her months, even years, of rehabilitation to get her back to the way she'd been before the accident – if ever. It would be a long, long time before she'd be able to walk, talk, even eat on her own again like she used to.

But she was alive. She was alive and she was conscious. It wasn't much of a consolation prize for poor Mrs Meducci, but it was something.

It was as I was reflecting over the vagaries of life that I heard a rustle. I turned my head just in time to catch Jesse trying to dematerialize.

'Oh, no, you don't,' I said, sitting up – and jolting my ribs quite painfully, I'd like to add. 'You come back here right now.'

He came back, a sheepish expression on his face.

'I thought you were asleep,' he said. 'So I decided to come back later.'

'Baloney,' I said. 'You saw I was *awake*, so you decided to come back later when you were sure I was asleep.' I couldn't believe it. I couldn't believe what I'd caught him trying to do. This hurt, I discovered, way more than my ribs. 'What, you're only going to visit me when I'm unconscious now? Is that it?'

'You've been through an ordeal,' Jesse said. He looked more uncomfortable than I'd ever seen him. 'Your mother – back at the house – I heard her tell everyone they weren't to do anything to upset you.'

'Seeing *you* won't upset me,' I said.

I was hurt. I really was. I mean, I'd known Jesse was mad at me for what I'd done – you know, that whole tricking-Michael-into-coming-out-to-the-Point-so-the-RLS-Angels-could-kill-him thing – but not even to want to *talk* to me any more . . .

Well, that was harsh.

203

The hurt I felt must have shown in my face since when Jesse spoke, it was in the gentlest voice I'd ever heard him use.

'Susannah,' he said. 'I—'

'No,' I interrupted him. 'Let me go first. Jesse, I'm sorry. I'm sorry for that whole thing last night. It was all my fault. I can't believe I did it. And I'll never, ever forgive myself for dragging you into it.'

'Susannah—'

'I am the worst mediator,' I went on. Once I had the ball rolling, I found it was hard to stop it. 'The worst one that ever lived. I should be thrown out of the mediator organization. Seriously. I can't believe I actually did something that stupid. And I wouldn't blame you if you never spoke to me again. Only—' I looked up at him, aware that there were tears in my eyes. Only this time, I wasn't ashamed to let him see them. 'It's just that you've got to understand: he tried to kill my family. And I couldn't let him get away with that. Can you understand that?'

Jesse did something then that he'd never done before. I doubt he'll ever do it again, either.

And it happened so fast, I wasn't even sure afterward if it had really happened, or if, in my drugged-out state, I imagined it.

But I'm pretty sure he reached out and touched my cheek.

That's all. Sorry if I got your hopes up. He just touched my cheek, the only part of me, I imagine, that wasn't scraped, bruised or broken.

But I didn't care. *He'd touched my cheek.* Grazed it, actually, with the backs of his fingers, not the tips. Then he dropped his hand.

'Yes, *querida*,' he said. 'I understand.'

My heart started beating so fast, I was certain he could hear it. Plus, I probably don't need to tell you, my ribs really, really ached. Each pulse seemed to send my heart slamming into them.

'And the only reason I got so angry was because I didn't want to see *this* happen to you.'

On the word *this*, he gestured toward my face. I must, I realized, have looked pretty bad.

But I didn't care. He'd touched my cheek. His touch had been gentle, and, for a ghost, warm.

Am I pathetic, or what, that a simple gesture like that could make me so head-over-heels happy?

I said, idiotically, 'I'll be all right. I won't even need any plastic surgery, they said.'

As if a guy born in 1830 even knows what plastic surgery is. God, can I spoil a mood, or what?

Still, Jesse didn't exactly draw away. He stood there looking down at me like he wanted to say more. I was perfectly willing to let him, too. Especially if he called me *querida* again.

Only it turned out he didn't call me anything. Because at that moment Gina came bursting back into the room clutching two cans of soda in her hands.

'Guess what?' she said as Jesse shimmered, and then, with a smile to me, disappeared. 'I ran into your mom in the hallway, and she said to tell you your second MRI came out normal, and you can start getting ready to go home. She's having all the paperwork done right now. Isn't that great?'

I grinned at her, even though doing so hurt my split lip.

'Great,' I said.

Gina looked at me curiously. 'What are you so happy about?' she wanted to know.

I continued to grin at her. 'You just said I get to go home.'

'Yeah, but you looked happy before I said that.' Gina narrowed her eyes at me. 'Suze. What gives? What's going on?'

'Oh,' I said, still smiling. 'Nothing.'

See what happens next in
The Mediator 4: Young Blood

One

Summer. Season of long, slow days and short, hot nights.

Back in Brooklyn, where I spent my first fifteen of them, summer – when it hadn't meant camp – had meant hanging out on the stoop with my best friend Gina her brothers, waiting for the ice-cream truck to come by. When it wasn't too hot, we played a game called War, dividing into teams with the other kids in the neighbourhood and shooting each other with imaginary guns.

When we got older, of course, we quit playing War. Gina and I also started laying off the ice cream.

Not that it mattered. None of the neighbourhood guys, the ones we used to play with, wanted anything to do with us. Well, with *me*, anyway. I don't think they'd have minded renewing acquaintances with Gina, but by the time they finally noticed what a babe she'd grown into, she'd set her sights way higher than guys from the 'hood.

I don't know what I expected from my sixteenth summer, my first since moving to California to live with my mom and her new husband . . . and, oh, yeah, his sons. I guess I envisioned the same long, slow days. Only these, in my mind, would be spent at the beach rather than on an apartment building's front stoop.

207

And as for those short, hot nights, well, I had plans for those, as well. All I needed was a boyfriend.

But as it happened, neither the beach nor the boyfriend materialized, the latter because the guy I liked? Yeah, he so wasn't interested. At least, as far as I could tell. And the former because . . .

Well, because I was forced to get a job.

That's right: a *job*.

I was horrified when one night at dinner, around the beginning of May, my stepfather Andy asked me if I'd put in any summer employment applications anywhere. I was all, 'What are you *talking* about?'

But it soon became clear that, like the many other sacrifices I'd been asked to make since my mother met, fell in love with, and married Andy Ackerman – host of a popular cable television home-improvement programme, native Californian, and father of three – my long hot summer lazing at the beach with my friends was not to be.

In the Ackerman household, it soon unfolded, you had two alternatives for how you spent your summer break: a job, or remedial tutoring. Only Doc, my youngest stepbrother – known as David to everyone but me – was exempt from either of these, as he was too young to work, and he had made good enough grades that he'd been accepted into a month-long computer camp, at which he was presumably learning skills that would make him the next Bill Gates – only hopefully without the bad haircut and Wal-Mart-y sweaters.

My second-youngest stepbrother, Dopey (also known as Brad) was not so lucky. Dopey had managed to flunk both English and Spanish – an astounding feat, in my opinion, English being his native language – and so was being forced by his father to attend summer school five days a week . . .

when he wasn't being used as unpaid slave labour on the project Andy had undertaken while his TV show was on summer hiatus: tearing down a large portion of our house's backyard deck and installing a hot tub.

Given the alternative – employment or summer school – I chose to seek employment.

I got a job at the same place my oldest stepbrother, Sleepy, works every summer. He, in fact, recommended me, an act which, at the time, simultaneously stunned and touched me. It wasn't until later that I found out that he had received a small bonus for every person he recommended who was later hired.

Whatever. What it actually boils down to is this: Sleepy – Jake, as he is known to his friends and the rest of the family – and I are now proud employees of the Pebble Beach Hotel and Golf Resort, Sleepy as a lifeguard at one of the resort's many pools, and me as . . .

Well, I signed away my summer to become a hotel staff babysitter.

OK. You can stop laughing now.

Even I will admit that it's not the kind of job I ever thought I'd be suited for, since I am not long on patience and am certainly not over fond of having my hair spat up in. But allow me to point out that it does pay ten dollars an hour, and that that does not include tips.

And let me just say that the people who stay at the Pebble Beach Hotel and Golf Resort are . . . Yeah, they are the kind of people who tend to tip. Generously.

The money, I must say, has gone a long way towards heal-ing my wounded pride. If I have to spend my summer in mindless drudgery, earning a hundred bucks a day – and fre-quently more – amply compensates for it. Because by the time the summer is over, I should have, without question, the most stunning fall wardrobe of anyone entering the junior class of the Junipero Serra Mission Academy.

So think about *that*, Kelly Prescott, while you spend your summer lounging by your father's pool. I've already got *four* pairs of Jimmy Choos, paid for *with my own money*.

What do you think about that, Little Miss Daddy's AmEx?

The only real problem with my summer job – besides the whiny children and their equally whiny, but loaded, parents, of course – is the fact that I am expected to report there at eight o'clock in the morning every day.

That's right. EIGHT A.M. No sleeping in for old Suze this summer.

I must say I find this a bit excessive. And believe me, I've complained. And yet the management staff at the Pebble Beach Hotel and Golf Resort have remained stubbornly unswayed by my persuasive arguments for refraining from offering babysitting services until nine.

And so it is that every morning (I can't even sleep in on Sundays, thanks to my stepfather's insistence that all of us gather around the dining table for the elaborate brunch he prepares; he seems to think we are the Camdens or the Waltons something) I am up before seven . . .

Which has, I've been surprised to learn, its advantages.

Although I would not list seeing Dopey without a shirt, sweating like a pig, and gulping OJ from the carton as one of them.

There are a lot of girls who go to my school who would, I know, pay money to see Dopey – and Sleepy, too, for that matter – without a shirt, sweat or no sweat. Kelly Prescott, for instance. And her best friend, and Dopey's sometime flame, Debbie Mancuso. I myself do not understand the attraction, but then I can only suppose that these girls have

210

not been around my stepbrothers after a meal in which beans played any sort of role on the menu.

Still, anyone who cared to see Dopey do his calendar pin-up imitation could easily do so for free, merely by stopping by our house any weekday morning. For it is in our backyard that Dopey has been, from approximately six in the morning until he has to leave for summer school at ten, stripped to the waist, and performing rigorous manual labour under the eagle eye of his father.

On this particular morning – the one where I caught him, once again, drinking directly from the juice carton, a habit of which my mother and I have been trying, with little success, to cure the entire Ackerman clan – Dopey had apparently been doing some digging, since he left a trail of mud along the kitchen floor, in addition to a dirt-encrusted object on what had once been an immaculate counter (I should know: it had been my turn to 409 it the night before).

'Oh,' I said, as I stepped into the kitchen. 'Isn't that a lovely picture.'

Dopey lowered the orange-juice container and looked at me.

'Don't you have somewhere to be?' he asked, wiping his mouth with the back of a wrist.

'Of course,' I said. 'But I was hoping that before I left, I could enjoy a nice glass of calcium-fortified juice. I see now that that will not be possible.'

Dopey shook the carton. 'There's still some left,' he said.

'Mixed with your backwash?' I heaved a shudder. 'I think not.'

Dopey opened his mouth to say something – presumably his usual suggestion that I chew on some piece of his anatomy – but his father's voice called from outside the sliding glass doors to the deck.

'Brad,' Andy yelled. 'That's enough of a break. Get back out here and help me lower this.'

Dopey slammed down the carton of OJ. Before he could stalk from the room, however, I stopped him with a polite, 'Excuse me?'

Because he wore no shirt, I could see the muscles in Dopey's neck and shoulders tense as I spoke.

'All right already,' he said, spinning around and heading back towards the juice carton. 'I'll put it away. Jeez, why are you always *on* me about crap like—'

'I don't care about *that*,' I interrupted him, pointing at the juice carton – although it had to have been making the counter sticky. 'I want to know what *that* is.'

Dopey looked where I'd moved my finger. He blinked down at the dirt-encrusted oblong object.

'I dunno,' he said. 'I found it buried in the yard while I was digging out one of the posts.'

I gingerly lifted what appeared to be a metal box, about six inches long by two inches thick, heavily rusted and covered in mud. There were a few places where the mud had rubbed off, though, and there you could see some words painted on the box. The few I could make out were *delicious aroma* and *quality assured*. When I shook the box, it rattled. There was something inside.

'What's in it?' I asked Dopey.

He shrugged. 'How should I know? It's rusted shut. I was gonna take a—'

I never did find out what Dopey was going to do to the box, since his older brother Sleepy walked into the kitchen at that moment, reached for the orange-juice carton, opened it, and downed the remaining contents. When he was through, he crumpled the carton, threw it into the trash compactor, and then, apparently noticing my appalled expression, said, '*What?*'

212

I don't get what girls see in them. Seriously. They are like *animals*.

And not the cute fuzzy kind, either.

Meanwhile, outside, Andy was calling imperiously for Dopey again.

Dopey muttered some extremely colourful four-letter words beneath his breath, then shouted, 'I'm *coming*, already,' and stomped outside.

It was already seven forty-five, so Sleepy and I really had to 'motor', as he put it, to get to the resort on time. But though my eldest stepbrother has a tendency to sleepwalk through life, there's nothing somnambulistic about his driving. I punched in at work with five minutes to spare.

The Pebble Beach Hotel and Golf Resort prides itself on its efficiency. And it is, in fact, a very smoothly run operation. As a staff babysitter, it's my responsibility, after punching in, to ask for my assignment for the day. That's when I find out whether I'll be washing strained carrots or burger fixings out of my hair after work. On the whole, I prefer burgers, but there's something to be said for strained carrots: generally the people who eat them can't talk back to you.

When I heard my assignment for that particular day, however, I was disappointed, even though it was a burger-eater.

'Simon, Susannah,' Caitlin called. 'You're assigned to Slater, Jack.'

'For God's sake, Caitlin,' I said to Caitlin, who was my supervisor. 'I was stuck with Jack Slater yesterday. *And* the day before.'

Caitlin is only two years older than me, but she treats me like I'm twelve. In fact, I'm sure the only reason she tolerates me is because of Sleepy: she is as warm for his form as every other girl on this planet . . . except, of course, me.

'Jack's parents,' Caitlin informed me, without even look-ing up from her clipboard, 'requested you, Suze.'

'Couldn't you have said I was already taken?'

Caitlin did look up then. She looked at me with cool, blue contact-lensed eyes. 'Suze,' she said. 'They *like* you.'

I fiddled with my bathing-suit straps. I was wearing the regulation navy-blue swimsuit beneath my regulation navy-blue Oxford T-shirt and khaki shorts. With *pleats*, no less. Appalling.

I mentioned the uniform, right? I mean, the part where I have to wear a uniform to work? No kidding. Every day. A uniform.

If I'd known about the uniform beforehand, I never would have applied for the job.

'Yeah,' I said. 'I know they like me.'

The feeling isn't mutual. It isn't that I don't like Jack, although he's easily the whiniest little kid I have ever met. I mean, you can see why he's that way – just take a look at his parents, a pair of career-obsessed physicians who think dumping their kid off with a hotel babysitter for days on end while they go sailing and golfing is a fine family vacation.

It's actually Jack's older brother I have the problem with. Well, not necessarily a *problem* . . .

More like I would just rather avoid seeing him while I am wearing my incredibly unstylish Pebble Beach Hotel and Golf Resort uniform khaki shorts.

Yeah. The ones with the pleats in them.

Except, of course, that every time I've run into the guy since he and his family arrived at the resort last week, I've been wearing the stupid things.

Not that I care, particularly, what Paul Slater thinks about me. I mean, my heart, to coin a phrase, belongs to another.

Too bad he shows no signs whatsoever of actually wanting it. My heart, that is.

Still, Paul – that's his name; Jack's older brother, I mean: Paul Slater – is pretty incredible. I mean, it isn't just that he's a hottie. Oh, no. Paul's hot *and* funny. Every time I go to pick Jack up or drop him off at his family's hotel suite, and his brother Paul happens to be there, he always has some flippant remark to make about the hotel or his parents or himself. Not mean or anything. Just funny.

And I think he's smart, too, because whenever he isn't on the golf course with his dad or playing tennis with his mom, he's at the pool reading. And not your typical pool book, either. No Clancy or Crichton or King for Paul. Oh, no. We're talking stuff by guys like Nietzsche, or Kierkegaard.

Seriously. It's almost enough to make you think he's not from California.

And of course it turns out, he's not: the Slaters are visiting from Seattle.

So you see, it wasn't just that Jack Slater is the whiniest kid I've ever met: there was also the fact that I wasn't really all that enthused about his hottie brother seeing me, yet again, in shorts that make my butt look roughly the size of Montana.

But Caitlin was totally uninterested in my personal feelings on the matter.

'Suze,' Caitlin said, looking down at her clipboard again. 'Nobody likes Jack. But the fact is, Dr and Mrs Slater like you. So you're spending the day with Jack. Capeesh?'

I sighed gustily, but what could I do? Aside from my pride, my tan was the only thing that was really going to suffer from spending yet another day with Jack. The kid doesn't like swimming, or bike riding, or Rollerblading, or frisbee tossing, or anything, really, to do with the great outdoors. His idea of a good time is to sit inside the hotel room and watch cartoons.

I'm not kidding, either. He is, without a doubt, the most boring kid I ever met. I find it hard to believe he and Paul came from the same gene pool.

'Besides,' Caitlin added, as I was standing there, fuming. 'Today is Jack's eighth birthday.'

I stared at her. 'His *birthday*? It's Jack's *birthday*, and his parents are leaving him with a sitter all day?'

Caitlin shot me a severe look. 'The Slaters say they'll be back in time to take him to dinner at the Grill.'

The Grill. Whoopee. The Grill is the fanciest restaurant at the resort, maybe even on the entire peninsula. The cheapest thing they serve there costs about fifteen dollars, and that's the house salad. The Grill is so *not* a fun place to take a kid on his eighth birthday. I mean, even Jack, the most boring child in the world, couldn't have a fun time there.

I don't get it. I really don't. I mean, what's wrong with these people? And how, seeing the way they treat their youngest child, had their other one managed to turn out so . . .

Well, *hot*?

At least, that was the word that flashed through my mind as Paul opened the door to his family's suite in response to my knock, then stood there grinning down at me, one hand in the pocket of his cream-coloured chinos, the other clutching a book by someone called Martin Heidegger.

Yeah, you know what the last book I read was? That'd be *Clifford*. That's right. The big red dog. And OK, I was reading it to a five-year-old, but still. Heidegger. Jeez.

'All right. Who called Room Service and ordered the pretty girl?' Paul wanted to know.

Well, OK, that wasn't funny. That was actually sort of sexually harassing, if you think about it. But the fact that the guy saying it was my age, about six feet tall, and olive-complected, with curly brown hair and eyes the colour of the mahogany desk in the hotel lobby, made it not so bad.

Not so bad. What am I talking about? The guy could sexually harass me anytime he wanted to. At least *someone* wanted to.

Just my luck it wasn't the guy I wanted.

I didn't admit this out loud, of course. What I said instead was, 'Ha ha. I'm here for Jack.'

Paul winced. 'Oh,' he said, shaking his head in mock disappointment. 'The little guy gets all the luck.'

He held the door open for me, and I stepped into the suite's plush living room. Jack was where he usually was, sprawled on the floor in front of the TV. He did not acknowledge my presence, as was his custom.

His mother, on the other hand, did acknowledge me: 'Oh, hi, Susan. Rick and Paul and I will be on the course all morning. And then the three of us are meeting for lunch at the Grotto, and then we've got appointments with our personal trainers. So if you could stay until we all get back, around seven, we'd appreciate it. Make sure Jack has a bath before changing for dinner. I've laid out a suit for him. It's his birthday, you know. OK, buh-bye, you two. Have fun, Jack.'

'How could he not?' Paul wanted to know, with a meaningful glance in my direction.

And then the Slaters left.

Jack remained where he was in front of the TV, not speaking to me, not even looking at me. As this was typical Jack behaviour, I was not alarmed.

I crossed the room – stepping over Jack on my way – and went to fling open the wide French doors that led out on to a terrace overlooking the sea. Rick and Nancy Slater were paying six hundred dollars a night for their view, which was one of the Monterey Bay, sparkling turquoise under a cloudless blue sky. From their suite you could see the yellow slice of beach upon which, were it not for my well-meaning but misguided stepfather, I would have been whiling away my summer.

It isn't fair. It really isn't.

Mediator

YOUNG BLOOD

In memory of Marcia Mounsey

One

Summer. Season of long, slow days and short, hot nights.

Back in Brooklyn, where I spent my first fifteen of them, summer – when it hadn't meant camp – had meant hanging out on the stoop with my best friend Gina and her brothers, waiting for the ice-cream truck to come by. When it wasn't too hot, we played a game called War, dividing into teams with the other kids in the neighbourhood and shooting each other with imaginary guns.

When we got older, of course, we quit playing War. Gina and I also started laying off the ice cream.

Not that it mattered. None of the neighbourhood guys, the ones we used to play with, wanted anything to do with us. Well, with *me*, anyway. I don't think they'd have minded renewing acquaintances with Gina, but by the time they finally noticed what a babe she'd grown into, she'd set her sights way higher than guys from the 'hood.

I don't know what I expected from my sixteenth summer, my first since moving to California to live with my mom and her new husband . . . and, oh, yeah, his sons. I guess I envisioned the same long, slow days. Only these, in my mind, would be spent at the beach rather than on an apartment building's front stoop.

223

And as for those short, hot nights, well, I had plans for those, as well. All I needed was a boyfriend.

But as it happened, neither the beach nor the boyfriend materialized, the latter because the guy I liked? Yeah, he so wasn't interested. At least, as far as I could tell. And the former because . . .

Well, because I was forced to get a job.

That's right: a *job*.

I was horrified when one night at dinner, around the beginning of May, my stepfather Andy asked me if I'd put in any summer employment applications anywhere. I was all, 'What are you *talking* about?'

But it soon became clear that, like the many other sacrifices I'd been asked to make since my mother met, fell in love with, and married Andy Ackerman – host of a popular cable television home-improvement programme, native Californian, and father of three – my long hot summer lazing at the beach with my friends was not to be.

In the Ackerman household, it soon unfolded, you had two alternatives for how you spent your summer break: a job, or remedial tutoring. Only Doc, my youngest stepbrother – known as David to everyone but me – was exempt from either of these, as he was too young to work, and he had made good enough grades that he'd been accepted into a month-long computer camp, at which he was presumably learning skills that would make him the next Bill Gates – only hopefully without the bad haircut and Wal-Mart-y sweaters.

My second-youngest stepbrother, Dopey (also known as Brad) was not so lucky. Dopey had managed to flunk both English and Spanish – an astounding feat, in my opinion, English being his native language – and so was being forced by his father to attend summer school five days a week . . .

when he wasn't being used as unpaid slave labour on the project Andy had undertaken while his TV show was on summer hiatus: tearing down a large portion of our house's backyard deck and installing a hot tub.

Given the alternative – employment or summer school – I chose to seek employment.

I got a job at the same place my oldest stepbrother, Sleepy, works every summer. He, in fact, recommended me, an act which, at the time, simultaneously stunned and touched me. It wasn't until later that I found out that he had received a small bonus for every person he recommended who was later hired.

Whatever. What it actually boils down to is this: Sleepy – Jake, as he is known to his friends and the rest of the family – and I are now proud employees of the Pebble Beach Hotel and Golf Resort, Sleepy as a lifeguard at one of the resort's many pools, and me as . . .

Well, I signed away my summer to become a hotel staff babysitter.

OK. You can stop laughing now.

Even I will admit that it's not the kind of job I ever thought I'd be suited for, since I am not long on patience and am certainly not over fond of having my hair spat up in. But allow me to point out that it does pay ten dollars an hour, and that that does not include tips.

And let me just say that the people who stay at the Pebble Beach Hotel and Golf Resort are . . . Yeah, they are the kind of people who tend to tip. Generously.

The money, I must say, has gone a long way towards healing my wounded pride. If I have to spend my summer in mindless drudgery, earning a hundred bucks a day – and frequently more – amply compensates for it. Because by the time the summer is over, I should have, without question, the most stunning fall wardrobe of anyone entering the junior class of the Junipero Serra Mission Academy.

So think about *that*, Kelly Prescott, while you spend your summer lounging by your father's pool. I've already got *four* pairs of Jimmy Choos, paid for *with my own money*.

What do you think about that, Little Miss Daddy's AmEx?

The only real problem with my summer job – besides the whiny children and their equally whiny, but loaded, parents, of course – is the fact that I am expected to report there at eight o'clock in the morning every day.

That's right. EIGHT A.M. No sleeping in for old Suze this summer.

I must say I find this a bit excessive. And believe me, I've complained. And yet the management staff at the Pebble Beach Hotel and Golf Resort have remained stubbornly unswayed by my persuasive arguments for refraining from offering babysitting services until nine.

And so it is that every morning (I can't even sleep in on Sundays, thanks to my stepfather's insistence that all of us gather around the dining table for the elaborate brunch he prepares; he seems to think we are the Camdens or the Waltons something) I am up before seven . . .

Which has, I've been surprised to learn, its advantages.

Although I would not list seeing Dopey without a shirt, sweating like a pig, and gulping OJ from the carton as one of them.

There are a lot of girls who go to my school who would, I know, pay money to see Dopey – and Sleepy, too, for that matter – without a shirt, sweat or no sweat. Kelly Prescott, for instance. And her best friend, and Dopey's sometime flame, Debbie Mancuso. I myself do not understand the attraction, but then I can only suppose that these girls have

226

not been around my stepbrothers after a meal in which beans played any sort of role on the menu.

Still, anyone who cared to see Dopey do his calendar pin-up imitation could easily do so for free, merely by stopping by our house any weekday morning. For it is in our backyard that Dopey has been, from approximately six in the morning until he has to leave for summer school at ten, stripped to the waist, and performing rigorous manual labour under the eagle eye of his father.

On this particular morning – the one where I caught him, once again, drinking directly from the juice carton, a habit of which my mother and I have been trying, with little success, to cure the entire Ackerman clan – Dopey had apparently been doing some digging, since he left a trail of mud along the kitchen floor, in addition to a dirt-encrusted object on what had once been an immaculate counter (I should know: it had been my turn to 409 it the night before).

'Oh,' I said, as I stepped into the kitchen. 'Isn't that a lovely picture.'

Dopey lowered the orange-juice container and looked at me.

'Don't you have somewhere to be?' he asked, wiping his mouth with the back of a wrist.

'Of course,' I said. 'But I was hoping that before I left, I could enjoy a nice glass of calcium-fortified juice. I see now that that will not be possible.'

Dopey shook the carton. 'There's still some left,' he said.

'Mixed with your backwash?' I heaved a shudder. 'I think not.'

Dopey opened his mouth to say something – presumably his usual suggestion that I chew on some piece of his anatomy – but his father's voice called from outside the sliding glass doors to the deck.

'Brad,' Andy yelled. 'That's enough of a break. Get back out here and help me lower this.'

Dopey slammed down the carton of OJ. Before he could stalk from the room, however, I stopped him with a polite, 'Excuse me?'

Because he wore no shirt, I could see the muscles in Dopey's neck and shoulders tense as I spoke.

'All right already,' he said, spinning around and heading back towards the juice carton. 'I'll put it away. Jeez, why are you always *on* me about crap like—'

'I don't care about *that*,' I interrupted him, pointing at the juice carton – although it had to have been making the counter sticky. 'I want to know what *that* is.'

Dopey looked where I'd moved my finger. He blinked down at the dirt-encrusted oblong object.

'I dunno,' he said. 'I found it buried in the yard while I was digging out one of the posts.'

I gingerly lifted what appeared to be a metal box, about six inches long by two inches thick, heavily rusted and covered in mud. There were a few places where the mud had rubbed off, though, and there you could see some words painted on the box. The few I could make out were *delicious aroma* and *quality assured*. When I shook the box, it rattled. There was something inside.

'What's in it?' I asked Dopey.

He shrugged. 'How should I know? It's rusted shut. I was gonna take a—'

I never did find out what Dopey was going to do to the box, since his older brother Sleepy walked into the kitchen at that moment, reached for the orange-juice carton, opened it, and downed the remaining contents. When he was through, he crumpled the carton, threw it into the trash compactor, and then, apparently noticing my appalled expression, said, '*What?*'

228

I don't get what girls see in them. Seriously. They are like *animals*.

And not the cute fuzzy kind, either.

Meanwhile, outside, Andy was calling imperiously for Dopey again.

Dopey muttered some extremely colourful four-letter words beneath his breath, then shouted, 'I'm *coming*, already,' and stomped outside.

It was already seven forty-five, so Sleepy and I really had to 'motor', as he put it, to get to the resort on time. But though my eldest stepbrother has a tendency to sleepwalk through life, there's nothing somnambulistic about his driving. I punched in at work with five minutes to spare.

The Pebble Beach Hotel and Golf Resort prides itself on its efficiency. And it is, in fact, a very smoothly run operation. As a staff babysitter, it's my responsibility, after punching in, to ask for my assignment for the day. That's when I find out whether I'll be washing strained carrots or burger fixings out of my hair after work. On the whole, I prefer burgers, but there's something to be said for strained carrots: generally the people who eat them can't talk back to you.

When I heard my assignment for that particular day, however, I was disappointed, even though it was a burger-eater.

'Simon, Susannah,' Caitlin called. 'You're assigned to Slater, Jack.'

'For God's sake, Caitlin,' I said to Caitlin, who was my supervisor. 'I was stuck with Jack Slater yesterday. *And* the day before.'

Caitlin is only two years older than me, but she treats me like I'm twelve. In fact, I'm sure the only reason she tolerates me is because of Sleepy: she is as warm for his form as every other girl on this planet . . . except, of course, me.

229

'Jack's parents,' Caitlin informed me, without even looking up from her clipboard, 'requested you, Suze.'

'Couldn't you have said I was already taken?'

Caitlin did look up then. She looked at me with cool, blue contact-lensed eyes. 'Suze,' she said. 'They *like* you.'

I fiddled with my bathing-suit straps. I was wearing the regulation navy-blue swimsuit beneath my regulation navy-blue Oxford T-shirt and khaki shorts. With *pleats*, no less. Appalling.

I mentioned the uniform, right? I mean, the part where I have to wear a uniform to work? No kidding. Every day. A uniform.

If I'd known about the uniform beforehand, I never would have applied for the job.

'Yeah,' I said. 'I know they like me.'

The feeling isn't mutual. It isn't that I don't like Jack, although he's easily the whiniest little kid I have ever met. I mean, you can see why he's that way – just take a look at his parents, a pair of career-obsessed physicians who think dumping their kid off with a hotel babysitter for days on end while they go sailing and golfing is a fine family vacation.

It's actually Jack's older brother I have the problem with. Well, not necessarily a *problem* . . .

More like I would just rather avoid seeing him while I am wearing my incredibly unstylish Pebble Beach Hotel and Golf Resort uniform khaki shorts.

Yeah. The ones with the pleats in them.

Except, of course, that every time I've run into the guy since he and his family arrived at the resort last week, I've been wearing the stupid things.

Not that I care, particularly, what Paul Slater thinks about me. I mean, my heart, to coin a phrase, belongs to another.

Too bad he shows no signs whatsoever of actually wanting it. My heart, that is.

Still, Paul – that's his name; Jack's older brother, I mean: Paul Slater – is pretty incredible. I mean, it isn't just that he's a hottie. Oh, no. Paul's hot *and* funny. Every time I go to pick Jack up or drop him off at his family's hotel suite, and his brother Paul happens to be there, he always has some flippant remark to make about the hotel or his parents or himself. Not mean or anything. Just funny.

And I think he's smart, too, because whenever he isn't on the golf course with his dad or playing tennis with his mom, he's at the pool reading. And not your typical pool book, either. No Clancy or Crichton or King for Paul. Oh, no. We're talking stuff by guys like Nietzsche, or Kierkegaard.

Seriously. It's almost enough to make you think he's not from California.

And of course it turns out, he's not: the Slaters are visiting from Seattle.

So you see, it wasn't just that Jack Slater is the whiniest kid I've ever met: there was also the fact that I wasn't really all that enthused about his hottie brother seeing me, yet again, in shorts that make my butt look roughly the size of Montana.

But Caitlin was totally uninterested in my personal feelings on the matter.

'Suze,' Caitlin said, looking down at her clipboard again. 'Nobody likes Jack. But the fact is, Dr and Mrs Slater like you. So you're spending the day with Jack. Capeesh?'

I sighed gustily, but what could I do? Aside from my pride, my tan was the only thing that was really going to suffer from spending yet another day with Jack. The kid doesn't like swimming, or bike riding, or Rollerblading, or frisbee tossing, or anything, really, to do with the great outdoors. His idea of a good time is to sit inside the hotel room and watch cartoons.

I'm not kidding, either. He is, without a doubt, the most boring kid I ever met. I find it hard to believe he and Paul came from the same gene pool.

'Besides,' Caitlin added, as I was standing there, fuming. 'Today is Jack's eighth birthday.'

I stared at her. 'His *birthday*? It's Jack's *birthday*, and his parents are leaving him with a sitter all day?'

Caitlin shot me a severe look. 'The Slaters say they'll be back in time to take him to dinner at the Grill.'

The Grill. Whoopee. The Grill is the fanciest restaurant at the resort, maybe even on the entire peninsula. The cheapest thing they serve there costs about fifteen dollars, and that's the house salad. The Grill is so *not* a fun place to take a kid on his eighth birthday. I mean, even Jack, the most boring child in the world, couldn't have a fun time there.

I don't get it. I really don't. I mean, what's wrong with these people? And how, seeing the way they treat their youngest child, had their other one managed to turn out so . . .

Well, *hot*?

At least, that was the word that flashed through my mind as Paul opened the door to his family's suite in response to my knock, then stood there grinning down at me, one hand in the pocket of his cream-coloured chinos, the other clutching a book by someone called Martin Heidegger.

Yeah, you know what the last book I read was? That'd be *Clifford*. That's right. The big red dog. And OK, I was reading it to a five-year-old, but still. Heidegger. Jeez.

'All right. Who called Room Service and ordered the pretty girl?' Paul wanted to know.

Well, OK, that wasn't funny. That was actually sort of sexually harassing, if you think about it. But the fact that the guy saying it was my age, about six feet tall, and olive-complected, with curly brown hair and eyes the colour of the mahogany desk in the hotel lobby, made it not so bad.

Not so bad. What am I talking about? The guy could sexually harass me anytime he wanted to. At least *someone* wanted to.

Just my luck it wasn't the guy I wanted.

I didn't admit this out loud, of course. What I said instead was, 'Ha ha. I'm here for Jack.'

Paul winced. 'Oh,' he said, shaking his head in mock disappointment. 'The little guy gets all the luck.'

He held the door open for me, and I stepped into the suite's plush living room. Jack was where he usually was, sprawled on the floor in front of the TV. He did not acknowledge my presence, as was his custom.

His mother, on the other hand, did acknowledge me: 'Oh, hi, Susan. Rick and Paul and I will be on the course all morning. And then the three of us are meeting for lunch at the Grotto, and then we've got appointments with our personal trainers. So if you could stay until we all get back, around seven, we'd appreciate it. Make sure Jack has a bath before changing for dinner. I've laid out a suit for him. It's his birthday, you know. OK, buh-bye, you two. Have fun, Jack.'

'How could he not?' Paul wanted to know, with a meaningful glance in my direction.

And then the Slaters left.

Jack remained where he was in front of the TV, not speaking to me, not even looking at me. As this was typical Jack behaviour, I was not alarmed.

I crossed the room – stepping over Jack on my way – and went to fling open the wide French doors that led out on to a terrace overlooking the sea. Rick and Nancy Slater were paying six hundred dollars a night for their view, which

233

was one of the Monterey Bay, sparkling turquoise under a cloudless blue sky. From their suite you could see the yellow slice of beach upon which, were it not for my well-meaning but misguided stepfather, I would have been whiling away my summer.

It isn't fair. It really isn't.

'OK, big guy,' I said, after taking in the view for a minute or two and listening to the soothing pulse of the waves. 'Go put on your swim trunks. We're hitting the pool. It's too nice out to stay inside.'

Jack, as usual, looked as if I'd pinched him rather than suggested a fun day at the pool.

'But *why*?' he cried. 'You know I can't swim.'

'Which is exactly,' I said, 'why we're going. You're eight years old today. An eight-year-old who can't swim is nothing but a loser. You don't want to be a loser, do you?'

Jack opined that he preferred being a loser to going outdoors, a fact with which I was only too well acquainted.

'Jack,' I said, slumping down on to a couch near where he lay. 'What is your problem?'

Instead of responding, Jack rolled over on to his stomach and scowled at the carpet. I wasn't going to let up on him, though. I knew what I was talking about, with the loser thing. Being different in the American public – or even private – educational system is not cool. How Paul had ever allowed this to happen – his little brother's turning into a whiny little wimp you almost longed to slap – I couldn't fathom, but I knew good and well Rick and Nancy weren't doing anything to help rectify the matter. It was pretty much all up to me to save Jack Slater from becoming his school's human punch-bag.

Don't ask me why I even cared. Maybe because in a weird way, Jack reminded me a little of Doc, my youngest stepbrother, the one who is away at computer camp. A geek in the truest sense of the word, Doc is still one of my favourite people. I have even been making a concerted effort to call him by his name, David . . . at least to his face.

But Doc is – almost – able to get away with his bizarre behaviour because he has a photographic memory and a computer-like ability to process information. Jack, so far as I could tell, possessed no such skills. In fact, I had a feeling he was a bit dim. So really, he had no excuse for his eccentricities.

'What's the deal?' I asked him. 'Don't you *want* to learn how to swim and throw a frisbee, like a normal person?'

'You don't understand,' Jack said, not very distinctly, into the carpet. 'I'm *not* a normal person. I – I'm different from other people.'

'Of course you are,' I said, rolling my eyes. 'We're all special and unique, like snowflakes. But there's Different, and then there's Freakish. And you, Jack, are going to turn Freakish, if you don't watch out.'

'I – I already am freakish,' Jack said.

But he wouldn't elaborate, and I can't say I pressed too hard, trying to find out what he meant. Not that I imagined he might like to drown kittens in his spare time, or anything like that. I just figured he meant freakish in the general sense. I mean, we all feel like freaks from time to time. Jack maybe felt like one a bit more often than that, but then, with Rick and Nancy for parents, who wouldn't? He was probably constantly being asked why he couldn't be more like his older brother, Paul. That would be enough to make any kid feel a little insecure. I mean, come on. *Heidegger*? On summer *vacation*?

Give me *Clifford*, any day.

I told Jack that worrying so much was going to make him

old before his time. Then I ordered him to go and put on his swimsuit.

He did so, but he didn't exactly hurry, and when we finally got outside and on to the brick path to the pool, it was almost ten o'clock. The sun was beating down hard, though it wasn't uncomfortably hot yet. Actually, it hardly ever gets uncomfortably hot in Carmel, even in the middle of July. Back in Brooklyn, you can barely go outdoors in July, it's so muggy. In Carmel, however, there is next to no humidity, and there's always a cool breeze from the Pacific . . .

Perfect date weather, actually. If you happened to have one. A date, I mean. Which of course I don't. And probably never will – at least with the guy I want – if things keep up the way they've been going . . .

Anyway, Jack and I were tripping down the brick path to the pool when one of the gardeners stepped out from behind an enormous forsythia bush and nodded to me.

This wouldn't have been at all odd – I have actually gotten friendly with all of the landscaping staff, thanks to the many frisbees I have lost while playing with my charges – except for the fact that this particular gardener, Jorge, who had been expected to retire at the end of the summer, had instead suffered a heart attack a few days earlier, and, well . . .

Died.

Yet there was Jorge in his beige coveralls, holding a pair of hedge clippers and bobbing his head at me, just as he had the last time I'd seen him, on this very path, a few days before.

I wasn't too worried about Jack's reaction to having a dead man walk up and nod at us, since for the most part I'm the only one I know who can actually see them. The dead, I mean. So I was perfectly unprepared for what happened next . . .

236

Which was that Jack ripped his hand from mine and, with a strangled scream, ran for the pool.

This was odd, but then, so was Jack. I rolled my eyes at Jorge, then hurried after the kid, since I am, after all, getting paid to care for the living. The whole helping-out-the-dead thing has to play second fiddle so long as I'm on the Pebble Beach Hotel and Golf Resort time clock. The ghosts simply have to wait. I mean, it's not as if they're paying me. Ha! I wish.

I found Jack huddled on a deckchair, sobbing into his towel. Fortunately, it was still early enough that there weren't many people at the pool yet. Otherwise, I might have had some explaining to do.

But the only other person there was Sleepy, high up in his lifeguard chair. And it was pretty clear from the way Sleepy was resting his cheek in one hand that his shutters, behind the lenses of his Ray-Bans, were closed.

'Jack,' I said, sinking down on to the neighbouring deckchair. 'Jack, what's the matter?'

'I . . . I t-told you already,' Jack sobbed into his fluffy white towel. 'Suze . . . I'm not *like* other people. I'm like what you said. A . . . a . . . freak.'

I didn't know what he was talking about. I assumed he was merely continuing our conversation from the room.

'Jack,' I said. 'You're no more a freak than anybody else.'

'No,' he sobbed. 'I *am*. Don't you get it?' Then he lifted his head, looked me straight in the eye, and hissed, 'Suze, don't you know why I don't like to go outside?'

I shook my head. I didn't get it. Even then, I still didn't get it.

'Because when I go outside,' Jack whispered, '*I see dead people.*'

TWO

I swear that's what he said.

He said it just like the kid in that movie said it, too, with the same tears in his eyes, the same fear in his voice.

And I had much the same reaction as I had when watching the movie. I went, inwardly, *Freaking crybaby*.

Outwardly, however, I said only, 'So?'

I didn't mean to sound callous. Really. I was just so surprised. I mean, in all my sixteen years, I've only met one other person with the same ability I have – the ability to see and speak with the dead – and that person is a sixty-something-year-old priest who also happens to be principal of the school I am currently attending. I certainly never expected to meet up with a fellow mediator at the Pebble Beach Hotel and Golf Resort.

But Jack took offence at my 'So?' anyway.

'*So?*' Jack sat up. He was a skinny little kid, with a caved-in sort of chest, and curly brown hair like his brother's. Only Jack lacked his brother's nicely buffed shape, so the curly hair, which looked sublime on Paul, gave Jack the unfortunate appearance of a walking Q-tip.

I don't know. Maybe that's why Rick and Nancy don't want to hang around him. Jack's a little creepy-looking, and apparently has frequent dialogues with the dead. God knows it never made me Miss Popularity.

The talking-to-the-dead thing, I mean. I am not creepy-looking. In fact, when I am not wearing my uniform shorts, I am frequently complimented on my appearance by the occasional construction worker.

'Didn't you hear what I said?' Jack was depressed, you could tell. I was probably the first person he'd ever told about his unique problem who'd been completely unimpressed.

Poor kid. He had no idea who he was dealing with.

'I see dead people,' he said, rubbing his eyes with his fists. 'They come up and start talking to me. And they're *dead*.'

I leaned forward, resting my elbows on my knees.

'Jack,' I said.

'You don't believe me.' His chin started trembling. 'No one believes me. But it's true!'

Jack buried his face in his towel again. I glanced in Sleepy's direction. Still no sign that he was aware of either of us, much less that he found Jack's behaviour at all odd. The kid was murmuring about all the people who hadn't believed him over the years, a list which seemed to include not only his parents, but a whole stream of medical specialists Rick and Nancy had dragged him to, hoping to cure their younger child of this delusion he has – that he can speak to the dead.

Poor little guy. He hadn't realized, as I had from a very early age, that what he and I can do . . . well, you just don't talk about.

I sighed. Really, it would have been too much to ask, apparently, for me to have a *normal* summer. I mean, a summer without any paranormal incidents.

But then, I'd never had one of those before in my life. Why should my sixteenth summer be any different?

I reached out and laid a hand on one of Jack's thin, quivering shoulders.

'Jack,' I said. 'You saw that gardener just now, didn't you? The one with the hedge clippers?'

Jack lifted an astonished, tear-stained face from the terry cloth. He stared up at me in wonder.

'You . . . you saw him, too?'

'Yeah,' I said. 'That was Jorge. He used to work here. He died a couple days ago of a heart attack.'

'But how could you—' Jack shook his head slowly back and forth. 'I mean, he's . . . he's a ghost.'

'Well, yeah,' I said. 'He probably has something he needs us to do for him. He kicked off kind of suddenly, and there may be stuff, you know, he left unfinished. He came up to us because he wants our help.'

'That's . . .' Jack stared at me. 'That's why they come up to me? Because they want help?'

'Well, yeah,' I said. 'What else would they want?'

'I don't know.' Jack's lower lip started to tremble again. 'To kill me.'

I couldn't help smiling a little at that one. 'No, Jack,' I said. 'That's not why ghosts come up to you. Not because they want to kill you.' Not yet, anyway. The kid was too young to have made the kind of homicidal enemies I had. 'They come up to you because you're a mediator, like me.'

Tears trembled on the edges of Jack's long eyelashes as he gazed up at me. 'A . . . a what?'

Oh, for God's sake, I thought. Why me? I mean, really. Like my life's not complicated enough. Now I have to play Obi Wan Kenobi to this kid's Anakin Skywalker? It so isn't fair. When was I ever going to get the chance to be a normal teenage girl, to do the things normal teenage girls like to do, like go to parties and hang out at the beach, and, um, what else?

Oh, yeah, date. A date, with the boy I actually like, would be nice.

But do I get dates? Oh, no. What do I get instead?

Ghosts. Mainly ghosts looking for help cleaning up the messes they made when they were alive, but sometimes ghosts whose sole amusement appears to be making even bigger messes in the lives of the people they left behind. And this frequently includes mine.

I ask you, do I have a big sign on my forehead that says Maid Service? Why am I always the one who has to tidy up other people's messes?

Because I had the misfortune to be born a mediator.

I must say, I think I'm way better suited for the job than poor Jack. I mean, I saw my first ghost when I was two years old, and I can assure you, my initial reaction was not fear. Not that, at the age of two, I'd been able to help the poor suffering soul who approached me. But I hadn't shrieked and run away in terror, either.

It wasn't until later, after my dad – who passed away when I was six – came back and explained it that I began to fully understand what I was, and why I could see the dead, but others – like my mom, for instance – could not.

One thing I did know, though, from a very tender age: mentioning to anyone that I could see folks they couldn't? Yeah, not such a hot idea. Not if I didn't want to end up on the ninth floor of Bellevue, which is where they stick all the whackos in New York City.

Only Jack didn't seem to have quite the same instinctive sense of self-preservation I'd apparently been born with. He'd been opening up his trap about the whole ghost thing to anyone who would listen, with the inevitable result that his poor parents didn't want to have anything to do with him. I'd be willing to bet that kids his own age, figuring he was lying to get attention, felt the same way. In a sense, the little guy had brought all his current misfortunes down upon himself.

On the other hand, if you ask me, whoever is up there handing out the mediator badges needs to make a better effort to see that the folks who get awarded the job are mentally up to the challenge. I complain a lot about it, because it has put a significant cramp on my social life, but there is nothing about this whole mediator thing I do not feel perfectly capable of handling . . .

Well, except for one thing.

But I've been making a concerted effort not to think about that.

Or rather, *him*.

'A mediator,' I explained to Jack, 'is someone who helps people who have died to move on, into their next life.' Or wherever people go when they kick the bucket. But I didn't want to get into a whole metaphysical discussion with this kid. I mean, he is, after all, only eight.

'You mean like I'm supposed to help them go to heaven?' Jack asked.

'Well, yeah, I guess.' If there is one.

'But . . .' Jack shook his head. 'I don't know anything about heaven.'

'You don't have to.' I tried to think how to explain it to him, then decided showing was better than telling. That's what Mr Walden, who I had last year for English and World Civ, was always saying, anyway

'Look,' I said, taking Jack by the hand. 'Come on. Watch me, and you can see how it works.'

Jack put the brakes on right away, though.

242

'No,' he gasped, his brown eyes, so like his brother's, wild with fear. 'No, I don't want to.'

I yanked him to his feet. Hey, I never said I was cut out for this baby-sitting thing, remember?

'Come on,' I said again. 'Jorge won't hurt you. He's really nice. Let's see what he wants.'

I practically had to carry him, but I finally got Jack over to where we'd last seen Jorge. A moment later the gardener – or, I should say, his spirit – reappeared, and after a lot of polite nodding and smiling, we got down to business. It was kind of hard, considering that Jorge's English was about as good as my Spanish – which is to say, not good at all – but eventually, I was able to figure out what was keeping Jorge from moving on from this life to his next – whatever that might be: his sister had appropriated a rosary left by their mother for her first grandchild, Jorge's daughter.

'So,' I explained to Jack, as I steered him into the hotel lobby, 'what we have to do is get Jorge's sister to give the rosary back to Teresa, his daughter. Otherwise, Jorge will just keep hanging around and pestering us. Oh, and he won't be able to find eternal rest. Got it?'

Jack said nothing. He just wandered behind me in a daze. He had been silent as death during my conversation with Jorge, and now he looked as if someone had whacked him on the back of the head with a Wiffle Bat a couple of hundred times.

'Come here,' I said, and steered Jack into a fancy mahogany phone booth with a sliding glass door. After we'd both slipped through it, I pulled the door shut, then picked up the phone and fed a quarter into the slot. 'Watch and learn, grasshopper,' I said to him.

What followed was a fairly typical example of what I do on an almost daily basis. I called information, got the guilty

243

party's phone number, then phoned her. When she picked up, and I ascertained that she spoke enough English to understand me, I informed her of the facts as I knew them, without the least embellishment. When you are dealing with the undead, there's no need for exaggeration of any kind. The fact that someone who has died has contacted you with details no one but the deceased could know is generally enough. By the end of our conversation, an obviously flustered Marisol had assured me that the rosary would be delivered, that day, into Teresa's hands.

End of conversation. I thanked Jorge's sister and hung up.

'Now,' I explained, to Jack, 'if Marisol doesn't do it, we'll hear from Jorge again, and we'll have to resort to something a little more persuasive than a mere phone call. But she sounded pretty scared. It's spooky when a perfect stranger calls you and tells you she's spoken to your dead brother, and that he's mad at you. I bet she'll do it.'

Jack stared up at me. 'That's it?' he asked. 'That's all he wanted you to do? Get his sister to give the necklace back?'

'Rosary,' I corrected him. 'And yes, that was it.'

I didn't think it was important to add that this had been a particularly simple case. Usually the problems associated with people speaking from beyond the grave are a little more complicated and take a lot more than a simple phone call to settle. In fact, oftentimes fisticuffs are involved. I had only just recently recovered from a few broken ribs given to me by a group of ghosts who hadn't appreciated my attempts to help them into the afterlife one little bit, and had, in fact, ended up putting me in the hospital.

But Jack had plenty of time to learn that not all the undead were like Jorge. Besides, it was his birthday. I didn't want to bum him out.

So instead, I slid the phone-booth door open again and said, 'Let's go swimming.'

Jack was so stunned by the whole thing he didn't even protest. He still had questions, of course . . . questions I answered as patiently and thoroughly as I could. In between questions, I taught him to freestyle.

And I don't want to brag, or anything, but I have to say that, thanks to my careful instructions and calming influence, by the end of the day Jack Slater was acting like – and even swimming like – a normal eight-year-old.

I'm not kidding. The little dude had completely lightened up. He was even *laughing*. It was as if showing him that he had nothing to fear from the ghosts who had been plaguing him his whole life had lifted from him his fear of . . . well, everything. It wasn't long before he was running around the pool deck, doing cannonballs off the side, and annoying all the doctors' wives who were trying to tan themselves in the nearby lounge chairs. Just like any other eight-year-old boy.

He even struck up a conversation with a group of other kids who were being tended by one of my fellow sitters. And when one of them splashed water in Jack's face, instead of bursting into tears, as he would have done the day before, Jack splashed the kid back, causing Kim, my fellow sitter, who was treading water beside me, to ask, 'My God, Suze, what did you do to Jack Slater? He's acting almost . . . *normal*.'

I tried not to let my pride show.

'Oh, you know,' I said with a shrug. 'I just taught him to swim, is all. I guess that gave him some confidence.'

Kim watched as Jack and another boy, just to be irritating, did double cannonballs into a group of little girls, who shrieked and then tried to hit the boys with their foam floaties.

'God,' Kim said. 'I'll say. I can't believe it's even the same kid.'

Neither, it became apparent, could Jack's own family. I was teaching him the backstroke when I heard someone whistle, low and long, from the far side of the pool. Jack and I both looked up and saw Paul standing there, looking all Pete Sampras-y in white and holding a tennis racquet.

'Well, would you look at that,' Paul drawled. 'My brother, in a pool. And enjoying himself, no less. Has hell frozen over, or something?'

'Paul,' Jack screamed. 'Watch me! Watch me!'

And the next thing any of us knew, Jack was racing through the water towards his brother. I wouldn't exactly call what Jack was doing a proper crawl, but it was a close enough imitation of it to pass, even in an older brother's eyes. And if it wasn't pretty, there was no denying the kid was staying afloat. You had to give him that.

And Paul did. He squatted down and, when Jack's head bobbed up just beneath him, he reached down and pushed it under again. You know, in a playful way.

'Congrats, champ,' Paul said, when Jack resurfaced. 'I never thought I'd live to see the day you wouldn't be afraid to get your face wet.'

Jack, beaming, said, 'Watch me swim back!' and began to thrash through the water to the other side of the pool. Again, not pretty, but effective.

But Paul, instead of watching his brother swim, looked down at me, standing chest-high in the clear blue water.

'All right, Annie Sullivan,' he said. 'What have you done to Helen?'

I shrugged. Jack had never mentioned his brother's feelings on the whole *I see dead people* thing, so I didn't know if Paul was aware of Jack's ability or if he, like his parents, thought it was all in the kid's head. One of the points I'd tried to impress upon Jack was that the fewer people – particularly – adults – who knew, the better. I had forgotten to ask if Paul knew.

Or, more important, believed.

'Just taught him how to swim, is all,' I said, sweeping some of my wet hair from my face.

I won't lie or anything and say I was embarrassed for a hottie like Paul to see me in my swimsuit. I look a lot better in the navy blue one-piece suit the hotel forces us to wear than I do in those heinous shorts.

Plus my mascara is totally the waterproof kind. I mean, I'm not an idiot.

'My parents have been trying to get that kid to swim for six years,' Paul said. 'And you do it in one day?'

I smiled at him. 'I'm extremely persuasive,' I said.

Yeah, OK, I was flirting. So sue me. A girl has to have *some* fun.

'You,' Paul said, 'are nothing short of a miracle worker. Come have dinner with us tonight.'

All of a sudden, I didn't feel like flirting any more.

'Oh, no, thank you,' I said.

'Come on,' Paul said. I have to say that he looked exceptionally fine in his white shirt and shorts. They brought out the deepness of his tan, just like the late afternoon sunlight brought out the occasional strand of gold in his otherwise dark brown curls.

And a tan wasn't all Paul had that the other hottie in my life didn't: Paul also happened to have a heartbeat.

'Why not?' Paul was kneeling by the side of pool, one dark forearm resting across an equally dark knee. 'My parents will be delighted. And it's clear my brother can't live without you.

247

And we're going to the Grill. You can't turn down an invitation to the Grill.'

'I'm sorry,' I said. 'I really can't. Hotel policy. The staff aren't supposed to mingle with the guests.'

'Who said anything about mingling?' Paul wanted to know. 'I'm talking about eating. Come on. Give the kid a birthday treat.'

'I really can't,' I said, flashing him my best smile. 'I have to go. Sorry.'

And I swam over to where Jack was struggling to lift himself on to a huge pile of floaties he'd collected, and pretended to be too busy helping him to hear Paul calling to me.

Look, I know what you're thinking. You're thinking I said no because the whole thing would just be too *Dirty Dancing*, right? Summer fling at the resort, only with the roles reversed: you know, the poor working girl and the rich doctor's son, nobody puts Baby in the corner, blah blah blah. That kind of thing.

But that's not it. Not really. For one thing, I'm not even technically poor. I mean, I'm making ten bucks an hour here, plus tips. And my mom is a TV news anchorwoman, and my stepdad has his own show, too.

And OK, sure, it's only local news, and Andy's show is on cable, but come on. We have a house in the Carmel Hills.

And OK, yeah, the house is a converted hundred-and-fifty-year-old hotel. But we each have our own bedroom, and there are three cars parked in the driveway, none of which are propped up on cinderblocks. We don't exactly qualify for food stamps.

And it isn't even that other thing I mentioned, about there being a policy against staff mingling with the guests. There isn't any such policy.

As Kim felt obligated to point out to me a few minutes later.

'What is your glitch, Simon?' she wanted to know. 'That guy's got the hots for you, and you went completely Red Baron on him. I never saw anybody get shot down so fast.'

I busied myself scooping a drowning ant off the surface of the water. 'I'm, um, busy tonight,' I said.

'Don't give me that, Suze.' Although I had never met Kim before we'd started working together – she goes to Carmel Valley High, the public school my mother is convinced is riddled with drug addicts and gangbangers – we'd gotten pretty close due to our mutual dissatisfaction at being forced to rise so early in the morning for work. 'You aren't doing anything tonight. So what's with the anti-aircraft fire?'

I finally captured the ant. Keeping it cupped in my palm, I made my way towards the side of the pool.

'I don't know,' I said as I waded. 'He seems nice and all. The thing is –' I shook my hand out over the side of the pool, setting the ant free – 'I kind of like somebody else.'

Kim raised her eyebrows. One of them had a little hole in it where she normally wears a gold stud. Caitlin makes her take it out before work, though.

'Tell!' Kim commanded.

I glanced involuntarily up at Sleepy, dozing in his life-guard's chair. Kim let out a little shriek.

'Eew,' she cried. '*Him*? But he's your—'

I rolled my eyes. 'No, not *him*. God. Just . . . Look, I just like somebody else, OK? But it's like . . . it's a secret.'

Kim sucked in her breath. 'Ooh,' she said. 'The best kind. Does he go to the Academy?' When I shook my head, she tried, 'Robert Louis Stevenson School, then?'

Again, I shook my head.

Kim wrinkled up her nose. 'He doesn't go to CVHS, does he?'

I sighed. 'He isn't in high school, OK, Kim? I'd really rather—'

'Oh, my God,' Kim said. 'A *college* guy? You dog. My mom would *kill* me if she knew I was going with a college guy—'

'He's not in college, either, OK?' I could feel my cheeks growing warm. 'Look, the thing is, it's complicated. And I don't want to talk about it.'

Kim looked taken aback. 'Well, all right. God. Sorry.'

But she couldn't leave well enough alone.

'He's older, right?' she asked, less than a minute later. 'Like *way* older? That's OK, you know. I went out with an older guy, like, when I was fourteen. He was eighteen. My mom didn't know. So I can totally relate.'

'Somehow,' I said, 'I really don't think you can.'

She wrinkled her nose again. 'God,' she said. 'How old *is* he?'

I thought about telling her. I thought about going, Oh, I don't know. About a century and a half.

But I didn't. Instead I told Jack it was time to go inside, if he was going to have a bath before dinner.

'Jeez,' I heard Kim say as I got out. '*That* old, huh?'

Yeah. Unfortunately. *That* old.

Three

I don't even really know how it happened. I was being way careful, you know. Careful not to fall in love with Jesse, I mean.

And I'd been doing a really good job. I mean, I was getting out and meeting new people and doing new things, just like it says to do in *Cosmo*. I certainly wasn't sitting around mooning over him or anything.

And yeah, OK, the majority of guys I have met since moving to California have turned out either to have psychopathic killers stalking them, or were actually psychopathic killers themselves. But that's really not a very good excuse for falling in love with a ghost. It really isn't.

But that's what happened.

I can tell you the exact moment I knew it was all over, too. My battle to keep from falling in love with him, I mean. It was while I was in the hospital, recovering from that severe butt-kicking I mentioned before – the one I got courtesy of the ghosts of four RLS students who had been murdered a few weeks before school let out for the summer.

Anyway, Jesse showed up in my hospital room (Why not? He's a ghost. He can materialize anywhere he wants) to express his get-well wishes, which were extremely heartfelt and all, and while he was there, he happened, at one point, to reach out and touch my cheek.

That's all. He just touched my cheek, which was, I believe, the only part of me that was not black and blue at the time.

Big deal, right? So he touched my cheek. That's no reason to swoon.

But I did.

Oh, not literally. It wasn't like anybody had to wave smelling salts under my nose or anything, for God's sake. But after that, I was gone. Done for. Toast.

I flatter myself I've done a pretty good job of hiding it. He, I'm sure, has no idea. I still treat him as if he were . . . well, an ant that has fallen into my pool. You know, irritating, but not worth killing.

And I haven't told anyone. How can I? No one – except for Father Dominic, back at the Academy, and my youngest stepbrother, Doc – has any idea Jesse even exists. I mean, come on, the ghost of a guy who died a hundred and fifty years ago, and lives in my bedroom? If I mentioned it to anyone, they'd cart me off to the looney bin faster than you can say *Stir of Echoes*.

But it's there. Just because I haven't told anyone doesn't mean it isn't there, all the time, lurking in the back of my mind, like one of those 'N Sync songs you can't get out of your head.

And I have to tell you, it makes the idea of going out with other guys seem like . . . well, a big waste of time.

So I didn't jump at the chance to go out with Paul Slater (though if you ask me, having dinner with him *and* his parents *and* his little brother hardly qualifies as going out). Instead, I went home and had dinner with my own parents and brothers. Well, stepbrothers, anyway.

Dinner in the Ackerman household was always this

very big deal . . . until Andy started working on installing the hot tub. Since then, he has slacked off considerably in the culinary department, let me tell you. And since my mom is hardly what you'd call a cook, we've been enjoying a lot of takeouts lately. I thought we had hit rock bottom the night before, when we'd actually ordered from Peninsula Pizza, the place Sleepy works nights as a delivery guy.

But I didn't know how bad it could get until I walked in that night and saw a red-and-white bucket sitting in the middle of the table.

'Don't start,' my mother said when she noticed me.

I just shook my head. 'I guess if you peel the skin off, it's not that bad for you.'

'Give it to me,' Dopey said, glopping semi-congealed mashed potatoes on to his plate. 'I'll eat your skin.'

I could hardly control my gag reflex after that offer, but I managed, and I was reading the nutritional literature that came with our meal – 'The Colonel has never forgotten the delicious aromas that used to float from his mother's kitchen on the plantation back when he was a boy' – when I remembered the tin box, the contents of which had also been advertised as having a delicious aroma.

'Hey,' I said. 'So what was in that box you guys dug up?'

Dopey made a face. 'Nothing. Bunch of old letters.'

Andy looked sadly at his son. The truth is, I think even my stepfather has begun to realize what I have known since the day I met him: that his middle son is a bohunk.

'Not just a bunch of old letters, Brad,' Andy said. 'They're quite old, dated around the time this house was built – 1850. They're in extremely poor condition – falling apart, actually. I was thinking of taking them over to the historical society. They might want them, in spite of the condition. Or –'

Andy looked at me – 'I thought Father Dominic might be interested. You know what a history buff he is.'

Father Dom is a history buff, all right, but only because, as a mediator, like me, he has a tendency to run into people who have actually lived through historical events like the Alamo and the Lewis and Clark expedition. You know, folks who take the phrase *Been there, done that* to a whole new level.

'I'll give him a call,' I said as I accidentally dropped a piece of chicken into my lap, where it was immediately vacuumed up by the Ackermans' enormous dog, Max, who maintains a watchful position at my side during every meal.

It was only when Dopey chortled that I realized I'd said the wrong thing. Never having been a normal teenage girl, it is sometimes hard for me to imitate one. And normal teenage girls do not, I know, give their high school principals calls on any sort of regular basis.

I glared at Dopey from across the table.

'I was going to call him anyway,' I said, 'to find out what I'm supposed to do with the leftover cash from our class trip to Great America.'

'I'll take it,' Sleepy joked. Why did my mother have to marry into a family of comedians?

'Can I see them?' I asked, pointedly ignoring both my stepbrothers.

'See what, honey?' Andy asked me.

For a moment I forgot what we were talking about. *Honey?* Andy had never called me *honey* before. What was going on here? Were we – I shudder to think it – *bonding*? Excuse me, I already have one father, even if he is dead. He still pops by to visit me all too often.

'I think she means the letters,' my mother said, apparently not even noticing what her husband had just called me.

'Oh, sure,' Andy said. 'They're in our room.'

'Our room' is the bedroom Andy and my mother sleep in. I try never to go in there, because, well, frankly, the whole thing grosses me out. Yeah, sure, I'm glad that my mom's finally happy, after ten years of mourning the death of my dad. But does that mean I want to actually *see* her in bed with her new husband, watching *West Wing*? No thank you.

Still, after dinner, I steeled myself and went in there. My mom was at her dressing table taking off her make-up. She has to go to bed very early in order to be up in time for her stint on the morning news.

'Oh, hi, sweetie,' my mom said to me in a dazed, I'm-busy kind of way. 'They're over there, I think.'

I looked where she pointed on top of Andy's dresser and found the metal box Dopey had dug up along with a lot of other guy-type stuff, like loose change and matches and receipts.

Anyway, Andy had tried to clean the box up, and he'd done a pretty good job of it. You could read almost all the writing on it.

Which was kind of unfortunate, because what the writing said was way politically incorrect. *Try new Red Injun cigars!* it urged. There was even a picture of this very proud-looking Native American clutching a fistful of cigars where his bow and quiver ought to have been. *The delicious aroma will tempt even the choosiest smoker. As with all our products, quality assured.*

That was it. No surgeon general's warning about how smoking can kill. Nothing about fetal birth weight. Still, it was kind of strange how advertising from before they had TV – before they even had *radio* – was still basically the same as advertising today. Only, you know, now we know that naming your product after a race of people will probably offend them.

I opened the box and found the letters inside. Andy was

right about their poor condition. They were so yellowed that you could hardly peel them apart without having pieces crumble off. They had, I could see, been tied together with a ribbon, a silk one, which might have been another colour once, but was now an ugly brown.

There was a stack of letters, maybe five or six in all, in the box. I can't tell you, as I picked up the first one, what I thought I'd see. But I guess a part of me knew all along what I was going to find.

Even so, when I'd carefully unfolded the first one and read the words *Dear Hector*, I still felt like somebody had snuck up behind me and kicked me.

I had to sit down. I sank down into one of the armchairs my mom and Andy keep by the fireplace in their room, my eyes still glued to the yellowed page in front of me.

Jesse. These letters were to Jesse.

'Suze?' My mom glanced at me curiously. She was rubbing cream into her face. 'Are you all right?'

'Fine,' I said in a strangled voice. 'Is it OK . . . is it OK if I just sit here and read these for a minute?'

My mom began to slop cream on to her hands. 'Of course,' she said. 'You're sure you're all right? You look a little . . . pale.'

'I'm great,' I lied. 'Just great.'

Dear Hector, the first letter said. The handwriting was beautiful – loopy and old-fashioned, the kind of handwriting Sister Ernestine, back at school, used. I could read it quite easily, despite the fact that the letter was dated 8 May 1850.

Eighteen fifty! That was the year our house had been built, the first year it was in business as a boarding house for travellers to the Monterey Peninsula area. The year – I knew from when Doc and I looked it up – that Jesse or Hector (which is his real name; can you imagine? I mean, *Hector*) had mysteriously disappeared.

Though I happen to know there hadn't been anything mysterious about it. He'd been murdered in this very house . . . in fact, in my bedroom upstairs. Which is why, for the past century and a half, he's been hanging out there, waiting for . . .

Waiting for what?

Waiting for you, said a small voice in the back of my head. A mediator, to find these letters and avenge his death, so he can move on to wherever it is he's supposed to go next.

The thought struck me with terror. Really. It made my hands go all sweaty, even though it was cool in my mom and Andy's room, what with the air conditioning being on full blast. The back of my neck started feeling prickly and gross.

I forced myself to look back down at the letter. If Jesse was meant to move on, well, then I was just going to have to help him do it. That's my job, after all.

Except that I couldn't help thinking about Father Dom. A fellow mediator, he had admitted to me a few months ago that he had once had the misfortune to fall in love with a ghost, back when he'd been my age. Things hadn't worked out – how could they? – and he'd become a priest.

Got that? A *priest*. OK? That's how bad it had been. That's how hard the loss had been to get over. *He'd become a priest.*

Frankly, I don't see how I could ever become a nun. For one thing, I'm not even Catholic. And for another, I don't look very good with my hair pulled back. Really. That's why I've always avoided ponytails and headbands.

Stop it, I said to myself. Just stop it and read.

I read.

The letter was from someone called Maria. I don't know

much about Jesse's life before he died – he's not exactly big on discussing it – but I do know that Maria de Silva was the name of the girl Jesse had been on his way to marry when he'd disappeared. Some cousin of his. I'd seen a picture of her once in a book. She was pretty hot, you know, for a girl in a hoop skirt who lived before plastic surgery. Or Maybelline.

And you could tell by the way she wrote that she knew it, too. That she was hot, I mean. Her letter was all about the parties she'd been to, and who had said what about her new bonnet. Her *bonnet*, for crying out loud. I swear to God, it was like reading a letter from Kelly Prescott, except that it had a bunch of *hithers* and *alacks* in it, and no mention of Ricky Martin. Plus a lot of stuff was spelled wrong. Maria may have been a babe, but it was pretty clear, after reading her letters, she hadn't won too many spelling bees back at ye olde schoolhouse.

What struck me, as I read, was the fact that it really didn't seem possible that the girl who had written these letters was the same girl who had, I was pretty sure, ordered a hit on her fiancé. Because I happened to know that Maria hadn't wanted to marry Jesse at all. Her dad had arranged the whole thing. Maria had wanted to marry this other guy, this dude named Diego, who ran slaves for a living. A real charming guy. In fact, Diego was the one I suspected had killed Jesse.

Not, of course, that Jesse had ever mentioned any of this – or anything at all, for that matter, about his past. He is, and always has been, completely tight-lipped on the whole subject of how he'd died. Which I guess I can understand: getting murdered has to be a bit traumatizing.

But I must say it's kind of hard getting to the bottom of why he's still here after all this time when he won't contribute at all to the conversation. I had had to find out all of this stuff

258

from a book on the history of Salinas County that Doc had dug up out of the local library.

So I guess you could say that I read Maria's letters with a certain sense of foreboding. I mean, I was pretty much convinced I was going to find something in them that was going to prove Jesse had been murdered . . . and who'd done it.

But the last letter was just as fatuous as the other four. There was nothing, nothing at all to indicate any wrong-doing of any kind on Maria's part . . . except for maybe a complete inability to spell the word fiancé. And really, what sort of crime is that?

I folded the letters carefully again and stuck them back into the tin, realizing, as I did so, that the back of my neck, as well as my hands, was no longer sweating. Was I relieved that there was nothing incriminating here, nothing that helped solve the mystery of Jesse's death?

I guess so. Selfish of me, I know, but it's the truth. All I knew now was what Maria de Silva had worn to some party at the Spanish ambassador's house. Big deal. Why would anybody stick letters as innocuous as that into a cigar box and bury them? It made no sense.

'Interesting, aren't they?' my mother said when I stood up.

I jumped about a mile. I'd forgotten she was even there. She was in bed now, reading a book on how to be a more effective time manager.

'Yeah,' I said, putting the letters back on Andy's dresser. 'Really interesting. I'm so glad I know what the ambassador's son said when he saw Maria de Silva in her new silver gauze ballgown.'

My mom looked up at me curiously through the lenses of her reading glasses. 'Oh, did she mention her last name somewhere? Because Andy and I were wondering. We didn't see it. De Silva, did you say?'

I blinked. 'Um,' I said. 'No. Well, she didn't say. But Doc and I . . . I mean, David, he told me about this family, the de Silvas, that lived in Salinas around that time, and they had a daughter called Maria, and I just . . .' My voice trailed off as Andy came into the room.

'Hey, Suze,' he said, looking a little surprised to see me in his room, since I'd never set foot in there before. 'Did you see the letters? Neat, huh?'

Neat. Oh my God. Neat.

'Yeah,' I said. 'Gotta go. Goodnight.'

I couldn't get out of there fast enough. I don't know how kids whose parents have been married multiple times deal with it. I mean, my mother's only remarried once, and to a perfectly nice man. But still, it's just so *weird*.

But if I'd thought I could retreat to my room to be alone and think things over, I was wrong. Jesse was sitting on my window seat.

Sitting there looking like he always looked: totally hot, in the white open-necked shirt and black toreador pants he habitually wears – well, it's not like you can change clothes in the afterlife – with his short dark hair curling crisply against the back of his neck, and his liquid black eyes bright beneath equally inky brows, one of which bore a thin white scar . . .

A scar that, more times than I like to admit, I'd dreamed of tracing with my fingertips.

He looked up when I came in – he had Spike, my cat, on his lap – and said, 'This book is very difficult to understand.' He was reading a copy of *First Blood*, by David Morrell, which they based the movie *Rambo* on.

I blinked, trying to rouse myself from the dazed stupor the sight of him always seemed to put me in for a minute or so.

260

'If Sylvester Stallone understood it,' I said, 'I would think you could.'

Jesse ignored that. 'Marx predicted that the contradictions and weaknesses within the capitalist structure would cause increasingly severe economic crises and deepening impoverishment of the working class,' he said, 'which would eventually revolt and seize control of the means of production . . . which is precisely what happened in Vietnam. What induced the US government to think that they were justified in involving themselves in the struggle of the people of this developing nation to find economic solidarity?'

My shoulders sagged. Really, is it too much to ask that I be able to come home from a long day of work and relax? Oh, no. I have to come home and read a bunch of letters written to the love of my life by his fiancée, who, if I am correct, had him killed a hundred and fifty years ago.

Then, as if that is not bad enough, he wants me to explain the Vietnam War.

I really have to start hiding my textbooks from him. The thing is, he reads them and actually manages to retain what they say, and then applies that to other things he finds to read around the house.

Why he can't just watch TV, like a normal person, I do not know.

I went over to my bed and collapsed on to it, face first. I was, I should mention, still wearing my horrible shorts from the hotel. But I couldn't bring myself to care what Jesse thought about the size of my butt at that particular moment.

I guess it must have showed. Not my butt, I mean, but my general unhappiness with the way my summer was going.

'Are you all right?' Jesse wanted to know.

'Yes,' I said, into my pillows.

261

Jesse said, after a minute, 'Well, you don't seem all right. Are you sure nothing is wrong?'

Yes, something is wrong, I wanted to shriek at him. I just spent twenty minutes reading a bunch of private correspondence from your ex-fiancée, and might I add that she seems like a terrifically *boring* individual? How could you have ever been stupid enough to have agreed to marry her? Her and her stupid *bonnet*?

But the thing is, I didn't want Jesse to know I'd read his mail. I mean, we're basically room-mates and all, and there are certain things you just don't do. For instance, Jesse is always tactfully not around whenever I am changing and bathing and whatnot. And I am very careful to stock up on food and litter for Spike, who, unlike a normal animal, actually seems to prefer ghost company to human. He only tolerates me because I feed him.

Of course, Jesse has, in the past, felt no compunction about materializing in the back seats of cars in which I happened to have been making out with someone.

But I know Jesse would never read my mail, of which I get only a limited amount, mostly in the form of letters from my best friend Gina, back in Brooklyn. And I have to admit, I felt guilty for reading his, even though it was almost two hundred years old and there certainly wouldn't have been anything about me in it.

What surprised me was that Jesse, who is, after all, a ghost, and can go anywhere without being seen – except by me and Father Dom, of course, and now, I guess, by Jack – didn't know about the letters. Really, he seemed to have no idea both that they'd been found and that, just moments before, I'd been downstairs, reading them.

But then, *First Blood* is pretty engrossing, I suppose.

So instead of telling him what was *really* wrong with me –

you know, anything about the letters, and especially anything about the whole *I'm in love with you, only where can it go? Because you're not even alive and I'm the only one who can see you, and besides, it's clear you don't feel the same way about me. Do you? Well, do you?* thing – just said, 'Well, I met another mediator today, and I guess that kind of weirded me out.'

And then I rolled over and told him about Jack.

Jesse was very interested and told me I ought to call Father Dom with the news. What I wanted to do, of course, was call Father Dom and tell him about the letters. But I couldn't do that with Jesse in the room, because of course he'd know I'd been prying in his personal affairs, which, given his whole secrecy thing about how he'd died, I doubted he'd appreciate.

So I said, 'Good idea,' and picked up the phone and dialled Father D's number.

Only Father D didn't answer. Instead, a woman did. At first I freaked out, thinking Father Dominic was shacking up. But then I remembered that he lives in a rectory with a bunch of other people.

So I went, 'Is Father Dominic there?' hoping it was only a novice or something and would go away and get him without comment.

But it wasn't a novice. It was Sister Ernestine, who is the assistant principal of my high school, and who of course recognized my voice.

'Susannah Simon,' she said. 'What are you doing calling Father Dominic at home at this hour? Do you know what time it is, young lady? It is nearly ten o'clock!'

'I know,' I said. 'Only—'

'Besides, Father Dominic isn't here,' Sister Ernestine went on. 'He's on retreat.'

'Retreat?' I echoed, picturing Father Dominic sitting in

263

front of a campfire with a bunch of other priests, singing 'Kumbaya My Lord' and possibly wearing sandals.

Then I remembered that Father Dominic had mentioned that he would be going on a retreat for the principals of Catholic high schools. He'd even given me the number there, in case there was some kind of ghost emergency and I needed to reach him. I didn't count discovering a new mediator as an emergency, however . . . though doubtless Father Dom would. So I just thanked Sister Ernestine, apologized for disturbing her, and hung up.

'What is a retreat?' Jesse wanted to know.

So then I explained to him what a retreat is, but the whole time I was sitting there thinking about the time he'd touched my face in the hospital and wondering if it had been because he just felt sorry for me or if he actually liked me (as more than just as a friend – I know he likes me as a friend) or what.

Because the thing is, even though he's been dead for a hundred and fifty years, Jesse is really an extreme hottie – much hotter even than Paul Slater . . . or maybe I just think so because I'm in love with him.

But whatever. I mean, he really is like someone straight off The WB. He even has nice teeth for a guy born before they invented fluoride, very white and even and strong-looking. I mean, if there were any guys at the Mission Academy who looked even remotely like Jesse, going to school wouldn't seem at all like the massive waste of time it actually is.

But what good is it? I mean, him looking so good, and all? He's a *ghost*. I'm the only one who can see him. It's not like I'll ever be able to introduce him to my mother, or take him to the prom, or marry him, or whatever. *We have no future together.*

I have to remember that.

But sometimes it's really, really hard. Especially when he's sitting there in front of me, laughing at what I'm saying, and petting that stupid, smelly cat. Jesse was the first person I met when I moved to California, and he became my first real friend here. He has always been there when I needed him, which is way more than I can say for most of the living people I know. And if I had to choose one person to be marooned on a desert island with, I wouldn't even have to think about it: of course it would be Jesse.

This is what I was thinking as I explained about retreats. It was what I was thinking as I went on to explain what I knew about the Vietnam War, and then the eventual fall of communism in the former Soviet Union. It was what I was thinking as I brushed my teeth and got ready for bed. It was what I was thinking as I said good night to him and crawled under the covers and turned out the light. It was what I was thinking as sleep overcame me and blissfully blotted out all thought whatsoever . . . the time I spend sleeping being the only time, lately, when I can escape thoughts of Jesse.

But let me tell you, it came back in full force when, just a few hours later, I woke with a start to find a hand pressed over my mouth.

And, oh yeah, a knife held to my throat.

Four

Being a mediator, I am not unaccustomed to being woken in, shall we say, a less than gentle manner.

But this was a *lot* less gentle than usual. I mean, usually when someone wants your help, they go out of their way not to antagonize you . . . which waving a knife around has a tendency to do.

But as soon as I opened my eyes and saw who this knife-wielding individual was, I realized that probably what she wanted was not my help. No, probably what she wanted was to kill me.

Don't ask me how I knew. Undoubtedly those old mediator instincts at work.

Well, and the knife was a pretty significant indicator.

'Listen to me, you stupid girl,' Maria de Silva hissed at me. Maria de Silva *Diego*, I should say, since at the time of her death she was married to Felix Diego, the slave-runner. I know all this from that book Doc got out of the library called *My Monterey*, a history of Salinas County from 1800 to 1850. There'd even been that portrait of Maria in it.

Which was how I happened to know who was trying to kill me this time.

'If,' Maria hissed, 'you don't get your father and brother to stop digging that hole' – um, *step*father and *step*brother, I

266

wanted to correct her, only I couldn't, on account of the hand over my mouth – 'I'll make you sorry you were ever born. Got that?'

Pretty tough talk from a girl in a hoop skirt. Because that's what she was. A girl.

She hadn't been when she'd died. When she had died, around the turn of the century – last century, of course, not this one – Maria de Silva Diego had been around seventy or so.

But the ghost on top of me appeared to be my own age. Her hair was black, without a hint of grey, and she wore it in these very fancy ringlets on either side of her face. She appeared to have a lot going on in the jewellery department. There was this big fat ruby hanging from a gold chain round her long, slender neck – very *Titanic* and all – and she had some heavy-duty rings on her fingers. One of them was cutting into my gums.

That's the thing about ghosts, though – the thing that they always get wrong in the movies. When you die, your spirit does not take on the form your body had at the moment you croaked. You just don't ever see ghosts walking around with their guts spilling out, or their severed head in their hands, or whatever. If you did, Jack might have been justified in being such a little scaredy cat.

But it doesn't happen that way. Instead, your ghost appears in the form your body had when you were at your most vital, your most alive.

And I guess for Maria de Silva, that was when she was sixteen or so.

Hey, it was nice she had an option, you know? Jesse hadn't been allowed to live long enough to have much of a choice. Thanks to her.

'Oh, no, you don't,' Maria said, the backs of her rings

267

scraping against my teeth in a manner I would really have to describe as unpleasant. 'Don't even think about it.'

I don't know how she'd known, but I had been considering ramming my knees into her spine. The knife blade pressing against my jugular soon dissuaded me of that plan, however.

'You're going to make your father stop digging back there, and you're going to destroy those letters, understand, little girl?' Maria hissed. 'And you aren't going to say a word about them – or me – to Hector. Am I making myself clear?'

What could I do? She had a *knife* to my throat. And there was nothing in her manner at all reminiscent of the Maria de Silva who'd written those idiotic letters. This chick was not gushing about her new bonnet, if you get my drift. I hadn't any doubt at all that she not only knew how to use that knife, but that she fully intended to do so, if provoked.

I nodded to show her that I was perfectly willing, under the circumstances, to follow her orders.

'Good,' Maria de Silva said. And then she lifted her fingers from my mouth. I could taste blood.

She had straddled me – which accounted for all the lacy petticoat in my face, tickling my nose – and now she looked down at me, her pretty features twisted into an expression of disgust.

'And they said for me to look out,' she sneered. 'That you were a tricky one. But you aren't so tricky, are you? You're just a girl. A stupid little girl.'

She threw back her head and laughed.

And then she was gone. Just like that.

As soon as I felt like I could move again, I got out of bed and went into my bathroom, where I turned on the light and looked at my reflection in the mirror above my sink.

No. It hadn't been a nightmare. There was blood between my teeth where Maria de Silva's ring had cut into me.

I rinsed until all the blood was gone, then turned off the bathroom light and came back into my room. I think I was in a daze or something. I couldn't quite register what had just happened. Maria de Silva. Maria de Silva, Jesse's fiancée – I think it would be safe to say ex-fiancée, under the circumstances – had just appeared in my room and threatened me. *Me.* Sweet little old *me.*

It was a lot to process, especially considering it was, oh, I don't know, four in the morning?

And yet it turned out I was in for yet another late-night shock. No sooner had I stepped from the bathroom than I noticed someone was leaning against one of the posts to the canopy over my bed.

Only it wasn't just someone, it was Jesse. And when he saw me, he straightened up.

'Are you all right?' he asked, worriedly. 'I thought I . . . Susannah, was somebody just here?'

Uh, your knife-wielding ex-girlfriend, you mean?

That's what I thought. What I said was, 'No.'

OK. Don't start with me. The reason I didn't tell him had nothing to do with Maria's threat.

No, it was the other thing Maria had said. About telling Andy to quit digging in the backyard. Because that could mean only one thing: that there was something buried in the backyard Maria didn't want anybody to find.

And I had a feeling I knew what that something was.

I also had a feeling that that something was the reason Jesse had been hanging around the Carmel Hills for so long.

I should have blurted this all out to Jesse, right? I mean, come on: he had a right to know. It was something that very directly concerned him.

But it was also something that, I was fairly sure, was going to take him away from me forever.

Yeah, I know: if I really loved him, I'd have been willing to set him free, like in that poem that's always on those posters with the seagulls flying in the wind: *If you love something, set it free. If it was meant to be, it will come back to you.*

Let me tell you something. That poem is stupid, all right? And it so totally does not apply in this situation. Because once Jesse gets set free, he is never coming back to me. Because he won't be able to. Because he'll be in heaven, or another life, or whatever.

And then I'll have to become a nun.

God. *God*, everything sucks.

I crawled back into bed.

'Look, Jesse,' I said, pulling the covers up to my chin. I had on a T-shirt and boxers, but, you know, no bra or anything. Not that he could tell, in the dark and all, but you never know. 'I'm really tired.'

'Oh,' he said. 'Of course. But . . . You're sure there wasn't anyone in here? Because I could swear I—'

I waited expectantly for him to finish. Just how would he end that sentence? *I could swear I heard the sweet dulcet tones of the woman I once loved? I could swear I smelled her perfume* – which, by the way, was of orange blossoms?

But he didn't say either of those things. Instead, looking really confused, he said, 'Sorry,' and disappeared, exactly the way his ex-girlfriend had disappeared. In fact, you'd think they might have run into each other, wouldn't you, out there on the spiritual plane, with all of this materializing and dematerializing?

But apparently not.

I won't lie and tell you that I dropped back off to sleep right away. I didn't, I was really, really tired, but my mind just

270

kept repeating what Maria had said, over and over. What on earth was she so hot and bothered about, anyway? Those letters didn't have anything the least bit incriminating in them. I mean, if it's true that she had Jesse iced so she could marry her boyfriend Diego instead of him.

And if those letters were so important, why hadn't she had them destroyed properly all those years ago? Why were they buried in our backyard in a cigar box?

But that wasn't what was really bothering me. What really bothered me was the fact that she wanted me to get Andy to stop digging altogether. Because that could only mean one thing:

There was, something even more incriminating back there.

Like a body.

And I didn't even want to *think* about whose.

And when I woke up again a few hours later, after finally managing to nod off, I still didn't want to think about it.

But one thing I did know: I was not going to ask Andy to stop digging (like he'd even listen to me if I did), nor was I going to destroy those letters. No freaking way.

In fact, I took personal possession of them, just in case, telling Andy that I'd deliver them to the historical society myself. I figured they'd be safe there, in case old Maria Diego got up to anything. Andy looked surprised, but not enough actually to ask me what I was up to. He was too busy yelling at Dopey for shovelling in the wrong place.

When I got to the Pebble Beach Hotel and Golf Resort that morning, it was to be greeted by Caitlin with an accusatory, 'Well, I don't know what you did to Jack Slater, but his family asked that you be assigned to watch him for the rest of their stay . . . until Sunday, actually.'

I wasn't surprised. Nor did I mind, particularly. The Paul

271

factor was troubling, of course, but now that I knew the reason behind Jack's odd behaviour, I genuinely liked the kid.

And he, it became clear, the moment I set foot inside his family's suite, was wild about me. No more lying on the floor in front of the TV for him. Jack was in his swimsuit and ready to go.

'Can you teach me the butterfly today, Suze?' he wanted to know. 'I've always wanted to know how to do the butterfly.'

'Susan,' his mother said to me, in a whispered aside, right before she ran off to her hair appointment (neither Paul nor his father were around, much to my relief, having had a seven-o'clock tee time). 'I can't thank you enough for what you've done for Jack. I don't know what you said to him yesterday, but he is like a different child. I have never seen him so happy. You know, he really is the most remarkably sensitive person. Such an imagination, too. Always thinking he's seeing . . . well, dead people. Has he mentioned this to you?'

I said nonchalantly that he had.

'Well, we've been at our wits' end. We must have had thirty different doctors look at him, and no one – *no one* – seemed able to get through to him. Then you came along, and . . .' Nancy Slater looked down at me with carefully made-up blue eyes. 'Well, I don't know how we'll ever be able to thank you, Susan.'

You could start, I thought, by calling me by my right name. But I didn't really care. I just said, 'No problem, Mrs Slater,' and went and got Jack and headed with him back to the pool.

Jack *was* like a different kid. There was no denying that. Even Sleepy, roused from his semi-permanent doze by Jack's happy splashing, asked me if that was the same boy he'd seen me with the morning before, and when I told him it was, actually looked incredulous for a second or two before going back to sleep. The things that had once frightened Jack – basically, everything – no longer seemed to bother him in the least.

And so when, after burgers at the Pool House, I suggested he and I take the hotel shuttle bus into town, he didn't even protest. He even commented that the plan 'sounded like fun'.

Fun. From Jack. Really, maybe mediating isn't my calling at all. Maybe I should be a teacher, or a child psychologist, or something. Seriously.

Jack wasn't particularly thrilled, however, when, once we got into town, we headed towards the building that houses the Carmel-by-the-Sea Historical Society. He wanted to go to the beach, but when I told him that it was to help a ghost and that we'd go to the beach afterwards, he was OK with it.

I'm not really a historical-society type of gal, but even I have to admit it was kind of cool, looking at all the old photos on the walls of the place, photos of Carmel and Salinas County a hundred years earlier, before all the strip malls and Safeways opened, when it was all just fields dotted with cypress trees, like in that book they made us read in the eighth grade, *The Red Pony*. They had some pretty cool stuff there – not much, really, from Jesse's time, but a lot from later on, like after the Civil War. Jack and I were admiring something called a stereo-viewer, which is what people used for entertainment before movies, when this untidy-looking bald man came out of his office and peered at us through glasses with lenses as thick as Coke-bottle bottoms and said, 'Yes, you wanted to see me?'

I said we wanted to see someone in charge. He said that was him, and introduced himself as Dr Clive Clemmings, PhD. So I told Dr Clive Clemmings, PhD, who I was and where I lived, and took the cigar tin from my JanSport back-pack (Kate Spade really doesn't go with pleat-front khaki shorts) and showed him the letters . . .

And he freaked out.

I mean it. He *freaked out.* He was so excited, he told the old lady at the reception desk to hold his calls (she looked up, astonished, from the romance novel she was reading; it was clear that Dr Clive Clemmings, PhD, must not get many calls) and ushered Jack and me back into his private office . . .

Where I nearly had a coronary. Because there, above Clive Clemmings's desk, was Maria de Silva's portrait, the one I had seen in that book Doc had taken out of the library.

The painter had done, I realized, an extraordinarily good job. He'd gotten it completely right, down to the artfully ringleted hair and the gold and ruby necklace round her elegantly curved neck, not to mention her snooty expression . . .

'That's her!' I cried, completely involuntarily, stabbing my finger at the painting.

Jack looked up at me as if I'd gone mental – which I suppose I momentarily had – but Clive Clemmings only glanced over his shoulder at the portrait and said, 'Yes, Maria Diego. Quite the jewel in the crown of our collection, that painting. Rescued it from being sold at a *garage sale* by one of her grandchildren, can you imagine? Down on his luck, poor old fellow. Disgraceful, when you think about it. None of the Diegos ever amounted to much, however. You know what they say about bad blood. And Felix Diego—'

Dr Clive had opened the cigar box and, using some special tweezery-looking things, unfolded the first letter. 'Oh, my,' he breathed, looking down at it.

'Yeah,' I said. 'It's from her.' I nodded up at the painting. 'Maria de Silva. It's a bunch of letters she wrote to Jesse – I mean, to Hector de Silva, her cousin, who she was supposed to marry, only he—'

'Disappeared.' Clive Clemmings stared at me. He had to be, if I guessed, in his thirties or so – despite the very wide spot of bare scalp along the top of his head – and though by no means attractive, he did not look so utterly repulsive just then as he had before. A look of total astonishment, which certainly does not become many, did wonders for him.

'My God,' he said. '*Where* did you find these?'

And so I told him again, and he got even more excited, and told us to wait in his office while he went and got something.

So we waited. Jack was very good while we did so. He only said, 'When can we go to the beach already?' twice.

When Dr Clive Clemmings, PhD, came back, he was holding a tray and a bunch of latex gloves, which he told us we had to put on if we were going to touch anything. Jack was pretty bored by that time, so he elected to go back out into the main room to play with the stereo-viewer some more. Only I donned the gloves.

But was I glad I did. Because what Clive Clemmings let me touch when I had them on was everything the historical society had collected over the years that had anything whatsoever to do with Maria de Silva.

Which was, let me tell you, quite a lot.

But the things in the collection that most interested me were a tiny painting – a miniature, Clive Clemmings said it was called – of Jesse (or Hector de Silva, as Dr Clive referred to him; apparently only Jesse's immediate family ever called him Jesse . . . his family, and me, of course) and five letters, in much better condition than the ones from the cigar box.

The miniature was perfect, like a little photograph. People could really paint back in those days, I guess. It was totally

Jesse. It captured him perfectly. He had on that look he gets when I'm telling him about some great conquest I had made at an outlet – you know, scoring a Prada handbag for fifty per cent off, or something. Like he couldn't care less.

In the painting, which was just of Jesse's head and shoulders, he was wearing something Clive Clemmings called a cravat, which was supposedly something all the guys wore back then, this big frilly white thing that wrapped round the neck a few times. It would have looked ridiculous on Dopey or Sleepy or even Clive Clemmings, in spite of his PhD.

But on Jesse, of course, it looked great.

Well, what wouldn't?

The letters were almost better than the painting, though, in a way. That's because they were all addressed to Maria de Silva . . . and signed by someone named Hector.

I pored over them, and I can't say that at the time I felt a lick of guilt about it, either. They were much more interesting than Maria's letters – although, like hers, not the least romantic. No, Jesse just wrote – very wittily, I might add – about the goings-on at his family's ranch and the funny things his sisters did. (It turns out he had five of them. Sisters, I mean. All younger, ranging in age, the year Jesse died, from sixteen to six. But had he ever mentioned this to me before? Oh, please.) There was also some stuff about local politics and how hard it was to keep good ranch hands on the job what with the gold rush on and all of them hurrying off to stake claims.

The thing was, the way Jesse wrote, you could practically hear him saying all this stuff. It was all very friendly and chatty and nice. Much better than Maria's braggy letters.

And nothing was spelled wrong, either.

As I read through Jesse's letters, Dr Clive rattled on about how now that he had Maria's letters to Hector, he was going to add them to this exhibit he was planning for the fall tourist season, an exhibit on the whole de Silva clan and their importance to the growth of Salinas County over the years.

'If only,' he said wistfully, 'there were any of them left alive. De Silvas, I mean. It would be lovely to have them as guest speakers.'

This got my attention. 'There have to be some left,' I said. 'Didn't Maria and that Diego guy have like thirty-seven kids or something?'

Clive Clemmings looked stern. As a historian – and especially a PhD – he did not seem to appreciate exaggeration of any kind.

'They had eleven children,' he corrected me. 'And they are not, strictly, de Silvas, but Diegos. The de Silva family unfortunately ran very strongly to daughters. I'm afraid Hector de Silva was the last male in the line. And of course we'll never know if he sired any male offspring. If he did, it certainly wasn't in Northern California.'

'Of course he didn't,' I said, perhaps more defensively than I ought to have. But I was peeved. Aside from the obvious sexism of the whole 'last male in the line' thing, I took issue with the guy's assumption that Jesse might have been off procreating somewhere when, in fact, he had been foully murdered. 'He was killed right in my own house!'

Clive Clemmings looked at me with raised eyebrows. It was only then that I realized what I had said.

'Hector de Silva,' Dr Clive said, sounding a lot like Sister Ernestine when we grew restless during the *begats* in Religion class, 'disappeared shortly before his wedding to his cousin Maria and was never heard from again.'

I couldn't very well sit there and go, *Yeah, but his ghost lives in my bedroom, and he told me* . . .

Instead, I said, 'I thought the, um, perception was that

Maria had her boyfriend, that Diego dude, kill Hector so she didn't have to marry him.'

Clive Clemmings looked annoyed. 'That is only a theory put forward by my grandfather, Colonel Harold Clemmings, who wrote—'

'*My Monterey*,' I finished for him. 'Yeah, that's what I meant. That guy's your grandfather?'

'Yes,' Dr Clive said, but he didn't look too happy about it. 'He passed away a good many years ago. And I can't say that I agree with his theory, Miss, er, Ackerman.' I had donated Maria's letters in my stepfather's name, so Dr Clive, sexist thing that he was, assumed that that was my name, too. 'Nor can I say that his book sold at all well. My grandfather was extremely interested in the history of his community, but he was not an educated man, like myself. He did not possess even a BA, let alone a PhD. It has always been my belief – not to mention that of most local historians, with the sole exception of my grandfather – that young Mr de Silva developed what is commonly referred to as "cold feet" –' Dr Clive made little quotation marks in the air with his fingers '– a few days before the wedding and, unable to face his family's embarrassment over his jilting the young woman in such a manner, went off in search of a claim of his own, perhaps near San Francisco . . .'

It's amazing, but for a moment I actually envisioned sinking those tweezery things Clive Clemmings had made me use to turn the pages of Jesse's letters straight into his eyes. If I could have got them past the lenses of those goobery glasses, that is.

Instead, I pulled myself together and said, with all the dignity I could muster while sitting there in a pair of khaki shorts with pleats down the front, 'And do you really believe, in your heart of hearts, Clive, that the person who wrote these letters would do something like that? Go away without a word to his family? To his little sisters, whom he clearly loved, and about whom he wrote so affectionately? Do you really think that the reason these letters turned up in my backyard is because *he* buried them there? Or do you find it beyond the realm of possibility that the reason they turned up there is because *he's* buried there somewhere, and if my stepfather digs deep enough, he just might find him?'

My voice had risen shrilly. I supposed I was getting a little hysterical over the whole thing. So sue me.

'Will *that* make you see that your grandfather was a *hundred per cent right*?' I shrieked. 'When my stepfather finds Hector de Silva's *rotting corpse*?'

Clive Clemmings looked more astonished than ever before. 'My dear Miss Ackerman!' he cried.

I think he said this because he'd realized, at the exact same moment as I had, that I was crying.

Which was actually pretty strange, because I am not a crier. I mean, yeah, sure, I cry when I bang my head on one of the kitchen-cabinet doors or see one of those drippy Kodak commercials or whatever. But I don't, you know, go around weeping at the drop of a hat.

But there I was, sitting in the office of Dr Clive Clemmings, PhD, bawling my eyes out. Good going, Suze. Real professional. Way to show Jack how to mediate.

'Well,' I said in a shaky voice as I stripped off my latex gloves and stood up, 'allow me to assure you, Clive, that you are very, very wrong. Jesse – I mean Hector – would never do something like that. That might be what *she* wants you to believe –' I nodded towards the painting above our heads, the sight of which I was now beginning to hate with a sort of passion – 'but it isn't the truth. Jesse – I mean, Hector – isn't . . . *wasn't* like that. If he'd gotten "cold feet" like you say –' I made the same stupid quotation marks in the air '– then he'd have called the whole thing off. And, yeah, his family might have been embarrassed, but they'd have forgiven him, because they clearly loved him as much as he loved them, and—'

But then I couldn't talk any more, because I was crying so hard. It was maddening. I couldn't believe it. Crying. *Crying* in front of this clown.

So instead I turned around and stormed out of the room.

Not very dignified, I guess, considering that the last thing Dr Clive Clemmings, PhD, saw of me was my butt, which must have looked enormous in those stupid shorts.

But I got the point across.

I think.

Of course, in the end, it turned out not to matter. But at the time, I had no way of knowing that.

And neither, unfortunately, did poor Dr Clive Clemmings, PhD.

Five

God, I hate crying. It's so humiliating. And I swear I hardly ever do it.

I guess, though, that the stress of being assaulted in the dead of night by the knife-wielding ex-girlfriend of the guy I love finally got to me. I pretty much didn't stop crying until Jack, in desperation, bought me a Yoo-hoo from Jimmy's Quik-Mart, on our way down to the beach.

That and a Butterfinger bar soon had me feeling like myself again, and it wasn't long before Jack and I were frolicking in the waves, making fun of the tourists, and placing penny bets on which surfer would be knocked off his board first. We had such a good time that it wasn't until the sun started setting that I realized I had to get Jack back to the hotel.

Not that anybody had missed us, we discovered when we got there. As I dropped Jack off at his family's suite, his mother popped her head in from the terrace, where she and Dr Rick were enjoying cocktails, and said, 'Oh, it's you, is it, Jack? Hurry and change for dinner, will you? We're meeting the Robertsons. Thank you, Susan, and see you in the morning.'

I waved and left, relieved that I'd managed to avoid Paul. After my unexpectedly traumatic afternoon, I did not think I could handle a confrontation with Mr Tennis Whites.

But my relief turned out to be precipitous, since, as I was sitting in the front seat of the Land Rover, waiting for Sleepy to tear himself away from Caitlin, who seemed to have something terribly urgent to discuss with him just as we were leaving, someone tapped on my rolled-up window. I looked around, and there was Paul, wearing a *tie*, of all things, and a dark blue sports jacket.

I pushed the button that rolled the window down.

'Um,' I said. 'Hi.'

'Hi,' he said. He was smiling pleasantly. The last of the day's sunlight picked up the gold highlights in his brown curls. He really was, I had to admit, good-looking. Kelly Prescott would have eaten him up with a spoon. 'I suppose you already have plans for tonight,' he said.

I didn't, of course, but I replied quickly, 'Yes.'

'I figured.' His smile was still pleasant. 'What about tomorrow night?'

Look, I know I'm a freak, all right? You don't have to tell me. There I was, and this totally hot, totally nice guy was asking me out, and all I could think about was a guy who, let's face it, is dead. All right? *Jesse is dead*. It's stupid – stupid, stupid, *stupid* – of me to turn down a date with a live guy when the only other guy I have in my life is dead.

But that's exactly what I did. I went, Gee, sorry, Paul. I have plans tomorrow night, too.'

I didn't even care if it sounded like I was lying. That's how screwed up I am. I just could not drum up the slightest bit of interest.

But I guess that was a pretty big mistake. I guess Mr Paul Slater isn't used to girls turning down his invitations to dinner, or whatever. Because he went, no longer smiling pleasantly – or at all, actually: 'Well, that's too bad. It's especially too bad considering the fact that now I guess I'm going to have to tell your supervisor about how you took my little brother off hotel property today without my parents' permission.'

I just stared at him through the open window. I couldn't even figure out what he was talking about, at first. Then I remembered the shuttle bus, and the historical society, and the beach.

I almost burst out laughing. Seriously. I mean, if Paul Slater thought my getting in trouble for taking a kid off hotel property without his parents' permission was the worst thing that could happen to me – that had even happened to me *today* – he was way, way off base. For crying out loud, a woman who'd been been dead for nearly a hundred years had held a knife to my throat in my own bedroom, not twenty-four hours earlier. Did he really think I was going to care if *Caitlin* issued me a *reprimand*?

'Go ahead,' I said. 'And when you tell her, be sure to mention that for the first time in his life, your brother actually had a good time.'

I hit the button to roll up the window – I mean, really, what was this guy's damage? – but Paul stuck his hand through it and rested his fingers on the glass. I let go of the button. I mean, I just wanted him to go away, not get maimed for life.

'Yeah,' Paul said. 'I've been meaning to ask you about that. Jack tells me that you told him he's a medium.'

'Mediator,' I corrected him before I could stop myself. And so much for Jack keeping the whole thing a secret, like I'd advised him to. When was this kid going to learn that going around telling people he can talk to ghosts wasn't going to endear him to anyone?

'Whatever,' Paul said. 'I guess you must think making fun of someone who has a mental disorder is pretty amusing.'

I couldn't believe it. I really couldn't. It was like something out of a TV show. Not on The WB, though, or even Fox. It was totally PAX.

'I do not think your brother has a mental disorder,' I said.

'Oh, don't you?' Paul looked all knowing. 'He tells you he sees dead people, and you think he's playing with a full deck?'

I shook my head. 'Jack might be able to see dead people, Paul. You don't know. I mean, you can't prove he *can't* see dead people.'

Oh, brilliant argument, Suze. Where the hell was Sleepy? Come on, already. Get me out of here.

'Suze,' Paul said, looking at me all searchingly. 'Please. Dead people? You really believe that? You really believe my brother can see – can speak to – the dead?'

'I've heard of weirder things,' I said. I glanced over at Sleepy. Caitlin was smiling up at him and shaking her blonde Jennifer Aniston mane all over the place. Oh my God, enough with the flirting already. Just ask him out and get it over with so I can go . . .

'Yeah, well, you shouldn't be encouraging him,' Paul said. 'It's about the worst thing you can do, according to his doctors.'

'Yeah?' I was getting kind of pissed off now. I mean, what did Paul Slater know about anything, anyway? Just because his father's a brain surgeon or whatever who can afford a week at the Pebble Beach Hotel and Golf Resort doesn't make him right all the time. 'Well, Jack seems fine to me. You might even learn a thing or two from him, Paul. At least he has an open mind.'

Paul just shook his head in disbelief. 'What are you saying, Suze? That *you* believe in ghosts?'

Finally, *finally*, Sleepy said goodbye to Caitlin and turned back towards the car.

'Yeah,' I said. 'I do. What about you, Paul?'

Paul just blinked at me. 'What about me?'

'Do you believe?'

His curled upper lip was all the reply I needed. Not caring if I severed his hand, I hit the window button. Paul pulled his fingers out just in time. I guess he thought I wasn't the finger-severing type.

Is he ever wrong.

Why are boys so difficult? I mean, really. When they aren't drinking directly out of the carton or leaving the toilet seat up, they are getting all offended because you won't go out with them and threatening to rat you out to your supervisor. Hasn't it occurred to any of them that this is not the way to our hearts?

And the problem is, they are just going to keep on doing it, as long as stupid girls like Kelly Prescott keep agreeing to go out with them anyway, in spite of their defects.

I sulked all the way home. Even Sleepy noticed.

'What's with you?' he wanted to know.

'That stupid Paul Slater's mad because I won't go out with him,' I said, even though I generally make it a policy not to share my personal problems with any of my stepbrothers except, occasionally, Doc, and then only because his IQ is so much higher than mine. 'He says he's going to tell Caitlin I took his little brother off hotel property without his parents' permission, which I did, but only to take him to the beach.' And to the Carmel-by-the-Sea Historical Society. But I didn't mention that.

Sleepy went, 'No kidding? That's pretty low. Well, don't worry about it. I'll smooth things over with Caitlin for you, if you want.'

I was shocked. I had only mentioned it because I was feeling so down in the dumps. I hadn't actually expected Sleepy to *help*, or anything.

'Really? You really will?'

'Sure,' Sleepy said with a shrug. 'I'm seeing her tonight after I get off from delivering.' Sleepy lifeguards by day and delivers pizzas by night. Originally he was saving up for a Camaro. Now he is saving up to get his own apartment, since there are no dorms at the community college he'll be attending and Andy says he isn't going to pay for Sleepy to have his own place unless he pulls his grades up.

I couldn't believe it. I said, 'Thanks,' in a stunned way.

'What's wrong with that Slater guy, anyway?' Sleepy wanted to know. 'I thought he'd be just your type. You know, smart and all.'

'Nothing's wrong with him,' I grumbled, fiddling with my seat belt. 'I just . . . I sort of like someone else.'

Sleepy lifted up his eyebrows behind his Ray-Bans. 'Oh? Anyone I know?'

I said shortly, 'No.'

'I don't know, Suze,' he said. 'Try me. Between the pizza gig and school, I know most everybody.'

'You definitely,' I said, 'do not know this guy.'

Sleepy frowned. 'Why? Is he some kind of gangbanger?'

I rolled my eyes. Sleepy has been convinced since almost the day we first met that I am in a gang. Seriously. As if gang members wear Stila. I am so sure.

'Does he live in the Valley?' Sleepy wanted to know. 'Suze, I'm telling you right now, if I find out you're going out with a gangbanger from the Valley—'

'God,' I yelled. 'Would you stop? He isn't a gangbanger, and neither am I! And he doesn't live in the Valley. You don't know him, OK? Just forget we had this conversation.'

See? See what I mean? See why things will never, ever

work out between me and Jesse? Because I can't pull him out and go, *Here he is, this is the guy I like, and he isn't a gangbanger, and he doesn't live in the Valley.*

I have just got to learn to keep my mouth shut, same as Jack.

When we got home, we were informed that dinner wasn't ready yet. That was because Andy was waist deep in the hole he and Dopey had made in the backyard. I went out and looked at it for a while, chewing on my thumbnail. It was very creepy, looking into that hole. Almost as creepy as the prospect of going to bed in a few hours, knowing that Maria was probably going to show up again.

And that, seeing as how I hadn't done a single thing she'd asked, this time she'd probably cut up a lot more than just my gums.

It was around then that the phone rang. It was my friend CeeCee, wanting to know if I cared to join her and Adam McTavish at the Coffee Clutch to drink iced tea and talk bad about everyone we know. I said yes right away because I hadn't heard from either of them in so long. CeeCee was doing a summer internship at the *Carmel Pine Cone* (the name of the local newspaper; can you imagine?) and Adam had been at his grandparents' house in Martha's Vineyard for most of the summer. The minute I heard her voice I realized how much I'd missed CeeCee, and how great it would be to tell her about vile Paul Slater and his tricks.

But then, of course, I realized I'd have to tell her the part about Paul's little brother, and how he really can speak to the dead, or the story wouldn't have half as much pathos, and the fact is, CeeCee is not the type who believes in ghosts, or anything, for that matter, that she can't see with her own two eyes, which makes the fact that she goes to Catholic school problematic, what with Sister Ernestine urging us all the time about Faith and the Holy Spirit.

But whatever. It was better than standing around at home, looking at a giant hole.

I hurried upstairs and slipped out of my uniform and into one of the cute J. Crew slip dresses I'd ordered and never gotten a chance to wear since I've spent the whole summer in my heinous khaki shorts. No sign of Jesse, but that was just as well, as I wouldn't have known what to say to him anyway. I felt totally guilty for having read his letters, even though at the same time I was glad I had done it, because knowing about his sisters and his problems on the ranch and all made me feel closer to him in a way.

Only it was a fake kind of close because he didn't know I knew. And if he had wanted me to know, don't you think he would have told me? But he never wants to talk about himself. Instead, he always wants to talk about things like the rise of the Third Reich and how could we as a country have possibly sat around and let six million Jews get gassed before doing anything about it?

You know. Things like that.

Actually, some of the things Jesse wants to discuss are very hard to explain. I'd have much rather talked about his sisters. For instance, had he found living with five girls as trying as I find living with three boys? I would imagine probably not, given the reverse toilet-seat situation. Did they even have toilets back then? Or did they just go in those nasty outhouses, like on *Little House on the Prairie*?

God, no wonder Maria was in such a bad mood.

Well, that and the whole being dead thing.

Anyway, Mom and Andy let me go out to eat with my friends because there was nothing for dinner. Family meals really weren't the same, anyway, without Doc. I was surprised to find that I actually missed him and couldn't wait for him to come home. He was the only one of my step-brothers who did not enrage me on any sort of regular basis.

Even though I couldn't really tell CeeCee about Paul, I did have a good time. It was good to see her, and Adam, who, of all the boys I know, acts the least like one, though he isn't gay or anything, and actually takes great umbrage if you suggest it. So does CeeCee, who has been in love with Adam since like forever. I had great hopes that Adam might return her feelings, but I could tell things had kind of cooled off – at least on his part – since he'd been away.

As soon as he got up to go to the bathroom, I asked CeeCee what was up with that, and she launched into this whole thing about how she thinks Adam met someone in Martha's Vineyard. I have to say, it was kind of nice listening to someone else complain for a while. I mean, my life pretty much sucks and all, but at least I know Jesse's not screwing around on me with some girl in Martha's Vineyard.

At least, I don't think so. Who knows where he goes when he isn't hanging around my room? It could be Martha's Vineyard, after all.

See? See how this relationship is never going to work?

Anyway, CeeCee and Adam and I hadn't seen each other in a long time, so there were quite a few people we needed to say bad things about, primarily Kelly Prescott, so when I got home, it was almost eleven . . . late for me, what with my having to be at work by eight.

Still, I was glad I'd gone out, as it had taken my mind off what I suspected awaited me in a few hours: another visit from the ravishing Mrs Diego.

But as I was washing my hair before bed, it occurred to me that there was no reason why I had to make things easy for Miss Maria. I mean, why should I be victimized in my own bed?

No reason. No reason at all. I did not have to put up with that kind of nonsense. Because that's what it was. Nonsense.

Well, sort of scary nonsense, but still nonsense, all the same.

So when I turned out the light that night, it was with a definite sense of satisfaction. I was, I felt, well protected from anything Maria might pull. I had with me beneath the covers a veritable arsenal of weapons, including an axe, a hammer, and something I could not identify that I had taken from Andy's workshop, but which had evil-looking spikes on it. Furthermore, I had Max the dog with me. He would, I knew, awaken me as soon as anything otherworldly showed up, being extremely sensitive to such things.

And, oh, yes, I slept in Doc's room.

I know. I know. Cowardly in the extreme. But why should I have stayed in my own bed and waited for her, like a lame duck, when I could sleep in Doc's bed and maybe throw her off the scent? I mean, it wasn't like I was looking for a fight or anything. Well, except for the whole not-doing-a-thing-she-said thing. I guess that was sort of indicative of looking for a fight. But not, you know, actively.

Because, I have to tell you, while ordinarily I might have gone out looking for Maria de Silva's grave, so I could just, you know, have it out with her then and there, this was a little different. Because of Jesse. Don't ask me why, but I just didn't think I had it in me to go and rough up his ex, the way I would have if she didn't have this connection to him. I can't say I'm really used to waiting for ghosts to come to me . . .

But this. This was different.

Anyway, I had just snuggled down between Doc's sheets (freshly laundered – I wasn't taking any chances. I don't know what goes on in the beds of twelve-year-old boys, and frankly, I don't want to know) and was blinking in the darkness at the odd things Doc has hanging from his ceiling, a model of the solar system and all of that, when Max started to growl.

He did it so low that at first I didn't hear it. But since I had pulled him into bed with me (not that there was a lot of room, what with the axe and the hammer and the spiky thing) I could *feel* the growl reverberating through his big canine chest.

Then it got louder, and the hair on Max's back started standing up. That's when I knew we were in for either an earthquake or a nocturnal visitation from the former belle of Salinas County.

I sat up, grabbing the spiky thing and holding it like a baseball bat, looking around wildly while saying to Max in a low voice, 'Good boy. It's OK, boy. Everything's going to be all right, boy,' and telling myself that I believed it.

That's when someone materialized in front of me. And I swung the spiky thing as I hard as I could.

Six

'Susannah!' Jesse cried from where he'd leaped to avoid being struck. 'What are you *doing*?'

I nearly dropped the spiky thing, I was so relieved it was him.

Max went wild with whining and growling. The poor thing was clearly having some sort of doggie nervous breakdown. In order not to risk his waking everyone in the house, and then having to explain why I was sleeping in my stepbrother's bed with a bunch of Andy's tools, I let him out of the room. As I did so, Jesse took the spiky thing from me and looked down at it curiously.

'Susannah,' he said when I'd closed the door again, 'why are you sleeping in David's room, armed with a pick?'

I raised my eyebrows, looking way more surprised than the occasion warranted. 'Is *that* what that is? I was wondering.'

Jesse just shook his head at me. 'Susannah,' he said, 'tell me what is going on. Now.'

'Nothing,' I said, my voice sounding too squeaky and high-pitched even to my own ears. I hurried forward and got back into Doc's bed, stubbing my toe on the hammer but not saying anything, since I didn't want Jesse to know it was there. Finding me in my stepbrother's bed with a pick was one thing. Finding me in my stepbrother's bed with a pick, an axe, and a hammer was something else entirely.

'Susannah.' Jesse sounded really mad, and he doesn't get mad all that often. Except, of course, when he finds me sucking face with strange boys in the driveway, that is. 'Is that an *axe*?'

Damn! I shoved it back down beneath the covers. 'I can explain,' I said.

He leaned the pick against the side of the bed and folded his arms across his chest. 'I'd like to hear it,' he said.

'Well.' I took a deep breath. 'It's like this.'

And then I couldn't think of any way to explain it, other than the truth.

And I couldn't tell him that.

Jesse must have read in my face the fact that I was trying to think up a lie, since he suddenly unfolded his arms and leaned forward, placing one hand on either side of the headboard behind me, and sort of capturing me between his arms, though he wasn't actually touching me. This was very unnerving and caused me to slump down very low against Doc's pillows.

But even that didn't really do any good, since Jesse's face was still only about six inches from mine.

'Susannah,' he said. He was *really* mad now. Fed up, even, you might say. 'What is happening here? Last night I could swear I felt . . . a presence in your room. And then tonight you are sleeping in here, with picks and axes? What is it that you aren't telling me? And why? Why can't you tell me?'

I had sunk down as low as I could, but there was no escaping Jesse's angry face, unless I threw the sheet up over my head. And that, of course, wouldn't be at all dignified.

'Look,' I said as reasonably as I could, considering that

there was a hammer digging into my foot. 'It's not that I don't want to tell you. It's just that I'm afraid that if I do . . .'

And then, don't ask me how, the whole thing just came tumbling out. Really. It was incredible. It was like he'd pushed a button on my forehead that said Information Please, and out it all came.

I told him everything, about the letters, the trip to the historical society, everything, finishing up with, 'And the thing is, I didn't want you to know, because if your body really is buried out there, and they find it, well, that means that there's no reason for you to hang around here any more, and I know it's selfish, but I would really miss you, so I was hoping if I didn't mention it you wouldn't find out and everything could just go on like normal.'

But Jesse didn't have at all the sort of reaction to this information that I thought he would. He didn't sweep me into his arms and kiss me passionately like in the movies, or even call me *querida*, whatever it means, and stroke my hair, which was wet from my shower.

Instead, he just started laughing.

Which I didn't really appreciate. I mean, after everything I had gone through for him in the past twenty-four hours, you would think he would show a bit more gratitude than to sit there and laugh. Especially when my life might very well be in mortal peril.

I mentioned this to him, but that only made him laugh harder.

Finally, when he was through laughing – which didn't happen until I'd pulled the hammer out from under the covers, something that sent him into fresh peals, but what was I supposed to do? It was still digging into me – he did reach out and sort of ruffle my hair, but there wasn't anything the least bit romantic about it, since I had put Kiehl's leave-in conditioner on it and I'm pretty sure it got on his fingers.

That just made me madder at him than ever, even though technically it wasn't his fault. So I took the axe out from beneath the sheets, too, and then pulled the covers up over my head and rolled over and wouldn't talk to him any more. Or look at him. Very mature, I know, but I was peeved.

'Susannah,' he said in a voice that was a little hoarse from all the laughing he'd been doing. I felt like punching him. I really did. 'Don't be like that. I'm sorry. I'm sorry I laughed. It's just that I didn't understand a word you just said, you were talking so fast. And then when you pulled out that hammer—'

'Go away,' I said.

'Come on, Susannah,' Jesse said in his silkiest, most persuasive voice – which he was using on purpose to make me go all squishy. Except that it wasn't going to work this time. 'Let go of the sheet.'

'No,' I said, clutching the sheet tighter as he plucked at it. 'I said go away.'

'No, I won't go away. Sit up. I want to talk to you seriously now, but how can I do that when you won't look at me? Turn around.'

'No,' I said. I was really mad. I mean, you would have been, too. That Maria was one scary individual. And he'd been going to marry her! Well, a hundred and fifty years ago, anyway. Had he even *known* her? Known that she wasn't anything like the girl who'd written those idiotic letters to him? What had he been thinking, anyway?

'Why don't you just go hang out with Maria,' I suggested to him acidly. 'Maybe you two could sit around and sharpen her knives together and have some more laughs at my expense. Ha ha, you could say. That mediator is so funny.'

295

'Maria?' Jesse pulled on the sheet some more. 'What are you talking about, knives?'

OK. So I hadn't been totally up front with him. I hadn't told him the whole story. Yeah, the part about the letters and the historical society and the hole and all. But the part about Maria showing up with the knife – the reason, in fact, that I was sleeping in Doc's bed with a bunch of tools? Hadn't mentioned that part.

Because I'd known how he was going to react. Exactly the way he did.

'Maria and knives?' he echoed. 'No. No.'

That did it. I rolled over and said to him, very sarcastically, 'Oh, OK, Jesse. So that knife she held to my throat last night, that must have been an *imaginary* knife. And I must have *imagined* it when she threatened to kill me, too.'

I started to roll back over in a huff, but this time he caught me before I turned all the way and swung me back around to face him. He wasn't, I saw with some satisfaction, laughing now. Or even smiling.

'A knife?' He was looking down at me like he wasn't sure he'd heard me right. 'Maria was here? With a knife? Why?'

'You tell me,' I said, even though I knew the answer perfectly well. 'Someone's been dead and gone for as long as she has, it would have to take something pretty big to bring her back.'

Jesse just stared down at me with those dark, liquid eyes of his. If he knew anything, he wasn't saying. Not just yet.

'She – she tried to hurt you?'

I nodded, and had the satisfaction of feeling his grip on my shoulders tighten.

'Yes,' I said. 'And she held it right here –' I pointed to my jugular – 'and she said if I didn't tell Andy to stop digging, she was going to k—'

Kill me, was what I was going to say, but I didn't get a chance to, because Jesse snatched me up – really, snatched, that's the only way to describe it – and held on to me very tightly for someone who had thought the whole thing a big funny joke just a few seconds before.

This was, I must say, extremely gratifying. It got even more gratifying when Jesse said some stuff – though I didn't know what it was, because it was in Spanish – into my wet hair.

But that death grip (excuse the pun) he had me in didn't need any translating: he was scared. Scared for *me*.

'It was a really *large* knife,' I said, enjoying the feel of his big strong shoulder beneath my cheek. I could totally get used to this. 'And very pointy.'

'*Querida*,' he said. OK, that word I understood. Well, sort of. He kissed the top of my head.

This was good. This was *very* good. I decided to go in for the kill.

'And then,' I said, doing a very good imitation of sounding like I was crying, or at least, was pretty close to doing so, 'she put her hand over my face to keep me from screaming, and one of her rings cut me and made my mouth all bloody.'

Oops. This one did not have the desired effect. I should probably not have brought up my bloody mouth, since instead of kissing me there, which was what I'd been aiming for, he pulled me away from him so he could look down into my face.

'Susannah, why didn't you tell me any of this last night?' He looked genuinely baffled. 'I asked you if something was wrong, and you never said a word.'

Hello? Hadn't he heard anything I just said?

'Because.' I was speaking through gritted teeth, but you would have, too, if the man of your dreams was holding you in his arms and all he wanted to do was talk. And about his ex-girlfriend's attempt to murder you, no less.

'It obviously has something to do with why you're here,' I said. 'Why you're still here, I mean, in this house, and why you've been here so long. Jesse, don't you see? If they find your body, that proves you were murdered, and that means Colonel Clemmings was right.'

Jesse's bewilderment seemed to increase, rather than lessen, thanks to this explanation.

'Colonel who?' he said.

'Colonel Clemmings,' I said. 'Author of *My Monterey*. His theory of why you disappeared is not that you got cold feet about marrying Maria and went off to San Francisco to stake a claim, but that that Diego guy killed you so he could marry Maria himself. And if they find your body, Jesse, that will prove you were murdered. And the most likely suspects are, of course, Maria and that Diego dude.'

But instead of being dazzled by my excellent sleuthing skills, Jesse asked, in a shocked voice, 'How do you know about him? About Diego?'

'I told you.' God, this was irritating. When were we going to get to the kissing? 'It's from a book Doc got out of the library. *My Monterey*, by Colonel Harold Clemmings.'

'But Doc – I mean, David – is at camp, I thought.'

I said, frustratedly, 'This was a long time ago. When I first got here. Last January.'

Jesse didn't let go of me or anything, but he had an extremely odd look on his face.

'Are you saying that you've known about this . . . how I died . . . all along?'

'Yes,' I said, a little defensively. I was getting the feeling that maybe he thought I'd done something wrong, prying into his death. 'But, Jesse, that's my job. That's what mediators *do*. I can't help it.'

'Why did you keep asking me about how I died, then,' he demanded, 'if you already knew?'

I said, still on the defensive side, 'Well, I didn't know. Not for sure. I still don't. But Jesse—' I wanted to make sure he understood this part, so I pulled back (and he unfortunately let go of me, but what could I do?) and sat up on my heels and said, very slowly and carefully, 'If they find your body out there, not only is Maria going to be really mad, but you . . . you're going to move on. You know? From here. Because that's what's been holding you back, Jesse. The mystery of what happened to you. Once your body is found, though, that mystery will be solved. And you'll go. And that's why I couldn't tell you, you see? Because I don't want you to go. Because I l—'

Oh my God, I almost said it. I can't even tell you how close I came to saying it. I got out the L and then the O just seemed to follow.

But at the last minute I was able to save it. I turned it to '—*like* having you around and I would really hate not seeing you any more.'

Swift, huh? That was a close one.

Because one thing I know for sure about guys, along with their inability to use a glass and lower the toilet seat and refill ice trays once they are empty: they really cannot handle the L word. I mean, it says so in just about every article I've ever read.

And you have to figure this is true of all guys, even guys who were born a hundred and fifty years ago.

And I guess my not using the L word paid off, since Jesse reached out and touched my cheek with his fingertips – just like he had done that day in the hospital.

'Susannah,' he said. 'Finding my body is not going to change anything.'

'Um,' I said. 'Excuse me, Jesse, but I think I know what I'm talking about. I've been a mediator for sixteen years.'

'Susannah,' he said. 'I have been dead for a hundred and fifty years. I think I know what *I* am talking about. And I can assure you, this mystery about my death you speak of . . . that is not why I, as you put it, am hanging around here.'

A funny thing happened then. Just like in Clive Clemmings's office, earlier that day, I just started crying. Really. Just like that.

Oh, I wasn't sobbing like a baby or anything, but my eyes filled up with tears and I got that bad prickly feeling behind my nose, and my throat started to hurt. It was weird, because I'd just, you know, been trying to *act* as if I were crying, and then all of a sudden, I really was.

'Jesse,' I said in this horrible sniffly kind of voice (acting like you're going to cry is way preferable to actually crying, as there is much less mucus involved), 'I'm sorry, but that's just not possible. I mean, I *know*. I've done this a hundred times. When they find your body out there, that is it. You're gone.'

'Susannah,' he said again. And this time he didn't just touch my cheek. He reached up and cupped the side of my face with one hand . . .

Although the romantic effect was somewhat ruined by the fact that he was half laughing at me. To give him credit, though, he looked as if he were trying just as hard not to laugh as I was trying not to cry.

'I promise you, Susannah,' he said, with a lot of pauses between the words to give them emphasis, 'that I am not going anywhere, whether or not your stepfather finds my body in the backyard. All right?'

I didn't believe him, of course. I wanted to and all, but the truth is, he didn't know what he was talking about.

What could I do, though? I had no choice but to be brave about it. I mean, I couldn't very well just sit there and cry my eyes out over it. What kind of fool would I seem then?

So I said, unfortunately in a very mucusy manner, since by that time the tears were sort of spilling out, 'Really? You promise?'

Jesse grinned and let go of my face. Then he reached into his pocket and pulled out a small, lace-trimmed thing I recognized. Maria de Silva's handkerchief. He'd used it before to bind up various cuts and scrapes I'd sustained in the line of mediation duty. Now he used it to wipe my tears.

'I swear,' he said, laughing. But just a little.

In the end, he persuaded me to come back to my own bed. He said he'd make sure his ex-girlfriend didn't come after me in the night. Only he didn't call her his ex-girlfriend. He just called her Maria. I still wanted to ask him what he'd been thinking, going out with a ferret-faced ice bitch like her, but there never really seemed to be a right moment.

Is there ever a right moment to ask someone why they were going to marry the person who had had them killed?

Probably not.

I don't know how Jesse thought he was going to stop Maria if she came back. True, he had been dead a lot longer than she had, so he had had a little more practice at the whole ghost thing. It seemed pretty likely, in fact, that Maria's haunting of me was her first and only visit back to this world from whatever spiritual plane she'd inhabited since her death. The longer someone has been a ghost, the more powerful they tend to be.

Unless, of course, like Maria, they happened to be filled with rage.

But Jesse and I had, together, fought ghosts every bit as angry as Maria, and won. We would win this time, too, I knew, so long as we stuck together.

It was definitely strange going to bed knowing someone was going to be sitting there, watching me sleep. But after I got used to the idea, it was sort of nice, knowing he was there with Spike on the daybed, reading a book he'd found in Doc's room called *A Thousand Years* by the light of his own spectral glow. It would have been more romantic if he'd just sat there gazing longingly at my face, but beggars can't be choosers, and how many other girls do you know who have boys perfectly willing to sit in their bedrooms and watch for evil trespassers all night? I bet you can't even name one.

I suppose eventually I must have fallen asleep, since when I opened my eyes again it was morning, and Jesse was still there. He had finished *A Thousand Years* and had moved on to a book from one of my shelves called *Bridges of Madison County*, which he seemed to find excruciatingly amusing, although he was trying not to laugh loud enough to wake me.

God, how embarrassing.

I didn't realize then that it was the last time I'd ever see him.

Seven

My day pretty much went downhill from there.

I guess while Maria wasn't that interested in renewing her acquaintance with her ex, she was still plenty interested in torturing me. I got my first inkling of this when I opened the refrigerator and pulled out the brand-new carton of orange juice someone had bought to replace the one finished off by Dopey and Sleepy the day before.

I had just opened it when Dopey stomped in, snatched the carton from me, and lifted it to his lips.

I started to go, 'Hey!' in an irritated voice, but the word soon turned into a shriek of disgust and terror when what poured into my stepbrother's mouth was not juice, but bugs.

Hundreds of bugs. Thousands of bugs. *Live* bugs, wriggling and crawling and falling from his open mouth.

Dopey realized what was happening about a split second after I did. He threw the carton down and ran to the sink, spitting out as many of the black beetles that had fallen into his mouth as he could. Meanwhile, they were still swarming over the sides of the carton on to the floor.

I don't know how I summoned the inner strength to do what I did next. If there's one thing I hate, it's bugs. Next to poison oak, it is one of the main reasons I spend so little time in the great outdoors. I mean, I do not mind the odd ant drowning in a pool or a butterfly landing on my shoulder, but show me a mosquito or, God forbid, a cockroach, and I am out the door.

Still, despite my near crippling fear of anything smaller than a peanut, I picked up that carton and poured its contents down the sink, then, quicker than you can say Raid, flicked on the disposal.

'Ohmygawd!' Dopey was yelling, as he continued to spit into the sink. 'Ohmyfreakingawd.'

Only he didn't say freaking. Under the circumstances, I didn't blame him.

Our shrieking had brought Sleepy and my stepfather into the kitchen. They just stood there staring at the hundreds of black beetles that had escaped death by the kitchen drain and were scurrying around the terracotta tiles. At least until I yelled, 'Step on them!'

Then we all started stomping on as many of the disgusting things as we could.

When we were through, only a couple ended up getting away, the ones that had the sense to make for the crack beneath the fridge, and one or two that made it all the way to the open sliding glass doors to the deck. It had been arduous, disgusting work, and we all stood around panting . . . except for Dopey, who, with a groan, rushed off into the bathroom, presumably to rinse with Listerine, or maybe to check for any antennas that might have gotten caught between his teeth.

'Well,' Andy said, when I explained what had happened. 'That's the last time I buy organic.'

Which was kind of funny, in a sick way. Except that I happened to know that organic or frozen from concentrate, it wouldn't have made any difference: a poltergeist had been at work.

Andy looked at the mess on the floor and said in a sort of dazed voice, 'We have to get this cleaned up before your mother gets home.'

He had that right. You think I've got a thing about bugs? You should see my mother. We are neither of us what you would call nature lovers.

We threw ourselves into our work, scrubbing and scouring bug guts off the tiles, while I made subtle suggestions that we order in for all our meals, not just supper, for the time being. I wasn't sure if Maria had gotten her hands on any other foodstuffs, but I suspected nothing in the pantry or refrigerator was going to be safe.

Andy was only too willing to go along with this, blathering on about how insect infestations can destroy entire crops, and how many homes he'd worked on had been destroyed by termites, and how important it was to have your house regularly fumigated.

But fumigation, I wanted to say to him, doesn't do any good when the bugs are the result of a vengeful ghost.

But of course I didn't mention this. I highly doubt he would have understood what I was talking about. Andy doesn't believe in ghosts.

Must be nice to have that luxury.

When Sleepy and I finally got to work, it appeared briefly that things were looking up, since we did not even get in trouble for being late. This was, of course, on account of Sleepy having Caitlin so firmly in his thrall. So you see, there are *some* advantages to having stepbrothers.

There did not even seem to have been a complaint from the Slaters about my having taken Jack off hotel property without their permission, since I was told to go straight to their suite. This, I thought to myself as I made my way down the thickly carpeted hotel corridors to their rooms, really is too good to be true, and just goes to show that behind every cloud is a slice of clear blue sky.

At least, that's what I was thinking as I knocked on their door. When it swung open, however, to reveal not just Jack, but both Slater brothers dressed in swimwear, I began to have my doubts.

Jack pounced on me like a kitten on a ball of yarn.

'Guess what?' he cried. 'Paul's not playing golf or tennis or anything today. He wants to spend the whole day with *us*. Isn't that great?'

'Um,' I said.

'Yeah, Suze,' Paul said. He had on long baggy swimtrunks (proving that it could have been worse: he could have been wearing one of those micro Speedos) and a towel wrapped round his neck and nothing else, except a smirk. 'Isn't that great?'

'Um,' I said. 'Yeah. Great.'

Dr and Mrs Slater scooted past us in their golf clothes. 'You kids have fun now,' Nancy called. 'Suze, we've got lessons all day. You'll stay until five, won't you?' Then, without waiting for an answer, she said, 'OK, buh-bye,' took her husband by the arm, and left.

OK, I said to myself. I can handle this. Already that morning I'd handled a swarm of bugs. I mean, despite the fact that every once in a while I thought I felt one crawling on me and jumped, only to find it was just my own hair or whatever, I had recovered pretty well. Far better, probably, than Dopey ever would.

So I could certainly handle having Paul Slater around all day bugging me. Um, I mean bothering me.

Right? No problem.

Except that it *was* a problem. Because Jack kept wanting to talk about the whole mediator thing, and I kept muttering for him to shut up, and then he'd go, 'Oh, it's OK, Suze, Paul knows.'

Which was the point. Paul wasn't *supposed* to know. It was supposed to be our secret, mine and Jack's. I didn't want stupid, non-believing, since-you-won't-go-out-with-me-I'm-telling-on-you Paul to have any part of it. Especially since every time Jack mentioned anything about it, Paul lowered his Armanis and looked at me over the top of the frames, all expectantly, waiting to hear what I'd say.

What could I do? I pretended I didn't know what Jack was talking about. Which was frustrating to him, of course, but what else was I supposed to do? I didn't want Paul knowing my business. I mean, my own mother doesn't know. Why on earth would I tell *Paul*?

Fortunately, after the first six or seven times Jack tried to mention anything mediator related and I ignored him, he seemed to get the message and shut up. It helped that the pool had gotten very crowded with other little kids and their parents and sitters, so he had plenty to distract him.

But it was still a little unnerving, leaning there against the side of the pool with Kim, who'd shown up with her charges, to glance at Paul every so often and see him stretched out on a deckchair, his face turned in my direction. Especially since I had the feeling that Paul, unlike Sleepy, up in his chair, was wide awake behind the dark lenses of his sunglasses.

Then again, as Kim put it, 'Hey, if a hottie like that wants to look at me, he can look all he wants.'

But of course, it's different for Kim. She doesn't have the ghost of a hundred-and-fifty-year-old hottie living in her bedroom.

All in all, I would say the morning turned out pretty wretchedly, considering. I figured that, after lunch, the day could only get better.

Was I ever wrong. After lunch was when the cops showed up.

I was stretched out on a lounge chair of my own, keeping one eye on Jack, who was playing a pretty rambunctious game of Marco Polo with Kim's kids, and another on Paul, who was pretending to read a copy of *The Nation*, but who was, as Kim pointed out, spying on us over the top of the pages, when Caitlin appeared, looking visibly upset, followed by two burly members of the Carmel police.

I assumed that they were merely passing through, on the way to the men's locker room, where there'd been an occasional break-in. Imagine my great surprise when Caitlin led the cops right up to me and said in a shaking voice, 'This is Susannah Simon, Officers.'

I hurried to climb into my hideous khaki shorts, while Kim, in the lounge chair beside mine, gaped up at the cops like they were mermen risen from the sea or something.

'Miss Simon,' the taller of the cops said. 'We'd just like a word with you for a moment, if you don't mind.'

I've talked to more than my fair share of cops in my time. Not because I hang out with gangbangers, as Sleepy likes to think, but because in mediating, one often is forced to, well, bend the law a little.

For instance, let's say Marisol had not turned that rosary over to Jorge's daughter. Well, in order to carry out Jorge's last wishes, I would have been forced to break into Marisol's home, take the rosary myself, and mail it to Teresa anonymously. Anyone can see how something like that, which is really for the greater good in the vast scheme of things, might be misinterpreted by local law enforcement as a crime.

So, yes, the fact of the matter is, I have been hauled before the cops any number of times, much to my poor mother's chagrin. However, with the exception of that unfortunate incident that had landed me in the hospital some months previously, I had not done anything lately, that I could think of, that could even remotely be construed as unlawful.

So it was with some curiosity, but little trepidation, that I followed the officers – Knightley and Jones – out of the pool area and behind the Pool House Grill, by the Dumpsters, the closest area where, I suppose, the officers felt we could be assured total privacy for our little chat.

'Miss Simon,' Officer Knightley, the taller policeman, began, as I watched a lizard dart out of the shade of a nearby rhododendron, look at us in alarm, and then dart back into the shadows. 'Are you acquainted with a Dr Clive Clemmings?'

I was shocked into admitting that I was. The last thing I had expected Officer Knightley to mention was Dr Clive Clemmings, PhD. I was thinking something more along the lines of, oh, I don't know. Taking an eight-year-old off hotel property without his parents' permission.

Stupid, I know, but Paul had really rattled me with that one.

'Why?' I asked. 'Is he – Mr Clemmings – all right?'

'Unfortunately, no,' Officer Jones said. 'He's dead.'

'Dead?' I wanted to reach out for something to hold on to. Unfortunately there wasn't anything to grab except a Dumpster, and since it was filled with the remains of that afternoon's lunch, I didn't want to touch it.

I settled for sinking down on to the curb.

Clive Clemmings? My mind was racing. Clive Clemmings *dead*? How? *Why*? I hadn't liked Clive Clemmings, of course. I'd been hoping that when Jesse's body turned up, I could go back to his office and rub it in his face. You know, the whole part about Jesse having been murdered after all.

Only now it looked as if I wouldn't get the chance.

'What happened?' I asked, gazing up at the cops bewilderedly.

'We're not sure, precisely,' Officer Knightley said. 'He was found this morning at his desk at the historical society, dead from an apparent heart attack. According to the receptionist's sign-in log, you were one of the few people who saw him yesterday.'

Only then did I remember that the lady behind the reception desk had made me sign in. Damn!

'Well,' I said, heartily – but not too heartily, I hoped. 'He was fine when I talked to him.'

'Yes,' Officer Knightley said. 'We're aware of that. It's not Dr Clemmings's death we're here about.'

'It isn't?' Wait a minute. What was going on?

'Miss Simon,' Officer Jones said. 'When Dr Clemmings was found this morning, it was also discovered than an item of particular value to the historical society was missing. Something you apparently looked at, with Dr Clemmings, just yesterday.'

The letters. Maria's letters. They were gone. They had to be. She had come and taken them, and Clive Clemmings had caught a glimpse of her somehow and had had a heart attack from the shock of seeing the woman in the portrait behind his desk walking around his office.

'A small painting.' Officer Knightley had to refer to his notepad. 'A miniature of someone named Hector de Silva. The receptionist, Mrs Lampbert, says Dr Clemmings told her you were particularly interested in it.'

This information, so unexpected, shook me. Jesse's *portrait*? Jesse's portrait was gone from the collection? But who would have taken *that*? And *why*?

I did not have to feign my innocence for once as I stammered, 'I – I looked at the painting, yes. But I didn't take

310

it or anything. I mean, when I left, Mr – Dr Clemmings was putting it away.'

Officers Knightley and Jones exchanged glances. Before they could say anything more, however, someone came around the corner of the Pool House.

It was Paul Slater.

'Is there a problem with my brother's babysitter, Officers?' he demanded in a bored voice that suggested – to me, anyway – that the Slater family's employees were often being dragged off for questioning by members of law enforcement.

'Excuse me,' Officer Knightley said, sounding really very offended. 'But as soon as we are done questioning this witness, we—'

Paul whipped off his sunglasses and barked, 'Are you aware that Miss Simon is a minor? Shouldn't you be questioning her in the presence of her parents?'

Officer Jones blinked a few times. 'Pardon me, uh, sir,' he began, though it was clear he didn't really consider Paul a sir, seeing as how he was under eighteen and all. 'The young lady isn't under arrest. We're just asking her a few—'

'If she isn't under arrest,' Paul said swiftly, 'then she doesn't have to speak to you at all, does she?'

Officers Knightley and Jones looked at one another again. Then Officer Knightley said, 'Well, no. But there has been a death and a theft, and we have reason to believe she might have information—'

Paul looked at me. 'Suze,' he said, 'have these gentlemen read you your rights?'

'Um,' I said. 'No.'

'Do you want to talk to them?'

'Um,' I said, glancing nervously from Officer Knightley to Officer Jones, and then back again. 'Not really.'

'Then you don't have to.'

Paul leaned down and took hold of my arm.

'Say goodbye to the nice police officers,' he said, pulling me to my feet.

I looked up at the police officers. 'Uh,' I said to them. 'I'm very sorry Dr Clemmings is dead, but I swear I don't know what happened to him, or that painting, either. Bye.'

Then I let Paul Slater pull me back out to the pool.

I am not normally so docile, but I have to tell you, I was in shock. Maybe it was post-being-questioned-by-the-police-but-not-taken-down-to-the-station-house exhilaration, but once we were out of the sight of Officers Knightley and Jones, I whirled around and grabbed Paul's wrist.

'All right,' I said. 'What was all that about?'

Paul had put his sunglasses back on, so it was hard to read the expression in his eyes, but I think he was amused.

'All what?' he asked.

'All that,' I said, nodding towards the back of the Pool House. 'That whole Lone-Ranger-to-the-rescue thing. Correct me if I'm wrong, but wasn't it just yesterday that you were going to turn me over to the authorities yourself? Or rat me out to my boss, anyway?'

Paul shrugged. 'Yes,' he said. 'A certain someone pointed out to me, however, that you catch more flies with honey than you do with vinegar.'

At the time, all I felt was a little miffed at being called a fly. It didn't even occur to me to wonder who that 'certain someone' might have been.

It wasn't long before I found out, however.

Eight

OK, so I went out with him.

So what?

So what does that make me? I mean, the guy asked me if I wanted to go with him for a burger after I dumped his brother back off with his parents at five, and I said yes.

Why shouldn't I have said yes? What did I have to look forward to at home, huh? Certainly not any hope of dinner. Roach à la mode? Spider fricassée?

Oh, yeah, and a ghost who had her fiancé murdered and was going to try to off me next, at her earliest opportunity.

I thought maybe I'd misjudged Paul. Maybe I hadn't been fair. I mean, yeah, he had been kind of stalkerish the day before, but he more than made up for it with the whole rescuing-me-from-the-police thing.

And he didn't make a single move on me. Not one. When I said I wanted to go home, he said no problem, and took me home.

It certainly wasn't his fault that when we drove up to my house, he couldn't pull into the driveway on account of all the police cars and ambulances parked there.

I swear, one thing I am getting with my summer job money is a cellphone. Because stuff keeps on happening, and

I have no idea, because I'm off having burgers with someone at Friday's.

I jumped out of the car and ran up to where I saw all the people standing. When I reached the caution tape, which was strung up all round the hole where the hot tub was supposed to go, someone grabbed me by the waist and spun me around before I had a chance to do what I intended, which was, although I'm not too clear on this, scramble down into the hole, to join the people I saw down at the bottom of it, bending over something that I was pretty sure was a body.

But, like I said, someone stopped me.

'Whoa, tiger,' that someone said, swinging me around. It turned out to be Andy, looking extremely dirty and sweaty and unlike his normal self. 'Hang on. Nothing for you to see there.'

'Andy.' The sun hadn't quite set, but I was having trouble seeing anyway. It was like I was in a tunnel, and all I could see was this bright pinprick of light at the end of it. 'Andy, where's my mom?'

'Your mom's fine,' Andy said. 'Everyone's fine.'

The pinprick started getting a little wider. I could see my mom's face now, peering at me worriedly from the deck, with Dopey behind her, wearing his usual sneer.

'Then what—' I saw the men in the bottom of the hole lift up a stretcher. On the stretcher was a black body bag like the kind you always see on TV. 'Who is that?' I wanted to know.

'Well, we're not sure,' my stepfather said. 'But whoever he is, he's been there a very long time, so chances are, he isn't anyone we know.'

Dopey's face loomed large in my line of vision.

'It's a skeleton,' he informed me with a good deal of relish. He appeared to have gotten over the fact that only that morning he'd had a mouth full of beetles, and was back to

314

his normal insufferable self. 'It was totally awesome, Suze, you should have been here. My shovel went right through his skull. It cracked like it was an egg or something.'

Well, that was enough for me. My tunnel vision came right back, but not soon enough to miss something that tumbled from the stretcher as it went past me. My gaze locked on it and followed it as it fluttered to the ground, landing very near my feet. It was only a deeply stained and extremely threadbare piece of material, no bigger than my hand. A rag, it looked like, though you could see that at one time it had had lace round its edges. Little bits of lace still clung to it like burrs, especially round the corner where, very faintly, you could read three embroidered initials:

MDS.

Maria de Silva. It was the handkerchief Jesse had used last night to dry my tears. Only it was the real handkerchief, frayed and brown with age.

And it had fallen out of the jumble of decaying material holding Jesse's bones together.

I turned around and threw up Friday's bacon cheese-burger and potato skins all over the side of the house.

Needless to say, no one except my mother was very sympathetic about this. Dopey declared it the most disgusting thing he had ever seen. Apparently he'd forgotten what he'd had in his mouth less then twelve hours before. Andy simply went and got the hose, and Sleepy, equally unimpressed, said he had to get going or he'd be late delivering 'za.

My mother insisted on putting me to bed, even though having her in my room just then was about the last thing I wanted. I mean, I had just seen them removing Jesse's body from my backyard. I would have liked to have discussed this disturbing sight with him, but how could I do that with my mother there?

I figured if I just let her fuss over me for half an hour, she'd go. But she stayed much longer than that, making me take a shower and change out of my uniform and into a silky pair of lounging pyjamas she'd bought me for Valentine's Day (pathetically, it was the only Valentine I received). Then she insisted on combing my hair out, like she used to when I was a little kid.

She wanted to talk, too, of course. She had plenty to say on the subject of the skeleton Andy and Dopey had found, insisting it was only 'some poor man' who had gotten killed in a shoot-out back in the days when our home was a boarding house for mercenaries and gunslingers and the odd rancher's son. She said the police would insist on treating it as a homicide until the coroner had determined how long the body had been there, but since, she went on, the fellow still had his spurs on (spurs!) she assumed they would come to the same conclusion she had: that this guy had been dead for a lot longer than any of us had been alive.

She tried to make me feel better. But how could she? She didn't have any idea why I was so upset. I mean, I'm not Jack. I had never blabbed to her about my secret talent. My mom didn't know that I knew whose skeleton that was. She didn't know that just twelve hours ago he had been sitting on my daybed, laughing at *Bridges of Madison County*. And that a few hours before that, he had kissed me – albeit on the top of my head, but still.

I mean, come on. You'd be upset, too.

Finally, finally she left. I heaved a sigh of relief, thinking I could relax, you know.

But no. Oh, no. Because my mother didn't retreat with the intention of leaving me alone. I found that out the hard way a couple of minutes later when the phone rang, and Andy hollered up the stairs that it was for me. I really did not feel like talking to anyone, but what could I do? Andy had already said I was home. So I picked up, and whose cheerful little voice do I hear on the other end?

That's right.

Doc's.

'Suze, how are you doing?' my youngest stepbrother wanted to know. Although clearly he already knew. How I was doing, I mean. Obviously, my mother had called him at camp – who gets calls from their stepmother at *camp*, I ask you? – and told him to call me. Because of course she knows. She knows he's the only one of my stepbrothers I can stand, and I'm sure she thought I might tell him whatever it was that was bothering me, and then she could pump him for information later.

My mother isn't an award-winning television news journalist for nothing, you know.

'Suze?' Doc sounded concerned. 'Your mom told me about . . . what happened. Do you want me to come home?'

I flopped back down on my pillows. 'Home? No, I don't want you to come home. Why would I want you to come home?'

'Well,' Doc said. He lowered his voice as if he suspected someone was listening in. 'Because of Jesse.'

Out of all the people I live with, Doc was the only one who had the slightest idea that We Are Not Alone. Doc believed . . . and he had good reason to. Once when I'd been in a real jam, Jesse had gone to him. Scared out of his wits, Doc had nevertheless come through for me.

And now he was offering to do so again.

Only what could he do? Nothing. Worse than nothing, he could actually get hurt. I mean, look at what had happened to Dopey that morning. Did I want to see Doc with a faceful of bugs? No way.

'No,' I said, quickly. 'No, Doc – I mean, David. That isn't necessary. You stay where you are. Things are fine here. Really.'

Doc sounded disappointed. 'Suze, things are *not* fine. Do you want to talk about it, at least?'

Oh, yeah. I want to discuss my love life – or lack thereof – with my twelve-year-old stepbrother.

'Not really,' I said.

'Look, Suze,' Doc said. 'I know it had to be upsetting. I mean, seeing his skeleton like that. But you've got to remember that our bodies are simply the vessel – and a very crude one, at that – in which our souls are carried while we're alive on earth. Jesse's body . . . well, it doesn't have anything to do with him any more.'

Easy for him to say, I thought miserably. He'd never gotten a look at Jesse's abs.

Not that, if he had, they would have interested Doc much, of course.

'Really,' Doc went on, 'if you think about it, that's probably not the only body Jesse's going to have. According to the Hindus, we shed our outer shells – our bodies – several times. In fact, we keep doing so, depending on our karma, until we finally get it right, thus achieving liberation from the cycle of rebirth.'

'Oh?' I stared at the canopy over my bed. I really could not believe I was having this conversation. And with a twelve-year-old. 'Do we?'

'Sure. Most of us, anyway. I mean, unless we get it right the first time. But that hardly ever happens. See, what's going on with Jesse is that his karma is all messed up, and he got bumped off the path to nirvana. He just needs to find his way back into the body he's supposed to get after, you know, his last one, and then he'll be fine.'

'David,' I said. 'Are you sure you're at computer camp? Because it sounds to me like maybe Mom and Andy dropped you off at yoga camp by mistake.'

'Suze,' Doc said with a sigh. 'Look. All I'm saying is, that skeleton you saw, it wasn't Jesse, all right? It has nothing to do with him any more. So don't let it upset you. OK?'

I decided it was high time to change the subject.

'So,' I said. 'Any cute girls at that camp?'

'Suze,' he said severely. 'Don't—'

'I knew it,' I said. 'What's her name?'

'Shut up,' Doc said. 'Look, I gotta go. But remember what I said, will you? I'll be home Sunday, so we can talk more then.'

'Fine,' I said. 'See you then.'

'See you. And Suze?'

'Yeah, Doc – I mean, David?'

'Be careful, OK? That Diego – the guy from that book, who supposedly killed Jesse? – he seemed kind of . . . mean. You might want to watch your back or . . . well, whatever.'

Whatever was right.

But I didn't say so to Doc. Instead, I said goodbye. What else could I say? Felix Diego isn't the half of it, sonny? I was too upset even to entertain the idea that I might possibly have a second hostile spirit to deal with.

But I didn't even know what upset was until Spike came scrambling through my open window, looked around expectantly, and miaowed . . .

And Jesse didn't show up.

Not even after I called out his name.

They don't, as a rule. Ghosts, I mean. Come when you call them.

But for the most part, Jesse does. Although lately he's been showing up before I even had a chance to call him, when I've

319

only *thought* about calling him. Then *wham*, next thing I knew, there he was.

Except not this time.

Nothing. Not a flicker.

Well, I said to myself as I fed Spike his can of food and tried to remain calm. That's OK. I mean, it doesn't mean anything. Maybe he's busy. I mean, that was his skeleton down there. Maybe he's following it to wherever they're taking it. To the morgue or whatever. It's probably very traumatic, watching people dig up your body. Jesse didn't know anything about Hinduism and karma. At least, that I knew of. To him, his body had probably been a lot more than just a vessel for his soul.

That's where he was. The morgue. Watching what they did with his remains.

But when the hours passed, and it got dark out, and Spike, who usually goes out prowling at night for small vermin and any Chihuahuas he can find, actually climbed on to my bed, where I sat leafing sightlessly through magazines, and butted his head against my hand . . .

Well, that's when I knew.

That's when I knew something was really, really wrong. Because that cat hates my guts, even though I'm the one who feeds him. If he's climbing up on to my bed and butting his head against my hand, well, I'm sorry, that means the universe as I know it is crumbling.

Because Jesse isn't coming back.

Except, I kept telling myself as my panic mounted, he promised. He *swore*.

But as the minutes ticked past and there was still no sign of him, I knew. I just knew. He was gone. They'd found his body, and that meant he was no longer missing, and that meant there was no need for him to hang around my room. Not any more, just like I'd tried to explain to him last night.

Only he had sounded so sure . . . so sure that that wasn't it. He had laughed. He had *laughed* when I first said it, like it was ridiculous.

But then where was he? If he wasn't gone – to heaven, or to his next life (not to hell; there's no place, I'm sure, for Jesse in hell, if there is a hell) – then *where was he*?

I tried calling my dad. Not on the phone or anything, because of course my dad can't be reached that way, being dead. I tried calling to him wherever he was, out there on the astral plane.

Only of course he didn't come, either. But then, he never does. Well, sometimes he does. But rarely, and not this time.

I just want you to know that I don't normally freak out like this. I mean, normally, I am very much a woman of action. Something happens and, well, I go kick some butts. That's how it usually works.

But this . . .

For some reason, I couldn't think straight. I really couldn't. I was just sitting there in my hunter-green lounging pyjamas, going, *What should I do? What should I do?*

Seriously. It was not good.

Which was why I did what I did next. If I couldn't figure out what to do myself, well, I needed someone to tell me what to do. And I knew just the someone who could.

I had to talk quietly because of course by that time it was past eleven, and everyone in the house but me was asleep.

'Is Father Dominic there?' I asked.

The person on the other end of the phone – an older man, from the sound of it – went, 'What's that, honey? I can barely hear you.'

'Father Dominic,' I said, speaking as loudly as I dared.

321

'Please, I need to speak to Father Dominic right away. Is he there?'

'Sure, honey,' the man on the phone said. Then I heard him yell, 'Dom! Hey, Dom! Phone for you!'

Dom? How *dare* that man call Father Dominic *Dom?* Talk about disrespectful.

But all my indignation melted when I heard Father Dominic's soft, deep voice. I hadn't realized how much I'd missed him, not seeing him every day over the summer like I do during the school year. 'Hello?'

'Father Dom,' I said. No, I didn't say it. I'll admit it: I wept it. I was a basket case.

'Susannah?' Father Dominic sounded shocked. 'What's wrong? Why are you crying? Are you all right?'

'Yes,' I said. All right, not said: sobbed. 'It's not me. It's J-Jesse.'

'Jesse?' Father Dom's voice took on the note it always did when the subject of Jesse came up. It'd taken him a while to warm up to Jesse. I guess I could see why. Father D is not only a priest, he's also the principal of a Catholic school. He's not supposed to approve of stuff like girls and guys sharing a bedroom . . . even if the guy is, you know, dead.

And I could understand it, because it's different with mediators than it is with everyone else. Everyone else just walks through ghosts. They do it all the time, and they don't even know it. Oh, maybe they feel a cold spot, or they think they've glimpsed something out of the corner of their eye, but when they turn around, no one is there.

It's different for mediators. For us, ghosts are made up of matter, not shrouds of mist. I can't put my hand through Jesse, though anyone else could. Well, anyone else but Jack and Father Dom.

So it's understandable why Father Dom's never been too

wild about Jesse, even though the guy's saved my life more times than I can count. Because whatever else he is, Jesse's still a guy, and he's living in my bedroom, and . . . . well, you get the picture.

Not, of course, that there'd been anything going on – much to my chagrin.

The thing was, now there never would be. I mean, now I'd never even know if something *could* have happened. Because he's gone.

I didn't mention any of this to Father Dom, of course. I just told him what had happened, about Maria and the knife and the bugs, and about Clive Clemmings being dead and the missing portrait, and how they'd found Jesse's body and now he was gone.

'And he promised me,' I finished, somewhat incoherently, because I was crying so hard. 'He *swore* that wasn't it, that that wasn't what was holding him here. But now he's gone, and—'

Father Dominic's voice was soothing and controlled in comparison to my hiccupy ramblings.

'All right, Susannah,' he said. 'I understand. I understand. Obviously there are forces at work here that are beyond Jesse's control and, well, beyond yours, too, I might add. I'm glad you called me. You were right to call me. Listen, now, and do exactly as I say.'

I sniffled. It felt so good – I can't even describe to you how good it felt – to have someone telling me what to do. Really. Ordinarily the last thing I want is to be told what to do. But in this case, I really, really appreciated it. I clung to the phone, waiting breathlessly for Father Dominic's instructions.

'You're in your room, I suppose?' Father D said.

I nodded, realized he couldn't see me, and said, 'Yes.'

'Good. Wake your family and tell them exactly what you just told me. Then get out of the house. Get out of that house, Susannah, just as quickly as you can.'

I took the phone away from my ear and looked at the receiver as if it had just started bleating in my ear like a sheep. Seriously. Because that would have made about as much sense as what Father Dom just said.

I put the receiver back to my ear.

'Susannah?' Father Dom was saying. 'Did you hear me? I am perfectly serious about this. One man is already dead. I do not doubt that someone in your family will be next if you do not get them out of there.'

I know I was a wreck and all. But I wasn't *that* much of a wreck.

'Father D,' I said. 'I can't *tell* them—'

'Yes, you can, Susannah,' Father Dominic said. 'I always thought it was wrong of you to keep your gift a secret from your mother all these years. It's time you told her.'

'As *if*,' I said, into the phone.

'Susannah,' Father D said. 'The insects were only the beginning. If this de Silva woman is taking demonic possession of your household, horrors such as . . . well, horrors such as you or I could never even imagine are going to begin—'

'Demonic possession of my household?' I gripped the phone tighter. 'Listen, Father D, she may have got my boyfriend, but she is *not* getting my house.'

Father Dominic sounded tired. 'Susannah,' he said. 'Please, just do as I say. Get yourself and your family out of there, before harm comes to any of you. I understand that you are upset about Jesse, but the fact is, Susannah, that he is dead and you, at least for the time being, are still alive. We've got to do whatever we can to see that you remain that way. I will leave here now, but I'm a six-hour drive away. I promise I will be there in the morning. A thorough administration of holy water should drive away any evil spirits remaining in the house, but—'

Spike had padded across the room towards me. I thought he was going to bite me, as usual, but he didn't. Instead, he trotted right up to my face and let out a very loud, very plaintive cry.

'Good God,' Father Dominic cried into the phone. 'Is that her? Is she there already?'

I reached out and scratched Spike behind his one remaining ear, amazed he was even letting me touch him. 'No,' I said. 'That was Spike. He misses Jesse.'

Father Dominic said, 'Susannah, I know how painful this must be for you. But you must know that wherever Jesse is now, he's better off than he's been for the past hundred and fifty years, living in limbo between this world and the next. I know it's difficult, but you must try to be happy for him, and know that, above all, he would want you to take care of yourself, Susannah. He would want you to keep yourself and your family safe—'

As I listened to Father Dom, I realized he was right. That *was* what Jesse would have wanted. And there I was, sitting around in a pair of lounging pyjamas when there was work to be done.

'Father D,' I said, interrupting him. 'In the cemetery, over at the Mission. Are there any de Silvas buried there?'

Father Dominic, startled from his safety-first lecture, said, 'I – de Silva? Really, Susannah, I don't know. I don't think—'

'Oh, wait,' I said. 'I keep forgetting, she married a Diego. There's a Diego crypt, isn't there?' I tried to picture the cemetery, which was a small one, surrounded by high walls, directly behind the basilica down at the Mission where Father Dominic works and I go to school. There are only a small number of graves there, mainly of the monks who had first worked with Junipero Serra, the guy who'd founded the Carmel Mission back in the 1700s.

But a few wealthy landowners in the 1800s had managed to get a mausoleum or two squeezed in by donating a size-able portion of their fortunes to the church.

And the biggest one – if I remembered correctly from the time Mr Walden, our World Civ teacher, had taken us to the cemetery to give us a taste of our local history – had the word Diego carved into the door.

'Susannah,' Father Dominic said. For the first time, there was a note of something other than urgency in his voice. Now he sounded frightened. 'Susannah, I know what you are thinking, and I . . . I forbid it! You are not to go near that cemetery, do you understand me? You are not to go near that crypt! It is much too dangerous . . .'

Just the way I like it.

But that's not what I said out loud. Aloud I said, 'OK, Father D. You're right. I'll wake my mom up. I'll tell her everything. And I'll get everyone out of the house.'

Father Dominic was so astonished, he didn't say anything for a minute. When he was finally able to find his voice, he said, 'Good. Well . . . good, then. Yes. Get everyone out of the house. Don't do anything foolish, Susannah, like call upon the ghost of this woman, until I get there. Promise me.'

Promise me. Like promises mean anything any more. Look at Jesse. He'd promised me he wasn't going to go away, and where was he?

Gone. Gone forever.

And I'd been too much of a coward ever to tell him how I really felt about him.

And now I'd never get the chance to.

'Sure,' I said to Father Dominic. 'I promise.'

But I think even he knew I didn't mean it.

Nine

Ghost busting is a tricky business.

You'd think it would be easy, right? Like if a ghost's bothering you, you just, you know, bust its chops and it'll go away.

Yeah. Doesn't work that way much, unfortunately.

Which is not to say that busting someone's chops does not have therapeutic value. Especially for someone who, like me, might be grieving. Because that's what I was doing, of course. Grieving for Jesse.

Except – and I don't know if this applies to all mediators or just me – I don't really grieve like a normal person. I mean, I sat around and cried my eyes out after the realization first hit me that I was never going to see Jesse again.

But then something happened. I stopped feeling sad and started feeling mad.

Really mad. There I was, and it was after midnight, and I was extremely angry.

It wasn't that I didn't want to keep my promise to Father D. I really did. But I just couldn't.

Any more than Jesse could apparently keep his promise to me.

So it was only about fifteen minutes after my phone call to Father D that I emerged from my bathroom – Jesse was gone, of course, so I could have changed in my room, but old habits die hard – in full ghost-busting regalia, including my tool belt and hooded sweatshirt, which even I will admit might seem a bit excessive for California in July. But it was night-time, and that mist rolling in from the ocean in the wee hours can be chilly.

I don't want you to think I didn't give serious thought to what Father D had said about my telling my mom everything and getting her and the Ackermans out of there. I really did think about it.

It's just that the more I thought about it, the more ridiculous it sounded. I mean, first of all, my mom is a television news journalist. She simply is not the type to believe in ghosts. She only believes in what she can see or, barring that, what has been proven to exist by science. The one time I did try to tell her, she totally did not understand. And I realized then that she never would.

So how could I possibly go busting into her bedroom and tell her and her new husband that they have to get out of the house because a vengeful spirit is after me? She would be on the phone to her therapist back in New York, looking for communities where I could go to 'rest,' so fast you wouldn't believe it.

So that plan was out.

But that was all right, because I had a much better one. One that, really, I should have thought of right away, but I guess that whole seeing-the-skeleton-of-the-guy-I-love-being-hauled-out-of-a-hole-in-my-backyard thing really got to me, and so I didn't think of it until I was on the phone with Father D.

But once I'd come up with it, I realized it really was the perfect plan. Instead of waiting for Maria to come to me, I was simply going to go to her and, well . . .

Send her back from where she came.

Or reduce her to a mound of quivering gelatinous goo. Whichever came first.

Because even though ghosts are, of course, already dead, they can still feel pain, just as people who lose a limb can still feel it itching from time to time. Ghosts know, when you plunge a knife into their sternum, that it *should* hurt, and so it does. The wound will even bleed for a while.

Then, of course, they get over the shock of it, and the wound disappears. Which is discouraging, since the wounds they, in their turn, inflict upon me do not heal half so fast.

But whatever. It works. More or less.

The wound Maria de Silva had inflicted on me wasn't visible, but that didn't matter. What I was going to do to her certainly would be. With any luck, that husband of hers would be around and I could do the same to him.

And what was going to happen if things didn't work out that way, and the two of them got the best of me?

Well, that was the coolest part of the whole thing: I didn't even care. Really. I had cried out every last ounce of emotion in me, and now, I simply didn't care. It didn't matter. It really didn't.

I was numb.

So numb that, when I swung my legs out my bedroom window and landed on the roof of the front porch – my usual form of exit when I didn't want anyone inside to be aware I was up to something – I didn't even care about the things that normally really mean stuff to me, like the moon, for instance, hanging over the bay, casting everything into black and grey shadow, and the scent of the giant pine to one side of the porch. It didn't matter. None of it mattered.

I had just crossed the porch roof and was preparing to swing down from it when a glow that was brighter than the

330

moon but much weaker than, say, the overhead in my bedroom, appeared behind me.

OK, I'll admit it. I thought it was Jesse. Don't ask me why. I mean, it went against all logic. But whatever. My heart gave a happy lurch and I spun around . . .

Maria was standing not five feet from me on the sloping, pine needle-strewn roof. She looked just as she had in that portrait over Clive Clemmings's desk: elegant and otherworldly.

Well, and why not? She isn't of this world, now, is she?

'Going somewhere, Susannah?' she asked me in her brittle, only slightly accented English.

'I was,' I said, pushing my sweatshirt hood back. I had pulled my hair into a ponytail. Unattractive, I know, but I needed all the peripheral vision I could get. 'But now that you're here, I see I don't have to. I can kick your bony butt here just as well as down at your stinking grave.'

Maria raised her delicately arched black eyebrows. 'Such language,' she said. I swear, if she'd had a fan on her, she'd have been using it, just like Scarlett O'Hara. 'And what could I possibly have done to warrant such an unladylike tongue-lashing? You'll catch more flies with honey, you know, than vinegar.'

'You know good and well what you did,' I said, taking a step towards her. 'Let's start with the bugs in the orange juice.'

She reached up and coyly smoothed back a strand of shining black hair that had escaped from her side ringlets.

'Yes,' she said. 'I thought you might like that one.'

'But killing Dr Clemmings?' I took another step forward. 'That was even better. Because I imagine you didn't have to kill him at all, did you? You just wanted the painting, right? The one of Jesse?'

331

She made what in magazines they call a moue out of her mouth: you know, she kind of pursed her lips and looked pleased with herself at the same time.

'Yes,' she said. 'At first I wasn't going to kill him. But when I saw the portrait – *my* portrait – above his desk, well, how could I not? He is not even related to me. Why should he have such a fine painting – and in his miserable little office, as well? That painting used to grace my dining room. It hung in splendour over a table with seating for twenty.'

'Yeah, well,' I said. 'My understanding is that none of your descendants wanted it. Your kids turned out to be nothing but a bunch of lowlifes and goons. Sounds like your parenting skills left a bit to be desired.'

For the first time, Maria actually looked annoyed. She started to say something, but I interrupted her.

'What I don't get,' I said, 'is what you wanted the painting for. The one of Jesse. I mean, what good is it to you? Unless you only took it to get me in trouble.'

'Wouldn't that be reason enough?' Maria enquired with a sneer.

'I suppose so,' I said. 'Except that it didn't work.'

'*Yet*,' Maria said, with a certain amount of emphasis. 'There is still time.'

I shook my head. I just shook my head as I looked at her. 'Gosh,' I said, mostly to myself. 'Gosh, I'm going to hurt you.'

'Oh, yes.' Maria tittered behind one lace-gloved hand. 'I forgot. You must be very angry with me. He's gone, isn't he? Hector, I mean. That must be a great blow for you. I know how *fond* you were of him.'

I could have jumped her right then. I probably should have. But it occurred to me that she might, you know, have some information on Jesse – how he was, or even where he was. Lame, I know, but look at it this way: on top of the whole, you know, love thing, he was one of the best friends I ever had.

'Yeah,' I said. 'Well, I guess slave-runners aren't really my cup of tea. That is who you married instead, right? A slave-runner. Your father must have been so proud.'

That wiped the grin right off her face.

'You leave my father out of this,' she snarled.

'Oh, why?' I asked. 'Tell me something, is he sore at you? Your dad, I mean. You know, for having Jesse killed? Because I imagine he would be. I mean, basically, thanks to you, the de Silva family line ran out. And your kids with that Diego dude turned out to be, as we've already discussed, major losers. I bet whenever you run into your dad out there, you know, on the spiritual plane, he doesn't even say hi any more, does he? That's gotta hurt.'

I'm not sure how much of that, if any, Maria actually understood. Still, she seemed plenty mad.

'You!' she cried. 'I warned you! I told you to make your family stop with their digging, but did you listen to me? It is your fault you've lost your precious Hector. If you had only listened, he would be here still. But no. You think, because you are this mediator – this special person who can commu-nicate with spirits – that you are better than us . . . better than me! But you are nothing – nothing, do you hear? Who are the Simons? Who are they? No one! I, Maria Teresa de Silva, am a descendant of royalty – of kings and princes!'

I just laughed. I mean, seriously. Come on.

'Oh, yeah,' I said. 'And that sure was some princely be-haviour, killing your boyfriend like that.'

Maria's scowl was like a dark storm cloud over her head. 'Hector died,' she hissed in a scary voice, 'because he dared to break off our betrothal. He thought to disgrace me in

333

front of everyone. Me! Knowing, as he did, of the royal lineage running through my blood. To suggest that I would—'

Whoa. This was a new one. 'Wait a minute. He did *what?*'

But Maria was off on a rant.

'As if I, Maria de Silva, would allow myself to be so humiliated. He sought to return my letters and asked for his own – and his ring – back. He could not, he said, marry me, after what he had heard about me and Diego.' She laughed, not pleasantly. 'As if he did not know to whom he was speaking! As if he did not know he was speaking to a de Silva!'

I cleared my throat. 'Um,' I said. 'I'm pretty sure he knew. I mean, that was his last name, too. Weren't the two of you cousins or something?'

Maria made a face. 'Yes. I am ashamed to say I shared a name – and grandparents – with that—' She called Jesse something in Spanish that did not sound at all flattering. 'He did not know with whom he was trifling. There was not a man in the county who would not have killed for the honour of marrying me.'

'And it certainly appears,' I couldn't help pointing out, 'that at least one man in the county was killed for refusing that honour.'

'Why shouldn't he have died?' Maria demanded. 'For insulting me in such a manner?'

'Um,' I said, 'how about because murder is illegal? And because having a guy killed because he doesn't want to marry you is the act of a freaking lunatic, which is exactly what you are. Funny how that part didn't trickle down through the annals of history. But don't worry. I'll make sure I get the word out.'

Maria's face changed. Before, she'd looked disgusted and irritated. Now she looked murderous.

Which was kind of funny. If this chick thought anybody in the world cared about what some prissy broad had done a century and a half ago, she was mightily mistaken. She had managed to kill the one person to whom this piece of information might have been remotely interesting – Dr Clive Clemmings, PhD.

But she was still apparently high on the whole 'we de Silvas are descended from Spanish royalty' thing, since she whirled on me, petticoats flying, and went, in this scary voice, 'Stupid girl! I said to Diego that you were far too much of a fool to cause trouble for us, but I see now that I was wrong. You are everything I have heard about mediators – interfering, loathsome creature!'

I was flattered. I truly was. No one had ever called me loathsome before.

'If *I'm* loathsome,' I said, 'what does that make you? Oh, wait, don't tell me, I already know. A two-faced backstabbing bitch, right?'

The next thing I knew, she'd pulled that knife from her sleeve and was once more pointing it at my throat.

'I will not stab you in the back,' Maria assured me. 'It is your face I intend to carve.'

'Go ahead,' I said. I reached out and seized the wrist of the hand that was clutching the knife. 'You want to know what your big mistake was?' She grunted as, with a neat move I'd learned in tae kwon do, I twisted her arm behind her back. 'Saying my losing Jesse was my fault. Because I was feeling sorry for you before. But now I'm just mad.'

Then, sinking one knee into Maria de Silva's spine, I sent her sprawling, face down, on to the porch roof.

'And when I'm mad,' I said as I prised the knife from her fingers with my free hand, 'I don't really know what comes over me. But I just sort of start hitting people. Really, really hard.'

Maria wasn't taking any of this quietly. She was shrieking her head off – mostly in Spanish, though, so I just ignored her. I was the only one who could hear her, anyway.

'I told my mom's therapist about it,' I informed her as I flung the knife, as hard as I could, into the backyard, still keeping her pinned down with the weight of my knee. 'And you know what she said? She said the trigger to my rage mechanism is oversensitive.'

Now that I was rid of the knife, I leaned forward and, with the hand I wasn't using to keep Maria's arm bent back against her spine, I seized a handful of those glossy black ringlets and jerked her head towards me.

'But you know what I said to her?' I asked Maria. 'I said, it's not that the trigger to my rage mechanism is oversensitive. It's that people . . . just . . . keep . . . pissing . . . me . . . off.'

To emphasize each of the last six syllables of that sentence, I rammed Maria de Silva's face into the roof tiles. When I dragged her head up after the sixth time, she was bleeding heavily from the nose and mouth. I observed this with great detachment, like it was someone else who had caused it and not me.

'Oh,' I said. 'Look at that. That is just so interfering and loathsome of me.'

Then I smashed her face against the roof a few more times, saying, 'This one is for jumping me while I was asleep and *holding a knife to my throat*. And this one is for making Dopey *eat bugs*, and this one is for making me have to clean up *bug guts*, and this one is for killing *Clive*, and oh yeah, this one is for *Jesse*—'

I won't say I was out of my mind with rage. I was mad. I was plenty mad. But I knew exactly what I was doing.

And it wasn't pretty. Hey, I'll be the first to admit that. I mean, violence is never the answer, right? Unless of course the person you're beating on is already dead.

But just because a hundred and fifty years ago this chick had had a good friend of mine offed, for no other reason than that he had very rightly wanted out of a marriage with her, she didn't deserve to have her face bashed in.

No way. What she deserved was to have every bone in her body broken.

Unfortunately, however, when I finally let go of Maria's hair and stood up to do just that, I noticed a sudden glow to my left.

Jesse, I thought, my heart doing another one of those speeding-up, skidding things.

But of course it wasn't Jesse. When I turned my head, what I saw materializing there was a very tall man in a dark moustache and goatee, dressed in clothes that were somewhat similar to Jesse's, only a lot fancier – like he was a costume-party Zorro or something. His snug black trousers had this elaborate silver filigree pattern going down the side of each leg, and his white shirt had those puffy sleeves pirates always wear in movies. He had a lot of silver scrollwork on his holster, too, and all around the brim of his black cowboy hat.

And he didn't look very happy to see me.

'OK,' I said, putting my hands on my hips. 'Wait, don't tell me. Diego, am I right?'

Under the pencil-thin moustache, his upper lip curled.

'I thought I told you,' he said to Maria, who was sitting up and holding her sleeve to her bleeding nose, 'to leave this one to me.'

Maria was making a lot of very unattractive snuffling noises. You could tell she'd never had her nose broken before, because she wasn't tipping her head back to stop the bleeding.

Amateur.

'I thought she might be more amusing,' Maria said in a voice laced with pain – and regret – 'to play with.'

Diego shook his head disgustedly. 'No,' he said. 'With mediators we do not play. I thought that was made clear to you from the start. They are entirely too dangerous.'

'I'm sorry, Diego.' Maria's voice took on a whiny quality I had not heard before. I realized she was one of those girls who has a 'guy' voice, one she uses only when men are around. 'I should have done as you said.'

It was my turn to be disgusted.

'Hello,' I said to Maria. 'This is the twenty-first century. Women are allowed to think for themselves now, you know.'

Maria just glared at me over the sleeve she was holding to her bleeding nose.

'Kill her for me,' she said in that whiny little-girl voice.

Diego took a step towards me, wearing an expression that told me he was only too happy to oblige his lady love.

'Oh, what?' I said. I wasn't even scared. I didn't care any more. The numbness in my heart had pretty much taken over my whole body. 'You always do what she tells you? You know, we have a word for that now. It's called being whipped.'

Apparently he was either unacquainted with this expression, or he just didn't care, since he kept coming at me. Diego was wearing spurs, and they clanged ominously against the roof tiles as he approached.

'You know,' I said, holding my ground. 'I gotta tell you. The goatee thing? Yeah, way over. And you know a little jewellery really does go a long way. Just something you might want to consider. I'm actually glad you stopped by, because I have a couple things I've been meaning to say to you. Number one, about your wife. Yeah, she's a skank. And number two, you know that whole thing where you killed Jesse and then buried his remains out back there? Yeah, way uncool. Because you see, now I have to—'

Only I never got a chance to tell Felix Diego what I was going to have to do him. That's because he interrupted me. He said, in this deep and surprisingly menacing voice, for a guy with a goatee, 'It has long been my conviction that the only good mediator is a dead one.'

Then, before I could so much as twitch, he threw his arms round me. I thought he was trying to give me a hug or something, which would have been pretty weird.

But that wasn't what he was doing at all. No, what he was doing, actually, was throwing me off the porch roof.

Oh, yes. He threw me right into the hole where the hot tub was supposed to go. Right where they'd uncovered Jesse's remains, just that afternoon . . .

Which I thought was kind of ironic, actually. At least, while I was still capable of thought.

Which wasn't for long, since I lost consciousness shortly after slamming into the ground.

Ten

Here's the thing about mediators:

We're hard to kill.

I'm serious. You wouldn't believe the number of times I've been knocked down, dragged, stomped on, punched, kicked, bitten, clawed, whacked on the head, held underwater, shot at, and, oh, yeah, thrown off roofs.

But have I ever died? Have I ever sustained a life-threatening injury?

No. I've broken bones – plenty of them. I've got scars galore.

But the fact is, whoever – or whatever – created us mediators did give us one natural weapon, at least, in our fight against the undead. No, not superhuman strength, though that would have been handy. No, what we've got, Father Dom and I – and Jack, too, probably, although I doubt he's had an opportunity to test it out yet – is a hide tough enough to take all the abuse that gets heaped on us and then some.

Which was why even though by rights a fall like the one I took should have killed me, it didn't. Not even close.

Not, of course, that Maria de Silva and her paramour didn't think they'd been successful. They must have, or they'd have stuck around to finish the job. But when I woke up hours later, groggy and with a headache you would not believe, they were nowhere to be seen.

Clearly, I had won the first round. Well, in a manner of speaking, anyway. I mean, I wasn't dead, and that, in my book, is always a plus.

What I was, was concussed. I knew right away because I get them all the time. Concussions, I mean.

Well, all right, twice.

Anyway, it's not so pleasant, being concussed. Basically, you feel pukey and sore all over, but, not surprisingly, your head really hurts more than anything. In my case, it was even worse in that I'd been lying at the bottom of that hole for so long, the dew had had a chance to fall. It had collected on my clothes and soaked them through and made them feel very heavy. So dragging myself out of that pit Andy and Dopey had dug became a real chore.

In fact, it was dawn before I finally managed to let myself back into the house – thank God Sleepy had left the front door unlocked when he'd come in from his big date. Still, I had to climb all those stairs. It was pretty slow going. At least when I got to my room and was finally able to peel off all of my sodden, muddy clothes, I didn't have to worry, for once, about Jesse seeing me in my altogether.

Because of course Jesse was gone.

I tried not to think about that as I crawled into bed and shut my eyes. This strategy – the not-thinking-about-Jesse-being-gone strategy – seemed to work pretty well. I was asleep, I think, before that thought had really had a chance to sink in again.

I didn't wake up until well past eight. Apparently Sleepy had tried to get me up for work, but I was too far gone. They let me sleep in, I guess, because they all assumed I was still upset about what had happened the day before, about the skeleton they'd found in the backyard.

I only wish that was all I had to be upset about.

When the phone rang a little after nine and Andy called up the stairs that it was for me, I was already up, standing in my bathroom in my sweats, examining the enormous bruise that had developed beneath my bangs. I looked like an alien. I'm not kidding. It was a wonder, really, I hadn't broken my neck. I was convinced that Maria and her boyfriend thought that's exactly what I'd done. It was the only reason I was still alive. The two of them were so cocky, they hadn't stuck around to make sure I was well and truly dead.

They'd obviously never met a mediator before. It takes a lot more than a fall off a roof to kill one of us.

'Susannah.' Father Dominic's voice, when I picked up the phone, was filled with concern. 'Thank God you're all right. I was so worried . . . But you didn't, did you? Go to the cemetery last night?'

'No,' I said. There hadn't been any reason to go there, in the end. The cemetery had come to me.

But I didn't say that to Father D. Instead, I asked, 'Are you back in town?'

'I'm back. You didn't tell them, did you? Your family, I mean.'

'Um,' I said, uncertainly.

'Susannah, you must. You really must. They have a right to know. We're dealing with a very serious haunting here. You could be killed, Susannah—'

I refrained from mentioning that I'd actually already come pretty close.

At that moment, the call waiting went off. I said, 'Father D, can you hold on a second?' and hit the receiver.

342

A high-pitched, vaguely familiar voice spoke in my ear, but for the life of me, I could not place it right away.

'Suze? Is that you? Are you all right? Are you sick or something?'

'Um,' I said, extremely puzzled. 'Yeah. I guess. Sort of. Who is this?'

The voice said, very indignantly, 'It's me! Jack!'

Oh, God. Jack. Work. Right.

'Jack,' I said. 'How did you get my home number?'

'You gave it to Paul,' Jack said. 'Yesterday. Don't you remember?'

I did not, of course. All I could really remember from yesterday was that Clive Clemmings was dead, Jesse's portrait was missing . . .

And that Jesse, of course, was gone. Forever.

Oh, and the whole part where the ghost of Felix Diego tried to split my head open.

'Oh,' I said. 'Yeah. OK. Look, Jack, I have someone on the other—'

'Suze,' Jack interrupted. 'You were supposed to teach me to do underwater somersaults today.'

'I know,' I said. 'I'm really sorry. I just . . . I just really couldn't face coming in to work today, bud. I'm sorry. It's nothing against you or anything. I just really need a day off.'

'You sound so sad,' Jack said, sounding pretty sad himself. 'I thought you'd be really happy.'

'You did?' I wondered if Father D was still waiting on the other line or if he'd hung up in a huff. I was, I realized, treating him pretty badly. After all, he'd cut his little retreat short for me. 'How come?'

'On account of how I—'

That's when I saw it. Just the faintest glow, over by the daybed. Jesse? Again my heart gave one of those lurches. It

343

was really getting pathetic, how much I kept hoping, every time I saw the slightest shimmer, that it would be Jesse.

It wasn't.

It wasn't Maria or Diego either – thank God. Surely not even they would be bold enough to try to take a whack at me in broad daylight . . .

'Jack,' I said, into the phone. 'I have to go.'

'Wait, Suze, I—'

But I'd hung up. That's because sitting there on my daybed, looking deeply unhappy, was Dr Clive Clemmings, PhD.

Just my luck: Wish for a Jesse. Get a Clive.

'Oh,' he said, blinking behind the lenses of his Coke-bottle-bottom glasses. He seemed almost as surprised to see me as I was to see him materialize there in my bedroom. 'It's *you.*'

I just shook my head. Sometimes my bedroom feels like Grand Central Station. 'Well, I simply didn't—' Clive Clemmings fiddled with his bow tie. 'I mean, when they said I should contact a mediator, I didn't . . . I mean, I never expected—'

'—that the mediator would be me,' I finished for him. 'Yeah. I get that a lot.'

'It's only,' Clive said, apologetically, 'that you're so . . .'

I just glared at him. I really wasn't in the mood. Can you blame me? What with the concussion, and all? 'That I'm so what?' I demanded. 'Female? Is that it? Or are you going to try to convince me you're shocked by my preternatural intelligence?'

'Er,' Clive Clemmings said. 'Young. I meant that . . . it's just that you're so young.'

I sank down on to the window seat. Really, what had I ever done to deserve this? I mean, nobody wants to be visited by

344

the spectre of a guy like Clive. I'm almost positive nobody ever wanted him to visit when he was alive. So why me?

Oh, yeah. The mediator thing.

'To what do I owe the pleasure, Clive?' I probably should have called him Dr Clemmings, but I had too much of a headache to be respectful to my elders.

'Well, I hardly know,' Clive said. 'I mean, suddenly, Mrs Lampbert – that's my receptionist, don't you know? – she isn't answering when I call her, and when people telephone for me, well, she tells them . . . the most horrible thing, actually. I simply don't know what's come over her.' Clive cleared his throat. 'You see, she's saying that I'm—'

'Dead,' I finished for him.

Clive eyes grew perceptibly bigger behind his glasses.

'Why,' he said, 'that's extraordinary. How could you know that? Well, yes, of course, you are the mediator, after all. They said you'd understand. But really, Miss Ackerman, I've had the most trying few days. I don't feel at all like myself, and I—'

'That,' I interrupted him, 'is because you're dead.'

Ordinarily, I might have been a little nicer about it, but I guess I still felt a little kernel of resentment towards old Clive for his cavalier dismissal of my suggestion that Jesse might have been murdered.

'But that's not possible,' Clive said. He tugged on his bow tie. 'I mean, look at me. I am clearly here. You are speaking to me—'

'Yeah,' I said. 'Because I'm a mediator, Clive. That's my job. To help people like you move on after they've . . . you know.' Since he clearly did not know, I elaborated: 'Croaked.'

Clive blinked rapidly several times in succession. 'I . . . I . . . Oh, dear.'

'Yeah,' I said. 'See? Now let's see if we can figure out why you're here and not in happy historian heaven. What's the last thing you remember?'

Clive dropped his hand from his chin. 'Pardon?'

'What's the last thing you remember,' I repeated, 'from before you found yourself . . . well, invisible to Mrs Lampbert?'

'Oh.' Clive reached up to scratch his bald head. 'Well, I was sitting at my desk, and I was looking at those letters you brought me. Quite kind of your stepfather to think of us. People so often overlook their community's historical society, when you know, really, without us, the fabric of the local lore would be permanently—'

'Clive,' I said. I knew I sounded cranky, but I couldn't help it. 'Look, I haven't even had breakfast yet. Can you get a move on, please?'

'Oh.' He blinked some more. 'Yes. Of course. Well, as I was saying, I was examining the letters you brought me. Ever since you left my office the other day, I've been thinking about what you said . . . about Hector de Silva, I mean. It does seem a bit unlikely that a fellow who wrote so lovingly of his family would simply walk out on them without a word. And the fact that you found Maria's letters buried in the yard of what was once a well-known boarding house . . . Well, I must say, upon further consideration, the whole thing struck me as extremely odd. I'd picked up my dictaphone and was just making a few notes for Mrs Lampbert to type up later when I suddenly felt . . . well, a chill. As if someone had turned the air-conditioning up very high. Although I can assure you Mrs Lampbert knows better than that. Some of our artefacts must be kept in highly controlled atmospheric climates, and she would never—'

'It wasn't the air-conditioning,' I said flatly.

346

He stared at me, clearly startled. 'No. No, it wasn't. Because a moment later, I caught the faintest whiff of orange blossoms. And you know Maria Diego was quite well known for wearing orange blossom-scented toilet water. It was so odd. Because a second later, I could swear that for a moment . . .' The look in his eyes, behind the thick lenses of those glasses, grew faraway. 'Well, for a moment, I could have sworn I saw her. Just out of the corner of my eye. Maria de Silva Diego . . .'

The faraway look left his eyes. When his gaze next fastened on to mine, it was laser sharp.

'And then I felt,' he told me, in a tightly controlled voice, 'a shooting pain, all up and down my arm. I knew what it was, of course. Congenital heart disease runs in my family. It killed my grandfather, you know, shortly after his book was first published. But I, unlike him, have been extremely diligent with my diet and exercise regimen. It could only have been the shock, you know, of seeing – thinking I was seeing anyway – something that wasn't – that couldn't possibly—'

He broke off, then continued, 'Well, I reached for the telephone to call 911 at once, but it . . . well, the telephone sort of . . . leaped off my desk.'

I just looked at him. I had to admit, by this time I was feeling sorry for him. I mean, he had been murdered, just like Jesse. And by the same hand, too. Well, more or less.

'I couldn't reach it,' Clive said sadly. 'The telephone, I mean. And that . . . that's the last thing I remember.'

I licked my lips. 'Clive,' I said. 'What were you saying? Into the dictaphone. Right before you saw her. Maria de Silva, I mean.'

'What was I saying? Oh, of course. I was saying that though it would bear further investigation, it did seem to me as if what you suggested, and what my grandfather always believed, might possibly have merit . . .'

I shook my head. I couldn't believe it.

'She killed you,' I murmured.

'Oh.' Clive was no longer blinking or tugging on his bow tie. He just sat there, looking like a scarecrow somebody had pulled the pole out from under. 'Yes. I suppose you could say that. But only in a manner of speaking. I mean, it was the shock, after all. But it's not as if she—'

'To keep you from telling anyone what I said.' In spite of my headache, I was getting mad all over again. 'And she probably killed your grandfather, too, the same way.'

Clive did blink then, questioningly. 'My . . . my grandfather? You think so? Well, I must say . . . I mean, his death was rather sudden, but there was no sign of—' His expression changed. 'Oh. Oh, I see. You think my grandfather was killed by the ghost of Maria de Silva Diego to keep him from writing further about his theory concerning her cousin's disappearance?'

'That's one way of putting it,' I said. 'She didn't want him going around telling the truth about what happened to Jesse.'

'Jesse?' Clive echoed. 'Who is Jesse?'

We were both nearly startled out of our wits by a sudden knock on my door.

'Suze?' my stepfather called. 'Can I come in?'

Clive, in a flurry of agitation, dematerialized. I said come in, and the door opened, and Andy stood there, looking awkward. He never comes into my room, except occasionally to fix things.

'Uh, Suze?' he said. 'Yeah, um, you have a visitor. Father Dominic is—'

Andy didn't finish because Father Dominic appeared just behind him.

I can't really explain why I did what I did then. There is no other explanation for it other than the simple fact that, well, in the six months I'd known him, I'd come to really feel something for the old guy.

In any case, at the sight of him, I jumped up from the window seat, completely involuntarily, and hurled myself at him. Father Dominic looked more than a little surprised at this unbridled display of emotion, as I am normally somewhat reserved.

'Oh, Father D,' I said, into Father Dominic's shirt-front. 'I'm so glad to see you.'

I was, too. Finally – *finally* – some normalcy was returning to my world, which seemed to have gone into a complete tailspin in the past twenty-four hours. Father Dominic was back. Father Dominic would take care of everything. He always did. Just standing there with my arms round him and my head against his chest, smelling his priestly smell, which was of Woolite and, more faintly, the cigarette he'd snuck in the car on his way over, I felt like everything was going to be all right.

'Oh,' Father Dominic said. I could feel his voice reverberating inside his chest, along with the small noises his stomach was making as it digested whatever it was he'd scarfed down for breakfast. 'Dear.'

Father Dom patted me awkwardly on the shoulder.

Behind us, I heard Dopey say, 'What's with *her*?'

Andy told him to be quiet.

'Aw, come on,' Dopey said. 'She can't still be upset over that stupid skeleton we found. I mean, that kind of thing shouldn't bother the Queen of the Night Peo—'

Dopey broke off with a cry of pain. I glanced around Father D's shoulder and saw Andy pulling his second-oldest son down the hallway by the rim of his ear.

'Cut it out, Dad,' Dopey was bellowing. 'Ow! Dad, cut it out!'

A door slammed. Down the hall in Dopey's room, Andy was reading him the riot act.

I let go of Father D.

'You've been smoking,' I said.

'Just a little,' he admitted. Seeing my expression, he shrugged helplessly. 'Well, it was a long drive. And I was certain that by the time I got here, I'd find you all murdered in your beds. You really have the most alarming way, Susannah, of getting yourself into scrapes . . .'

'I know.' I sighed, and went to sit on the window seat, circling one knee with my arms. I was in sweats, and I hadn't bothered putting on make-up or even washing my hair. What was the point?

Father D didn't seem to notice my heinous appearance. He went on, as if we were back in his office, discussing student government fund-raising, or something completely innocuous like that, 'I've brought some holy water. It's in my car. I'll tell your stepfather that you asked me to bless the house, on account of yesterday's, er, discovery. He might wonder at your suddenly embracing the Church, but you'll just have to start insisting upon saying grace at supper time – or perhaps even attending Mass from time to time – to convince him of your sincerity. I've been doing a bit of reading on those two – Maria de Silva and this Diego person – and they were quite devout. Murderers, it appears, but also churchgoers. They will, I think, be quite reluctant to enter a home that has been sanctified by a priest.' Father Dominic looked down at me with concern. 'It's what could happen when you set foot anywhere outside this house that's worrying me. The minute you – Good heavens, Susannah.' Father

Dominic broke off and peered down at me curiously. 'What on earth happened to your forehead?'

I reached up and touched the bruise beneath my bangs.

'Oh,' I said, wincing a little. The wound was still tender. 'Nothing. Look, Father D—'

'That isn't nothing.' Father Dominic took a step forward, then inhaled sharply. 'Susannah! Where in heaven's name did you get that nasty bruise?'

'It's nothing,' I said, scraping my bangs down over my eyes. 'It's just a little token of Felix Diego's esteem.'

'That mark is hardly nothing,' Father Dominic declared. 'Susannah, has it occurred to you that you might have a concussion? We should have that X-rayed immediately—'

'Father Dominic—'

'No arguments, Susannah,' Father D said. 'Put some shoes on. I'm going to go have a word with your stepfather, and then we're going down to the Carmel Hosp—'

The phone jangled noisily. I told you. Grand Central Station. I picked it up, mostly to give myself time to think of an excuse why I didn't need to go to the hospital. A trip to the emergency room was going to require a story about how I'd come to obtain this latest injury, and frankly, I was running out of good lies.

'Hello?' I said into the receiver while Father D scowled down at me.

'Suze?' That all-too-familiar high-pitched little voice. 'It's me again. Jack.'

'Jack,' I said, tiredly. 'Look, I told you before. I'm really not feeling well—'

'That's just it,' Jack said. 'I got to thinking that maybe you hadn't heard. And then I thought I'd call and tell you. Because I know you'll feel better when I tell you.'

'Tell me what, Jack?'

351

'About how I mediated that ghost for you,' Jack said.

God, my head was pounding. I was so not in the mood for this. 'Oh, yeah? What ghost was that, Jack?'

'You know,' Jack said. 'That guy who was bugging you. That Hector guy.'

I nearly dropped the phone. I did drop it, actually, but I flung out my hands and caught the receiver before it hit the floor. Then I held it back up to my ear with both hands so I would be sure not to drop it again – and make certain I was hearing him right. I did all this with Father Dominic watching me.

'Jack,' I said, feeling like all the wind had been knocked out of me. 'What are you talking about?'

'That guy,' Jack said. His childish lisp had gone indignant. 'You know, the one who wouldn't leave you alone. That lady Maria told me—'

'Maria?' I had forgotten all about my headache, all about Father Dom. I practically yelled into the phone, 'Jack, what are you talking about? Maria who?'

'That old-fashioned lady ghost,' Jack said, sounding taken aback. And why not? I was shouting like a lunatic. 'The nice one whose picture was in that bald guy's office. She told me that this Hector guy – the one from the other picture, the little picture – was bugging you, and that if I wanted to give you a nice surprise, I should exer– I should exor– I should—'

'Exorcise him?' My knuckles had gone white round the receiver. 'Exorcise him, Jack? Is that what you did?'

'Yeah,' Jack said, sounding pleased with himself. 'Yeah, that's what it was. I exorcised him.'

Eleven

I sank down on to the window seat.

'What—' My lips felt numb. I don't know if it was a complication of my concussion or what, but all of a sudden I couldn't feel my lips. 'What did you say, Jack?'

'I exorcised him for you.' Jack sounded immensely pleased with himself. 'All by myself, too. Well, that lady helped a little. Did it work? Is he gone?'

Across my room, Father Dominic was looking at me questioningly. Small wonder. My conversation, from his end, had to sound completely bizarre. I hadn't, after all, had a chance to tell him about Jack.

'Suze?' Jack said. 'Are you still there?'

'When?' I murmured through my numb lips.

Jack went, 'What?'

'When, Jack,' I said. 'When did you do this?'

'Oh. Last night. While you were out with my brother. See, that Maria lady, she came over, and she brought that picture, and some candles, and then she told me what to say, and so I said it, and it was really cool, because this red smoke started coming out of the candles, and then it swirled and swirled, and then over our heads this big hole opened up in the air, and I looked up inside it, and it was really dark, and then I said some more words, and then that guy appeared, and he got sucked up right inside.'

I didn't say anything. What could I say? The kid had just described an exorcism – at least, all the ones I'd ever experienced. He wasn't making it up. He had exorcised Jesse. He had exorcised *Jesse*. Jesse had been *exorcised*.

'Suze,' Jack said. 'Suze, are you still there?'

'I'm still here,' I said. I guess I must have looked pretty awful, since Father Dom came and sat down on the window seat next to me, looking all worried.

And why not? I was in shock.

And this was a different kind of shock than I'd ever felt before. This wasn't like being thrown off a roof or having a knife held to my throat. This was worse.

Because I couldn't believe it. I simply couldn't believe it. Jesse had kept his promise. He hadn't disappeared because his remains had, at long last, been found, proving he'd been murdered. He'd disappeared because Maria de Silva had had him exorcised . . .

'You're not mad at me, are you?' Jack asked worriedly. 'I mean, I did the right thing, right? That Maria lady said Hector was really mean to you, and you would be really thankful—' There was a noise in the background, and then Jack said, 'That's Caitlin. She wants to know when you're coming back. She wants to know if you can maybe come in this afternoon, because she has to—'

But I never did learn what Caitlin had to do. That's because I had hung up. I just couldn't listen to that sweet little voice telling me these horrible, awful things for one second more.

The thing was, it wouldn't sink in. It just wouldn't. I understood intellectually what Jack had just said, but emotionally, it wasn't registering.

Jesse had *not* moved on from this plane to the next – not of his own free will. He had been ripped from his existence here the same way he'd been ripped from life, and, ultimately, by the very same hands.

And why?

For the same reason he'd been killed: to keep him from embarrassing Maria de Silva.

'Susannah.' Father Dominic's voice was gentle. 'Who is Jack?'

I glanced up, startled. I had practically forgotten Father D was in the room. But he wasn't just in the room. He was sitting right beside me, his blue eyes filled with bewildered concern.

'Susannah,' he said. Father Dom never calls me Suze, like everyone else does. I asked him why once, and he told me it was because he thought Suze sounded vulgar. Vulgar! That really cracked me up at the time. He's so funny, so old-fashioned.

Jesse never called me Suze, either.

'Jack's a mediator,' I said. 'He's eight years old. I've been babysitting for him up at the resort.'

Father Dominic looked surprised. 'A mediator? Really? How extraordinary.' Then his look of surprise turned back to one of concern. 'You ought to have called me straight away, Susannah, the moment you realized it. There aren't many mediators in the world. I would like very much to speak to him. Show him the ropes, as it were. You know, there's such a lot to learn for a young mediator. It mightn't be wise for you to undertake educating one, Susannah, given your own comparative youth . . .'

'Yeah,' I said, with a bitter laugh. To my bemusement, the sound caught in my throat on a sort of sob. 'You can say that again.'

I couldn't believe it. I was crying again.

What *was* this, anyway? I mean, this crying thing? I go for months dry as a bone, and then all of a sudden, I'm weeping at the drop of a hat.

'Susannah.' Father Dominic reached out and grabbed my arm. He gave me a little shake. I could tell by his expression he was really astonished. Like I said, I never cry. 'Susannah, what is it? Are you *crying*, Susannah?'

I could only nod.

'But why, Susannah?' Father Dom asked urgently. 'Why? Jesse? It's a hard thing, and I know you'll miss him, but—'

'You don't understand,' I blurted. I was having trouble seeing. Everything had gotten very fuzzy. I couldn't see my bed or even the patterns on the pillows on the window seat, and they were much closer. I raised my hands to my face, thinking maybe Father Dom had been right, and that I should get that X-ray after all. Something was evidently wrong with my vision.

But when my fingers encountered wetness on my cheeks, I was forced to admit the truth. There wasn't anything wrong with my vision. My eyes were simply overflowing with tears.

'Oh, Father,' I said, and for the second time in half an hour, I threw my arms round a priest's neck. My forehead collided with his glasses, and they went all crooked. To say that Father Dominic was startled by this gesture would be an understatement of the grossest kind.

But judging by the way he froze up when I uttered them, he was even more surprised by the words that came out of my mouth.

'He exorcised Jesse, Father D. Maria de Silva tricked him into doing it. She told Jack that Jesse had been b-bothering me, and that he'd b-be doing me a favour, getting rid of him.

Oh, Father Dominic—' My voice rose to a wail. 'What am I going to do?'

Poor Father Dominic. I highly doubt he has hysterically weeping women throwing their arms round him all that often. You can totally tell. He didn't know how to react at all. I mean, he patted me on the shoulder and said, 'Shhh, everything will be all right,' and stuff, but you could tell he was really uncomfortable. I guess he was afraid Andy was going to walk by and think I was crying because of something Father Dominic had said.

Which was ridiculous, of course. As if anything anybody *said* could make me cry.

After a few minutes of Father Dom saying, 'Shhh, everything will be all right,' and being all stiff, I couldn't help laughing.

Seriously. I mean, it was funny. In a sad, pathetic kind of way.

'Father Dominic,' I said, pulling away and looking up at him through my streaming eyes. 'Are you joking? Everything is *not* going to be all right. OK? Nothing is *ever* going to be all right *ever* again.'

Father Dominic might not have been a very good hugger, but he was all there in the hanky department. He fished his out and started dabbing my face with it. I'd seen him do this before with the little kids at school, the kindergartners who were crying over dropped ice-cream cones or whatever. He really had the whole dabbing thing down.

'Now, Susannah,' he said as he dabbed. 'That isn't true. You know that isn't true.'

'Father,' I said. 'I know it *is* true. Jesse is gone, and it is totally my fault.'

'How is it your fault?' Father Dominic looked down at me disapprovingly. 'Susannah, it isn't your fault at all.'

'Yes, it is. You said so yourself. I should have called you the minute I realized the truth about Jack. But I didn't. I thought I could handle him myself. I thought it was no big deal. And now look what happened. Jesse's gone. *Forever.*'

'It is a tragedy,' Father Dominic said. 'I cannot think of a greater injustice. Jesse was a very good friend to you . . . to both of us. But the fact is, Susannah –' He'd managed to clean up almost all my tears, and now he put his handkerchief away – 'he spent a good many years wandering in a sort of half-life. Now his struggles are over, and he can perhaps begin to enjoy his just rewards.'

I narrowed my eyes at him. What was he *talking* about?

He must have read the scepticism in my face, since he said, 'Well, think about it, Susannah. For one hundred and fifty years, Jesse was trapped in a sort of netherworld between his past life and his next. Though you can lament the manner in which it happened, he has, at last, made the leap to his final destination—'

I jerked away from Father D. In fact, I jerked away from the window seat. I stood up, strode away a few paces, and then whirled around, astounded by what I'd just heard.

'What are you talking about?' I demanded. 'Jesse was here for a *reason*. I don't know what it was, and I'm not sure he did, either. But whatever it was, he was supposed to stay here, in this "netherworld", until he'd worked it out. Now he'll never be able to. Now he'll never know why he was here for all that time.'

'I understand that, Susannah,' Father Dominic said in a voice I found infuriatingly calm. 'And as I said before, it is unfortunate – a tragedy. But regardless, Jesse has moved on, and we should at least be glad he's found eternal peace—'

'Oh my *God*!' I was shouting again, but I didn't care. I was enraged. 'Eternal peace? How do you *know* that's what he's found? You can't know that.'

'No,' Father Dominic said. I could tell he was choosing his words with care now. Like I was a bomb that might go off if he used the wrong one.

'You're right,' Father D said quietly. 'I can't know that. But that is the difference between you and me, Susannah. You see, I have faith.'

I was across the room in three quick strides. I don't know what I was going to do. I certainly wasn't going to hit him. I mean, the trigger to my anger mechanism might be over-sensitive, but I'm not about to go around punching priests. Well, at least not Father Dom. He is my homeboy, as we used to say back in Brooklyn.

Still, I think I was going to shake him. I was going to put my hands on his shoulders and attempt to shake some sense in him, since reasoning did not appear to be working. I mean, seriously, faith. *Faith!* As if *faith* ever worked better than a good ass-kicking.

But before I could lay a hand on him, I heard someone behind me clear his throat. I looked around, and there was Andy, in his toolbelt and jeans and a T-shirt that said *Welcome to Duck Bill Flats*, standing in my open doorway and looking concerned.

'Suze,' he said. 'Father Dominic. Is everything all right in here? I thought I heard some shouting.'

Father Dominic stood up.

'Yes,' he said, looking grave. 'Well, Susannah is – and very rightly, too – concerned about the, er, unfortunate discovery in your backyard yesterday. She has asked me, Andrew, to perform a house blessing, and I of course said I would. I've left my Bible in the car, however . . .'

Andy perked right up. 'You want me to go get it for you, Father?' he asked.

'Oh, that would be wonderful, Andrew,' Father D said. 'Just wonderful. It should be on the front seat. If you could bring that to me, I'll get to work straight away.'

'No problem, Father,' Andy said, and he went away, looking all happy. Which is easy to be if you, like Andy, haven't the slightest clue what's going on in your own house. I mean, Andy doesn't believe. He doesn't know there's a plane of existence other than this one. He doesn't know people from that other plane are trying to kill me.

Or that I was once in love with the guy whose bones he dug up yesterday.

'Father D,' I said, the minute I heard Andy's feet hit the stairs.

'Susannah,' he said tiredly. He was trying to head me off at the pass, I could tell. 'I understand how difficult this is for you. Jesse was very special. I know he meant a great deal to you—'

I couldn't believe this. 'Father D—'

'—but the fact is, Susannah, Jesse is in a better place now.' Father Dominic, as he spoke, walked across my room, stooped down by the door, and pulled out a black bag he'd apparently set down in the hallway. He lifted the bag, set it down again on my unmade bed, and opened it. Then he started taking things out of it.

'You and I,' he went on, 'are just going to have to have faith in that thought, and move on.'

I put my hands on my hips. I don't know if it was the concussion or the fact that my boyfriend had been exorcised, but my bitch quotient was set on high, I think.

'I have faith, Father Dom,' I informed him. 'I have plenty

of faith. I have faith in myself, and I have faith in you. That's how I know that we can fix this.'

Father Dominic's baby blues widened behind the lenses of his bifocals as he lifted a purple ribbony thing to his lips, kissed it, then slipped it round his neck. 'Fix this? Fix what? Whatever do you mean, Susannah?'

'You know what I mean,' I said, because he did.

'I—' Father Dominic took a metal thing that looked like an ice-cream scooper out of his bag, along with a jar of what I could only suppose was holy water. 'I realize, of course,' he said, 'that Maria de Silva Diego will have to be dealt with. That is troubling, but I think you and I are both perfectly well equipped to handle the situation. And the boy, Jack, will have to be seen to and adequately indoctrinated in the appropriate methods of mediation, of which exorcism, as you know, should only be used as a last resort. But—'

'That's not it,' I said.

Father Dominic looked up from his house-blessing preparation. 'It isn't?' he echoed questioningly.

'No,' I repeated. 'And don't pretend like you don't know what I'm talking about.'

He blinked a few times, reminding me of Clive Clemmings.

'I can't say that I do know, Susannah,' he said. 'What are you talking about?'

'Getting him back,' I said.

'Getting who back, Susannah?' Father Dom's all-night driving marathon was starting to show. He looked tired. He was a handsome guy, for someone in his sixties. I was pretty sure half the nuns and most of the female portion of the Mission's congregation were in love with him. Not that Father D would ever notice. The knowledge that he was a middle-aged hottie would only embarrass Father D.

361

'You know who,' I said.

'Jesse? Getting Jesse back?' Father Dominic stood there, the stole round his neck and the dipper thing in one hand. He looked bewildered. 'Susannah, you know as well as I do that once spirits find their way out of this world, we lose all contact with them. They're gone. They've moved on.'

'I know. I didn't say it was going to be easy. In fact, I can think of only one way to do it, and even then, well, it'll be risky. But with your help, Father D, it just might work.'

'My help?' Father Dominic looked confused. 'My help with what?'

'Father D,' I said, 'I want you to exorcise me.'

Twelve

'For the last time, Susannah,' Father Dominic said. This time he pounded on the steering wheel for emphasis as he said it. 'What you are asking is impossible.'

I rolled my eyes. 'Hello? What happened to faith? I thought if you had faith, anything was possible.'

Father D didn't like having his own words tossed back at him. I could tell by the way he was grimacing at the reflection of the cars behind us in his rear-view mirror.

'Then let me say that what you are suggesting has a very unlikely chance of succeeding.' Driving in Carmel-by-the-Sea is no joke, since the houses have no numbers, and the tourists can't, for the life of them, figure out where they're going. And the traffic is, of course, ninety-eight per cent tourists. Father D was frustrated enough by our efforts to get where we were going. My announcement back in my bedroom that I wanted him to exorcise me wasn't helping his mood much, either.

'Not to mention the fact that it is unethical, immoral, and probably quite dangerous,' he concluded, as he waved at a minivan to go ahead and go around us.

'Right,' I said. 'But it's not *impossible*.'

'You seem to be forgetting something,' Father D said. 'You are not a ghost, nor are you possessed by one.'

'I know. But I *have* a spirit, right? I mean, a soul. So why can't you exorcise it? Then I can go, you know, have a look around, see if I can find him, and if I do, bring him back.' I added as an afterthought, 'If he wants to come, of course.'

'Susannah.' Father Dom was really fed up with me, you could totally tell. It had been all right, back at the house, when I'd been crying and everything. But then I'd gotten this terrific idea.

Only Father Dominic didn't think the idea was so terrific, see. I personally found it brilliant. I couldn't believe I hadn't thought of it before. I guess my brain had gotten a little squashed, what with the concussion.

But there was no reason why my plan shouldn't work. No reason at all.

Except that Father Dominic would have no part of it.

'No,' he said. Which was what he'd been saying ever since I first mentioned it. 'What you are suggesting, Susannah, has never been done before. There isn't the slightest guarantee it will work. Or that, if it does, you will be able to return to your body.'

'That,' I said calmly, 'is where the rope comes in.'

'No!' Father Dominic shouted.

He had to slam on the brakes at that very moment because a tour bus came barrelling along from out of nowhere, and, there being no traffic lights in downtown Carmel, there were often differences of opinion over whose turn it was at four-way stops. I heard the holy water, still in its jar in his black bag on the back seat, slosh around.

You wouldn't have thought there'd be any left, what with the dousing Father D had given our house. That stuff had been seriously flying. I hoped he was right about Maria and Felix being too Catholic to dare to cross the threshold of a newly blessed home. Because if he was wrong, I'd pretty

364

much made a big ass out of myself in front of Dopey for no reason. Dopey had been all, 'Whatcha doing *that* for, Father D?' when Father Dominic got to his room with the aspergillum, which turned out to be what the dippy thing was called.

'Because your sister asked me to,' Father Dom replied as he flicked holy water all over Dopey's weight bench — probably the only time that thing had ever come close to being cleaned.

'Suze asked you to bless my room?' I could hear Dopey's voice all the way down the hall, in my own room. I'm sure neither of them knew I was listening.

'She asked me to bless the house,' Father Dominic said. 'She was very disturbed by the discovery of the skeleton in your backyard, as I'm sure you know. I would greatly appreciate it if you would show her a little extra kindness for the next few days, Bradley.'

Bradley! In my room, I started cracking up. Bradley! Who knew?

I don't know what Dopey said in reply to Father Dom's suggestion that he be nicer to me, because I took the opportunity to shower and change into civilized clothing. I figured twelve hours was more than enough to go around in sweats. Any more than that and you are, quite frankly, wallowing in your own sorrow. Jesse would not want my grieving over him to affect my by-now-famous sense of fashion.

Besides, I had a plan.

So it was that, showered, made up, and attired in what I considered to be the height of mediator chic in the form of a slip dress and sandals, I felt prepared to take on not only the minions of Satan but the staff at the *Carmel Pine Cone*, in front of whose office Father D had promised to drop me. I had not only figured out, you see, a way to get Jesse back: I'd figured out a way to avenge Clive Clemmings's death, not to mention his grandfather's.

Oh, yes. I still had it. But good.

'It is out of the question, Susannah,' Father Dominic said. 'So put the idea from your head. Wherever he is now, Jesse is in a better place than he was. Let him rest there.'

'Fine,' I said. We pulled up in front of a low building, heavily shaded by pine trees. The offices of the local rag.

'Fine,' Father Dominic said, putting his car into Park. 'I'll wait out here for you. It would probably be better if I didn't come in, I suppose.'

'Probably,' I said. 'And there's no need to wait. I'll find my own way home.' I undid my seat belt.

'Susannah,' Father Dominic said.

I lifted my sunglasses and peered at him. 'Yes?'

'I'll wait here for you,' he said. 'We still have a good deal of work to do, you and I.'

I screwed up my face. 'We do?'

'Maria and Diego,' Father D reminded me gently. 'You are protected from them at home now, but they are still at large, and will, I think, be excessively angry when they realize you are not dead—' I had finally broken down and explained to him what had happened to my head. 'We need to make preparations, you and I, to deal with them.'

'Oh,' I said. 'That.'

I had, of course, forgotten all about it. Not because I did not feel Maria and her husband needed to be dealt with, but because I knew my idea of dealing with them and Father D's idea were not exactly going to gel. I mean, priests aren't really big on beating adversaries into bloody pulps. They're more into gentle reasoning.

'Sure,' I said. 'Yeah. We should get right on that.'

'And of course—' Father D looked really odd. I realized

why when the next words that came out of his mouth were, 'We've got to decide what's to be done with Jesse's remains.'

Jesse's remains. The words hit me like twin punches. Jesse's remains. Oh God.

'I was thinking,' Father Dominic said, still choosing his words with elaborate care, 'of putting in a formal request with the coroner's office to have the remains transferred to the church for burial in the Mission cemetery. Do you agree with me that that would be appropriate?'

Something hard grew in my throat. I tried to swallow it down.

'Yes,' I said. It came out sounding funny, though. 'What about a headstone?'

Father Dominic said, 'Well, that might be difficult, seeing as how I highly doubt the coroner will be able to make a positive identification.'

Right. They didn't have dental X-rays back when Jesse'd been alive.

'Maybe,' Father Dominic said, 'a simple cross . . .'

'No,' I said. 'A headstone. I have three thousand dollars.' More if I took back all those Jimmy Choos. Good thing I'd saved the receipts. Who needed a fall wardrobe, anyway? 'Do you think that would cover it?'

'Oh,' Father Dominic said, looking taken aback. 'Susannah, I—'

'You can let me know,' I said. Suddenly, I didn't think I could sit there on the street any more, discussing this with him. I opened the passenger door. 'I better go. See you in a few.'

And I started to get out of the car.

But not soon enough. Father D called my name again.

'Father D,' I began impatiently, but he held up a hand.

'Just hear me out, Susannah,' he said. 'It isn't that I don't wish there was something we could do to bring Jesse back. I, too, wish that he could, as you said, have found his own way to wherever it was he was supposed to have gone after death. I do. I truly do. I just don't think that going to the extreme you're suggesting is . . . well, necessary. And I certainly don't think it's what he would have wanted, your risking your life for his sake.'

I thought about that. I really did. Father D was absolutely right, of course. Jesse would not have wanted me to risk my life for him, not ever. Especially considering the fact that he doesn't even have one any more. A life, I mean.

But let's face it, Jesse's from a slightly different era. Back when he was born, girls spent all their time at quilting bees. They didn't exactly go around routinely kicking butt the way we do now.

And even though Jesse's seen me kick butt a million times, it still makes him nervous, you can totally tell. You would think he'd be used to it by now, but no. I mean, he was even surprised when he heard about Maria and her knife. I guess that's kind of understandable. Come on, little Miss Hoop Skirt, poppin' a blade?

Still, even after a century and a half of knowing she was the one who had ordered the hit on him, that completely blew his mind. I mean, that sexism thing, they drive that stuff down deep. It hasn't been easy, curing him of it.

Anyway, all I'm saying is, Father D's right: Jesse definitely would not want me to risk my life for him.

But we don't always get what we want, do we?

'Fine,' I said again. You would have thought that Father D would notice how accommodating I'd become all of a sudden. I mean, didn't he realize that he wasn't the only person in town who could help me? I had an ace up my sleeve, and he didn't even know it.

'Be back in a flash,' I said with a full-on, hundred-watt smile.

Then I turned and went into the offices of the *Carmel Pine Cone* like I was just going in there to place a personal ad or something.

What I was doing, of course, was something way more insidious.

'Is CeeCee Wells here?' I asked the pimply kid at the reception desk.

He looked up, startled. I don't know what freaked him out more, my slip dress or the fact that I'd asked to see CeeCee.

'Over there,' he said, pointing. His voice wobbled all over the place.

'Thanks,' I said, and started down a long and quite messy corridor, passing a lot of industrious journalists who were eagerly tapping out their stories on the recent spate of wind-chime thefts off people's front porches, and the more alarming problem of parking in front of the post office.

CeeCee was in a cubicle in the back. It appeared to be the photocopier cubicle, because that was what she was doing: photocopying.

'Oh my God,' she said, when she saw me. 'What are you doing here?'

She didn't say it in an unhappy way, though.

'Slumming,' I said, and settled myself into an office chair beside the fax machine.

'I can see that,' CeeCee said. She was taking her role as girl reporter very seriously. Her long, stick-straight white hair was coiled up on top of her hair with a Number 2 pencil, and there was a smudge of toner on one pink cheek. 'Why aren't you at the resort?'

'Mental-health day,' I said. 'On account of the dead body they found in our backyard yesterday.'

CeeCee dropped a ream of paper.

'Oh my God!' she gushed. 'That was *you*? I mean, there's a mention of a coroner's call up to the hills in the Police Beat section, but somebody said it must have been a Native American burial site or something . . .'

'Oh, no,' I said. 'Not unless the Native Americans around here wore spurs.'

'Spurs?' CeeCee reached for a notepad that was resting on top of the copier, then pulled the pencil from the knot on top of her head, causing her long hair to fall down around her shoulders. Because she is an albino, CeeCee keeps the vast majority of her skin protected from the sun at all times, even when she's working inside an office. Today was no exception. In spite of the heat outside, she was wearing jeans and a brown button-up sweater.

On the other hand, the air-conditioning in the place had to be on high. It was like an icebox in there.

'Spill,' CeeCee said, perching on the edge of the table that supported the fax machine.

I did. I spilled it all. Everything, from the letters Dopey had found to my trip to Clive's office to his untimely death the day before. I mentioned Clive's grandfather's book and Jesse and the historically significant role my house had played in his murder. I told her about Maria and Diego and their no-account kids, the fact that Jesse's portrait was now missing from the historical society, and my suspicions that the skeleton found in my backyard belonged to him.

When I was through, CeeCee raised her gaze from the notepad and went, 'Geez, Simon. This could be a movie of the week.'

'Lifetime channel,' I agreed.

CeeCee pointed at me with the pencil. 'Tiffani-Amber Thiessen could play Maria!'

'So,' I said. 'Are you going to print it?'

'Heck, yeah,' CeeCee said. 'I mean, it's got everything. Romance and murder and intrigue and local interest. Too bad almost everybody involved has been dead a hundred years, or more. Still, if I can get confirmation from the coroner that your skeleton belonged to a male in his twenties . . . Any idea how they did it? Killed him, I mean?'

I thought about Dopey and his shovel. 'Well,' I said, 'if they shot him – you know, in the head – I doubt the coroner will be able to tell, thanks to Brad's ham-fisted digging technique.'

CeeCee looked at me. 'You want to borrow my sweater?'

Surprised, I shook my head. 'Why?'

'You're shivering.'

I was, but not because I was cold.

'I'm OK,' I said. 'Look, CeeCee, it's really important you get them to run this story. And they have to do it soon. Like tomorrow.'

She said, not looking up again from her notepad, 'Oh, I know. And I think it'd go great alongside Dr Clemmings's obituary, you know? The project he was working on when he died. That kind of thing.'

'So,' I said, 'it'll run tomorrow? Do you think it'll run tomorrow?'

CeeCee shrugged. 'They won't want to run it until they get the coroner's report on the body. And that could take weeks.'

Weeks? I didn't have weeks. And though CeeCee didn't know it, she didn't have weeks either.

I was shaking uncontrollably now. Because I had realized, of course, what I'd just done: put CeeCee in the same kind of jeopardy I'd put Clive Clemmings in. Clive had been just fine until Maria had overheard him telling his dictaphone what I'd said about Jesse. Then faster than you could say *The Haunting*, he was suffering from a massive, paranormally induced coronary. Had I just sentenced CeeCee to the same gruesome end? While I highly doubted Maria was going to ransack the offices of the *Carmel Pine Cone* the way she had the Carmel Historical Society, there was still a chance she might find out what I had done.

I needed that story to run right away. The sooner people found out the truth about Maria and Felix Diego, the better my chances of them not killing me – or the people I cared about.

'It's got to run tomorrow,' I said. 'Please, CeeCee. Can't you call the coroner and get some kind of unofficial statement?'

CeeCee did look up from her notebook then. She looked up and said, 'Suze. What is the rush? These people have been dead for like forever. What does it matter?'

'It matters,' I said. My teeth were starting to chatter. 'It just really matters, OK, CeeCee? Please, *please* see what you can do to put a rush on it. And promise you won't talk about it. The story, I mean. Outside these offices. It's really important that you keep it to yourself.'

CeeCee reached out and laid a hand on my bare shoulder. Her fingers were very warm and soft. 'Suze,' she said, peering down at me sort of intently. 'What did you do to your head? Where'd that giant bruise under your bangs come from?'

I pushed self-consciously at my hair.

'Oh,' I said. 'I tripped. I fell into a hole. The hole they found the body in, isn't that funny?'

CeeCee didn't seem to think it was funny at all. She went, 'Have you had a doctor look at that? Because it looks pretty bad. You might have a concussion, or something.'

'I'm fine,' I said, standing up. 'Really. It's nothing. Look, I better go. Remember what I said, will you? About the story, I mean. It's really important that you don't mention it to anyone. And that you get them to run it as soon as possible. I need a lot of people to see it. A *lot* of people. They need to see the truth. You know. About the Diegos.'

CeeCee stared at me. 'Suze,' she said. 'Are you sure you're all right? I mean, since when do you care about the local gentry?'

I stammered, as I backed out of the cubicle, 'Well, since meeting Dr Clemmings, I guess. I mean, it's a real tragedy that people so often overlook their community's historical society, when you know, really, without it, the fabric of the—'

'You,' CeeCee interrupted, 'need to go home and take an Advil.'

'You're right,' I said, picking up my purse. It matched my slip dress, pink, with little flowers embroidered on it. I was overcompensating for all the days I'd had to wear those khaki shorts. 'I'll go. See you later.'

Then I got the hell out of there before my head exploded in front of everybody.

But on my way back to Father Dominic's car I realized that the reason I'd been shivering back in the photocopying cubicle hadn't been due to the excessive air-conditioning, the fact that Jesse was gone, or even the fact that two homicidal ghosts were actively trying to kill me.

No, I was shivering because of what I knew I was about to do.

When I got to Father Dom's car, I bent down and said through the open passenger window, 'Hey.'

Father Dominic started and hurled something out the driver's-side window.

But it was too late. I'd already seen what he'd been up to. Plus I could smell it.

'Hey,' I said again. 'Give me one of those.'

'Susannah.' Father Dominic looked stern. 'Don't be ridiculous. Smoking is an awful habit. Believe me, you do not want to pick it up. How did things go with Miss Wells?'

'Um,' I said. 'Fine.' I'm pretty sure it's a sin to tell a lie to a priest, even a white lie that can't possibly hurt him. But what was I supposed to do? I know him, see. And I know he's going to be completely rigid on the whole exorcism thing.

So what else could I do?

'She wants me to stick around, actually,' I said, 'and help her write it. The story, I mean.'

Father Dominic's white eyebrows met over his silver frames. 'Susannah,' he said. 'We have a great deal to do this afternoon, you and I—'

'Yeah,' I said. 'I know. But this is pretty important. How about I meet you back at your office at the Mission at five?'

Father Dominic hesitated. I could tell he thought I was up to something. Don't ask me how. I mean, I can be quite the angelic type, when I put my mind to it.

'Five o'clock,' he said, finally. 'And not a minute later or, Susannah, I'm telling you right now, I will telephone your parents and tell them everything.'

'Five o'clock,' I said. 'Promise.'

I waved as he drove away, and then, just in case he was looking in his rear-view mirror, made as if to go back into the newspaper building.

But instead I slipped around the back of it, then headed towards the Pebble Beach Hotel and Golf Resort.

I had some unfinished business there.

Thirteen

He wasn't in the pool.

He wasn't eating burgers at the Pool House.

He wasn't on the tennis courts, at the stables, or in the pro shop.

Finally, I decided to check his room, although it didn't make any sense at all that he'd be there. Not on a gloriously sunny day like this one.

But when the door to his suite swung open to my knock, that's exactly where I found him. He was, Caitlin informed me tersely, taking a nap.

'Taking a nap?' I stared at her. 'Caitlin, he's an eight-*year*-old, not an eight-*month*-old.'

'He said he was tired,' Caitlin snapped at me. 'And what are you doing here, anyway? I thought you were supposed to be sick.'

'I *am* sick,' I said, pushing past her into the suite.

Caitlin eyed me disapprovingly. You could tell she was jealous of my slip dress and delicate pink sandals, not to mention my bag. I mean, compared to her, in her regulation Oxford T and pleated khakis, I looked like Gwyneth Paltrow. Only with better hair, of course.

'You don't look very sick to me,' Caitlin declared.

'Oh, yeah?' I lifted up my bangs so she could see my fore-head.

She sucked in her breath and made an oh-that-must-have-hurt face. 'My God,' she said. 'How'd you do that?'

I thought about saying it was a job-related injury of some kind, so I could milk some disability out of her, but I didn't think it would work. Instead, I just said I'd tripped.

'So what are you doing here?' Caitlin wanted to know. 'I mean, if you're not here to work.'

'Well,' I said. 'That's the thing. I felt really guilty, you know, saddling you with Jack, so I got my mom to drop me off here after she took me to the doctor. I'll stay with him for the rest of the day, if you want.'

Caitlin looked dubious. 'I don't know,' she said. 'You're not in uniform—'

'Well, I wasn't going to wear my uniform to the *doctor's* office,' I squealed. Really, it was amazing how these elaborate lies were tripping off my tongue. I could hardly believe it myself, and I was the one making them up. 'I mean, come on. But look, he told me I'm fine, so there's no reason I can't take over for you. We'll just stay here in the suite, if you're that nervous about people seeing me out of uniform. No problem.'

Caitlin glanced at my forehead again. 'You're not on any kind of painkiller for that, are you? Because I can't have you babysitting all whacked up on Scooby Snacks.'

I held up the first three fingers of my right hand in the international symbol for scouting.

'On my honour,' I said, 'I am not whacked up on Scooby Snacks.'

Caitlin glanced at the closed door to Jack's room. 'Well,' she said, hesitantly.

'Oh, come on,' I said. 'I could really use the dough. And don't you and Jake have a date tonight?'

Her gaze skittered towards me. 'Well,' she said, blushing. Seriously. She *blushed*.

'Yeah,' she said. 'Actually, we do.'

God. It had only been a guess.

'Don't you want to cut out a little early,' I said, 'to make yourself, you know, all glam for him?'

She giggled. Caitlin actually giggled. I am telling you, my stepbrothers ought to come with government warning labels: Caution, hazardous when mixed with oestrogen.

'OK,' she said, and started heading for the door. 'My boss'll kill me, though, if he sees you without your uniform, so you've got to stay in the room. Promise?'

I had made and broken so many promises in the past twenty-four hours, I didn't think one more could hurt. I went, 'Sure thing, Caitlin.'

And then I walked her to the door.

As soon as she was gone, I put down my purse and went into Jack's room. I did not knock first. There is nothing an eight-year-old boy's got that I haven't seen before. Besides, I was still a bit hacked with the little creep.

Jack may have been told to take a nap, but he certainly wasn't doing so. When I walked into his room, he thrust whatever it was he'd been playing with under the blankets and lifted his head from the pillow with his face all screwed up like he was sleepy.

Then he saw it was me, threw the covers back, and revealed that not only was he fully dressed, but that he'd been playing with his Gameboy.

'Suze!' he shouted, when he saw me. 'You came back!'

'Yeah,' I said. It was dark in his room. I went to the French doors and threw open the heavy drapes to let in the sunlight. 'I came back.'

'I thought,' Jack said, jumping up and down excitedly on the bed, 'that you were mad at me.'

'I *am* mad at you,' I said, turning around to look at him. The sight of that sparkling sea had dazzled my eyes, though, so I couldn't see him very well.

'What do you mean?' Jack stopped jumping. 'What do you mean you're mad at me?'

Look, I wasn't going to screw around with the kid, OK? I just wish everyone had been as straight with me when I was his age. It is possible I wouldn't be so quick with my fists if I didn't have this pent-up inner rage from having been lied to so much as an eight-year-old. *Yes, Suze, of* course *there's really a Santa Claus*, but *No, there's no such thing as ghosts*. And then the clincher, *No, this shot I'm about to give you isn't going to hurt a* bit.

'That ghost you exorcised?' I said, facing him with my hands on my hips. 'He was my friend. My *best* friend.'

I wasn't going to say boyfriend, or anything, because that wasn't true. But the hurt I was feeling must have shown in my voice, since Jack's lower lip started to jut out a little.

'What do you mean?' he wanted to know. 'What do you mean, he was your friend? That's not what that lady said. The lady said—'

'That lady is a liar. That lady,' I said, coming swiftly towards the bed and lifting up my bangs, 'did *this* to me last night. See? Or at least, her husband did. All she tried to do was stab me with a knife.'

Jack, standing on the bed, was taller than I was. He looked down at the bruise on my forehead with something like horror.

'Oh, Suze,' he breathed. 'Oh, Suze.'

'You screwed up,' I said to him, dropping my hand. 'You

didn't mean to. I understand that Maria tricked you. But you still screwed up, Jack.'

Now his lower lip was trembling. So was his whole chin, actually. And his eyes had filled up with tears.

'I'm sorry, Suze,' he said. His voice had gone about three pitches higher than usual. 'Suze, I'm so sorry!'

He was trying really hard not to cry. He wasn't succeeding, though. Tears were spilling out of his eyes and rolling down his chubby cheeks . . . the only part of him that was chubby, except maybe for his Albert Einstein hair.

And even though I didn't want to, I found myself wrapping my arms round him and patting him on the back as he sobbed into my neck, telling him everything was going to be all right.

Just like, I realized, with something akin to horror, Father Dominic had done to me!

And just like him, I was completely lying. Because everything was *not* going to be all right. Not for me, at least. Not ever again. Unless I did something about it, and fast.

'Look,' I said, after a few minutes of letting Jack wail. 'Stop crying. We have work to do.'

Jack lifted his head from my shoulder – which he had, by the way, gotten all wet with snot and tears and stuff, since my dress was sleeveless.

'What . . . what do you mean?' His eyes were red and squinty from crying. I was lucky nobody walked in right then. I definitely would have been convicted of child abuse or something.

'I'm going to try to get Jesse back,' I explained, swinging Jack down from the bed. 'And you're going to help me.'

Jack went, 'Who's Jesse?'

I explained. At least, I tried to. I told him that Jesse was the guy he had exorcised, and that he had been my friend, and that exorcising people was wrong, unless they'd done something very very bad, such as tried to kill you, which was, Jack explained, what Maria had told him Jesse'd tried to do to me.

So then I told Jack that ghosts are just like people, some of them are OK, but some of them are liars. If he had ever met Jesse, I assured him, he'd have known right away he was no killer.

Maria de Silva, on the other hand . . .

'But she seemed so nice,' Jack said. 'I mean, she's so pretty and everything.'

Men. I'm serious. Even at the age of eight. It's pathetic.

'Jack,' I said to him. 'Have you ever heard the expression, Don't judge a book by its cover?'

Jack wrinkled his nose. 'I don't like to read much.'

'Well,' I said. We had gone out into the living room, and now I picked up my purse and opened it. 'You're going to have to do some reading if we're going to get Jesse back. I'm going to need you to read this.'

And I passed him an index card on which I'd scrawled some words. Jack squinted down at it.

'What is this?' he demanded. 'This isn't English.'

'No,' I said. I started taking other things out of my purse. 'It's Portuguese.'

'What's that?' Jack asked.

'It's a language,' I explained, 'that they speak in Portugal. Also in Brazil, and a few other places.'

'Oh,' Jack said, then pointed at a small Tupperware container I'd taken from my purse. 'What's *that*?'

'Oh,' I said. 'Chicken blood.'

Jack made a face. 'Eew!'

'Look,' I said. 'If we're going to do this exorcism, we're

going to do it right. And to do it right, you need chicken blood.'

Jack said, 'I didn't use chicken blood when Maria was here.'

'Yeah,' I said. 'Well, Maria does things her way, and I do things my way. Now let's go into the bathroom to do this. I have to paint stuff on the floor with the chicken blood, and I highly doubt the housekeeping staff will appreciate it if we do it here on the carpet.'

Jack followed me into the bathroom that joined his room to his brother's. In the part of my brain that wasn't concentrating on what I was doing, I kind of wondered where Paul was. It was strange he hadn't called after that whole thing where he'd dropped me off at my house and there'd been all those cop cars and stuff in front of it. I mean, you'd have thought he'd wonder, at least, what that had been all about.

But I hadn't heard a peep out of him.

Not that I cared. I had way more important things to worry about. But it was still kind of odd.

'There,' I said, when we had everything set up. It took an hour, but when we were done, we had a fairly decent example of how an exorcism – the Brazilian voodoo variety, anyway – is supposed to look. At least according to a book I'd read on the subject once.

With the chicken blood I'd procured from the meat counter of one of the gourmet shops downtown, I'd made these special symbols in the middle of the bathroom floor, and around them I'd stuck assorted candles (the votive kind, the only ones I could get at short notice, between the offices of the *Carmel Pine Cone* and the hotel; they were cinnamon scented, too, so the bathroom smelled sort of like Christmas . . . well, except for the not-so-festive fragrance of chicken blood).

In spite of the amateurishness with which it had been thrown together, it was, in fact, a working portal to the afterlife – or at least it would be, once Jack did his part with the notecard. I'd gone over the pronunciation of each word, and he seemed to have it down pretty well. The only thing he couldn't seem to get around was the fact that the person we were exorcising was, well, me.

'But you're *alive*,' he kept saying. 'If I exorcise your spirit from you, won't you be dead?'

Actually, this was a thought that had not really occurred to me. What *would* happen to my body after my spirit had left it? Would I be dead?

No, that was impossible. My heart and lungs wouldn't stop working just because my soul was gone. Probably I'd just lie there, like someone in a coma.

This was not, however, very comforting to Jack.

'But what if you don't come back?' he wanted to know.

'I'm going to come back,' I said. 'I told you. The only reason I *can* come back is that I do have a living body to return to. I just want to have a look around out there and see if Jesse's OK. If he is, fine. If not . . . well, I'll try to bring him back with me.'

'But you just said the only reason you can come back is because you have a living body to return to. Jesse doesn't. So how can he come back?'

This was, of course, a good question. That was probably why it put me in such a bad mood.

'Look,' I said, finally. 'Nobody has ever tried this before, so far as I know. Maybe you don't have to have a body to come back. I don't know, OK? But I can't not try just because I don't know the answer. Where would we be if Christopher Columbus hadn't tried? Huh?'

Jack looked thoughtful. 'Living in Spain right now?'

'Very funny,' I said. It was at this point that I took the last thing from my bag and tied one end round my waist. I tied the other end to Jack's wrist.

'What's the rope for?' he asked, looking down at it.

'So I can find my way back to you,' I said.

Jack looked confused. 'But if just your spirit's going, what's the point of tying a rope round your body? You said your body wasn't going anywhere.'

'Jack,' I said from between gritted teeth. 'Just reel me back in if I'm gone more than half an hour, all right?' I figured half an hour was about as long as anybody's soul could be separated from their body. On TV I was always seeing stuff about little kids who'd slipped into icy water and drowned and been technically dead for up to forty minutes, yet recovered without any brain damage or anything. So I figured half an hour was cutting it as close as I could.

'But how—'

'Oh my God,' I snapped at him. 'Just do it, OK?'

Jack glowered at me. Hey, just because we're both mediators doesn't mean we get along all the time.

'OK,' he said. Under his breath, I heard him mutter, 'You don't have to be such a witch about it.'

Only he didn't say witch. Really, it is shocking, the words kids are using these days.

'All right,' I said. I stepped into the centre of the circle of candles and stood in the middle of all the chicken-blood symbols. 'Here goes nothing.'

Jack looked down at his notecard. Then he looked back up at me.

'Shouldn't you lie down?' he asked. 'I mean, if it's gonna be like you're in a coma, I don't want you to fall down and hurt yourself.'

He was right. I didn't want my hair to catch on fire or any-thing.

On the other hand, I didn't want to get chicken blood on my dress. I mean, it was an expensive one. Ninety-five dollars at Urban Outfitters.

Then I thought, Suze, what is wrong with you? It's just a dress. You're doing this for Jesse. Isn't he worth more than ninety-five dollars?

So I started to lie down.

But I had only managed to get down on one knee when there was a terrific thumping on the door to the suite.

I'll admit it. I panicked. I figured it was the fire depart-ment or somebody responding to a report of smoke from someone whose bathroom vent adjoined Jack's.

'Quick,' I hissed at him. 'Blow out all the candles!'

While Jack hurried to do as I said, I stumbled to the door.

'Who is it?' I called sweetly when I got there.

'Susannah,' an all-too-familiar voice said. 'Open the door this instant.'

Fourteen

If you ask me, Father D way overreacted.

I mean, first of all, I had the situation completely under control.

And second, it wasn't as if we'd sacrificed any small animals, or whatever. I mean, the chicken had already been dead.

So all that stomping around and calling us names was really unnecessary.

Not that he called Jack any names. No, most of the names were hurled at me. Apparently, if I am intent on destroying myself, that is one thing. But to force a small boy to aid in my self-destruction? That is just despicable.

And my pointing out that the small boy was the one who'd created the need for me to behave self-destructively? Yeah, that didn't go over too well.

But what the whole thing did do was illustrate to Father Dominic just how serious I was about my plan. I guess it finally got through to him that I was going to do my best to find Jesse, with or without his help.

So he decided that, under those circumstances, he had better help, if only to improve my chances of not hurting myself, or anybody else.

'It will not,' he said, looking all tight-lipped about it as he unlocked the doors to the basilica, 'be any fly-by-night oper-ation, either. None of this Brazilian voodoo business. We are going to perform a decent Christian exorcism, or none at all.'

Really, if you think about it, I probably have the most bizarre conversations of anyone on the planet. Seriously. I mean, a *decent Christian exorcism*?

But it isn't just the conversations I have that are bizarre. I mean, the circumstances under which I have them are pretty bizarre, too. For instance, I was having this one in a dark empty church. Dark because it was after midnight, and empty for the same reason.

'And you are going to have adult supervision,' Father Dominic went on as he ushered me inside. 'How you could have expected that boy to successfully perform so complic-ated a procedure, I simply cannot imagine . . .'

He had been ranting in that particular vain all afternoon. All the way up until Jack's parents – not to mention Paul – had gotten back to the suite, as a matter of fact. Father D hadn't, of course, been able to whisk me off right away the way he'd wanted to, because of Jack. Instead, Jack and I had been forced to clean up the mess we'd made – it is no joke sponging chicken blood out from between bathroom tiles, let me tell you – and then we'd had to sit and wait for Dr and Mrs Slater to return from their tennis lesson. Jack's parents had looked a little surprised to find the three of us sitting there on the couch. I mean, think about it: a babysitter, a boy, and a priest? Talk about feeling as if you were whacked up on Scooby Snacks.

But what was I supposed to do? Father D wouldn't leave without me. He didn't trust me not to try exorcising myself.

So the three of us sat there while Father D lectured us on the fine art of mediation. He talked for two hours. I'm not kidding. *Two hours.* I can tell you, Jack was probably regretting ever having told me about the whole *I see dead people* thing by the end of it. He was probably all, *Uh, yeah, about the dead people? Joking, guys. I was joking . . .*

But I don't know; maybe it was good the little guy got the do's and don'ts. God knew I hadn't been too lucid with my own Intro to Mediation. I mean, if I'd been a little clearer on the finer points, maybe this whole thing with Jesse would never have—

But whatever. You can only beat yourself up so much. I was fully aware the entire mess was my own fault. That's why I was so intent on fixing it.

Oh, and the part about my being in love with the guy? Yeah, that had a little something to do with it, too.

Anyway, that's what we were doing when Jack's parents walked in: listening to Father D drone on about responsibility and courtesy when dealing with the undead.

Father Dominic dried up when Dr and Mrs Slater, followed by Paul, came into the suite. They, in turn, stopped chatting about their dinner plans and just stood there, staring.

Paul was the one who came out of it first.

'Suze,' he said, smiling. 'What a surprise. I thought you weren't feeling well.'

'I recovered,' I said, standing up. 'Dr and Mrs Slater, Paul, this is, um, the principal of my school, Father Dominic. He was nice enough to give me a ride over so that I could, um, visit Jack . . .'

'How do you do?' Father Dominic got quickly to his feet. Like I said, Father D's no slouch in the looks department. He cut a pretty impressive figure, all snowy-topped six feet of him. He didn't look like the kind of guy you'd feel funny about finding in your hotel suite with your eight-year-old and his babysitter, which is saying quite a lot, you know.

When Dr and Mrs S heard that Father D was affiliated with the Junipero Serra Mission, they got all chummy and started saying how they'd been on the tour, and how impressive it was and all. I guess they didn't want him to think they were the kind of people who came to a town with a historically significant slice of Americana attached to it, and then spent the whole time they were there playing golf and downing mimosas.

While his parents and Father D schmoozed, Paul sidled up to me and whispered, 'What are you doing tonight?'

I thought about telling him the truth: 'Oh, nothing. Just having my soul exorcised so I can roam around purgatory, looking for the ghost of the dead cowboy who used to live in my bedroom.'

But that, you know, might have sounded flippant, or like one of those made-up excuses girls use. You know, the old 'I'm washing my hair' put-down. So I just said, 'I've got plans.'

Paul went, 'Too bad. I was hoping we could take a drive up to Big Sur and watch the sunset, then maybe grab something to eat.'

'Sorry,' I said, with a smile. 'Sounds great, but like I said, I've got plans.'

Most guys would have dropped it after that, but Paul, for some reason, did not. He even reached out and casually draped an arm round my shoulders . . . if you can do something like that casually. Somehow, though, he pulled it off. Maybe because he's from Seattle.

'Suze,' he said, dipping his voice low, so that no one else in the room could overhear him – especially his little brother, who was clearly straining his neck in an effort to do so. 'It's

Friday night. We're leaving day after tomorrow. You and I might never see each other again. Come on. Throw a guy a bone, will you?'

I don't have guys pursuing me all that often – at least, not hotties like Paul. I mean, most of the guys who've liked me since I moved to California . . . well, there've been some serious relationship issues, such as the fact that they ended up serving long prison terms for murder.

So this was pretty new for me. I was impressed in spite of myself.

Still, I'm not a dope. Even if I hadn't been in love with somebody else, Paul Slater was from out of town. It's easy for guys who are leaving in a couple of days to give a girl the rush. I mean, come on: they don't have to commit.

'Gosh,' I said. 'That is just so sweet. But you know what? I really do have other plans.' I stepped out from beneath his arm and totally interrupted Dr Slater's in-depth description of that day's golf score – bogey, bogey, par, par. 'Can you give me a lift home, Father D?'

Father Dominic said he could, of course, and we left. I noticed Paul giving me the old hairy eyeball as we said our goodbyes, but I figured it was because he was hacked at me for turning down his dinner invitation.

I didn't know it was for entirely different reasons. At least, not then. Although, of course, I should have. I really should have.

Anyway, Father D lectured me all the way home. He was way mad, madder than he'd ever been with me before, and I've done some stuff that's gotten him plenty peeved. I wanted to know how he'd figured out I was at the hotel and not back at the paper helping CeeCee write her story, like I'd said I'd be, and he said it hadn't been hard: he just remembered that CeeCee was a straight-A student who surely wouldn't need *my* help writing anything, and turned his car around. When he found out I'd left ten minutes earlier, he tried to think where he would have gone under similar circumstances, back when he was my age.

'The hotel was the obvious choice,' Father Dominic informed me as we pulled up in front of my house. No ambulances this time, I was relieved to note. Just the shady pine trees and the tinny sound of the radio Andy was listening to in the backyard as he worked on the deck. A sleepy summer evening. Not at all the kind of night you'd think of when you heard the word exorcism.

'You are not,' Father D went on, 'precisely unpredictable, Susannah.'

Predictable I may be, but it has apparently worked to my advantage, since right before I got out of the car, Father D went, 'I'll return at midnight to bring you down to the Mission.'

I looked at him in surprise. 'The Mission?'

'If we're going to perform an exorcism,' he said, tersely, 'we're going to do it correctly, in a house of the Lord. Unfortunately the monsignor, as you know, is sure to frown on such a use of Church property, so while I dislike having to resort to subterfuge, I can see that you will not be swayed from this course, and so it will unfortunately be necessary in this case. I want to make certain there's no chance of Sister Ernestine or anyone else discovering us. Therefore, midnight it will have to be.'

And midnight, therefore, it was.

I can't really tell you what I did in the meantime. I was too nervous, really, to do much of anything. We had takeout for dinner. I don't know what it was. I hardly tasted it. It was just me and my mom and Andy, since Sleepy had a date with Caitlin, and Dopey was with his latest skank.

The only thing I know for sure is that CeeCee called with the news that the story on the dysfunctional de Silva/Diego family was going to run in the Sunday edition of the paper.

'It'll reach thirty-five thousand people,' CeeCee assured me. 'Way more than our circulation during the week. More people subscribe to the Sunday paper, because of the funnies and all.'

The coroner, she informed me, had come through with a tentative confirmation of my story: the skeleton found in my backyard was between one hundred and fifty to one hundred and seventy-five years old, and belonged to a male of twenty to twenty-five years of age.

'Race,' CeeCee went on, 'is difficult to determine due to the damage to the skull from Brad's shovel. But they were certain about the cause of death.'

I clutched the receiver to my ear, conscious that my mother and Andy, over at the dinner table, could hear every word.

'Oh?' I said, trying to keep my tone light. But I could feel myself getting cold again, just like I had that afternoon in the photocopy cubicle.

'Asphyxiation,' CeeCee said. 'There's like some bone in the neck they can tell by.'

'So he was . . .'

'Strangled,' CeeCee said matter-of-factly. 'Hey, what are you doing tonight, anyway? Wanna hang? Adam's got some family thing he has to go to. We could rent a movie—'

'No,' I said. 'No, I can't. Thanks, CeeCee. Thanks a lot.'

I hung up the phone.

Strangled. Jesse had died from being strangled. By Felix Diego. Funny, I had somehow always figured he'd been shot to death. But strangling made more sense: people would have heard a shot and come to investigate. Then there'd

391

have been no question about what happened to Hector de Silva.

But strangling someone? That was pretty much silent. Felix could easily have strangled Jesse in his sleep, then carried his dead body into the backyard and then buried it, along with his belongings. No one would have been the wiser . . .

I guess I must have stood there looking down at the phone for a while, since my mom went, 'Suze? Are you all right, honey?'

I jumped and went, 'Yeah, Mom. Sure. I'm fine.'

But I hadn't been fine then. And I certainly wasn't fine now.

I had only been to the Mission after dark a couple times before, and it was still as creepy now as it had been then . . . long shadows, dark recesses, spooky noises as our footsteps echoed down the aisle between the pews. There was this statue of the Virgin Mary right by the doorway, and Adam had told me once that if you walked by it while thinking an impure thought, the statue would weep blood.

Well, my thoughts as I walked into the basilica weren't exactly impure, but I noticed as I passed the Virgin Mary that she looked more particularly prone to weeping blood than usual. Or maybe it was just the dark.

In any case, I was creeped out. Above my head yawned the huge dome you could see, glowing red in the sun and blue in the moon, from my bedroom window, while before me loomed the chancel in which the altar glowed, swathed in white.

Father Dom had been busy, I saw when I entered the church. Candles had been set up in a wide circle just before the altar rail. Father Dominic, still muttering to himself

392

about my need for adult supervision, stooped down and began lighting the wicks.

'That's where you're – I mean, we're – going to do it?' I asked.

Father Dominic straightened and surveyed his handiwork.

'Yes,' he said. Then, misreading my expression, he added dourly, 'Don't let the absence of chicken blood fool you, Susannah. I assure you the Catholic exorcism ceremony is highly effective.'

'No,' I said quickly. 'It's just that . . .'

I looked at the floor in the middle of the circle of candles. The floor looked very hard – way harder than the bathroom floor back at the hotel. That was tile. This was marble. Remembering what Jack had said, I went, 'What if I fall down? I might conk my head again.'

'Fortunately, you will be lying down,' Father D said.

'Can't I have a pillow or something?' I asked. 'I mean, come on. That floor looks cold.' I glanced at the altar cloth. 'How about that? Can I lie on that?'

Father Dominic looked pretty shocked for a guy who was about to exorcise a girl who was neither possessed nor dead.

'For goodness' sake, Susannah,' he said. 'That would be sacrilegious.'

Instead he went and got some choir robes for me. I made a nice little bed on the floor between all the candles, then lay down on it. It was actually quite comfortable.

Too bad my heart was pounding way too hard for me ever to have been able to doze off.

'All right, Susannah,' Father D said. He wasn't happy with me. He hadn't been happy with me, I knew, for some time. But he was bowing to the inevitable.

Still, he seemed to feel one last lecture was necessary.

'I am willing to help you with this ridiculous scheme of

yours, but only because I realize that if I do not, you will try to do it on your own, or with, God forbid, that boy's help.' Father D was looking at me very sternly from where he stood. 'But do not think for one minute that I approve.'

I opened my mouth to argue, but Father Dominic held up one hand.

'No,' he said. 'Allow me to finish, please. What Maria de Silva did was wrong, and I realize you are only trying to correct that wrong. But I am afraid I cannot see any of this ending happily. It is my experience, Susannah – and I hope you will agree that my experience is significantly greater than yours – that once spirits are exorcised, they stay that way.'

Again I opened my mouth, and again Father D shushed me.

'Where you are going,' he went on, 'will be like a waiting area for spirits who have passed from the astral plane but have not yet reached their final destination. If Jesse is still there, and you manage to find him – and you understand that I consider this a very great if, because I don't think you're going to – do not be surprised if he chooses to stay where he is.'

'Father D,' I began, rising up on to my elbows, but he shook his head.

'It might be his only chance, Susannah,' Father Dominic said sombrely, 'of ever moving on.'

'No,' I said. 'That's not true. There's a reason, see, that he's hung around my house for so long. All he has to do is figure out what that reason is, and he'll be able to move on on his own—'

'Susannah,' Father Dominic interrupted. 'I'm sure it isn't that simple—'

'He has a right,' I insisted through gritted teeth, 'to decide for himself.'

'I agree,' Father Dominic said. 'That's what I'm trying to say, Susannah. If you find him, you must let him decide. And you mustn't . . . well, you mustn't attempt to use any sort of, er . . .'

I just blinked up at him. 'Father D,' I said. 'What are you talking about?'

'Well, it's only that . . .' Father Dominic looked more embarrassed than I had ever seen him. I could not, for the life of me, figure out what was wrong with him. 'I see that you changed . . .'

I looked down at myself. I had changed out of my pink slip dress and into a black one that had little red rosebuds embroidered on it. This I had paired with some totally cute Prada slides. I had had a hard enough time choosing an ensemble. I mean, what do you wear to an exorcism? I totally did not need Father D dissing my duds.

'What?' I demanded defensively. 'What's wrong with it? Too funereal? It's too funereal, isn't it? I *knew* black was all wrong for the occasion.'

'Nothing's wrong with it,' Father Dominic said. 'It's simply that . . . Susannah, you mustn't attempt to use your, um, sexual wiles to influence Jesse's decision.'

My mouth dropped open. OK. Now I was mad.

'Father Dominic!' I sat up and yelled. After that, though, I was completely speechless. I couldn't think of anything to say except, 'As *if*!'

'Susannah,' Father Dominic said severely. 'Don't pretend you don't know what I mean. I know you care about Jesse. All I'm asking is that you don't use your –' he cleared his throat – 'feminine charms to manipulate his—'

'Like I *could*,' I grumbled.

'Yes.' Father Dominic's tone was firm. 'You could. All I'm asking is that you don't. For the good of both of you. *Don't.*'

'Fine,' I said. 'I won't. I wasn't planning to.'

'I'm delighted to hear that,' Father Dominic said. He opened a small, leather-bound book and began flipping through the pages. 'Shall we begin, then?'

'I suppose.' Still grumbling, I lay back down. I couldn't believe Father D had just suggested what he had – that I would use my sex appeal to lure Jesse back to me. Ha! Father D was overlooking two simple things: one being that I'm not so sure I have sex appeal, and two, that if I do, Jesse had certainly never noticed.

Still, Father Dominic had felt obliged to say something about it, which must mean he'd noticed something. Must be the dress. Not bad for fifty-nine ninety-five.

As I lay there, a slow grin crept over my face. Father D had used the word *sexual*. About *me*!

Excellent.

Father D began reading from his little book. As he read, he swung this metal ball that had smoke coming out of it. The smoke was from the incense burning inside the metal ball. Let me tell you, it stank.

I couldn't understand what Father D was saying, since it was all in Latin. It sounded nice, though. I lay there in my black slip dress and wondered if I ought to have worn trousers. I mean, who knew what I was going to find up there? What if I had to do some climbing? People might see my underwear.

You would have thought I'd be pondering more profound thoughts than this, but I am very sorry to report that the most deepest thing I thought about while Father Dominic was exorcising my soul was that when this was all over, and Jesse was home, and Maria and Felix had been locked back up in their crypt, where they belonged, I was going to have to take a really long soak in that hot tub Andy was installing, because, let me you tell you, I was *sore*.

And then something started happening above my head. A section of the domed ceiling disappeared, and was replaced by all this smoke. Then I realized it was the smoke from the incense Father D was waving around. It was curling like a tornado above my head.

Then, in the centre of the tornado, I saw the night sky. Really. Like the dome over the top of the basilica wasn't there any more. I could see stars twinkling coldly. I didn't recognize any constellations, even though Jesse had been trying to teach them to me. Back in Brooklyn, you couldn't see the stars so well, because of the city lights. So other than the Big Dipper, which you can always see, I don't know the names of any of the constellations.

It didn't matter. This wasn't the sky I was seeing. Not Earth's sky, anyway. It was something else. Someplace else.

'Susannah,' Father Dominic said gently.

I started, then looked at him. I had been, I realized, half asleep, staring up at that sky.

'What?' I asked.

'It's time,' Father Dominic said.

Fifteen

Father Dominic looks funny, I thought. Why does he look so funny?

I realized why when I sat up. That's because only part of me sat up. The rest of me stayed where I was, lying on the choir robes with my eyes closed.

You know on *Sabrina the Teenage Witch* when she splits into two people, so one can go to the party with Harvey and the other can go to the witch convention with her aunts? That's what had happened to me. I was two people now.

Except that only one of them was conscious. The other half was just lying there with her eyes closed. And you know what? That bruise on my forehead really did look disgusting. No wonder everyone who saw it recoiled in horror.

'Susannah,' Father Dominic said. 'Are you all right?'

I tore my gaze from my unconscious self.

'Fine,' I said. I looked down at my spiritual self, which appeared to me to be exactly the same as the person beneath me, except that I was glowing a little. An excellent fashion accessory, by the way, if you can get it. You know, that all-over spectral glow can really do things for a girl's complexion.

Plus something else. The bruise on my forehead? Yeah, it didn't hurt any more.

'You don't have much time,' Father Dominic said. 'Just half an hour.'

I blinked at him. 'How am I supposed to know when half an hour is up? I don't have a watch.' I don't wear one because somehow they always end up getting smashed by some recalcitrant spirit. Besides, who wants to know what time it is? The news is almost always disappointing.

'Wear mine,' Father Dom said, and he took off his enormous steel-link man watch and gave it to me.

It was the first object I picked up in my new ghostly state. It felt absurdly heavy. Still, I managed to fasten it round my wrist, where it jangled loosely, like a bracelet. Or a prison shackle.

'OK,' I said, looking up at that hole above me. 'Here goes nothing.'

I had to climb, of course. Don't ask me why I hadn't thought of this. I mean, I had to reach up and grab the edges of that hole in time and space and boost myself up into it. And in a slip dress, no less.

Whatever. I was about halfway in when I heard a familiar voice shriek my name.

Father Dominic spun around. I leaned down from the hole – through which I could only see fog, grey fog that spritzed my face damply – and saw Jack, of all people, running down the church aisle towards us, his pale face white with fear, and something trailing behind him.

Father Dominic reached out and caught him just before he flung himself on my unconscious form. He obviously didn't see my legs dangling from the enormous tear in the church ceiling.

'What are you doing here?' Father Dominic demanded, his face almost as white as the kid's. 'Do you have any idea what time it is? Do your parents know you're here? They must be worried sick—'

'They're – they're asleep,' Jack panted. 'Please, Suze forgot . . . she forgot her rope.' Jack held up the long white object that had been skittering along behind him as he'd run between the pews. It was my rope from our first attempt to exorcise me. 'How is she going to find her way back without her rope?'

Father Dominic took the rope from Jack without a word of thanks. 'It was very wrong of you, Jack,' he said disapprovingly, 'to come here. What could you have been thinking? I told you it was going to be very dangerous.'

'But . . .' Jack kept looking at my unconscious half. 'Her rope. She forgot her rope.'

'Here,' I called, from my celestial hole. 'Toss it up here.'

Jack looked up at me, and the anxiety left his face.

'Suze!' he yelled delightedly. 'You're a ghost!'

'Shhh!' Father Dominic looked pained. 'Really, young man, you must keep your voice down.'

'Hi, Jack,' I said from my hole. 'Thanks for bringing the rope. How'd you get down here, anyway?'

'Hotel shuttle,' Jack said proudly. 'I snuck on to it. It was coming into town to pick up a lot of drunk people. When it stopped near the Mission, I snuck off.'

I couldn't have been prouder if he'd been my own son. 'Good thinking,' I said.

'This,' Father Dominic moaned, 'is the last thing we need right now. Here, Susannah, take the rope, and for the love of God, hurry—'

I leaned down and grabbed the end of the rope, then tied it securely round my waist. 'OK,' I said. 'If I'm not back in half an hour, start pulling.'

'Twenty-five minutes,' Father Dominic corrected me. 'We

lost time, thanks to this young man's interruption.' He took a pocket watch from his coat with the hand that wasn't clutching the other end of the rope. 'Go now, Susannah,' he urged me.

'Right,' I said. 'OK. Be right back.'

And then I swung my legs into the hole. When I looked down, I could see Father Dominic and Jack standing there, peering up at me. And I could also see me, asleep like Snow White, in a circle of dancing candle flames. Although I doubt Snow White ever wore Prada.

I got up and looked around me. Nothing.

I'm serious. There was nothing there. Just that black sky, through which a few stars burned coldly. And then there was the fog. Thick, ever-moving, cool fog. I should have, I thought to myself with a shiver, worn a sweater. The fog seemed to weigh down the air I was taking into my lungs. It also seemed to serve as a muffler. I couldn't hear a sound, not even my own footsteps.

Oh, well. Twenty-five minutes wasn't long. I sucked in a chestful of damp air and yelled, 'Jesse!'

It was a highly effective move. Not that Jesse showed up. Oh, no. But this other guy did.

In a gladiator outfit, no less.

I'm not even kidding. He looked like the guy from my mom's American Express card (which I frequently borrow, with her permission, of course). You know, the broom sticking out of his helmet, the leather miniskirt, the big sword. I couldn't see his feet on account of the fog, but I assumed that, if I could, he'd be wearing lace-up sandals (so unflattering on people with fat knees).

'You,' he said, in this deep, no-nonsense voice, 'do not belong here.'

401

See. I knew the slip dress had been a mistake. But who knew purgatory had a dress code?

'I know,' I said, giving him my best smile. Maybe Father D was right. Maybe I do have a tendency to use my sexuality to get what I want. I was certainly laying on the girlie thing thick for the Russell Crowe type in front of me.

'The thing is,' I said, fingering my rope, 'I'm looking for a friend. Maybe you know him. Jesse de Silva? He showed up here last night, I think. He's about twenty, six feet tall, black hair, dark eyes—' Killer abs?

Russell Crowe must not have been listening closely, since all he said was, 'You do not belong here,' again.

OK, the slip dress had definitely been a mistake. Because how was I supposed to kick this guy out of my way without splitting the skirt?

'Look, mister,' I said, striding up to him and trying not to notice that his pectoral muscles were so pronounced, his breasts were bigger than mine. Way bigger. 'I told you. I'm looking for someone. Now either you tell me if you've seen him, or you get out of my face, OK? I'm a mediator, all right? I have just as much right to be here as you.'

I did not, of course, know if this was true, but heck, I've been a mediator all my life, and I haven't gotten squat for it. As far as I was concerned, somebody owed me, but big.

The gladiator seemed to agree. He went, in a completely different tone, 'A mediator?' He looked down at me as if I were a monkey that had suddenly sat up and started saying the Pledge of Allegiance.

Still, I must have done something right, since he said slowly, 'I know the one of whom you speak.'

Then he seemed to come to a decision. Stepping to one side, he said in a commanding voice, 'Go now. Do not open any doors. He will come.'

I stared at him. Whoa. 'Are you . . . are you serious?'

For the first time, he showed some personality. He went, 'Do I seem to be joking to you?'

'Um,' I said. 'No.'

'Because I am the gatekeeper. I do not joke. Go now.' He pointed. 'You have not much time.'

Off in the distance, in the direction he was pointing, I saw something. I don't know what it was, but it was something other than fog. I felt like hugging my new gladiator friend, but I restrained myself. He didn't seem the touchy-feely sort.

'Thanks,' I said. 'Thanks a whole lot.'

'Hurry,' the gatekeeper said. 'And remember, whatever you do, do not go towards the light.'

I had given the rope a yank so that Father D would give me some slack. Now I just stood there with it in my hands, staring at the gladiator.

'Don't go in the light?' I echoed. 'You're not serious.'

I swear to you, he sounded indignant. 'I told you before, I do not joke. Why do you think I would say something I do not mean?'

I wanted to tell him that the whole don't-go-into-the-light thing was way overplayed. I mean, *Poltergeist One* through *Three* had pretty much run that line into the ground.

But who knew? Maybe the guy who wrote those movies was a mediator. Maybe he and the gatekeeper were pals or something.

'OK,' I said, sidling past him. 'Gotcha. Don't go in the light.'

'Or open any doors,' the gatekeeper reminded me.

'No doors,' I said, pointing at him and winking. 'You got it.'

Then I turned around, and the fog was gone.

Well, not gone, really. I mean, it was still there, licking at

403

my heels. But most of it had given way, so that I could see I was in a corridor lined with doors. There was no ceiling overhead, just those coldly winking stars and inky black sky. Still, the long corridor of closed doors seemed to stretch out forever before me.

And I wasn't supposed to open any of those doors. Or go into the light.

Well, the second part was easy. I didn't see any light to go towards. But how was I not supposed to open one of those doors? I mean, really. What was going on behind them? What would I find if I opened one, just a crack, and peeked in? Alternate universe? The planet Vulcan? Maybe a world where Suze Simon was a normal girl, not a mediator? Maybe one where Suze Simon was homecoming queen and the most popular person in the whole school, and Jesse wasn't a ghost and could actually take her to dances and had his own car and didn't live in her bedroom?

Then I stopped wondering what was behind all those doors. That's because coming down the hallway towards me – as if he'd just materialized there from out of nowhere – came Jesse.

He looked pretty surprised to see me. I don't know if it was the fact that I was standing there in what was, I suppose, heaven's waiting room, or if it was the attractive length of cord round my waist, which did not, I have to admit, go with the rest of my outfit.

Whatever it was, he looked pretty shocked.

'Oh,' I said, reaching up to make sure my bangs were covering my unsightly bruise. 'Hi.'

Jesse froze in his tracks and just stared at me. It was like he couldn't believe what he was seeing. He didn't look any different from the last time I'd seen him. I mean, the last time I'd seen his ghost. The last time I'd seen him, of course, it had been a view of his rotten corpse, and the sight had, of course, made me lose my supper.

But this Jesse was a lot easier on the eyes.

Still, if I'd expected any sort of joyful reunion – a hug or, God forbid, a kiss – I was in for a disappointment. He just stood there, staring at me like I'd grown two heads since the last time we'd bumped into each other.

'Susannah,' he breathed. 'What are you doing here? Are you – you're not—'

I caught his meaning at once and went, with a nervous laugh, 'Dead? Me? No, no, no. No. I just, um, I came up here because I wanted to, um, you know, see if you were all right . . .'

OK, could I be any lamer? I mean, seriously. I had pictured this moment in my head a thousand times since I'd first decided I was going to come after him, and in all my fantasies, no explanations were ever necessary. Jesse just threw his arms round me and started kissing me. On the lips.

This, though. This was way awkward. I wished I'd prepared a speech.

'Um,' I said. What I really wished was that I could stop saying *um*. 'See, the thing is, I wanted to make sure you were here because you wanted to be. Because if you don't want to be, well, Father Dom and I thought maybe it would be possible for you to come back. To, um, finish whatever it is, you know, that was keeping you down there. In my world, I mean. Our world,' I corrected myself, quickly, remembering Father Dominic's warning. 'Our world, I mean.'

Jesse continued to just stare at me.

'Susannah,' he said. His voice sounded weird. I figured out why a second later, when he asked, 'Weren't you the one who sent me here?'

I gaped at him. 'What? What are you talking about?'

Now I knew what was so weird about his voice. It was filled with hurt. 'Didn't you,' he asked, 'have me exorcised?'

'Me?' My own voice rocketed up about ten octaves. 'Me? Jesse, of course not. I would never do that. I mean, you know I would never do something like that. That kid Jack did it. Your girlfriend Maria made him do it. She was trying to get rid of you. She told Jack you were bothering me, and he didn't know any better, so he exorcised you, and then Felix Diego threw me off the porch roof, and Jesse, they found your body, I mean your bones, and I saw them and I threw up all over the side of the house, and Spike really misses you and I was just thinking, you know, if you wanted to come back, you could, because that's why I've got this rope, so we can find our way back.'

I was babbling. I have a tendency to do this even when I am not standing in purgatory. But I couldn't help myself. Everything was just kind of spilling out. Well, not everything. I mean, I totally wasn't going to tell him *why* I wanted him to come back. I wasn't going to mention the L word or anything. And not even because of Father D's warning, either.

'That is,' I went on, 'if you want to come back. I could see why you'd want to stay here. I mean, after a hundred and fifty years and all, it's probably a relief. I imagine they'll be moving you along soon, and you'll be getting a new life, or going up to heaven, or whatever. But I was just thinking, you know, it wasn't fair of Maria to do what she did to you – twice – and that if you want to come back and figure out what it was you were, you know, doing down there on earth for so long, well, I'd just give you a hand, if I could.'

I looked down at Father D's watch. It was easier than looking into Jesse's face, and seeing that he still wore that inscrutable expression, as if he couldn't quite believe what he was seeing. And hearing.

'The only thing is,' I said, 'I can be separated from my body for half an hour before I wind up permanently detached, and we only have fifteen minutes left. So you have to hurry up and decide. What's it going to be?'

Was that, I wondered, unfeminine enough for Father Dom? I was so totally not working it. No one could accuse me even of *smiling*. I was the picture of a professional mediator.

Only I didn't know how long I was going to be able to maintain my businesslike persona. Especially when Jesse reached out, like he did just then, and laid a hand on my arm.

'Susannah,' he said, and now his voice wasn't filled with hurt at all, but something that, if I wasn't mistaken, sounded a lot like anger. 'Are you saying you *died* for me?'

'Um,' I said, wondering if it would count as using my feminine wiles if *he* was the one who touched *me*. 'Well, not technically. Yet. But if we hang around here much longer—'

The hand on my arm tightened. 'Let's go,' he said.

I wasn't sure he really understood the situation. 'Jesse,' I said. 'I can find my own way back, OK? I'm like this with the gatekeeper.' I held up crossed fingers. 'If you want to come with me because you want to go back, that's fine, but if you just want to walk me back to my hole, believe me, I can get there on my own.'

Jesse just said, 'Susannah. Shut up.'

And then, still keeping one hand on my arm, he grabbed the rope and started following it, back in the direction from which I'd come.

Oh, I thought as he propelled me along. OK. Great. Now he's mad at me. Here I risk my life – because let's face it, that's what I was doing – and he's *mad* at me because of it. I actually should have thought of this. I mean, risking your life for a guy is practically like using the L word. Worse, even. How was I going to get out of this one?

I said, 'Jesse, don't flatter yourself that I did this for you. I mean, it has been nothing but one giant pain in the neck, having you for a room-mate. Do you think I like having to come home from school or from work or whatever and having to explain stuff like the Bay of Pigs to you? Believe me, life with you is no picnic.'

He didn't say anything. He just kept pulling me along.

'Or what about Tad?' I said, bringing up what I knew was a sore subject. 'I mean, you think I like having you tag along on my dates? Having you out of my life is going to make things a lot simpler, so don't think, you know, I did this for you. I only did it because that stupid cat of yours has been crying its head off. And also because anything I can do to make your stupid girlfriend mad, I will.'

'*Nombre de Dios*, Susannah,' Jesse muttered. 'Maria's not my girlfriend.'

'Well, she certainly used to be,' I said. 'And what about that, anyway? That girl is a full-on skank, Jesse. I can't believe you ever agreed to marry her. I mean, what were you thinking, anyway? Couldn't you see what she was like underneath all that lace?'

'Things,' Jesse said through gritted teeth, 'were different back then, Susannah.'

'Oh, yeah? So different that you couldn't tell the girl you were about to marry was a big old—'

'I hardly knew her,' Jesse said, hauling me to a stop and glaring down at me. 'All right?'

'Nice try,' I said. 'You two were cousins. Which is a whole

408

other issue which, if you really want to know, completely grosses me—'

'Yes, we were cousins,' Jesse interrupted, giving my arm a shake. 'But like I said before, things were different back then, Susannah. If we had more time, I'd tell you—'

'Oh, no, you don't. We still have –' I looked down at Father D's watch – 'twelve minutes left. You tell me now.'

'Susannah—'

'*Now*, Jesse, or I swear, I'm not budging.'

He actually groaned in frustration, and said what I think must have been a very bad word, only I don't know for sure, since it was in Spanish. They don't teach us swears in Spanish at school.

'Fine,' he said, dropping my arm. 'You want to know? You want to know how it was back then? It was different, all right? California was different. Completely different. There was none of this mingling of the sexes. Boys and girls did not play together, did not sit side by side in classrooms. The only time I was ever in the same room with Maria was at meals, or sometimes dances. And then we were surrounded by other people. I doubt I ever heard her speak more than a few words—'

'Well, they were evidently pretty impressive ones, since you agreed to marry her.'

Jesse ran a hand through his hair and made another exclamation in Spanish. 'Of course I agreed to marry her,' he said. 'My father wanted it, her father wanted it. How could I say no? I didn't want to say no. I didn't know – not then – what she was. It was only later, when I got her letters, that I realized—'

'That she can't spell?'

He ignored me. '– that the two of us had nothing in common, and never would. But even then, I would not have

409

disgraced my family by breaking things off with her. Not for that.'

'But when you heard she wasn't as pure as the driven snow?' I folded my arms across my chest and glared at him, sexist product of the nineteenth century that he was. 'That's when you decided she wasn't good wife material?'

'When I heard rumours about Maria and Felix Diego,' he said, impatiently, 'I was unhappy. I knew Diego. He was not a good man. He was cruel and . . . Well, he was always looking for ways to make money. And Maria had a lot of money. He wanted to marry her – you can guess why – so when I found out, I decided it might be better to end it, yes—'

'But Diego got to know you first,' I said, a throb in my voice.

'Susannah.' He stared down at me. 'I've had a century and a half to get used to being dead. It no longer matters to me who killed me, or why. What's important to me right now is seeing that you do not end up the same way. Now will you move, or do I have to carry you?'

'OK,' I said, letting him pull me along again. 'But I just want to get one thing straight. I did not do all this – you know, get myself exorcised and come up here and all – because I'm in love with you or anything like that.'

'I would not,' he said grimly, 'as you say, flatter myself.'

'Damn straight,' I said. I wondered if I was still being unfeminine enough. Actually, I was beginning to think I was being a little *too* unfeminine. Hostile, actually, was what I was being. 'Because I'm not. I came because of the cat. The cat really misses you.'

'You shouldn't have come at all,' Jesse said under his breath. Still, I heard him anyway. It wasn't like there was a whole lot of other noise up there. We had left the corridor – it had disappeared, I saw, the minute we turned our backs to

410

it – and were back in the fog again, following the rope that, thankfully, Jack had remembered. 'I cannot believe that Father Dominic allowed it.'

'Hey,' I said. 'Leave Father D out of it. This is all your fault, you know. None of this would have happened if you had just been open and honest with me from the beginning about how you died. Then I could have at least told Andy to dig elsewhere. And I'd have been prepared to deal with Maria and her bohunk husband. I don't know why they are so strung out about people finding out they're a couple of murderers, but they are very intent on keeping what happened to you a big old myst—'

'That,' Jesse said, 'is because to them, no time has passed since their deaths. They were at rest until it became evident that my body was about to be found, which would inevitably open up speculation as to the cause of my demise. They do not understand that more than a century has passed since then. They are trying to preserve their places in the community, as the leading citizens they once were.'

'Tell me about it,' I said, fingering my bruise. 'They think it's still eighteen fifty, and they're afraid of the neighbours finding out they offed you. Well, it's all going to blow up in their faces in a day or so. The truth is coming out, courtesy of the *Carmel Pine Cone*—'

Jesse spun me around to face him. He looked madder than ever. 'Susannah,' he said. 'What are you talking about?'

'I told the whole story to CeeCee,' I explained, unable to keep a note of self-congratulation from creeping into my voice. 'She's interning at the paper for the summer. She says they're running the story – the real story, about what happened to you – on Sunday.'

Seeing his expression growing, if anything, even darker, I added, 'Jesse, I had to. Maria killed the guy at the historical

411

society – the one she stole your picture from in order to do the exorcism. I'm pretty sure she killed his grandfather, too. Maria and that husband of hers have killed everybody who has ever tried to tell the truth about what really happened to you that night. But she's not going to be able to do it any more. That story is going to go out to thirty-five thousand people. More even, because they'll post it on the paper's website. Maria isn't going to be able to kill everybody who reads it.'

Jesse shook his head. 'No, Susannah. She'll just settle for killing you.'

'Jesse,' I said. 'She can't kill me. She's already tried. I've got news for you: I am really, really hard to kill.'

'Maybe not,' Jesse said. He held something out in his hand. I looked down at it. To my surprise, I saw that it was the rope we'd been following.

Only instead of the end disappearing down into the hole through which I'd climbed, it sat, frayed, in Jesse's hand. As if it had been cut.

Cut with a knife.

Sixteen

I stared down at the end of the rope in horror.

It's funny. You know what the first thing that popped into my head was?

'But Father Dom said,' I cried, 'that Maria and Felix were good Catholics. So what are they doing down in that church?'

Jesse had a little more presence of mind than I did. He reached out and seized my wrist, twisting it so he could see the face of Father Dominic's watch.

'How much more time do you have?' he demanded. 'How many more minutes?'

I swallowed. 'Eight,' I said. 'But the whole reason Father Dom blessed my house was so they wouldn't try to come in, and then look what they do. They come into a church—'

Jesse looked around. 'We'll find the way out,' he said. 'Don't worry, Susannah. It has to be around here somewhere. We'll find it.'

But we wouldn't. I knew that. There was no point, I knew, even in looking. What with the fog covering the ground so thickly, there was no chance we'd ever find the hole through which I'd climbed.

No. Susannah Simon, who'd been so hard to kill, was effectively dead already.

413

I started untying the rope from round my waist. If I was going to meet my maker, I at least wanted to look my best.

'It must be here,' Jesse was saying as he waved at the fog, trying to part it in order to see beneath it. 'Susannah, it must be.'

I thought about Father Dominic. And Jack. Poor Jack. If that rope had been cut, it could only have been because something catastrophic had happened down in the church. Maria de Silva, that practising Catholic Father D had been so convinced would never dare launch an attack on consecrated ground, had not been as frightened of offending the Lord as Father Dominic had assumed she'd be. I hoped he and Jack were all right. Her problem was with me, not them.

'Susannah.' Jesse was peering down at me. 'Susannah, why aren't you looking? You cannot give up, Susannah. We'll find it. I know we'll find it.'

I just looked at him. I wasn't even seeing him, really. I was thinking about my mother. How was Father Dominic going to explain it? I mean, if he wasn't already dead himself. My mom was going to be really, really suspicious if my body was found in the basilica. I mean, I wouldn't even go to church on Sunday. Why would I be there on a Friday night?

'Susannah!' Jesse had reached out and seized me by both my shoulders. Now he gave me a shake with enough force to send my hair flying into my face. 'Susannah, are you listening to me? We only have five more minutes. We've got to find a way out. Call him.'

I blinked up at him, confusedly pushing my long dark hair from my eyes. That was one thing, anyway. I'd never have to worry about finding the perfect shade to cover my grey. I'd never turn grey now.

'Call who?' I asked dazedly.

'*The gatekeeper*,' Jesse said through gritted teeth. 'You said he was your friend. Maybe he'll show us the way.'

I looked into Jesse's eyes. I saw something in them I'd never seen before. I realized, in a rush, what that something was.

Fear. Jesse was afraid.

And suddenly I was afraid, too. Before I'd just been shocked. Now I was scared. Because if Jesse was afraid, well, that meant something really, really bad was about to happen. Because Jesse does not scare easily.

'*Call him*,' Jesse said, again.

I tore my gaze from his and looked around. Everywhere – everywhere I looked – I saw only fog, night sky, and more fog. No gatekeeper. No hole back to the Junipero Serra Mission church. No hallway filled with doors. Nothing.

And then, suddenly, there was something. A figure, striding towards us. I was filled with relief. The gatekeeper, at last. He would help me. I knew he would . . .

Except that, as he came closer, I saw it wasn't the gatekeeper at all. This guy didn't have anything on his head except hair. Curly brown hair. Just like—

'Paul?' I burst out incredulously.

I couldn't believe it. Paul. Paul Slater. Paul Slater was coming towards us. But how—

'Suze,' he said conversationally as he strolled up. His hands were in the pockets of his chinos, and his Brooks Brothers shirt was untucked. He looked as if he had just breezed in from a long day on the golf course.

Paul Slater. *Paul Slater.*

'What are you doing here?' I asked. 'Are you . . . are you dead?'

'I was about to ask you the same question,' Paul said. He

looked at Jesse, who was still clutching my shoulders. 'Who's your friend? He *is* a friend, I assume.'

'I—' I glanced from Jesse to Paul and then back again. 'I came up here to get him,' I explained. 'He's my friend. My friend Jesse. Jack accidentally exorcised him, and—'

'Ah,' Paul said, rolling back and forth on his heels. 'Yes. I told you that you should have left well enough alone with Jack. He'll never be one of us, you know.'

I just stared at him. I could not figure out what was happening. Paul Slater, here? It didn't make any sense. Not unless he was dead. 'One of . . . what?'

'One of us,' Paul repeated. 'I told you, Suze. All this do-gooding, mediator nonsense. I can't believe you fell for it.' He shook his head, chuckling a little. 'I would have thought you were smarter than that. I mean, the old man, I can understand. He's from a completely different world – a different generation. And Jack, of course, is . . . well, clearly unsuited for this sort of thing. But you, Suze. I'd have expected more from you.'

Jesse let go of my shoulders but kept one hand firmly round one of my wrists . . . the wrist with Father Dominic's watch on it. 'This,' he said, 'is not the gatekeeper, I take it.'

'No,' I said. 'This is Jack's brother, Paul. Paul?' I looked at him. 'How did you get here? Are you dead?'

Paul rolled his eyes. 'No. Please. And you didn't need to go through all that rigmarole to get here, either. You can, like me, come and go from here when you please, Suze. You've just been spending so much time "helping" –' he made quotation marks in the air with his fingers – 'lost souls like that one –' he nodded his head in Jesse's direction – 'you've never had a chance to concentrate on discovering your real potential.'

I stared at him. 'You told me . . . you told me you don't believe in ghosts.'

416

He smiled like a kid with his hand caught in the cookie jar. 'I should have been more specific,' he said. 'I don't believe in letting them walk all over me, like you clearly seem to.' His gaze roved over Jesse contemptuously.

I was still having trouble processing what I was seeing . . . and hearing.

'But . . . but isn't that what mediators are supposed to do?' I stammered. 'Help lost souls?'

Paul heaved a shudder, as if the fog swirling around us had suddenly grown colder. 'Hardly,' he said. 'Well, maybe the old man. And the boy. But not me. And certainly not you, Susannah. And if you'd bothered giving me the time of day, instead of being so caught up trying to rescue this one –' he sneered in Jesse's direction – 'I might have been able to show you precisely what you're capable of. Which is so much more than you can begin to imagine.'

A glance at Jesse told me that I had better cut this little conversation short if I didn't want any bloodshed. I could see a muscle I'd never noticed before leaping in Jesse's jaw.

'Paul,' I said. 'I want you to know that it really means a lot to me, the fact that you, apparently, have your finger on the pulse of the mystical world. But right now, if I don't get back to earth, I'm going to wake up dead. Not to mention the fact that if I'm not mistaken, your little brother might be having a really hard time down there with a guy named Diego and a chick in a hoop skirt.'

Paul nodded. 'Yes,' he said. 'Thanks to you and your refusal to acknowledge your true calling, Jack's life is in danger, as is, incidentally, the priest's.'

Jesse made a sudden motion towards Paul, which I cut short by holding up a restraining hand.

'How about giving us some help then, huh, Paul, if you know so much?' I asked. It was no joke, holding Jesse back.

417

He seemed ready to tear the guy's head off. 'How do we get out of here?'

Paul shrugged. 'Oh, is that all you want to know?' he asked. 'That's easy. Just go into the light.'

'Go into the—' I broke off, furious. '*Paul!*'

He chuckled. 'Sorry,' he said. 'I just wanted to know if you'd seen the movie.'

But he wasn't chuckling a bit a split second later when Jesse suddenly launched himself at him.

I'm serious. It was way WWF. One minute Paul was standing there, smirking, and the next, Jesse's fist was sinking into his tanned, handsome face.

Well, I'd tried to stop him. Paul was, after all, probably my only way out of there. But I can't say I really minded when I heard the sound of nasal cartilage tearing.

Paul was pretty much a baby about the whole thing. He started cursing and saying stuff like, 'You broke my nose! I can't believe you broke my nose!'

'I'll break more than your nose,' Jesse declared, clutching Paul by his shirt collar and waving his blood-smeared fist in front of his eyes, 'if you don't tell us how to get out of here *now.*'

How Paul might have responded to this interesting threat I never did find out. That's because I heard a sweetly familiar voice call my name. I turned around, and there, running towards me through the mist, was Jack.

Round his waist was a rope.

'Suze,' he called. 'Come quick! That mean lady ghost you warned me about, she cut your rope, and now she and that other one are beating up Father Dominic!' Then he stopped running, took in the sight of Jesse still clutching a bloody-faced Paul, and said, curiously, 'Paul? What are *you* doing here?'

A moment passed. A heartbeat, really – if I'd had one, which, of course, I didn't. No one moved. No one breathed. No one blinked.

Then Paul looked up at Jesse and said, 'You'll regret this. Do you understand? I'll make you sorry.'

Jesse just laughed, without the slightest trace of humour, and said, 'You're welcome to try.'

Then he tossed Paul aside as if he were a used tissue, strode forward, seized my wrist, and dragged me towards Jack.

'Take us to them,' he said to the little boy.

And Jack, slipping his hand into mine, did so, without looking back at his brother. Not even once.

Which told me, I realized, just about everything – except what I really wanted to know:

Just who – or, more aptly, *what* – was Paul Slater?

But I didn't have time to stay and find out. Father Dominic's watch gave me a minute to return to my body, or be placed in the difficult position of not having one . . . which was going to make starting the eleventh grade in the fall a real problem.

Fortunately, the hole was not far from where we'd been standing. When we got to it and I looked down, I couldn't see Father Dominic anywhere. I could hear the sounds of a struggle, though – breaking glass, heavy objects hitting the floor, wood splintering.

And I could see my body, stretched out beneath me as if I were sleeping, and sleeping so deeply I wasn't stirring at the sound of all that racket. Not a twitch.

Somehow, it seemed a much longer way down than it had climbing up.

I turned to look at Jack. 'You should go first,' I said. 'We'll lower you with the rope—'

But both he and Jesse shouted, 'No!' at the same time.

And the next thing I knew, I was falling. Really. Down and down I tumbled, and while I couldn't see much as I fell, I could see what I was about to land on, and let me tell you, I did not relish crushing my own . . .

But I didn't. Just like in dreams I've had where I've been falling, I opened my eyes at the moment of impact, and found myself blinking up at Jesse's and Jack's faces, peering down at me over the rim of the hole Father Dom had created with his chanting.

I was inside myself again. And I was in one piece. I could tell as I reached down to make sure my legs were still there. They were. Everything was functional. Even the bruise on my head hurt again.

And when, a second later, a statue of the Virgin Mary – the one Adam had told me had wept blood – landed across my stomach, well, that really hurt, too.

'There she is,' Maria de Silva cried. 'Get her!'

I have to tell you, I am getting really tired of people – particularly dead people – trying to kill me. Paul is right: I *am* a do-gooder. I do nothing but try to help people, and what do I get for my efforts? Virgin Mary statues in the midriff. It isn't fair.

To show just how unfair I thought it all was, I heaved the statue off me, scrambled to my feet, and grabbed Maria by the back of her skirt. Apparently, recalling her last incident with me, she decided to make a run for it. Too late, though.

'You know, Maria,' I said conversationally as I reeled her in by her flounces, the way a fisherman reels in a really big trout. 'Girls like you really irritate me. I mean, it's not just that you get guys to do your dirty work for you, instead of doing it yourself. It's this whole I'm-so-much-better-than-you-because-I'm-a-de-Silva thing that really bugs me.

420

Because this is America.' I reached out and grabbed a fistful of her glossy black curls. 'And in America, we're all created equal, whether our last name is de Silva or Simon.'

'Yes?' Maria cried, lashing out with her knife. She'd apparently gotten it back. 'Well, do you want to know what irritates me about you? You think that just because you are a mediator, you are better than me.'

I have to tell you, that one cracked me up.

'Now that's not true,' I said, ducking as she took a swipe at me with her blade. 'I don't think I'm better than you because I'm a mediator, Maria. I think I'm better than you because I do not go around agreeing to marry guys I'm not in love with.'

In a flash, I had her arm pinned behind her waist again. The knife fell to the floor with a clatter. 'And even if I did,' I went on, 'I wouldn't have them murdered just so I could marry somebody else. Because –' keeping a firm grip on her hair with my other hand, I steered her towards the altar rail – 'I believe the key to a successful relationship is communication. If you had simply communicated with Jesse better, none of this would be happening now. I mean, that's your real problem right there, Maria. Communication goes two ways. Somebody has to talk. And somebody has to listen.'

Seeing what I was about to do, Maria shrieked, 'Diego!'

But it was too late. I had already rammed her face, hard, into the altar rail.

'The thing is,' I explained as I pulled her head back from the rail to examine the extent of the damage, 'you won't listen, either, will you? I mean, I told you not to mess with me. And –' I leaned forward to whisper her in her ear – 'I think I specified that you not mess with my boyfriend, either. But did you listen? No . . . you . . . did . . . not.'

I accompanied each of those last four words with a blow

421

to Maria's face. Cruel, I know, but let's face it: she totally deserved it. The bitch had tried to kill me, not once, but twice.

Not that I'm counting or anything.

Here's the thing about chicks who were brought up in the nineteenth century: they're sneaky. I'll give them that. They have the whole back-stabbing, attacking people while they're asleep thing down pretty pat.

But as far as actual hand-to-hand combat goes? Yeah, not so good at that. I broke her neck pretty easily just by stomping on it. In Prada slides, too!

It was a shame her neck wouldn't stay broken for long.

But while I had her nicely subdued, I looked around to see if Jack had made it down OK . . .

And the news was not good. Oh, Jack was fine. It was just that he was hunched over Father Dominic, who was far from it. He was lying in a crumpled heap to one side of the altar, looking way worse for wear. I climbed over the altar rail and went to him.

'Oh, Suze,' Jack wailed. 'I can't wake him up! I think he's—'

But even as he was speaking, Father Dom, his bifocals askew on his face, let out a moan.

'Father D?' I lifted his head and set it down gently in my lap. 'Father D, it's me, Suze. Can you hear me?'

Father D just moaned some more. But his eyelids fluttered, which I knew was a good sign.

'Jack,' I said. 'Run over there to that gold box beneath the crucifix – see it? – and pull out the decanter of wine you'll find there.'

Jack hurried to do as I had asked. I put my face close to Father Dominic's and whispered, 'You'll be OK. Hang on, Father D. Keep it together.'

A very loud splintering crash distracted me, and I glanced around the rest of the church with a sudden sinking feeling. Diego. He was here somewhere. I'd forgotten all about him—

But Jesse hadn't.

I don't know why, but I had simply assumed that Jesse had stayed up there in that creepy shadowland. He hadn't. He had slipped back into this world – the real world – without, apparently, much thought as to what he might be giving up in doing so.

On the other hand, down here he was getting to beat the crap out of the guy who killed him, so maybe he wasn't giving up all that much. In fact, he looked pretty intent on returning the favour – you know, killing the guy who'd killed him – except, of course, that he couldn't, since Diego was already dead.

Still, I had never seen anybody go after someone with such single-minded purpose. Jesse, I was convinced, wasn't going to be satisfied merely with breaking Felix Diego's neck. No, I think he wanted to rip out the guy's spine.

And he was doing a pretty job of it, too. Diego was bigger than Jesse, but he was also older, and not as quick on his feet. Plus, I think Jesse just plain wanted it more. To see his opponent decapitated, I mean. At least, if the energy with which he was swinging a jagged-edged piece of pew at Felix Diego's head was any indication.

'Here,' Jack said breathlessly as he brought the wine, in its crystal decanter, to me.

'Good,' I said. It wasn't whisky – isn't that what you're supposed to give unconscious people to rouse them? – but it had alcohol in it. 'Father D,' I said, raising his head and putting the unstoppered decanter to his lips. 'Drink some of this.'

Only it didn't work. Wine just dribbled down his chin and dripped on to his chest.

Meanwhile, Maria had begun to moan. Her broken neck was snapping back into place already. That's the thing about ghosts. They bounce back, and way too fast.

Jack glared at her as she tried to raise herself to her knees. 'Too bad we can't exorcise *her*,' he said, darkly.

I looked at him. 'Why can't we?' I asked.

Jack raised his eyebrows. 'I don't know. We don't have the chicken blood any more.'

'We don't need the chicken blood,' I said. 'We have that.' I nodded towards the circle of candles. Miraculously, in spite of all the fighting going on, they had remained standing.

'But we don't have a picture of her,' Jack said. 'Don't we need a picture of her?'

'Not,' I said, gently putting Father D's head back on the floor, 'if we don't have to summon her. And we don't. She's right here. Come on and help me move her.'

Jack took her feet. I took her torso. She moaned and fought us the whole way, but when we laid her on the choir robes, she must have felt as I did – that it was pretty darn comfortable – since she stopped struggling and just lay there. Above her head, the circle Father Dom had opened remained open, smoke – or fog, as I knew it was now – curling down from its outer edges in misty tendrils.

'How do we make it suck her in?' Jack wanted to know.

'I don't know.' I glanced at Jesse and Diego. They were still engaged in what appeared to be mortal combat. If I had thought Jesse had lost the upper hand, I'd have gone over and helped, but it appeared he was doing fine.

Besides, the guy had killed him. I figured it was payback time, and for that, Jesse did not need my help.

'The book!' I said, brightening. 'Father Dom read from a book. Look around. Do you see it?'

Jack found the small, black, leather-bound volume beneath the first pew. When he flipped through the pages, however, his face fell.

'Suze,' he said. 'It's not even in English.'

'That's OK,' I said, and I took it from him and turned to the page Father Dominic had marked. 'Here it is.'

And I began to read.

I'm not going to pretend I know Latin. I don't. I hadn't the slightest idea what I was saying.

But I guess pronunciation doesn't count when you are summoning the forces of darkness, since, as I spoke, those misty tendrils began to grow longer and longer, until finally they spilled out on to the floor and began to curl round Maria's limbs.

She didn't even seem to mind, either. It was like she was enjoying the way they felt around her wrists and ankles.

Well, the chick was kind of dominatrixy, if you asked me.

She didn't even struggle when, as I read further, the slack on the smoky tendrils tightened, and slowly, the fog began elevating her off the floor.

'Hey,' Jack said in an indignant voice. 'How come it didn't do that for you? How come you had to climb into the hole?'

I was afraid to reply, however. Who knew what would happen if I stopped reading?

So I kept on. And Maria soared higher and higher, until . . .

With a strangled cry, Diego broke away from Jesse and came racing towards us.

'You bitch!' he bellowed at me as he stared in horror at his wife's body, dangling in the air above us. 'Bring her down!'

Jesse, panting, his shirt torn down the middle and a thin ribbon of blood running down the side of his face from a cut in his forehead, came up behind Diego and said, 'You want your wife so badly, then why don't you go to her?'

And he shoved Felix Diego into the centre of the ring of candles.

A second later, tendrils of smoke shot down to curl round him, too.

Diego didn't take his exorcism as quietly as his wife. He did not appear to be enjoying himself one bit. He kicked and screamed and said quite a lot of stuff in Spanish that I didn't understand, but which Jesse surely did.

Still, Jesse's expression did not change, not even once. Every so often I looked up from what I was reading and checked. He watched the two lovers – the one who had killed him and the one who had ordered his death – disappear into the same hole we'd just climbed from.

Until finally, after I'd uttered a last 'Amen', they disappeared.

When the last echo of Diego's vengeful cries died away, silence filled the church. It was so pervasive a silence, it was actually a little overwhelming. I myself was reluctant to break it. But I felt like I had to.

'Jesse,' I said, softly.

But not softly enough. My whisper, in the stillness of the church, after all that violence, sounded like a scream.

Jesse tore his gaze from the hole through which Maria and Diego had disappeared and looked at me questioningly.

I nodded towards the hole. 'If you want to go back,' I said, though each word tasted, I was sure, like those beetles Dopey had accidentally poured into his mouth, 'now is the time, before it closes up again.'

Jesse looked up at the hole, and then at me, and then back at the hole.

And then back at me.

'No, thank you, *querida*,' he said, casually. 'I think I want to stay and see how it all ends.'

Seventeen

How it all ended that day was with Jack and Jesse and me helping Father Dominic, when he finally came around, to a phone, so that he could call the police and report that he'd stumbled across a pair of thieves looting the place.

A lie, yes. But how else was he going to explain all the damage Maria and Diego had done? Not to mention the bump on his noggin.

Then, once we were sure the police and an ambulance were on their way, Jesse and I left Father Dominic and waited with Jack for the cab we'd called, carefully not talking about the one thing I'm pretty sure we were all thinking: Paul.

Not that I didn't try to get Jack to tell me what was up with his brother and all. Basically, the conversation went like this:

Me: 'So, Jack. What is up with your brother?'

Jack (scowling): 'I don't want to talk about it.'

Me: 'I can fully appreciate that. However, he appears to be able to move freely between the realms of the living and the dead, and I find this alarming. Do you think it is possible that he is the son of Satan?'

Jesse: 'Susannah.'

Me: 'I mean that in the nicest possible way.'

Jack: 'I said I don't want to talk about it.'

Me: 'Which is perfectly understandable. But did you know before now that Paul is a mediator, too? Or were you as surprised as we were? Because you didn't seem very surprised when you ran into him, you know, up there.'

Jack: 'I really don't want to talk about this right now.'

Jesse: 'He doesn't want to talk about it, Susannah. Leave the boy alone.'

Which was easy for Jesse to say. Jesse didn't know what I did. Which was that Paul and Maria and Diego . . . they had all been in cahoots. It had taken me a while to realize it, but now that I had, I could have kicked myself for not seeing it before: Paul's keeping me occupied at Friday's while Maria had Jack perform the exorcism on Jesse. Paul's remark – 'It's easier to catch flies with honey than with vinegar.' Hadn't Maria said the exact same thing to me, not a few hours later?

The three of them – Paul, Maria, and Diego – had formed an unholy trinity, bound, apparently, by a common hatred of one person: Jesse.

But what possible reason could Paul, who'd never even met Jesse until that moment in purgatory, have to hate him? Now, of course, his dislike was understandable: Jesse had done him a very great bodily injury, something for which Paul has sworn to repay him next time he saw him. I'm sure Jesse wasn't taking it too seriously, but I was worried. I mean, I'd just gone to a lot of trouble to get Jesse out of one sticky situation. I wasn't too enthused about seeing him plunge straight into another one.

But it was no good. Jack wouldn't talk. The kid was traumatized. Well, sort of. He actually seemed like he'd had a pretty good time. He just didn't want to talk about his brother.

Which bummed me out. Because I had a lot of questions. For instance, if Paul was a mediator – and he had to be; how

429

else could he have been walking around up there? – why hadn't he helped his little brother out with the whole *I see dead people* thing, said a few words of encouragement, assured the poor kid he wasn't crazy?

But if I'd hoped to get any answers out of Jack on that account, I was sadly disappointed.

I guess if I'd had a brother like Paul, I probably wouldn't have wanted to talk about it, either.

Once Jack had been safely dropped off at the hotel, Jesse and I began the long walk home (I didn't have enough money on me for a ride from the hotel back to my house).

You might wonder what we talked about during that two-mile trek. A lot, surely, might have been discussed.

And yet, to tell you the truth, I can't remember. I don't think we really talked about anything important. What was there to say, really?

I snuck in as successfully as I'd snuck out. No one woke up, except the dog, and once he saw it was me, he went right back to sleep. No one had noticed that I'd been gone.

No one ever does.

Spike was the only one besides me who'd noticed Jesse was gone, and his joy at seeing him again was an embarrassment to felines everywhere. I could hear the stupid cat purring all the way across the room . . .

Although I didn't listen for long. That's because what happened was, I walked in, pulled down the bedclothes, slipped off my slides, and climbed into bed. I didn't even wash my face. I climbed into bed, looked one last time at Jesse as if to reassure myself he was really back, and then I went to sleep.

And I stayed asleep until Sunday.

My mother became convinced I was coming down with mono. At least until she saw the bruise on my forehead. Then she decided I was suffering from an aneurysm. Much

430

as I tried to convince her that neither of these things was true – that I was just really, really tired – she didn't believe me, and would, I'm convinced, have dragged me to the hospital Sunday morning for an MRI – hey, I had been asleep for almost two days – except that she and Andy had to drive up to Doc's camp to bring him home.

The thing is, I guess dying – even for just half an hour – can be very exhausting.

I woke ravenous with hunger. After my mom and Andy left – having extracted from me a promise that I would not leave the house all day, but would instead wait meekly for them to return, so that they could reassess my state of health at that time – I downed two bagels and a bowl of Special K before Sleepy and Dopey even showed up at the table, looking all tussle-headed and unkempt. I, on the other hand, had already showered and dressed, and was ready to face the day . . . or at least unemployment, since I wasn't certain the Pebble Beach Hotel and Golf Resort was going to extend my contract with them, due to my having missed two days of work in a row.

Sleepy, however, reassured me on that account.

'Naw, it's cool,' he said as he shovelled Cheerios into his mouth. 'I talked to Caitlin. I told her you were going through, you know, a thing. On account of the dead dude in the backyard. She was OK with it.'

'Really?' I wasn't actually listening to Sleepy. Instead, I was watching Dopey eat, always an awe-inspiring sight. He stuffed one entire half of a bagel into his mouth and seemed to swallow it whole. I wished I had a camera so I could record the event for posterity. Or at least prove to the next girl who declared my stepbrother a babe how wrong she was. I watched as, without lifting his gaze from the newspaper spread out before him, Dopey stuffed the other half of the bagel into his mouth and, again without chewing, ingested it, the way snakes devour rats.

It was the most disgusting thing I'd ever seen. Well, apart from the beetles in the orange-juice container.

'Oh.' Sleepy leaned back in his chair and plucked something from the counter behind him. 'And Caitlin said to give this to you. It's from the Slaters. They checked out yesterday.'

I caught the envelope he tossed. It was lumpy. There was something hard in it. *Susan*, it said, on the outside.

'They weren't supposed to check out until today,' I said, ripping the envelope apart.

'Well.' Sleepy shrugged. 'They left early. What can I tell you?'

I read the first letter enclosed in the envelope. It was from Mrs Slater. It said,

Dear Susan,
   What can I say? You did such wonders for our Jack. He is like a different boy. Things have always been much harder for Jack than for Paul. Jack just isn't as bright as Paul, I suppose. In any case, we were very sorry not to be able to say goodbye, but we did have to leave earlier than expected. Please accept this small token of our appreciation, and know that Rick and I are eternally in your debt.

                                   Nancy Slater

Folded into this note was a cheque for two hundred dollars.

I'm not kidding. That wasn't my pay for the week, either. That was my *tip*.

I laid the cheque and the letter down beside my cereal bowl and took the next note out of the envelope. It was from Jack.

432

Dear Suze,

You saved my life. I know you don't believe it, but you did. If you hadn't done what you did for me, I would still be afraid. I don't think I will ever be afraid again. Thank you, and I hope your head feels better. Write to me if you ever get a chance.

Love,
Jack

PS Please don't ask me any more about Paul. I'm sorry about what he did. I'm sure he didn't mean it. He is not so bad. J

Oh, right, I thought, cynically. Not so bad? The guy was a creep! He could walk freely within the land of the dead, and yet when his own brother was being terrified out of his wits by the fact that he could see dead people, the guy didn't lift a finger to explain. Not so bad. The guy was *very* bad. I sincerely hoped I never saw him again.

There was a second postscript to Jack's letter.

PPS I thought you might want to have this. I don't know what else to do with it. J

I tilted the envelope, and to my great surprise, out popped the miniature of Jesse I'd seen on Clive Clemmings's desk, back at the historical society. I looked down at it, stunned.

I would have to give it back. That was my first thought. I had to give it back. I mean, wouldn't I? You can't just keep things like that. That would be like stealing.

Except that somehow, I didn't think Clive would mind. Especially after Dopey looked up from the paper and went, 'Yo, we're in here.'

Sleepy glanced up from the automobile section he'd been

scanning, as usual, for a '67 black Camaro with less than fifty thousand miles.

'Get out,' he said, in a bored voice.

'No, seriously,' Dopey said. 'Look.'

He turned the paper around, and there was a picture of our house. Alongside it was a photo of Clive Clemmings and a reproduction of Maria's portrait.

I snatched the paper away from Dopey.

'Hey,' he yelled. 'I was reading that!'

'Let somebody who can pronounce all the big words have a try,' I said.

And then I read CeeCee's article out loud for both of them.

She'd written, basically, the same story I'd told her, starting with the discovery of Jesse's body – only she called him Hector, not Jesse, de Silva – and then going into Clive's grandfather's theory about his murder. She hit all the right points, hammering it home about Maria's two-faced treachery and Diego's overall ickiness. And without coming out and saying so in as many words, she managed to indicate that none of the couple's offspring ever amounted to much of anything.

Rock on, CeeCee.

She credited all of her information to the late Dr Clive Clemmings, PhD, who she claimed had been piecing together the mystery at the time of his death a few days earlier. I had a feeling that Clive, wherever he was, was going to be pleased. Not only did he come off looking like a hero for having solved a hundred-and-fifty-year-old murder mystery, but they'd also managed to find a photo of him in which he still had most of his hair.

'Hey,' Dopey said when I was finished reading. 'How

come they never mentioned me? I'm the one who found the skeleton.'

'Oh, yeah,' Sleepy said in disgust. 'Your role was really crucial. After all, if it wasn't for you, the guy's skull might still have been intact.'

Dopey launched himself at his older brother. As the two of them rolled around on the floor, making a thunderous noise their father would never have put up with if he'd been home, I set the paper aside and returned to my envelope from the Slaters. There was still one more slip of paper inside it.

Suze, the strong, slanting handwriting on it read. *Apparently, it was not to be . . . for now.*

Paul. I couldn't believe it. The note was from Paul.

I know you have questions. I also know you have courage. What I wonder is whether you have the courage to ask the question that is the hardest for someone of our . . . persuasion.

In the meantime, remember: if you give a man a fish, he'll eat for a day. But if you teach him to fish, he'll eat all the fish you might have caught for yourself.

Just a little something to keep in mind, Suze.

Paul

Gosh, I thought. What a charmer. No wonder we never clicked.

The hardest question of all? What was *that*? And what persuasion were we, precisely? What did this guy know that I didn't? Plenty, apparently.

One thing I did know, though. Whatever else Paul was – and I was not at all convinced he was a mediator – he was a jerk. I mean Paul had pretty much left Jack out to dry not once, but twice, first by never once bothering to say *Hey, don't worry, kid, for folks like you and me, it's normal to see dead people all over the place,* and the second time by leaving him alone in that church while those two psychos were tearing up the place.

Not to mention what, I was convinced, he'd done to Jesse, someone he had not even known.

And for that, I'd never forgive him.

And I certainly wasn't about to trust him. Or his opinions on fishing.

Disgusted as I was with him, however, I didn't throw his note away. It would, I decided, have to be shown to Father Dom, who, a phone call had reassured me, was doing well – just a little sore, was all.

While Sleepy and Dopey rolled around – Dopey yelling, 'Get offa me, homo' – I picked up my bounty and went back upstairs. Heck, it was my day off. I wasn't going to spend it indoors, despite my mother's orders. I decided to give CeeCee a call and see what she was up to. Maybe the two of us could hit the beach. I deserved, I thought, a little R and R.

When I got to my room, I saw that Jesse was already up. He doesn't usually pay morning visits. On the other hand, I don't normally sleep for thirty-six hours straight, so I guess neither of us was really sticking to the schedule.

In any case, I hadn't expected to see him there, and so I jumped about a foot and a half and quickly hid the hand carrying his miniature behind my back.

I mean, come on. I don't want him to think I *like* him or anything.

'You're awake,' he said from the window seat where he'd been sitting with Spike and a copy of Abby Hoffman's *Steal This Book* that I happen to know he'd stolen from my mother's bookshelf downstairs.

'Um,' I said, sidling over to my bed. Maybe, if I was quick

enough, I could thrust his picture under my pillow before he noticed. 'Yes, I am.'

'How do you feel?' he asked me.

'Me?' I asked, like there was somebody else in the room he could possibly have been asking.

Jesse laid the book down and looked at me with another one of those expressions on his face. You know, the kind I can never read.

'Yes, you,' he said. 'How do you feel?'

'Fine,' I said. I made it to the bed. I sat down on it, and quick as a mongoose – I've never seen one in action, but I've heard they're pretty fast – I thrust the cheque, the letters, and the miniature under my pillow. Then I relaxed.

'I feel great,' I said.

'Good,' he said. 'We need to talk.'

Suddenly I didn't feel so relaxed any more. In fact, I sprang to my feet. I don't know why, but my heart started beating very fast.

Talk? What does he want to talk about? My mind was going a hundred miles a second. I suppose we should talk about what happened. I mean, it was very scary and all of that, and I nearly died, and like Paul said, I do have a lot of questions—

But what if that was what Jesse wanted to talk about? The part where I nearly died, I mean?

I didn't want to talk about that. Because the fact is, that whole part, that part where I nearly died, well, I nearly died trying to save *him*. Seriously. I was hoping he hadn't noticed, but I could tell by the look on his face that he totally had. Noticed, I mean.

And now he wanted to talk about it. But how could I talk about it? Without letting it slip? The L word, I mean.

'You know what,' I said, very fast. 'I don't want to talk. Is that OK? I really, really don't want to talk. I am all talked out.'

Jesse lifted Spike off his lap and put him on the floor. Then he stood up.

What was he doing? I wondered. *What was he doing?*

I took a deep breath, and kept talking about not talking.

'I'm just – Look,' I said, as he took a step towards me. 'I'm just going to give CeeCee a call and maybe we'll go to the beach or something, because I really . . . I just need a day off.'

Another step towards me. Now he was right in front of me.

'Especially,' I said significantly, looking up at him, 'from talking. That's what I especially need a day off from. *Talking.*'

'Fine,' he said. He reached up and cupped my face in both his hands. 'We don't have to talk.'

And that's when he kissed me.

On the lips.

JINX

Meg Cabot

Does Jinx have bad luck – or special powers?

Misfortune has followed Jean Honeychurch all her life – which is why everyone calls her Jinx. And now her parents have shipped her off to New York to stay with relatives – including her sophisticated cousin, Tory – until the trouble she's caused back home dies down.

Could she even be . . . a WITCH?

Tory is far too cool to bother with Jinx – until Jinx's chronic bad luck wreaks havoc in Tory's perfect life. Only then does Jinx discover that beneath Tory's big-city glamour lies a world of hatred and revenge. Now it seems that the jinx that's driven Jean crazy may just be the only thing that can save her life . . .

A selected list of titles available from Macmillan Children's Books

The prices shown below are correct at the time of going to press. However, Macmillan Publishers reserves the right to show new retail prices on covers, which may differ from those previously advertised.

Meg Cabot

The Mediator:		
Love You to Death & High Stakes	978-0-330-51950-2	£6.99
The Mediator:		
Grave Doubts & Heaven Sent	978-0-330-51952-6	£6.99
Jinx	978-0-330-44201-5	£5.99
Airhead	978-0-330-45382-0	£6.99
Airhead: Being Nikki	978-0-330-45383-7	£6.99
All American Girl	978-0-330-41555-2	£5.99
All American Girl: Ready or Not	978-0-330-43834-6	£5.99
Avalon High	978-0-330-44687-7	£5.99
Teen Idol	978-0-330-43300-6	£5.99
How to Be Popular	978-0-330-44406-4	£5.99
Tommy Sullivan Is a Freak	978-0-330-44407-1	£5.99

All Pan Macmillan titles can be ordered from our website, www.panmacmillan.com, or from your local bookshop and are also available by post from:

Bookpost, PO Box 29, Douglas, Isle of Man IM99 1BQ

Credit cards accepted. For details:
Telephone: 01624 677237
Fax: 01624 670923
Email: bookshop@enterprise.net
www.bookpost.co.uk

Free postage and packing in the United Kingdom